## "Do you need something?"

He stepped inside and closed the door behind him. "You."

She couldn't have heard that right. All the adrenaline and crackling of her nerves had her brain misfiring. "What did you just say?"

"Nothing."

The mattress dipped from his weight and her body slid into his. "I can't seem to calm my nerves. I feel like I'm six seconds from flying apart."

His palm slipped over her thigh. "It's aftermath."

"Do you always feel like this?"

"Just sometimes." He slid his hand over hers and their fingers entwined. "Your nerve endings are on fire. The danger and fear, the sadness and pain. It's all mixing and getting jammed up inside you."

"How do I get rid of it?"

"Different things work for different people." His thumb rubbed against the back of her hand. Slow, lazy circles that soothed her even as her insides continued to churn.

Bold had worked for her once before. She tried it again. "Any ch____ ____ ____ ___ trick?"

# SHELTERED

### BY
### HelenKay DIMON

MILLS &
BOON

Published in Great Britain 2015
by Mills & Boon, an imprint of Harlequin (UK) Limited,
Eton House, 18-24 Paradise Road, Richmond, Surrey, TW9 1SR

© 2015 HelenKay Dimon

ISBN: 978-0-263-25312-2

46-0715

Harlequin (UK) Limited's policy is to use papers that are natural, renewable and recyclable products and made from wood grown in sustainable forests. The logging and manufacturing processes conform to the legal environmental regulations of the country of origin.

Printed and bound in Spain
by CPI, Barcelona

**HelenKay Dimon,** an award-winning author, spent twelve years in the most unromantic career ever—divorce lawyer. After dedicating all that effort to helping people terminate relationships, she is thrilled to deal in happy endings and write romance novels for a living. Now her days are filled with gardening, writing, reading and spending time with her family in and around San Diego. Stop by her website, www.helenkaydimon.com, and say hello.

Thank you to my husband, James,
for the trip to Oregon. All that beautiful open
space gave me tons of suspense ideas.

# Chapter One

For the third night in a row the wind and rain whipped up the Oregon Coast and smacked into the side of Lindsey Pike's small cottage. The temps dipped into lower than normal range for late summer, but that was only part of the reason for keeping her windows closed. The other sat about eleven miles away, up a steep hill and behind a locked gate.

But cool temperature or not, a steady banging put her already zapping nerves further on edge. The rattle came first, then the thud. That would teach her to wait on fixing the shutter in the family room until "sometime next week."

She leaned back into the stack of pillows piled behind her on her bed and reopened her book. After she stared at the same line for what felt like the billionth time, she decided maybe this wasn't the right night for dry research reading. She slipped her legs over the side of the bed and winced when her bare toes hit the chilled hardwood floor.

She made it two steps down the hallway in search of the perfect mindless magazine before she stilled. Something was off. In the air, in the tight space...something.

Up on the balls of her feet, she spun around, thinking to head back to the bedroom and to the gun she kept locked in a safe in her nightstand. Then it hit her. No banging. The wind still howled and the rafters shook now and then. But no more noise.

Torn between possibilities, she stood there. The poor shutter probably finally blew off. That meant hunting it down tomorrow and reattaching it, properly this time. Even as the rationale hung in her mind her unease increased. The slow churning of dread deep in her stomach spun faster. Yeah, she'd lived through paralyzing anxiety before and knew the sensation never led her wrong.

She turned back toward the family room and saw him. It...whatever. Big and looming and shadowed. Without thinking, she took off in a sprint in the opposite direction. Her feet tapped against the floor as she broke for the bedroom. For the gun and the phone. She'd use the lamp as a weapon if she had to. Anything to survive.

Footsteps thundered behind her, louder and faster. Just as she hit the doorway a hand fell on her shoulder. Fingers clenched against her pajama top and dragged it and her backward. She landed with a thump against a solid mass.

"Listen to me." The deep voice vibrated as he whispered.

"No." She scratched and clawed. "Let go!"

She wound up for the most deafening scream of her life, but it choked off in her throat when his hand landed on her mouth. "Lindsey, stop."

In the haze she didn't recognize the voice. Didn't matter if she did. Forget that he knew her name. This person broke in. She had to get him out or take him down. Those were the only two options. She would not be a victim again.

"Lindsey, it's me." He pulled her in tighter against

him, banding an arm around her middle and trapping her legs with one of his.

"Get out," she screamed, but the words got muffled against his palm.

She went with biting. Clamped down hard on the fleshy part of his hand and heard him swear as he jerked back. His arm loosened and she scrambled away. She couldn't get the bedroom door shut, but she could get to that lockbox.

Her heartbeat hammered in her ears as her fingers fumbled with the drawer pull. She'd barely opened it when the attacker knocked her back on the mattress. She flailed, kicking out, trying to land a punch or a hit, or anything that would slow him down or double him over.

Adrenaline pumped through her. Between the race down the hall and the fear pulling at her, she should be exhausted. Instead, energy pulsed through her. She believed she could lift the house, if needed. But first she had to move this guy.

She shoved a knee deep between his legs, but he reached down and caught the shot just in time. With her head shifting on the bed and her body in constant motion, she could barely see. All of her focus went into thinking and moving.

"Lindsey, it's Hank."

His frustration hit her. The words took another second. She maintained her tight grip on his wrist as she looked up. Her gaze went to the broad shoulders and coal-black hair. Those intense dark eyes.

Recognition struck. Right, Hank…something. He was the new handyman, the gofer, whatever his real title, for the New Foundations Retreat. The place she hated most but could not escape.

If he thought letting her make that connection in her

mind would make it easier to accept his presence, he was dead wrong. She put anyone affiliated with New Foundations in the "never trust" category. The scruffy rough-and-tumble look would not get him off that list, especially now.

She bucked her hips, trying to knock him off balance. "Get off."

When that failed, panic rolled through her. His weight anchored her to the bed, which left her few options.

"You need to listen," he said in a harsh whisper.

"No." She tried to wiggle her wrist free so she could scratch. If he'd put just a bit of space between their locked bodies, she would knee him hard enough to send him rolling on the floor.

Lightning lit up the room and a crack of thunder came right behind. She remembered childhood tales about the time between them having something to do with the distance you were from the storm. Probably hogwash, but she needed something mindless to block the blinding fear.

He touched her cheek and moved her head until she faced him. He stared down, as if willing her to believe. "Men are coming."

With that her body froze. "What?"

"Some people at New Foundations want to talk to you and I don't think they care if you want to listen."

A new wave of desperation hit her. Maybe he was there to warn her. Maybe he was there to help whoever was coming, if that threat was even true. Didn't matter, because she refused to stick around and see.

Inhaling and trying to calm her breathing, she didn't flinch away from his touch or try to get away. For a few seconds she put all her energy into convincing him. "I have to get out of here."

"I need to keep you safe." He nodded as the grip on her wrists eased. "That's why I'm here."

He broke in and scared the hell out of her. Those facts kept running through her mind and pushing out everything else. "You're one of them."

"Lindsey, no." He shook his head. "I am not here to hurt you."

The calm tone. The orders delivered in an even cadence. She'd experienced it all before, sometimes from well-meaning folks who promised they would help. But those other times weighed on her, had her skepticism snapping. "Why should I believe you?"

"Wish I had a good answer for that, but I don't." He hesitated and then lifted off her, inch by inch, until he balanced on his knees, straddling her. One quick glance down between his legs and he shifted to kneel to the side of her. "I'm only a few steps in front of them."

She'd never been one to get dizzy or faint. Not her style at all, but the oxygen seeped out of her until the room spun and bile raced up her throat. "Let me slip out the back."

"Would never work." He held up his hands as he stepped off the mattress and stood in front of her. "They need to think you're with me."

She jackknifed into a sitting position, ready to make a second grab for the nightstand depending on what he said next. "What?"

"Trust me."

That was never going to happen. Not for him. Not for anyone. Those days were long gone for her. "No way."

She barely got the words out before a crack sounded at the front of the house. A new surge of fear whipped through her.

He glanced behind him as he kept that hand out, gesturing for her to stay down. "Do not move."

From the bed? That wasn't happening either. "I will kill you first."

"And that would be your right if I tried to hurt you, but I won't." The words sounded good, but he started unbuttoning his shirt.

"What are you doing?" But she knew. Knew and would throw every single thing in the room at him, nailed down or not.

He left his blue long-sleeve shirt open over a T-shirt and reached for his belt. A few quick moves and he had the zipper down and the jeans on the floor. "Making it believable."

Her hand inched toward the lamp. The heavy base right to his skull might stop him. "Okay."

But he didn't come at her in his boxer briefs. He bent down and slipped something out of...a gun. With a touch of a finger to his lips he turned toward the doorway.

"Who's there?" His deep voice echoed down the hall.

She had no idea what was happening. Shadows moved outside her window. She assumed branches, but she didn't know. Everything blended together and morphed until the walls pounded in on her.

He kicked off his shoes and stepped into the hallway. The floorboards creaked under his weight.

She thought about diving out the window but had no idea what lurked out there. Forcing her mind to focus, she grabbed for the nightstand drawer. Punched in the lock code and had the gun loaded and in her hand as she crept out behind Hank.

"I am not going to let you touch my girlfriend." He kept his back against the wall as he slid farther down the hall toward the family room. "Leave now and this ends fine."

*My girlfriend?* Her mind stuck there and refused to unstick. The most she could do was stand up and get to the bedroom doorway.

She stopped in time to see the collision. Hank took one more step and a body smashed into him. She aimed her gun, but only darkness greeted her. The two men were locked in battle, rolling like a ball across her floor. She heard grunts and saw arms rise and fall. One back thumped against the hallway wall, then another.

Lightning flashed and she saw blond hair and a dark jacket. She didn't recognize the intruder. Only Hank. She could make him out as he landed punch after punch against the blond's jaw.

Thunder boomed and then an eerie quiet fell over the back of the house. The men tumbled as they slipped out of sight. Something fell to the floor with a crash, but the usual buzz of the lights and hum of the refrigerator had stopped. She reached out and flicked the switch by her head, but nothing happened. Either the storm knocked out the power or a group of men outside her home did. She hated both options.

Gripping the gun, she stepped into the hall and tried to make out one figure from the other. She didn't know Hank and didn't owe him anything, but he could have dragged her outside and handed her to the blond. He hadn't, and the confusion from that kept her from shooting him now.

But she could see shapes. Hank had the blond on the floor. Hank's legs pinned the guy, and an arm hooked around his neck. Looked to her as though her make-believe boyfriend had this one won. Nothing about that realization had her relaxing.

*Sheltered*

The scuffle continued. The blond's heels smacked against the floor. The battle seemed to be dying down until another figure stepped into the far end of the hall opposite her. Her insides chilled and her body shook hard enough for her teeth to rattle. She couldn't make out his face but got the impression he was staring at her. Waiting.

One swing of his arm and he knocked Hank's head into the wall. She aimed, ready to fire at anyone who came toward her. But the newest man reached down and dragged the blond to his feet. Then they were gone.

She stood there, unable to think. Unable to breathe.

"Lindsey?" Hank stumbled to his feet as he scooped his gun off the floor. "You okay?"

His voice snapped her out of her stupor. She reached inside her bedroom and ripped the emergency flashlight out of the socket, then grabbed the second one she kept just inside the bathroom door.

She fumbled to hold them both in one hand and aimed them in Hank's direction. He blinked as he rubbed one hand over the back of his head. The other one, the one with the weapon, dropped to his side.

His gaze traveled over her, and then he frowned. "Where did you get a gun?"

Not exactly the response she'd expected, but until he asked she forgot she held it. "It's mine."

"Maybe you could lower it."

She wanted to ask if he was okay. After all, unless he'd put on some great show, he'd just saved her from two intruders storming in and taking her away. But that wasn't where her mind went. "Who are you?"

At first she didn't think he heard her. He walked through the small house. Checked the front door. Looked outside.

He finally turned back to her. "You should think of me as Hank Fletcher. A handyman who blew into town looking for work. We met, started dating and now I'm at your house most nights."

Wrong answer, and that was before she got to the boyfriend thing. She ignored that part completely. "But that's not who you are."

"No."

At least he didn't lie or try to shrug her off. But she still wanted an answer. "Tell me or the gun stays up."

He leaned against the armrest of her couch. "Holt Kingston, undercover with the Corcoran Team, and right now the best hope you have of not being dragged up to the compound and questioned."

She had no idea what any of that meant but grabbed on to the "undercover" part and hoped that stood for police or law enforcement. Really, anyone with a gun and some authority who could help.

Going further, the idea of trusting him even the slightest bit brought her common sense to a screeching halt. But as much as it grated, there was something about him. It had been that way from the beginning. She'd seen him in town and driving the New Foundations truck and she couldn't stop watching. She chalked the reaction up to being cautious, but what she was thinking of doing right now, letting him in if only an inch, struck her as reckless.

Even now, standing there in his underwear, with this massive chest and...well, everything looked pretty big. Still, the fear that had gripped her body and held it to that spot in the hall eased away. Tension buzzed through the room, but the panic had subsided.

Ignoring the warning bells dinging in her head, she

verbally reached out. "So, you know New Foundations is a cult."

"Oh, Lindsey." He shook his head. "It's worse than that. So much more dangerous and threatening."

At least he understood that much about the place that starred in her nightmares. That was more than her father ever understood. "Okay, then."

His shoulders dropped a little, as if the tension stiffening them had ratcheted down. "So, we're good?"

No way was she going that far. Not yet. Probably not ever. "Let's just say I'm willing to hear you out."

"That's all I'm asking."

She let the hand with the gun drop to her side but didn't let go. "Talk fast."

## Chapter Two

Holt felt the tension ease from his shoulders the second she dropped the gun. The close call would teach him to break protocol. He'd overheard two New Foundations bruisers talking about grabbing Lindsey and snapped into action. Gone to her house and the rest was a combination of pure luck and timing.

Not that he usually dropped cover. He rescued for a living. That was what the Corcoran Team did. Worked undercover in off-the-books operations, preventing kidnappings before they happened and when called in too late, being the first to rush in and get victims out. Hired by governments and corporations, they performed work others couldn't.

His three-man team moved constantly but reported back to the main office in Annapolis. Connor Bowen owned the company and ran the show, including the four agents who worked out of Maryland. Holt only had to check in with one person—Connor—and the boss would not like how this assignment had spun out.

Holt could hardly admit getting his head turned by a pretty woman. And Lindsey Pike definitely qualified as that. She possessed a girl-next-door prettiness. The shiny brown hair with streaks of blond. The big green eyes. The confident way she moved around the town of Justice, Oregon, the most ill-named town ever.

She'd intrigued him from day one, and hearing she was in trouble tonight got him moving.

Now he figured he had about ten seconds to convince her that he was one of the good guys or see her whip out that gun again. Actually, from the frown, maybe more like five.

"Tell me exactly why you're here." Her expression didn't change. Those lips stayed in a flat line as a sort of grim determination moved over her.

No shock. No panic. That told him she knew exactly how dangerous the folks at New Foundations were. Maybe she'd expected them to hunt her down. Maybe she'd been poking at them. Either way, she appeared to possess the type of intel he needed.

In cases like this, with the adrenaline still pumping, the simple truth tended to work, so he went with it. "There were orders to bring you in."

"From?"

He had a feeling the call came from high up, but he couldn't pinpoint it yet. "I don't know."

If possible, her frown deepened. "Of course you do. Who told you to come after me?"

That explained it. She still viewed him as attacker, not rescuer. "No one. I overheard men talking at the compound and got here first to warn you."

"Compound." She scoffed. "The place almost sounds nice when you say it that way."

Not what he'd seen. Sure, on the surface, everything ticked along fine. The camp operated as a retreat. Cabins lined up in a serene wooded area. Communal gardens and shared meals in a dining hall. Staff had the option of living in less private bunkhouses a few hundred feet from the main area, behind the yoga studio.

It all seemed peaceful, the perfect place for people who were tired of being plugged in and those sick of government regulations or city life. But on the inside something festered. Groups of men would leave for hours at a time. The gun range had a steady stream of customers. So did the makeshift village built on the back of the property. The one where people practiced drills storming houses and learning how to fight off attacks.

But none of that worried Holt like the sheer amount of firepower he'd seen brought onto the property. He recognized the crates and couldn't come up with a single reason a retreat that featured yoga would also have grenade launchers.

Corcoran had been sent in after information leaked. But finding former members proved difficult. People went there and stayed, which had government officials thinking cult. That was what Holt had expected on this assignment, but now he knew better. New Foundations had the makings of a homegrown militia.

He stepped carefully with Lindsey now, hoping he'd finally found a thread he could pull to bring the place down. "Apparently you ticked off someone at the retreat."

"You have no idea."

But he wanted to know. With her, he guessed the direct question might not get the job done, so he verbally walked around it, hoping to land on the information he needed. "Were you a member?"

She tightened her grip on the gun. "For now, I think I'll ask the questions."

The woman played this well. He admired her refusal to get sucked in. "Why do you think I'll agree to that?"

"You are in my house. You dragged me out of bed, stripped down and—"

*"Fine." Round One to Lindsey.* "Go ahead."

Using the hand with the gun, she motioned for him to sit down on the couch. "What's the Corcoran Team?"

He settled for leaning against the armrest because he had a feeling he needed to be up and ready to fight with this woman. "Can't tell you that."

She stood right in front of him, close but not close enough for him to grab the gun or get a jump on her. If he didn't know better, he'd say she'd been trained. And if he was right that she'd spent some time at the retreat and lived to talk about it, her survival instincts might rival his own.

"Are you with the government?"

*"With?"* He knew what she was asking but didn't know if she knew.

"An FBI agent or something."

The out waited right there and he took it. "Or something."

She sighed at him. Threw out one of those long-suffering exhales that women did so well when men ticked them off. "I feel like we're going backward here."

"We'll get to all that, but first we're going to contact the police." He should have made the call as soon as the attackers left.

"No." That was all she said. A curt denial.

People generally didn't question his orders. Probably had something to do with his size and no-room-for-debate scowl. His sister said he'd inherited the look and demeanor from their dad. Holt knew that wasn't exactly a compliment.

"Excuse me?" He kept his voice deadly soft in an attempt to telegraph his mood to her.

Her eyebrow lifted. "Oh, I'm thinking you heard me."

This woman didn't scare easily. He had to admit he found that, along with everything else about her, smoking hot. The not-backing-down thing totally worked for him.

Not that he had time for anything but work, which led him right back to his point. "We need to file a report."

"We know who attacked. You just confirmed it. You came here to stop it…I guess."

Her refusal to get that point had his temper spiking, but he didn't let it show. He never let it show. He didn't need the West Point education and years in the army after to teach him how to remain calm. For him, playing this game amounted to common sense and he could pull off outward disinterest even while his insides churned. "The people at New Foundations can't know I'm onto them."

"Why?" Her tone now rang with interest, as if she were trying to fit the pieces together in her head.

"I'm working undercover, which means you can't say anything." He'd already blown that one, but since she hadn't shot in him in the head he believed he'd made the right call.

"Who would I tell?"

That wasn't exactly his point. "I have no idea."

She hesitated while her gaze toured his face. "Let's talk about the undercover thing for a bit."

*Yeah, enough sharing.* "After we call the police."

She shook her head. Looked even more determined to shut down his plan. "The police around here protect the people who run New Foundations. They have some sort of relationship that keeps the camp in business."

Holt got that. There would need to be some sort of quid pro quo for the retreat to operate in such an information vacuum. At least he hoped so. "I'm counting on that."

Her stance eased and some of the tension tightening her shoulders disappeared. "You lost me."

A quick once-over glance told him some of her fear had subsided. The glance also tugged on his concentration. Her pajamas, the lack of a bra…he noticed it all.

He forced his mind back to the conversation and off her body and that face…man, she was killing him. "We have one hope of keeping you safe."

"What's that?"

"Me."

She treated him to a second sigh, this one longer than the first. She also put her gun down on the table at the end of the couch. "I knew you were going to say that."

No need to spook her, so he didn't make a move or even look at the gun, even though it sat just inches from his thigh. "If they think we're dating, I become more helpful."

"How?" The skepticism in her voice slammed into him.

He gritted his teeth as he tried to ignore the attitude. "You stay protected."

"Why wouldn't they just grab me?"

A fine question, which led him to one of his own. "Why do they want to?"

"Don't know." She folded her arms across her midsection. "Ask them."

"Are you always this difficult?" She was almost as prickly as he was when it came to holding back information. He admired the skill even as it blocked him from getting the intel he needed.

"Yes."

The honesty was pretty hot, too. Still, Holt knew his

plan provided the right answer. "We call the police. We file a report. The report gets back to the New Foundations folks and my cover holds. With all that in place, it becomes that much harder for them to grab you."

She shrugged. "Or I could leave town."

A good plan. The smart one. For some reason not one he liked very much. "That's the better option, but I was betting you'd say no if I suggested it."

"Why?"

"In addition to the fact that you seem to question everything I say?"

The corner of her mouth lifted in what looked like an almost-smile. "I'm tempted to deny that, but I fear it would prove your point."

Since he felt as though he actually won that round, he answered the original question. "The people I'm protecting usually refuse to leave their homes, family, friends… you get the picture."

He'd heard the refrain so many times that he was starting to believe Connor's argument that people valued family and home above all else. Not one to stick around in one place for very long, Holt didn't really get it.

He had people in his life he'd die for and a job he loved, but the whole craving a home thing never registered with him. Maybe it stemmed from having a father more dedicated to the army than his kids.

Maybe it was what happened when the person you trusted most left you to die on an abandoned stretch of dirt road in Afghanistan. Holt suspected that didn't help, but it didn't really matter how he got to the emotional freeze-out, because that was his reality and he didn't see it changing.

"You do this a lot?" she asked.

"Rescue? Yeah, it's all I do." All he knew.

The final bit of tension zapping around the room ceased. "So you can actually shoot that thing?"

He followed her gaze to his gun. The one she could see. "Yes, ma'am."

"You're not a handyman."

It was his turn to shrug. "I'm handy."

"Oh, really?"

"I've got skills." He needed to pull back. Knew it but didn't.

Her expression changed then. "Are you flirting with me?"

*So tempting.* "That would be bad form, since two guys just tried to kick my butt." He needed to stay on his feet and aware, though he could understand why she asked. His gaze kept wandering. So did his thoughts.

Not good at all.

"I don't understand any of what's going on tonight. I've seen you around town. I stay away from the camp and never say anything about what goes on there." She broke away and walked toward the kitchen, then paced back.

She walked with her movements jerky for the first time. Frustration pulsed off her.

Yeah, he needed this intel. He felt for her, but she talked about knowing what happened in the camp. Didn't say she "heard" tales. No, she had personal knowledge. He'd bet on it. "You're saying you don't know what you did to upset the New Foundations people?"

"Of course I do."

Round and round they went. She gave new meaning to the term *pulling teeth.* "And?"

"My entire life is dedicated to ruining that place."

*Bingo.* "Well, then…"

She pointed in the general direction of the front door. "They don't know that."

"Clearly they do." And she had him curious. Her hatred sounded personal. That could mean she once lived there. She might know about former members. People his team needed to interview.

"You are not the only one working undercover. For me, it's more like working underground." She went back to pacing. "And up until tonight no one ever bothered me. I live just far enough away, keep my name out of the papers and protests. I drive miles outside of my way just so I can avoid driving near the entrance."

When he couldn't take the quiet tap of her bare feet against the hardwood one more second, he stepped in front of her. "Maybe someone recognized you."

He needed more details but decided not to press because whatever the reason, she'd landed on someone's radar screen. That meant the life she knew and protected was over.

Her head snapped up. "It could be worse than that."

"How?"

Tension tightened her features again. "Someone up there must have figured out who I really am."

# Chapter Three

Simon Falls leaned back in his desk chair. The only desk chair on the property. Everyone else preferred mats and cushy chairs. He wanted a stiff-backed seat that put him face-to-face with the monitors on the wall and in front of him. Security feeds, including two rotating video shots of places in town.

Now was not the time to descend into touchy-feely madness. He'd leave the talk about privacy and personal space to the workshop leaders. No one paid him to hold hands. His job came down to one simple idea: protect the camp at any cost. A task that would be easier if everyone did their job, which brought his mind back to this meeting.

He tapped his pen against the desk blotter as he stared at the two men he depended on to handle trouble. This time they'd failed him. He'd handed them one assignment—grab the girl and bring her back unharmed.

They'd run into trouble and had all sorts of excuses. Only one interested Simon.

"What man?" When neither underling answered him, Simon tried again. "At the house. Give me the identity."

"It was Hank Fletcher, one of the newer guys on our staff." Todd Burdock, the best shot in the camp, gave his assessment while standing at attention.

Simon turned the information over in his mind. "You're saying Hank is dating Lindsey Pike."

Todd frowned as if he were choosing his words carefully. "I'm saying he was sleeping over."

Grant Whiddle nodded. "No question they're together."

None of that information matched the surveillance. Simon watched Lindsey. Had watched her for months once the whispers started and the background investigation ran him into a wall. "Since when?"

Todd shook his hand. "I don't know."

Not a sufficient answer, and the man should know that. Simon did not countenance failure. Not here. Not on his watch. "Find out."

"We can call him in," Grant suggested.

Simon knew that was the exact wrong answer. That was the reason he ran camp security and the two in front of him didn't.

"Hank is not to know we were behind tonight's incident." That would make tracking impossible, and now Simon had a new person to track. "No, this needs to be handled differently. Who does Hank know at the compound?"

"No one. He sticks to himself," Todd said without giving eye contact. Then again, he never did.

But Hank was the issue here. A loner. No surprise there. They littered the camp. Disillusioned men who needed a purpose filled the beds and the coffers. They came with what little they owned and handed it over in exchange for a promise.

Simon remembered tagging Hank as one of those types during his interview. Dishonorably discharged for firing when any sane person would fire. He had potential plus a gift for shooting. And he might still work out, but that didn't mean the Lindsey Pike connection could be ignored.

"He lives at the bunkhouse." Simon knew because he'd assigned Hank the space. "Is this his first night away from the compound since arriving?"

Grant gave Todd a quick look before speaking. "No."

That didn't quite match up with Simon's view of the man or with what Simon saw on the monitors day after day. Hank did his job, never wavered, rarely asked questions. But everyone had an agenda, and Simon would find Hank's.

"We need a closer watch on him. I want every minute accounted for, including those with Lindsey." Especially those with Lindsey.

"So we're not bringing her up to camp now?" Grant asked.

The question screeched across Simon's nerves. So stupid. That was the problem with hired guns. They didn't always come with brains. "You can't very well try to drag her out of her house two nights in a row. She'll be expecting you."

Grant shook his head. "But we'll be expecting Hank this time. We can take another guy and—"

*Enough.* "The original mission is on hold until we know more about Hank." Simon dismissed them by returning to watch his monitors.

Todd cleared his voice. "She is potentially dangerous, sir."

"She is." Simon stared at the men again. "So am I. You would both be wise to remember that."

THE COUNTY SHERIFF'S office proved less helpful than Lindsey had expected. She didn't want to file a report or even involve law enforcement. That opened the door into an investigation, which meant someone could stumble over pieces of her past. Pieces she'd kept hidden for years.

"Vagrants." Deputy Carver made that announcement after his walk-through of her house.

The guy had been on the job for about eight months. He'd earned it the old-fashioned way, by taking over when his father had a heart attack. The elder Frank Carver went into the hospital and then rehab and now waited out his disability leave at home as he worked to get his strength back.

The younger Frank Carver stepped in. Never mind he was green and over his head, he'd grown up in this town. Knew everyone by name.

What Frank Carver, Jr., with his red hair and cheeks stained red the way they did anytime he talked with anyone, lacked in experience, he made up for in sheer shooting ability and endurance. He'd simply been tagging along after his father long enough to be considered a fixture. Combine that with the town's love and loyalty to his father, and the kid wasn't going anywhere.

He wasn't doing anything to help her either. She fought the urge to say "I told you so" to Holt. Settled for mouthing it instead.

The deputy had done exactly what she'd predicted—nothing. No forensics. No photos. He just walked around with Holt at his heels.

"No other answer, really." Deputy Carver took a closer look at the doorjamb. Studied it. Even got up on his tiptoes since the thick-soled shoes only put him at five nine, and that was just barely. "You said they weren't kids."

Holt stood there, studying whatever Deputy Carver studied and shaking his head. "These were grown men."

"Good thing you were here, then, Mr. Fletcher." Deputy Carver shot Holt a man-to-man look.

"You can call me Hank."

She was impressed Holt refrained from rolling his eyes. At six-foot-something, he towered over the kid. Also looked as if he could break the deputy in half. The contrast in their sizes and confidence, styles and stance could not have been more pronounced. At twenty-four, Frank Jr. had to be a decade or so younger than Holt, but the difference in maturity shone through.

Not that she was looking…but she couldn't really stop looking. Recognizing Holt standing in her house had shaken her. He didn't belong there. She'd locked the doors, performed her nightly safety check. But that wasn't what had her rattled to the point where her teeth still chattered.

No, she'd been thinking about him. A lot, every day, at odd times. Ever since she'd seen him in town weeks before, he'd played a role in her dreams. The quiet stranger who walked into town, didn't ask questions and swept her right into the bed. Pure fantasy wrapped in a tall, dark and dangerous package. The broad shoulders and trim waist, the coal-black hair and the hint in his features of Asian ancestry.

She blamed the dark eyes and brooding look. That was why she stared. She'd see him around town and she'd watch, her gaze following him, then skipping away when he'd look back. The whole thing made her feel like a naughty teen, but it had been so long since she'd felt anything for a man that she welcomed the sensation.

"I'd hate to think what could have happened," Deputy Carver said, droning on.

Holt waved the younger man off. "But it didn't, so we're good."

She tried to ignore the deputy's attempts at male bonding and the way both men talked around her, as if she weren't even in the room.

But this was her house. Her life. "For the record, I can use a gun."

"Of course." The deputy didn't even spare her a glance before talking to Holt again. "I don't think I've seen you around. Are you new in town?"

"I work odd jobs at New Foundations."

Lindsey couldn't figure out if this amounted to the deputy's attempt to question Holt or if the younger man was so enamored that the staring reflected some sort of weird hero worship. Either way, it was getting late and she needed to clean up and get to bed.

"Good work. Good people up there." Frank Jr. tucked the small pad of paper back into his pocket without ever taking a note.

"Yeah, right." Not that anyone asked her, but she threw the words out there anyway. When Holt smiled, she figured he at least got her point about being ignored.

"And you're with Ms. Pike." The comment came out of the blue.

Holt didn't show any outward reaction. She had to bite back a groan.

*Here we go.* "Are you asking about my love life?" She really wanted to know.

"Of course not." The deputy looked at her for the first time. A short look. Long enough to frown, but that was about it. "Just making an observation."

"We're together." Holt inched closer to her.

She hadn't actually noticed him moving, but one second he stood by the door and the next he stood beside her. She concentrated for a second, tried to block out the whoosh of blood through her ears and the comforting feel of his hand low on her back. Long fingers. A warm palm.

She almost choked, and not from fear. No, this churning felt much more like excitement.

"We'll let you know if we find anything, but I'm sure this was a once and done. Probably someone looking for drugs or money for drugs." The deputy took out his car keys. He hadn't run down the porch steps but looked two seconds away from taking off.

Holt's questions stopped him. "Is there a big drug problem around here?"

"Isn't there everywhere?" Frank Jr. asked as he glanced over his shoulder at them.

"Then it's good I'm living here now. With Lindsey." Holt's voice rang out.

He didn't yell, but he might as well have. It felt as if even the breeze stopped blowing. He sure had her attention.

The deputy turned the full way around and faced them. Kept his focus on Holt as an atta-boy grin crept across his lips. "Is that right?"

She had the opposite reaction. Shock rolled over her. Pretending to be her boyfriend was one thing, and she hadn't even agreed to that yet. Being her live-in sounded much bigger. To the people in town and everyone at the camp, it would be bigger. But she guessed that was the point.

She hadn't worked it all out in her head when Holt's fingers tightened against her back. Ready or not, it seemed he wanted her support. She coughed it up. "Uh, yeah."

The deputy just stared. Stood on the bottom step and looked them both up and down, never bothering to close his mouth or hide his delight at being the first to dig up this small-town gossip. "Then you have even less reason for worry."

"That's how I look at it." Holt nodded in what came off as a dismissal.

The deputy must have gotten the hint, because he walked the rest of the way down the steps and to his car. Didn't say anything about the attack in the house or give her any warning or advice. It was as if Holt had spoken and that resolved everything.

While she liked not having to answer questions, the way the whole scene rolled out had her feeling twitchy. Someone broke into *her* house and went after *her*, and only Holt mattered to the deputy.

She knew who—New Foundations—and why, but she doubted the deputy did. She'd done everything to keep her past and true identity hidden. Revealing it now out of frustration was not the right answer, so she let the whole thing drop.

Well, not all of it. There was still the small bit of gloating she planned to do. "That was a waste of time. I'll refrain from saying 'told you so' a few hundred times."

Holt took one step down. The move put them close to eye-to-eye. "Again, the point of that exercise was to send a message. We accomplished that."

"You want people to think we're not looking at New Foundations as the culprit." She got it. The more she thought about the long term, the more she appreciated Holt stepping in with a rational head.

She wasn't the type to run on emotions, but facing down men with a gun threw off her emotional balance. She still fought to regain a sense of normalcy...or what passed for normalcy for her.

"That and to establish me as the guy they have to get through before they can touch you," Holt said.

That part didn't quite fit together in her head. "Speaking of which—"

Holt leaned against the beam holding up this side of the porch. "When they think I live here it becomes less likely they come back."

"You think they'll just leave me alone?"

"No."

Not exactly the answer she'd expected. The guy could use a lesson or two in tact. "That's not very comforting."

"I was going for honest."

And she had to appreciate that. She'd spent a lot of her life trying to ferret out emotions and counteract the games people played. Holt appeared to be a straight shooter. She knew on one level she should love that, but when it came to being dragged out of her own house, she needed a little reassurance.

She also needed to set some ground rules.

"Then, honestly, you should know you're not living here." The last thing she needed was a walking, talking fantasy sleeping on her couch. Dreaming about him already messed with her sleep. Having him nearby, hearing him, smelling him, being able to look at him all the time, might just break her control.

Instead of commenting on her point, Holt crossed his arms over that impressive chest. "You danced around it before. Now tell me exactly why they want you. While you're at it, you can finally tell me what you meant an hour ago with that talk about your identity. Maybe start with how many you have."

Yeah, she could play this game, too. He stood on her turf. That should count for something. As far as she was concerned, he should go first. "Only if you tell me exactly what you're really doing here and why. You can also throw in who sent you. Maybe give me a list of what you've found out so far."

Standing there in the quiet he didn't say touché, but she sensed it.

"Impressive." He smiled. "I think we're at an impasse."

The twinkle in his dark eyes and that dimple in his cheek…oh, so tempting. She had to marshal all her resources to push back and fight off the energy zipping around inside her. "That still doesn't get you a bed for the night."

"I'll take the couch."

This guy had a ready response for everything. "Hank…Holt…" She actually didn't know which was right, let alone who he really was and if he could be trusted. Her instincts told her yes, but even letting him plant the seed about being in a relationship with her amounted to a big risk. "Okay, I give up. What do I call you?"

"In public, Hank. If it makes it easier and helps you remember not to slip up, always call me that."

She preferred Holt. The name fit him. It felt big and secure and special. Not that she could let him know any of that. "I don't know you."

He winked at her. "Right back at ya."

Maybe it was the voice, all rough and husky. Maybe it was the fact he could have hurt her a dozen times, dragged her right up to the compound or let the two goons who broke into her house do it. For whatever reason, a sense of calm washed over her when he came around.

She wished she knew why. "Why should I trust you?"

"You don't have a choice."

Wrong. That was the one thing—possibly the only helpful thing—she'd learned from her father. "People always have a choice."

Holt shrugged. "Fine. Leave town until it's safe."

He gave her the out and she should have grabbed it. The words sat right there on her tongue. She could leave, take a few days away and get her bearings. But the idea of leaving him, of running, made her stomach fall. "When will that be?"

"I don't know."

The guy did do honesty well. It didn't always serve his case, yet he stuck with it. She liked that about him. That and those shoulders…and the face…and the hair that looked so soft. "I have work to do."

"Which is what exactly?"

She couldn't exactly say: rescuing people from the camp. That would open a whole new line of questioning, and she was not ready to go there with him. Or with anyone. "We're spinning in circles."

His arms dropped to his sides and he moved in closer. "Look, I get that you're afraid and wary and don't know me. Up until a few hours ago I only knew you as the woman in town who looked so hot in dark jeans."

*Wait*… "What?"

He just kept talking. "Now I know you're messed up in New Foundations, which is a crappy thing to be. Some of the people up there are dangerous, possibly delusional."

They were all those things and more. She knew because she'd lived there, fought them. Escaped and hadn't stopped emotionally running since. "I need to stop them."

"You need to stay away and let me take care of them." His eyebrow lifted. "You just have to trust me."

She wanted to believe. She'd been in this battle so long exhaustion had crept into her bones. The idea of turning over the reins and walking away sounded like sweet relief. But she knew things that he didn't, and not seeing this through would slowly pick away at her.

No, she needed to bring down New Foundations on her own. Every cabin. Every workshop. Send every person home.

If only Holt didn't look so sincere. His laser-like gaze never slipped. He watched her until she started to squirm in her skin. She knew what he wanted and she couldn't give it to him. "You're asking a lot."

"I know."

His ready acceptance chipped away at her defenses, just as so much of him did. "You seem to take for granted I'll look at that face and those shoulders and fall in line."

He cleared his throat. "You like my shoulders?"

He stood very close now. Right there until only a few feet separated their bodies. His ego just might kill her.

Time to bring him back down to earth. "You're missing the point."

"I am here to assess what's happening at the compound, determine the danger level and, if necessary, get people out before things blow up. Literally."

That sounded so promising. She'd been stymied by her limited resources and inability to safely infiltrate the fence surrounding the place. To divulge everything to him might help her case against the camp, but it would put her identity at risk. The constant balancing act got old.

Still, if he really could help, really was willing to step in, she couldn't ignore that offer. "But you're not FBI."

He shook his head. "Not FBI or ATF."

"I want to believe you're one of the good guys." But that left a lot of other possibilities, both legitimate and not.

He held up three fingers. "Give me three days to prove it to you."

That icy reserve melted inside her. She felt that resistance give way and her need to say yes overwhelm her. With him she might make progress. He wasn't promising the impossible. He was offering protection, and right now it looked as if she needed it. Maybe together they could work through what the people at the camp knew and what they wanted.

At least that was her assessment. She still needed to know his. "And during those three days?"

His gaze bounced up and down her body, heating a trail as it went. "You get a pretend boyfriend with good shoulders."

He'd hit upon the one thing she could no longer resist. "Deal."

# Chapter Four

For the first time since throwing in with the Corcoran Team, Holt seriously considered not showing up at the prearranged time for a meeting the next morning. This one took place two towns over. He'd lost his tail easily and doubled back, circled around. Now he stood in the storage room of a hardware store with his men, waiting for them to snap out of their joint stupor.

He'd known the crap storm he'd wade into the second he opened his mouth and filled them in on what had happened last night, including the part where he camped out on Lindsey's couch. He stuck to the facts and rapid-fired his way through them in his oral report.

Fallout time.

"You did what?" Shane Baker, Holt's best friend and the man he trusted most in the world, looked as if he couldn't fight off his smile.

The openmouthed staring had given way to smirks, which meant Holt needed a new topic of conversation. "Let's move on."

"When do we get to give you a hard time for picking a woman over the job?"

Holt reassessed his decision to lay out all the facts. He should have skipped right over the Lindsey piece, but Shane was about to walk into town playing the role of an old military buddy. For the fake romantic relationship with Lindsey to work, Shane needed to play along. That meant coming clean...unfortunately.

"Never," Holt said, wondering how to regain control of the conversation. Taking on two of them made it tough.

The snorting sound came the second before Shane's response. "Wrong answer."

Cameron Roth, the team's flying expert, shook his head. "Sorry, man. It's happening."

Holt thought he'd at least have an ally in Cam. The guy had run into a similar situation with a woman and a mess followed by a rescue three months before. "Should we talk about you and Julia and how you had us all racing through an abandoned shipyard to save you?"

"Huh." Cam made a face. "That's not how I remember it."

Shane held up a hand. "Wait, are you comparing your situation with Lindsey to Cam's sad lovesick whining over Julia?"

Cam shook his head again. "I don't remember that either."

"Oh, please." Shane took a seat on a stack of boxes balanced against a wall. "You fell in love and got stupid."

Holt felt a punch of relief when Shane and Cam went after each other and jumped over him. Comparing his relationship with Lindsey to the one shared by Cam and Julia, a couple on the verge of getting engaged, did not amount to a good strategy. But he'd dodged that disaster.

Now he needed his men back on track, and fast. "We're on limited time here."

Fully engaged now, Shane crossed one ankle over the other and leaned in. "Then let's get back to your cover."

Not exactly where Holt wanted to take the next round of conversation. "What about it? It's intact."

"Do we know that or are you going to get called in to see the boss at the camp and get shot?" Cam asked.

"The thing with Lindsey makes me more interesting to management." Being followed ever since he left Lindsey's house clued Holt in. He'd gone from being one of the many faceless men roaming around the campground handling odd jobs to a person they watched.

Not that the person following him could be called an expert. No, the guy closed in too fast and showed too much interest. He also managed to pick a vehicle Holt recognized as regularly being parked in Simon Falls's private garage. Not a New Foundations company vehicle but one Holt had already staked out during his late-night recon on the property.

Shane frowned. "Which is the problem, since the point was to blend."

"This is better." Every minute Holt became more convinced and he'd get Connor on board in the next hour or so.

Lindsey's intel placed a target—whatever it was, and he'd get that out of her soon enough—on her forehead. That put Holt in the middle, and if he was going to sit there he might as well use the position.

The system worked like a circle. He wanted the information Lindsey possessed, and now someone at New Foundations would want to know what he knew. Either that or eliminate him, and Holt had no intention of letting that option happen.

Shane's frown deepened with each question. "How can the impromptu plan you're using now be better than the one we worked out for a week, taking all contingencies into account?"

All contingencies except Lindsey. Nothing prepared Holt for her, but he didn't volunteer that piece of information.

"Because under his new plan he gets to sleep at Lindsey's house." Cam twisted the top off the water bottle in his hand. "She is the prize here."

"It's not like that." And Holt would work very hard to keep it that way. He was not a dating guy and he never fooled around on a job.

Cam saluted him with the water bottle. "Yet."

The man-to-man look from Cam made Holt worry they'd never stay on task, so he looked to Shane for help. "I need you on this."

"What's the 'this' you're talking about?"

"Watching over Lindsey when I can't." Holt had to keep up the job at the camp. That meant leaving her without protection. Enter Hank Fletcher's old friend in town for a few weeks.

The cover gave Shane an excuse to hang around. Cam could continue to fly tourists around on the helicopter while really conducting aerial searches of the campground and surrounding areas.

"Does she know she's about to get a second roommate?" Shane asked.

Since she barely wanted one man in the house, Holt hadn't exactly jumped at offering details between coffee and cereal at the kitchen sink this morning. "No."

"Can I be there when she finds out you plan to spring me on her?" Shane's smile could only be described as annoying.

Holt hid a wince. "Go away."

"Make up your mind." Shane dragged out the singsongy voice. "You want me to stay. You want me to go."

"To the public we were in the military together. Met

there, served and remained friends through everything." Connor and Joel had set up the cover. "Now you're out and looking for a place to land, but you were there when I shot the locals in Afghanistan. You think I got a raw deal."

New Foundations sought out disgruntled men with skills. That meant Holt had needed a story that fit the type. And since he had a horror story of his own in his past, it wasn't all that hard to call up those feelings of frustration.

The difference was he didn't blame the army for what had happened to him. In real life, he'd been the one left to die by someone he trusted. In his cover story, he did the killing. He hated both end results, but he'd lived with the realities of one of them for years now.

"You said that's the story to the public. Interesting word choice." Cam and Shane started talking at the same time, but Cam rushed to finish first. "Are you saying you're going to tell Lindsey who I really am?"

Didn't matter who spoke up, because the answer didn't change. "She already knows my real name and about Corcoran."

"How did that happen again?" Cam asked.

And that brought them right back to where the conversation had started. Instead of staying on the ride, Holt jumped off and started doing what he did best— issuing orders.

He looked at Cam. "You keep up the flights. Take photos. Send them back to Joel and Connor and see if they can make sense of what you're seeing."

Joel Kidd took the lead on Corcoran's tech needs. He could make sense out of nonsense better than anyone Holt knew. And Connor was just about the most competent man on the planet. Holt trusted them to help all the way from Maryland.

"And what about Lindsey?"

"What are you talking about?" But Holt got Cam's point. Connor led Corcoran by a few simple rules to get the job done—collect all the information you can before going in, trust your team and know that Connor would come behind you and clean up the mess.

"The Maryland office, Joel in particular, needs to rip her life apart. Investigate her." Shane slipped into protocol-speak. When no one said anything, he looked around the closed-in room. "What, am I wrong?"

Cam shook his head. "He isn't."

Not in the mood for an argument, Holt conceded. He'd planned to conduct some research into Lindsey and her past. He'd just hoped to do it on a limited basis, without the entire Corcoran Team watching. Apparently that was not going to happen. "Fine."

"She's going to love it when she finds out we're digging into her past," Shane said.

Holt knew the easy answer for that. "We're not going to tell her."

"Yeah, I've found that's not the best strategy with women. You think it'll be fine, but it never works out that way." Cam clapped a hand against Holt's shoulder. "But you keep living in your fantasy world and thinking you control this thing with her."

"I can." Holt was impressed with how strong his voice sounded.

Cam shook his head. "I almost feel bad for you."

LINDSEY SLIPPED OUT onto her porch later that evening. The sun had started to set and a stray cool breeze kicked up. Summers this close to the water and tucked into the base of the woods meant still needing a sweater some nights.

For as long as she could remember, she'd loved sitting outside, watching the sun go down. After years of living at the campground and adhering to all the rules, she enjoyed her freedom. No early morning rising for chores and gun practice. No lectures.

But tonight the air carried a chill and it cut right through her. She'd spent the day making contingency plans if she had to move out without notice. She'd contacted the former New Foundations members she helped place in alternative living situations and gone over the go codes and emergency evacuation drills.

Somewhere in there she'd done some research on Holt and the Corcoran Team. Not that there was much to find on him, but she'd had some luck on his group.

She walked over to where he stood by the edge, staring out into the yard and across the black water of the small lake fifty feet in front of it. He leaned with his palms resting against the railing. The move had him bending slightly, showing off those shoulders and his very impressive backside.

The faded jeans balancing on those hips. The muscles rippling to the point she could see them through the thin fabric of his T-shirt. She'd never noticed a man's clothes before, but on him she noticed everything.

She stood even with him and listened to the sound of animals scurrying in the dark and the steady brush of leaves blowing in the wind. "So you're always going to be hanging around here when you're not working."

He nodded without looking at her. "For now, pretty much."

Even though his stance appeared relaxed, something about him seemed to be on high alert. She could feel the energy pulse off him. Watch his gaze as he scanned the area from one side to the other.

With him around she felt safe, and that was new. She'd learned early to depend on herself. Not expect anything. Hide and run and adapt. That had been her mantra to the day she found her way back to Justice, Oregon, only a few miles from the place that defined so much of who she was and how she saw the world.

As the months ticked by, exhaustion settled in. She helped other members of New Foundations get out. Laid the groundwork and found them new living arrangements. Through her past had the contacts to change identities and keep them safe.

She'd only worked with a few because breaking the silence barrier at the compound proved almost impossible. She had to wait until someone said something to someone and it filtered through contacts back to her. Then came weeks of secret meetings as she built trust.

The whole strategy could be tedious and never amounted to enough. The campground still loomed.

But last night, for the first time in years, she slept without moving and jerking and waking up every few hours. She wanted to think handling the two armed men who stormed her house had something to do with it, but she knew a large thank-you went to Holt. He'd stayed on her couch and kept his promises. Harm did not come knocking and he did not do anything to scare her.

And now they'd arrived at night number two. "I've decided it's okay for you to stay."

He threw her the side eye before going back to his visual tour of the property in front of them. "You just figured that out now?"

It was amazing how she could start thinking good things about him and working up a warm fuzzy feeling and then he'd talk and—boom—the goodwill fizzled. Communicating did not appear to be where they excelled. "I looked into the Corcoran Team."

He turned then. Stood up and gave her his full attention. "Okay."

"I'm thinking I saw a sanitized version, like the version you and your people were okay with me seeing, but I was able to find some references." After an internet search turned up bland and unhelpful results, she'd called in some favors to help her get through a firewall or two. She had a bit of inside information on the group.

"That's kind of the point. It's hard to work undercover, which we sometimes need to do, if everyone can find your face all over social media."

"Makes sense." And the information she'd found bore that out. The group had taken on huge companies and small governments, the NCIS and government contractors. The only allegiance the members appeared to have was to each other. "Even confirmed your existence on the team with your boss."

That had been an interesting exercise. She'd seen a few references to Connor Bowen, the owner and leader, and to one other member of the team, a former NCIS agent, but no one else. There could be two guys on the team or two hundred and there was no way for her to tell just by searching around.

The wall of secrecy extended to the team's location and exactly what they could do and how much the government knew about their work. There had been exactly one photo, an older one of Connor Bowen. He had the tall, dark and handsome thing down. Looking at Holt, Lindsey wondered if "speech-stealing hot" was some sort of job requirement for this group.

Connor's deep and reassuring voice had matched the

confident look he wore in the photo. He hadn't sounded all that shocked about Holt giving away his identity, but Connor had made her repeat three times the part about Holt playing the role of her fake boyfriend. She'd swear he'd laughed.

"Wait a minute." Holt shook his head as if trying to assess what she'd just said. "Connor actually talked with you?"

"Well, finding the number proved impossible. I had to call other agencies and do a bunch of internet searches, all which pointed to the fact the Corcoran Team didn't have a number I could access. To the extent anyone admitted Corcoran even existed. Then right when I gave up, the phone rang and Connor was on the line." The whole thing had a Big-Brother-is-watching feel that freaked her out. "Spooky, by the way."

"Joel tracks all searches for Corcoran. He lets people see only what he wants them to see so he can monitor and do some looking of his own."

She had no idea who that was, but her mind went to a bigger question. "Searches where?"

A faint smile crossed Holt's mouth. "Everywhere."

"The information lockdown is a bit intimidating." She could think of a few more words, but that seemed like the nicest.

"Just as Connor wants it."

"Well, he didn't seem happy about me bugging him, but yes. He answered my questions...sort of." The man had sounded downright stunned when she insisted she needed some sort of verification of Holt's identity. She could only assume other people saw Holt's imposing form and I'm-in-charge swagger and capitulated without a fight.

Not her. If he wanted that kind of woman, she was

not his type…not that he served as anything other than a bodyguard for her.

"I filled him in on the status of the assignment an hour ago." Holt started to say something else, then stopped.

"He must have called me right after that." Or at least that was what he'd told her. "Apparently you told him you broke cover."

Holt switched to frowning. Something he excelled at to the point of being an expert. "You're sounding sort of official there."

"I borrowed his phrase." If she could remember more, she'd throw them out, too.

"So now you know I'm legitimate and we can stop arguing about that, right?" Holt's gaze returned to the yard and the shuffling of dirt in the distance.

She shrugged even though the gesture was wasted. He didn't even give her eye contact. "For now."

Without seeming to move, he angled his body. Stood partway in front of her, blocking her body from the quiet night beyond them. "I'm at a disadvantage here. You know about me and you're not coughing up any details about yourself."

"Noticed that, did you?"

He winked at her. "Don't let the shoulders fool you. I'm not as slow as I look."

That zapped the amusement right out of her. "You're not going to forget I said that, are you?"

"No way."

She rushed to fix her mess. "What I meant was—"

He pinned her in place with a quick glance. "I know what you meant."

The guy could stop looking like that. So determined and…big. He crowded in on her on the large open porch without even moving. Something about the way he held his body and aimed that intense stare had her squirming.

"Clearly you don't have a problem with ego." She wished he taught a class in that, because she'd be in the front row.

"I know mutual attraction when I see and feel it."

"Mutual?" That struck her as such a tame term for the need that had pulsed through her ever since he arrived in town.

She knew how many times a day her mind wandered and his face popped into her head. From the first time she'd seen him, picking out a muffin and ordering black coffee from the deli she helped manage, her common sense took a nosedive. One look at him and every vow she'd ever made about staying focused on her quest died a withering death.

He shook his head. "You are not going to derail this conversation."

"I can try."

"You might…" His head snapped back in the direction he'd been looking for the past few minutes. Far left behind the shed.

"What is it?" She dropped her voice to a whisper that barely carried over the sound of her breathing.

"Company."

"Are you kidding?" She wanted to scream, shout… find her gun. She went with listening instead. Not her strongest skill, but at least it was something she could control while the world seemed to be bouncing around at random.

"I've been tracking the person for about fifteen minutes."

The constant visual search and the thrum of awareness running through him made sense. Still, the fact that the guy could chat while conducting surveillance and not show any signs of anxiety confused her. "While we were talking?"

"Then and before."

*Well, sure.* He acted as if that were normal. "You could warn a person."

"Time to move."

She almost didn't hear the whispered comment, but she did see the change come over him. It was as if he switched from being on watch to back to normal again, which made no sense to her at all.

"I think we should call it a night and go inside." His voice picked up a bit in volume. Not enough to be obvious, but a slight beat or two more than before.

She'd rather go with that gun idea. "Absolutely."

She pitched her voice nice and strong even as her insides shook. The touch of his hand right before he wrapped an arm around her shoulders helped. He guided them through the front door and inside. She didn't remember moving until he shut the door behind her.

He reached down to his ankle and pulled up with a gun in his hand. That was when she noticed he held two. His dark eyes flashed with fire as he morphed from the calm guy standing outside, getting some air, back to the fierce protector. She approved of the change. And she finally got it. The last part had been an act to let whoever lingered out there think he was safe.

He handed her a gun. "You know how to use it?"

"Yes." A whole range of guns. Guns, knives, some explosives. The New Foundations leadership didn't bother with subtleties back when she got stuck up there. You learned how to fight because weak people were useless to the cause. She just never really understood what the cause was supposed to be.

As soon as the gun hit her palm, she checked it. The magazine, the chamber. This weapon didn't belong to her, but she'd be able to pull the trigger. She was not afraid to do what had to be done to protect herself.

Holt positioned her in the doorway between the kitchen and the family room. She had her back against a solid wall and a clear view of the door and a patch of the front yard through the window within her line of sight.

This guy was good. He knew exactly how to keep on the offensive. She didn't think she could find him more attractive, but in that moment she did.

"Stay here." He held out a hand as if to keep her in place even though he never touched her. "Shoot anyone who is not me. Aim for the leg to make him hobble or the hand to make him drop the gun."

That bordered on insulting. "I'm a better shot than that."

"It's a risk to keep the guy breathing, but I need him alive for questioning." Holt delivered his comment and then slipped away from her.

For a big man, he moved without making a sound. Even the floorboards that usually creaked didn't. He shifted and stalked around her furniture and through the room until he disappeared.

She had two choices—sit and wait or track and help. She'd made a vow to step in and not remain silent years ago. She followed it now.

As she reached her kitchen, then the back door of the cottage, she visually searched for him. He'd have to be running to be gone, but she couldn't see him.

He'd congratulated her on her security system, then set up additional sensor lights that afternoon, insisting she had blind spots he needed to fix. One of those popped on behind the shed where she kept the lawn mower and other yard equipment.

She squinted, thinking she'd see movement. She could make out one dark blob...then another. They were nearly on top of each other.

She was halfway outside with the door banging behind her before she remembered Holt's words: stay here.

# Chapter Five

Holt heard the door slam a second before the sound of footsteps echoed around him. He focused, trying to pull the sounds apart. He had not one but two people out there with him in the dark. The only good news was that Lindsey was likely one of those people. He liked the odds of him against one attacker, but he hated the idea of her wandering into danger.

He ignored the sound of sneakers slipping against the wet grass and concentrated on what he could handle. Not her, but the man who had been lingering in the yard, hiding behind trees and leaning against the shed, while Holt watched him.

The guy had waited before moving in, but now he hid in that small building. The same one Lindsey said they used for storage. Holt would blow it up or drag him out. Whatever strategy would keep the guy from venturing near Lindsey worked for Holt.

But he had to move because even now she flew across the yard. She moved in a soundless blur. Once she got near him, whatever advantage he now held would be gone because she'd become his priority.

He signaled for her to stop but had no idea if she saw him. He didn't wait.

Weapon up, he slunk around the outside of the building, crouching low and placing careful quiet footsteps. If the attacker shot through the wall, he should miss. Most people shot at standing height. Holt hovered well below that.

By the time he got to the door, Lindsey stood fewer than fifteen feet away. He motioned for her to stop, and this time her forward momentum slammed to a halt. She stood there, frozen.

He didn't suffer from the same problem. He hit the watch alarm to bring Shane and Cam running. They'd come in stealth mode and assess the situation before doing anything that would derail the mission. They'd also make sure nothing happened to Lindsey if something did happen to him.

Then the silent countdown started. After one last glance at Lindsey to reassure himself she hadn't moved, Holt took off. Rounded the corner and hit the doorway with his shoulder. A huge splintering crack ripped through the air around them. Wood shredded and what was left of the door bounced against the inside wall.

Holt caught the bounce with his hip and went in shouting. In two steps he bulldozed over the figure looming on the other side of the door. Momentum kept them moving. Holt didn't stop until he had the man—and by the sheer size this was definitely a man—pinned against the riding lawn mower.

Holt had the guy's back resting on the seat and his feet scraping against the ground as he tried to get his footing. But Holt didn't give him the chance. He had wads of the guy's shirt in his fists as he leaned in.

The guy's fear hit Holt first. Panic and anger all wrapped up in one ball.

He flailed and called out, "Stop!"

The voice registered first. Holt recognized it as one

of the attackers from last night. Holt could tie the guy
back to the threats he'd overheard, then to the run on
Lindsey's house and now to her yard. The repeated shots
took guts. It suggested a dangerous level of desperation.

"Grant?" Holt called up the name out of nowhere.
Grant was the sidekick type. The guy who led with his
fists because he lacked the intuition and skills to be at
the top.

Lindsey's foot hit the threshold. Then she rushed
inside. "What's going on?"

Time to play the role of disgruntled and concerned
boyfriend. Holt didn't have much experience with this,
but he was just frustrated enough over Lindsey following him and walking straight into danger that he thought
he could fake it. "Go inside."

Grant tried to hold up one of his hands. "I can explain."

Holt used his knee to pin one of Grant's arms down.
The steering wheel took care of the other. "Do it now."

"I came looking for you." The words rushed out of
Grant as he stumbled to get them out.

"Why?" Holt angled his body so he stayed between
Grant and Lindsey.

Grant might be shaking and stuttering now, but that
all could be an act. The guy possessed one of those huge
lurking frames, as if he could get into uniform and walk
onto the front line of any professional football team and
fit in. That didn't mean he couldn't fake it all.

"You're supposed to be at the bunkhouse," he said.

This was a new rule. Holt wondered who added it and
why. "No one told me about any curfew."

"There isn't…" Grant exhaled as his head dropped
back against the metal. "Can you let me up?"

"No." That was just about the last thing Holt planned
to do this evening.

Lindsey reached over, coming far too close, and snatched the gun out of the large pocket of Grant's jacket. "I agree. You stay pinned down until you tell us why you're hanging out on my property."

Something about seeing her there, amid the chaos and fighting, snapped Holt back into perspective. He didn't need an arrest tonight. He needed an explanation.

"One more time." Holt eased up on the grip around Grant's neck.

"I can't breathe." He coughed, nearly doubling over.

Holt waited for Grant to stop with the theatrics.

"Again." Never one for an overabundance of words, Holt stuck with that.

"When you're new, the expectation is you'll stay around the bunkhouse. You've been going out and I was asked to make sure you were okay." The guy managed to shrug from his awkward position.

Holt wasn't impressed. From the way Lindsey frowned it didn't look as if she believed the line either.

"How did you know I was here?" Holt asked.

Grant smiled. "The leader sees all."

Now was not the time for enlightenment nonsense. "Try again."

"There are rumors about you and Ms. Pike."

It all sounded rational except that it wasn't. Holt didn't see how there could be gossip about anything, since the whole fake boyfriend thing had only come up last night. "Why not tell me today when we were up at camp?"

Lindsey snorted. "And if your visit is fact-finding and innocent, why not come to my front door?"

Yeah, Holt liked her point even better. "Answer that one."

He eased back so Grant could sit up. When he stopped there, Holt dragged the guy to his feet. He was younger and bigger but needed hours of training to be effective. Despite the time at the campground, from what Holt could see no one had taught Grant or anyone those skills. And Holt had no intention of doing it now.

Grant shrugged. "I didn't know if the rumors were true. I was trying to double-check."

Lindsey made a half-strangled noise. "By looking through windows?"

Holt had known she'd hate that, but the reality check could turn out to be a good thing. She needed to understand the danger and the players. Sometimes novices in matters like this caused the most trouble. He needed her protected and ready. Though the fury pounding off her suggested she could handle herself just fine.

"Maybe we should call in the sheriff," Lindsey said, selling it as if she thought law enforcement might help when she clearly didn't. "He's looking into a break-in here."

"That was not me." Grant held up both hands. "Checking up on you, that's all. I swear."

As if that didn't make it bad enough. Holt had no idea why this kid—and close-up, Holt could see he was just that, maybe in his midtwenties—thought that admission got him anywhere. At camp he was the gung-ho type. Tonight he cowered.

"Did someone tell you to come here?" Holt danced around the main question but wondered if he needed some work on the skills, since Lindsey flinched.

"No." Grant didn't break eye contact. Didn't get fidgety. "It was my idea."

Holt almost wondered if that was true. Anyone with true skills and experience would have come up with something better.

Backing away, Holt gave the guy a bit of breathing room. "I'm with Lindsey."

She frowned at him. "With?"

Holt refused to believe she didn't understand. "Dating."

"You're staying here?" Grant asked the question with a shake in his voice.

"The point is that you do not have her permission or mine to be around here." Holt decided to shake the kid. Dropped his voice low and menacing and shot Grant an expression that promised pain. "If I find you here again I won't need the sheriff. Do we understand each other?"

Grant didn't say anything. Just stood there, wide-eyed and unmoving.

"To be clear." Lindsey kept glaring at Grant. "I'll shoot you."

Holt had to smile at that. "Yes, she will."

"Okay, I get it." Grant swore under his breath. "Stay away."

"Right." Holt stepped back, leaving a slim trail for the guy to escape the shed. "Now go."

Grant didn't hesitate. He bolted around them, smacking into a ladder and running out before Holt could say anything else.

Quiet returned to the property as tension ramped up around them. Holt tried to find the right words to make her understand he was in charge, always and unquestionably.

She faced him. "That went well."

With that the anger whooshed right out of him. Something about seeing her with the gun and knowing she could and would use it if necessary had him relaxing. This woman would not hide under a bed. If threatened she'd come out fighting.

She got hotter with each passing second.

But Grant wasn't the only one who needed to "get" a few points. Holt needed Lindsey to get one major one, as well. "You were supposed to stay put."

"You should know that's not likely to ever happen." She waved a hand in front of him, up and down his torso. "This bossing-people-around thing you do doesn't work for me."

Yeah, she'd made that clear. Looked as though he had to find a new way of handling her, because his usual skill set kept misfiring. "Noted."

"We're in this together."

The words sent an odd sensation spinning through him. One he couldn't pinpoint or identify. "On that subject."

Wariness washed over her, changing everything from her facial expression to her stance. "I almost hate to ask, but what?"

*Smart woman.* "We're about to get company."

She looked around. "Another attacker?"

"No, but I'd say we have two seconds before you meet the rest of my team." Not that he thought bringing them all together was a great idea. He just didn't have a choice since he'd already sounded the silent alarm.

She tucked her hair behind her ear. "I'm not sure I'm ready."

"From what I've seen, you can handle anything." Including him...which scared him more than he wanted to admit.

SIMON PLANNED ON an evening of research. He had stacks of paperwork on Hank Fletcher. The guy left a trail. A difficult one, which was part of the reason Simon had thought the other man would fit in so well at New Foundations.

Give him a purpose and a home, build his confidence and loyalty. Hand him enough responsibility to feel secure, then begin to plant the seeds. Simon had been using the same system for years.

Some men took longer to convince. Some bought into the program from the beginning. No matter the amount of time it took, Simon won. The days of him waiting and following had long passed.

He had folders sitting on the edge of the desk. The content in front of him highlighted potential recruits. Most of the time people found their way to New Foundations without any help. The disenfranchised and disillusioned.

Every now and then they'd target someone and spend the time luring him or her, usually him, in. Simon set aside time tonight to analyze the people outlined in those folders, but Todd's call interrupted his plans.

Todd and Grant stood in front of his desk. Todd, tall and sure and full of fury, while Grant looked down and shuffled his feet. Simon had heard the report, but he wanted the live version.

"What happened tonight?" When no one talked, Simon's patience slipped. He looked from one to the other and settled on Grant. "Now."

His breath came out in a gasp. Then he started talking. "I went to Ms. Pike's house again."

The words grated across Simon's nerves. His orders had been clear. No one disobeyed his orders. "Why?"

"I thought I could gather some intel." Grant lifted his head and didn't break eye contact. "Show you what I could do."

An interesting idea, but Simon already knew what needed to be done. He did not need assistance from a novice. "What made you think you were qualified to devise strategy?"

Some of the color drained from Grant's face. "I've been trained."

Simon glanced at Todd. "Apparently not well enough, since this is your second failure in two days. Both of you."

So much promise, but Grant continued to be a disappointment. Simon teamed him up with Todd, thinking the match made sense, but Todd taught by yelling and hitting. Grant didn't appear to respond well to that tactic, which was unfortunate.

"Training or not, Hank found you and issued a threat," Todd grumbled.

"I will hear the explanation from Grant." Simon made a mental note that all the men needed a reminder lesson on boundaries. "Continue, Grant."

"I thought I could slip in, watch and report back." Grant shifted around, waved his hand. He'd gone from the collected man who welcomed the assignment of grabbing Lindsey to a man on the edge.

This would not do at all. Simon had no other choice but to make Grant an example. "But you did not ask my permission before acting. You know about the concept of chain of command from your time in the military."

There was no room for independent thinking in this group. They had one leader. One agenda.

"I thought—"

Simon gritted his teeth. "Do not waste my time with justifications."

All the life ran out of Grant. "No, sir."

Seeing the big man humbled in front of him gave Simon an idea. Grant might not be useful as a follower. Somewhere along the line he'd developed this sense that he could make calls, which was absolutely not the case. But that didn't mean he didn't have a use.

"You're dismissed. Go back to the bunkhouse."

Simon removed the man from his list of concerns with a flick of his hand. He turned to the man he normally could count on to get a job done. "Todd, you stay here."

Todd kept his attention forward, never looking at Grant as he slunk away.

"He lied about leaving. I thought he was going back to the dining hall," Todd said once the door closed behind him.

More excuses. Simon was not in the mood. "He was your responsibility."

"Yes."

"*You* failed me." Words Simon knew would race Todd to the edge of reason.

The man craved acceptance more than most. He'd grown up alone and lost his only home when an injury sidelined him in the middle of his top-tier security career. Simon took him in and invested the time his company refused to give him.

Bottom line: Todd owed him and knew it.

Todd visibly swallowed. "Yes, sir."

"You need to fix this."

Todd nodded. "I can work on his training and impose some discipline on Grant."

It was too late for that now. Simon had other plans. "Maybe there's another way Grant can help us with Ms. Pike."

Todd frowned. "Sir?"

The more Simon thought it through, the more he liked this alternative. There would be some loss and a need for retraining, but he'd get a lot more in return. "It's time to send Lindsey Pike a message."

Todd's frown didn't ease. "Okay."

"We'll use Grant to do it." Then she would be right where Simon wanted her—trapped.

## Chapter Six

Lindsey left home the next morning well before dawn. Holt had laid down all sorts of rules and regulations the night before. Talked about the places she could go and how she needed a bodyguard with her at all times. Generally bossed and pushed, even threatened to take her gun.

Not her favorite characteristics in a guy.

She'd nodded, gone to bed and beat him out of the house that morning. She knew he'd have to use the bathroom sometime. When he did, she took off on her hourlong drive into the mountains. She had a feeling the note of explanation she left would not make her return run any smoother.

She turned into the unpaved drive and went as far as she could in a car. The path led to a small cabin tucked into a round of towering trees. This place didn't have an official address. She'd discovered the hard way on a previous visit that it didn't have a working bathroom.

None of that mattered. She needed to see the man inside. Roger Wallace, nineteen in age but far younger than that in terms of social skills. He'd spent years at New Foundations. He'd moved in there with his uncle long after she got out. He was her first rescue. And he'd missed two check-ins.

She turned off the car and parked it by the gate. Once again she took out the burner phone and made the call. Left the emergency code...then waited. After a few minutes ticked by with no reply, she started walking. This was not the place one traveled without an invitation, but she knew the markers.

Before she rounded the first turn, she heard it. The rumble of an engine and the crunch of tires over gravel. Relief raced through her. Glancing back, she expected to see Roger's beat-up truck. Instead of blue with a smashed-in front fender, she saw a familiar black. Clean and shiny with Holt taking up the front seat.

She winced. Actually winced. Then she saw the expression on his face and had to fight the temptation to step back.

He slammed the door and stalked up the path toward her. Stepped over the gate without breaking stride and headed right for her. She knew she needed to shout out a warning about booby traps, but she doubted he'd hear her over the anger whirling around him. He came at her in a straight line, his attention never wavering and his frown growing more severe with each step.

She jumped on the offensive. "How did you find me?"

"No, Lindsey." He stopped right in front of her with his hands on his hips and the fury radiating off him. "We aren't doing it this way."

She could hear the tremble of anger in his voice. Not that the eyes flashing with fire didn't give him away.

But something about him verbally throwing elbows and insisting on always getting his way put her on the edge. He used that tone, and her immediate reaction was to deny him whatever he demanded. Since that felt juvenile and they did wade deeper into danger with every step, she treaded carefully. Went with a stall. "I have no idea what you mean."

"You were attacked."

She hadn't exactly forgotten. "I remember."

"Do you?" His voice stayed deadly soft.

She inhaled, pushing out her natural impulse to fight back, and tried to regain her control. Roger could be in trouble, and having Holt there might not be a terrible thing, now that he was already standing right there. "I'll explain if you calm down."

"You will explain even if I start shouting."

Holt wasn't exactly making it easy to take the high road. She did it anyway. "Roger hasn't checked in."

Holt didn't say anything for a second. Just stared at her while the deep frown lines on his face eased. Not much but a bit. "I need more details."

She toyed with the idea of telling him only enough to clue him in but not enough to overshare about Roger. She abandoned the idea as soon as she thought it. This wasn't the time. Knowing too much might endanger Roger's cover, but Holt possessed a protection power she didn't and she had to trust he would step up.

She stuck to the facts and recited them as if reading from a file. "Roger Wallace, a former resident at New Foundations. He lives out here. We have a check-in schedule and he missed it."

"How many times?"

She didn't pretend to misunderstand. Holt was collecting details and she appreciated the need. "Two."

"Has it ever happened before?"

Roger worked with her. He provided the information she needed to help others. He had trouble adjusting, but he could walk former members through the necessary life skills and he had volunteered to do that.

That meant she stayed in constant contact with Roger. Three days without a word was two days too long. They had a mandatory check-in time every other day. He'd never missed one. "No."

Holt's arms finally dropped to his sides. "We'll get back to the part about how you know him and who he is to you later."

That was exactly what she didn't want. "I don't think—"

"But right now we're going to check on him." Holt walked past her.

She grabbed his arm and dragged him to a halt. "Stop."

"Lindsey, do not test me. I am trying not to unleash on you for running out without telling me." He didn't pull out of her hold. His jaw had also unclenched.

She took that all as a good sign. "You would have insisted I not come here."

"Right." He jerked as if he wanted to take off again.

"Holt, stop." The man's stubborn nature made her head pound. "You are walking into danger."

"You're saying he'll shoot if he sees me?" Holt didn't seem all that concerned about the possibility.

From only a few days with him, she guessed he thought he could take on a bullet and win. Sometimes she wondered. The guy did possess this amazing sense of confidence. She watched him and felt safe and secure.

But there were explosives rigged and planted along the route to the house. She could look up and see it ahead, but getting there required twists and turns. Taking Roger out of the camp didn't change his us-against-them mind-set. "If you even get that far. He's got a system of traps out here."

"Then we're leaving." The news didn't faze him at all. He listened, nodded and reevaluated. "It's that simple."

She loved that about him. She threw roadblock after roadblock at him and he didn't shake. She'd never known a man like him. Her father had been weak and easy to turn. He'd heard about New Foundations and viewed it as some Nirvana. A place they could go and be safe.

"I know where the explosives are." She pointed to random spots on the ground. But they were only random if you didn't know the pattern. She did.

"We still need to go."

The words came out strong and sure, but a strange emotion moved over his face. She guessed the rescuer inside him battled with the guy who got the job done. She tried to make the fight a bit easier. "First, I'm attacked and now Roger missed a check-in."

Holt studied her. "You think he's in trouble."

"I know he is."

He nodded and stepped in closer. "Tell me about the booby traps."

She turned over his hand and traced a pattern on his palm. "The explosives are buried in an 'x' with a set of devices in the middle of the drive in a line from that tree." She pointed at a strange bush with red-brown leaves planted among the thick growth. A shock of color among all that green.

"Got it."

She knew he would, so she told him all of it. "There are trip wires and I don't know what else throughout the woods. If we stick to the path and use clues, mainly those posts, we'll be fine."

"You've done this before."

That didn't mean it didn't scare her, because it did. "I visit Roger in person out here every few weeks."

"Did you rescue him from the campground?" Holt's eyes narrowed. "Is that the big secret? Is that why someone up there wants to grab you?"

The reminder sent a tremble spinning through her. "Is now the right time for that discussion?"

"Probably not but it's happening later." He exhaled. "I don't like this."

"Because you insist on leading and hate not to be in charge?" But she knew that meant he agreed to go forward. Holt wasn't the type to run away from a potentially dangerous situation. Neither was she. Not anymore.

He glared at her. "Add that to the list of things we're going to argue about later."

She had a feeling he wouldn't forget that awful future conversation he kept referencing...unfortunately. "For the record, I'm not really looking forward to this discussion."

"You drew the battle line when you left that note." He scoffed. "You actually thought telling me not to worry would work?"

She couldn't really argue with any of his anger or her bad choices. She'd operated this morning as she always did, head down and moving forward. She acted alone because that was what she knew.

Getting used to having him around would take time. But the bigger concern was that she'd get accustomed to him being around just as he decided it was time to go.

No question she stood on the edge of heartache. She knew and saw the warning signs and didn't know how to avoid the danger.

"See those?" She pointed to the faded ribbons tied high up in the tree, then followed the nearly invisible line of wire toward the ground.

"Traps."

It had taken her forever to understand Roger's system. She talked tough, but Roger came out and walked her into the cabin almost every time she visited. "You recognize the setup?"

"Of course."

*Of course.* "Normal people aren't familiar with explosive devices."

The tightness around Holt's mouth finally eased. "I don't think we know the same people."

She started walking. "I don't—"

"No." He grabbed her back. Wrapped an arm around her waist and pulled her tight against his chest before she got more than a few feet away from him. "Do not put your foot down."

She looked a few steps in front of her and saw the disturbance in the rocks and dirt. Squinting, she noticed the thin wire. Tiny, almost a line in the dirt, but she recognized it. Not in this fashion, maybe, but Roger had shown her examples. She'd almost shuffled her way over a trip wire.

Her heartbeat thundered in her ears as she kept her death grip on his arm. "That wasn't supposed to be there."

As if she weighed less than a pillow, Holt tightened his hold and lifted her. He stepped back, taking them both out of the immediate danger of the wire.

The second those muscled arms enfolded her, the fear subsided. Her breath hiccupped out of her and she grabbed on. When he lowered her feet to the ground again, her knees buckled. All the strength left her muscles, and a sudden dizziness hit her. The mix of fear and relief had her leaning into him.

He glanced down at her with eyes filled with concern. "You okay?"

"Not really." Not when her bones had turned to jelly.

"Looks like your friend changed the pattern."

But that was the point. That didn't happen. Roger wouldn't put her at risk. He also wouldn't impose a communication blackout. The longer she stood there, the more worried she grew. "He wouldn't."

Holt didn't let go of her. Strong hands held on to her forearms, keeping her balanced. "This isn't like in the movies, Lindsey. You step on that and it explodes. There's no click or chance to defuse it. It will go off."

"I both hate and am grateful that you know that." And he seemed to know everything. When it came to fighting and surviving, he was the man she wanted by her side.

"We're changing this."

But he needed to understand she had an obligation to Roger. One she took seriously. She thought of him as a friend, though she wasn't sure if Roger knew how to have those. At the very least, he worked with her and she cared about him. She had to know he was safe. "We can't go back."

"Agreed. We need to see this through now." He stepped around her until she faced his back. "Follow behind me. Hook your finger through my belt loop and match your steps to mine. I lift my foot and you put yours in the exact same place."

This wasn't fair. She should take the risk, not him. But the determination in his voice suggested she not even try to argue the point. "Fine."

"We'll go slow."

And they did. It felt as if hours passed as they walked up the drive. More like lumbered. He measured every step and constantly scanned the area. Sometimes minutes ticked by between moves. Once or twice he shuffled his feet.

With every placement of his foot he made a mark. She guessed that was his form of leaving bread crumbs for them to find their way back again. Tedious or not, the process worked.

They got to the front of the cabin and she finally unclenched her fingers from his belt loops.

Instead of a feeling of relief and being ready to go, dread washed over her. The usual broken and cracked pots filled his porch, but there was no sign of Roger. His truck sat in its spot. She never quite understood how he got that thing in there, through the tangle of branches and over the explosives, but he did and refused to share the secret.

"This is bad." She whispered the comment before she could think it through. Didn't even know she was saying it until it spilled out. "The lack of gunfire."

"The front door is open."

She followed his gaze and stared at the green door. Didn't see anything wrong with it. "You can tell?"

"It's not lining up with the trim." He pointed as he talked. "I also see a trip wire at the top of the stairs. Is that normally there?"

"No, but how in the world can you—"

"Perfect eyesight and expensive training." Holt glanced around the wooded area one last time before turning to her. "Call for him."

"Roger?" She shouted his name two more times. Birds fluttered in the trees at the sound of her voice, but nothing and no one else moved. He didn't come out and threaten, which was what she expected him to do if he saw a stranger with her. He might even fire a warning shot first.

Holt swore and mumbled something about sleeping in. "Does this Roger have any friends he could be visiting?"

That was an easy one. "No."

"Let's go this way." Instead of walking up the front steps as she expected, as any regular person would do, Holt took them around to the side of the porch. He crouched down and peered under the slats. Used a stick he found on the ground to tap different sections of the wood. Whatever he saw or heard must have satisfied him, because he held out a hand to boost her up onto the railing. "Here."

Going first made her stomach tumble, and not in the good way. She feared setting her foot down the wrong way or putting too much weight on one board over another. So she sat there and waited for Holt to pop up over the side. He did and kept going. Straddled the railing and headed for the door with careful steps.

Holt pivoted around pots filled with dirt and others set up in what looked like a haphazard grouping but really served as yet another warning system for Roger. "Do you see anything out of the ordinary for this guy?"

She knew the place looked as if it had been left in disarray, but this was how it always looked to her. The tickling sensation at the back of her neck proved to be the bigger issue. She didn't ignore her body's panic signals. Not anymore.

She guessed Holt operated on what he could see and understand, but she told him the truth anyway. "No, but it doesn't feel right."

"I think we should follow your gut on this one." He delivered the surprise statement, then held out a hand to her. "Stay behind me and watch the path."

The comment and the feel of his palm against hers had barely registered when he pushed the door open. He didn't need to turn the knob. A gentle touch sent it swinging.

He took half a step and froze. "Damn."

"What?" She peeked over his shoulder and immediately regretted it. Her gaze went to the blob on the floor. Dark and huge, the stain grew as she watched. Then the reality hit her as a buzzing started in her head. "Is that…"

She couldn't say the word. Not when she was too busy trying not to heave.

"If I had to guess, I'd say blood." Holt squeezed her hand, then let go. "And too much of it."

She watched him reach for his phone. He pressed in a few numbers, then disconnected. Then he started taking photos.

Every choice struck her as sick and wrong. None of the callous indifference matched the man she'd seen in action over the past few days.

She grabbed his arm, thinking to spin him around. He didn't move while he shifted in front of her. "What are you doing?"

"I called in Cam and now I'm preserving the scene until he gets here."

None of the words made sense in her head. "What?"

"Cam is one of my men. You were supposed to meet him the other night but they—he and Shane—followed Grant back to the campground instead."

'I remember."

"We need experts to sift through the clues before Sheriff Carver and his band of misfits come storming in here." Holt didn't even blink. "Cam and Shane qualify as experts."

Just thinking about what could have happened to Roger and the need for more men started the world spinning. She reached out to lean against the doorway and spied a flannel shirt rolled up in a ball near her foot. "This is his—"

Holt stopped her before she could pick it up. "Don't touch anything."

"Evidence?"

"Or more traps. I don't know what we're looking at here."

Holt managed to lose her again. Seemed obvious to her. "A crime scene."

"Probably." He pointed at the lamp turned on its side and the couch cushions tossed and sitting at strange angles. "I'm trying to figure out if it looks staged."

A memory came zipping back. The car accident and the blood. How Roger siphoned off his own and saved it for weeks. "Oh."

Holt's gaze shot right to her. "Tell me."

"He faked his own death to get out of New Foundations." That was only a fraction of the weirdness. She delivered the rest. "I helped him do it. That's the mission that binds me to this area when I really want to move as far away as possible."

Holt being Holt, he didn't show much emotion. A deeper frown, maybe, but nothing in the way of shock. "I figured as much."

She'd told him this huge secret. A piece of information that should have unraveled who he thought she was and raised all sorts of questions. "That's all you have to say?"

He nodded. "When we talk later, that will be one of the topics."

That was starting to look like a really long future conversation. But she couldn't think about that now. Could barely think about anything as she stood there, trying to fight off the need to double over and try to catch her breath. "What now?"

"We back out and let my men check the scene. They'll grab anything that implicates you or points to Roger's past, since I'm thinking you want all that hidden."

She didn't fight it. "Yes."

"Then do not move." He took one step, and an agonizing creak rang out under his heel. "I mean it."

"I plan on listening to you from now on."

His eyes narrowed. "I want to believe you."

She didn't touch that. Watched him travel around the small two-room space instead. He conducted a visual tour of each surface and snapped photos before coming back to stand next to her. "There's no body. Plenty of signs of a struggle but no drag marks in or out."

She had no idea how he picked all that up in a two-minute visual scan. "That's a horrible sentence."

"I don't disagree." He glanced at his watch. "Time to go."

She didn't question him, mostly because she didn't want to stand in the middle of the macabre scene with the ransacked cabin and the papers strewn everywhere. And the blood. She might see that puddle every day for the rest of her life.

He made it sound easy, but retracing their steps took almost as long as getting to the cabin. It probably didn't help that she'd turned into a shaking mess. What little she was able to hold it together back at Roger's house abandoned her the farther away she got. A trembling started deep in her bones and moved through her entire body.

By the time she got back to her car and tried to pull out her keys, she was a mess. She dropped the set twice. The third time they jangled so loudly in her palm that Holt removed them with a gentle touch. When he suggested she ride with him and he have his men, whoever they were, return her car, she jumped at it.

The long drive back to her house passed in slow sections. She dreaded he'd start that conversation he was so desperate to have. But he didn't. He turned on the heat, despite the time of year, and let the radio play softly in the background.

It took until they'd almost reached home for her to realize this qualified as his attempt to put her at ease. He didn't rapid-fire questions at her or demand answers. He let her do battle with the adrenaline coursing through her.

She was about to thank him when she saw the man. Tall and almost as sturdy as Holt. This guy had light brown hair but stood in a battle position that was now so familiar to her—legs apart and hands on hips as the perfect scowl formed on his lips.

The man was handsome and muscular. Very fit. Had a bit of a boyish-charm look to him, while Holt wore that stern countenance a lot of the time. Still, she couldn't help thinking this guy and Holt knew each other. "Who is that?"

"He's with me." Holt parked the car and turned off the engine. "And it's very bad he's here."

That was the last thing she wanted to hear. She tried to form a question, but nothing came out. She used up all her energy opening the door and somehow getting out.

"What's up?" Holt frowned and walked at the same time. "You're supposed to be out with Cam conducting some forensics on that cabin."

"Ma'am." The guy nodded at her before returning his full attention to Holt. "We have a new problem."

Holt swore in a voice just above a whisper. "Another one?"

"What is it?" Lindsey asked at the same time.

The guy looked at her then. "There's a dead body on your property."

## Chapter Seven

So many questions bombarded Holt's brain. He wanted to know more about this Roger person and how he'd got out of the camp. Holt also needed more insight into Lindsey. He wanted to sleep with her. Kiss her, touch her, hold her in bed and talk with her. His sudden need for that last one made him twitchy, but there was so much about her, her life and this situation he didn't know.

Walking now between her and Shane struck Holt as strange. He'd introduced them and watched as they shook hands. Holt ignored the "nice job" man-to-man look Shane shot him.

They'd been friends for a long time. They'd known each other and served together for a short stint. Now they worked on the same team, spent a lot of their free time hanging out and had the same goals.

They also shared a similar sensibility about relationships. Neither wanted one. Cam had been with them right up until the point he'd met Julia and then lost his mind.

Holt had watched as the men of Corcoran—the toughest guys either of them knew—get ripped apart by their love for their women. Strong, intelligent men shredded and a mess as they ran around trying to get these amazing women back.

Holt and Shane joked about it. It was embarrassing and Holt didn't want any part of it.

The idea of being vulnerable for a woman, of putting everything on the line, had him mentally throwing up a wall. He liked all the women his friends ended up with and understood why the guys loved them. The matches made sense.

It was the wall of fire they walked through to be together that made no sense to Holt. Why would anyone willingly take that on? He'd never met any woman who turned him around and had him thinking that would be a good idea.

But then he met Lindsey.

She counted as a wild card. He'd never known anyone like her. Even now, as they walked the line of the property and closed in on a section by the water, Holt's mind rolled. He thought back to the things she'd said and the way she acted in danger. So in charge yet human. The combination had him dropping to his knees.

Not that he planned to let either of the people with him know. He'd rather welcome the silence.

"It's Roger," she whispered into the silence.

"We don't know that." Though Holt did think it had to be. A person didn't lose that much blood and live to talk about it. He might have faked his death before, but this was another level.

Shane pushed the branches aside and kept walking. Didn't say anything, as if leaving them to hold a private conversation even though he hovered right there.

She shook her head. "I should have checked in on him sooner."

Without thinking, Holt reached over and took her hand. Slipped his fingers through hers and felt the coolness of her skin and the jumpiness of her raw nerves.

She jerked at the contact but didn't let go. No, she tightened her hand around his and held on.

Since he couldn't think of anything smart to say and since he spent part of the time scanning the surroundings for signs of trouble, he figured silence was the best solution anyway. As they got closer to the lake's small shore, Holt saw the body. Crumpled in a heap as the water lapped over his legs.

Definitely a male and not a small one. His face was turned away and the body appeared to be soaked through, either from the night's rain or being in the lake. Too hard to tell without more tests. But Holt was looking at a large form wearing dark clothes, which described a lot of men in this part of Oregon.

Lindsey stopped. Holt didn't notice until he almost yanked hard on her arm. He dropped her hand and turned to her. Shane wore an expression of concern and Holt guessed he had one of his own.

He watched the color drain from her cheeks and he leaned in closer to make sure she didn't pass out or something equally bad. "What is it?"

"That's not Roger."

"That's good news, isn't it?" Shane asked.

Holt wasn't so sure. Roger as the victim made sense. They could make those connections and draw those lines. A dead stranger on her property brought up more questions and increased the danger level.

Holt preferred to fight against a known quantity. Someone with an agenda—revenge, greed, a cause or whatever—could be trapped if you found the right bait. Not so easy with the unknown.

Rather than guess, Holt snapped into action. He walked over to the body, careful not to disturb the scene more than necessary, and crouched down. His gaze traveled, looking for signs of injury other than the obvious gunshot wound to the back of the guy's head. Any identification would help, though the lake had likely carried that away.

He got his phone out, prepared to take photos and prints and send them back to Connor for analysis. When his gaze landed on the dead guy's face, Holt knew he didn't need to worry about the identification. His mind raced as he went through every interaction and conversation. He remembered the threats the last time they'd met.

One thing was clear, their lives were about to explode. Blow right out into the open. So much for Lindsey wanting to live under the radar. Those days might be over. Holt just hoped his cover held long enough to figure all this out.

He motioned for Shane to bring Lindsey closer.

She walked in measured steps with her hand locked on Shane's arm as she stumbled over the loose rocks. "What is it?"

"Not what, who." Holt stood up. "Grant."

"The guy that attacked you at the house and then you caught sneaking around?" Shane made a hmmphing sound as he dropped down to conduct his own visual inspection of the body.

"Gunshot to the back of the head," Holt said, stating the obvious.

Shane glanced up at Lindsey. "Holt said you're a good shot. Where's your gun?"

"At the house." She tore her attention away from the lifeless body and glared at Shane. "Do you think I did it?"

"No, but others might." Holt understood where Shane was going with his thinking and mentally followed along. This scene had all the hallmarks of a trap.

"Why would I kill this guy?" She yelled the question loud enough for her voice to carry through the trees. The steady clap of the water against the rocks played in the background as the breeze blew through, but she stood perfectly still.

Shane stood up. "Someone will have a theory."

"Meaning?" Some of the confidence left her voice.

Never one to mince words, Shane didn't do it now either. "You're about to be set up."

"That's ridiculous." Lindsey snorted. When the men continued to stand there, she looked to Holt, who nodded. "Wait, you agree?"

Holt realized he'd have to spell it out. This was a delicate balance between keeping her calm and telling her what she needed to do so she could act. Unfortunately, he didn't do delicate. "I think Grant here got on the wrong side of someone at the campground. Maybe this is payment for not grabbing you the other night."

"Okay." She made the word last for three syllables.

He could see she still didn't get it. Her brain probably rebelled because of all the violence she'd seen. He couldn't blame her for shutting down. Normal people didn't think things through, looking for every evil angle. "And now he's on your property."

"It's a message or the beginning of a trap, maybe both," Shane said, speaking slower and softer than usual. He didn't do delicate either, but he possessed more tact, which might help in this situation.

For a second Lindsey stared at the rhythmic falling of the small waves before turning back to Holt. "So, what do we do?"

"Go look for your gun and—"

Shane scoffed at that. "I'll bet you a thousand dollars it's not where you think it is."

She shook her head. "I have a security system."

"So?" Shane practically laughed. "I won't tell you how easy it is to manipulate and get around those."

*So much for tact.* Holt ignored the interruptions and got the rest of his thought out. "Then we call Deputy Carver."

Now he stood back and waited for Lindsey's reaction. He predicted it wouldn't be great. Not that he could blame her. They'd hit her with one bad piece after another. Anyone would buckle.

Instead of screaming the tall trees down around them, she shook her head. "He's useless."

Holt counted on that. Competency meant finding clues and solving the crime, and if someone really was leading law enforcement in Lindsey's direction, Holt needed to slow that progress down. He needed someone who lingered a step behind, and the deputy seemed like the man for the job. "Let's hope so, because I have a feeling we're going to need someone who's not smart enough to follow obvious clues."

Lindsey rolled her eyes. "Frank Jr. is perfect, then."

"Interesting reaction." Shane frowned. "Sounds like a town called Justice doesn't have much of it."

Holt couldn't agree more. "Which is why we're here to help."

SIMON TOOK ONE look at Deputy Carver and thought it was almost unfair how easy the next few minutes were going to be. The elder Carver was someone Simon understood well. He had a singular focus and knew the world didn't always break down into easily definable categories of right and wrong. He could not be managed, but his young son could be.

The young deputy was about to fall into a pile of

trouble if he didn't obey the simple rules. Simon motioned for him to take a seat.

"What is it?" Simon asked after growing weary of Frank just standing there, twisting his hands together.

"There's been some trouble on the Pike property."

Simon knew all about the body and the chaos. Lindsey would no longer be able to hide, which was exactly the point of the exercise. "We've talked about the pros and cons of you coming to my office during the day."

"I followed all the requirements you put in place. No one thinks I'm here on official business. I made it clear this was a social call."

Always nice to have rule-abiding people on his payroll. Simon got a special kick out of taking his relationship with Frank Sr. one generation down and influencing the son, as well. Some people proved easy to purchase. "Tell me about Lindsey Pike."

Frank Jr. lowered his arms and balanced his hands on the back of the chair in front of him. "There's been a murder and it impacts you."

Little slowed Simon down. This wouldn't either. "How?"

"The victim is Grant."

No surprise there. Simon had given the order. He was just grateful this one had been carried out. "Tell me exactly what you're saying."

"Someone shot Grant in the back of the head and dumped his body next to the waterline near Lindsey's cottage."

Simon didn't care about this news. It didn't impact him at all, except as he could use it to get what he wanted from Lindsey. "What did she see?"

The deputy frowned but was smart enough not to ask too many questions. "Nothing."

"And Hank?" They'd likely serve as alibis for each other. That didn't mean they weren't in it together. Or at least that was the seed he intended to plant...right now.

The deputy shook his head, as if trying to understand the question. "You know about those two?"

The profound lack of faith in him and his skills had Simon thinking he needed to show more strength. So few people even saw him outside camp. Inside he'd become a figurehead and an inspiration, both an example and an ongoing threat. "I know about everyone on my payroll. Every detail. Every secret they don't want me to know."

"There'll be an investigation."

They'd finally hit on a point that interested Simon. He leaned back in his chair. "Does Lindsey have an alibi?"

Frank Jr.'s hands tightened on the chair until his fingers turned red. "Excuse me?"

"I've heard she's an expert shot." The woman's skills in running and hiding proved impressive, but those days were coming to an end.

"As are a lot of people around in this county, including people who live on your property."

Simon couldn't afford to let the deputy's mind wander in that direction. "I wasn't going to mention this, but Grant had a problem at her house."

"Meaning?"

Just as expected, he took the bait. Simon had to bite back his smile of satisfaction. "He went over there to deliver some information to Hank about work. Hank and Lindsey took exception. They threatened him."

Frank Jr. leaned forward. "What did they say?"

"I wasn't there. I just got the impression Hank made the usual guy threats about staying away from his woman, but Lindsey...well..." Simon tapped his pen against the armrest. Drew out the scene, letting the deputy come to him for each morsel.

"What?"

"She threatened to shoot Grant."

The deputy's head snapped back. "Why would she?"

"I found out, too late, I might add, that Grant had a bit of a crush on her. He's been following her around, or I guess I should use past tense." Simon shook his head to complete the effect. "If I had known, I might have been able to turn this around before it became a tragedy."

The deputy pushed off from the chair and stood up straight again. "You mean Grant was stalking her."

"Nothing on that level. But you can imagine what the news about her dating Hank did to Grant."

"Did he say he was afraid of Hank?"

A reasonable assumption and Simon stored that information away for later. He could push the thinking in that direction if needed, but for now he wanted the spotlight on Lindsey. All the pressure on her. "More like afraid of Lindsey."

Frank Jr. nodded, looking every bit in charge and more like his father than ever. "I'll look into it."

Simon held up his hands. "That's all I'm asking."

# Chapter Eight

Hours after the police left and the van took Grant's body away, Lindsey paced her bedroom. The night had fallen and the house had gone to sleep. It was almost two in the morning and she couldn't close her eyes without seeing Grant's limp form. He'd scared her and come at her with a gun, but she hadn't wished him dead. She just wanted to be left alone.

Right now she needed to research or watch mindless television or do something to fill her head with something other than images of blood and gunshot wounds. Normally she'd wander into her family room and do things to keep her busy. Not tonight. Not with two men sacked out on her couch and floor.

After the awful day and all those questions from the deputy she almost felt bad about shutting down on Holt and asking for a few minutes alone. Those minutes turned into hours and now she hovered on the edge of going stir-crazy.

Her in the room with the big bed. Two big men trapped in her small family room with all her extra pillows and blankets, not that they seemed to care about the cramped quarters or lack of amenities. She thought there was probably a better solution, but she couldn't figure it out.

Well, that wasn't true. She knew what she wanted. Holt in here with her.

She thought it and two seconds later she heard a soft knock at her door. After a quick look down at her shorts pajamas, a pink version of the ones Holt had already seen, she reached over and turned the knob. Holt stood there wearing a T-shirt and boxers and nothing else. He had a gun in his hand and stared at her.

"Are you okay?" His voice was filled with concern.

She tried to think back to the past few minutes. She hadn't knocked anything over. She half wondered if she'd started talking out loud. It wouldn't be the first time. She considered it more or less a hazard of living alone. "Why?"

"You're walking around in here." He made a circle in the air with his finger. "Like, nonstop."

She glanced at her bare feet and curled her pink toenails under. There was no way she'd made enough noise to bring her armed bodyguards running. "You could hear that?"

His gaze dropped. Bounced down her body, then right back up again. "I'm aware of everything you do."

"That sounds odd." But not bad. The tone and words had her body warming from the inside out.

He blew out a long breath. "If you're okay I'll go."

"Stop." She caught his arm before he could execute the great escape. Without using any force, she had him turned around again. His eyebrows rose, but he didn't say anything, so she jumped back into talking. "You can stay for a few minutes."

He looked at the bed, then at her again. "I'm not sure that's a good idea."

The sudden need for him overwhelmed her. She craved his presence. But she knew where his mind went.

Hers drove there, too, but she mulled the possibilities over and arrived at a different conclusion.

She wanted him in here, with her. Tonight she needed comfort and reassurance, two things she'd blocked from her life for so long.

Dragging anyone else into her mess struck her as unfair. She lived with danger just out of reach but always waiting there to strike. Lately, it had walked right up to her door. The long hours of research and all the secrets. Sharing even a portion of that made anxiety churn deep in her belly.

But with Holt something changed. He knew danger, lived mired in it and didn't flinch. He would be the type to listen and help her meet her goal...after he lectured her to death about safety. Even with his hotness factor shooting off the charts, he came with some downsides. A stubbornness that matched hers was one.

She stepped back and held out a hand to him. "Just for a few minutes."

He seemed to hesitate, but at least he lowered his gun. "What exactly do you want me to do here?"

Being bold meant taking risks. She didn't do that in her personal life. She'd step right out on the line when it came to doing battle with New Foundations. She fought behind the scenes, but she did fight.

Romance, dating, all that took a backseat. Her experience was limited and she hadn't even been attracted to a man on any physical level in more than a year except for the usual "he's pretty cute" thoughts when she saw some guys around at times.

Still, she jumped in this time knowing he could turn her down and make every second of whatever time they had left together awkward. But from the heat banked in his eyes, she guessed he wouldn't. "Lie down with me until I fall asleep."

His features softened. "Are you scared? Because nothing is going to happen in this house with Shane and me here."

She knew that. When he'd promised her earlier that she wouldn't be arrested right there and then and dragged away from him, she believed that, too. He wanted her safe. She got that.

Whether she amounted to nothing more than a potential witness to him, she didn't know. But he meant more to her. He'd become a symbol of how things could be. Decent and strong. Most of the men she'd known in her life failed at both of those.

She didn't lower her hand. Not yet. "Please."

His gaze jumped back to the mattress before landing on her face again. "For a few minutes only, because I need to keep watch."

As excuses went, that was a strong one. She ignored it anyway. "Thanks."

He unloaded his weapon, then double-checked it before putting it on the table next to her bed. She was going to tell him about the drawer and the small gun safe in there until she remembered him searching through everything in the room with her once they found her gun missing.

Another fact that she could not think about right now. If she added up all the problems of the tragedies of the past few days, she might have to curl up in a ball in the corner. If her mind turned to Roger and what possibly happened to him, she froze.

She didn't have many friends, choosing instead to keep people at a distance and out of harm's way. She cared about Roger. He might not be able to articulate his feelings for her, but she knew he depended on her, and for him that meant something. And she might have failed him.

Holt turned back to her and took her hand. "Lindsey?"

She shook her head, pushing out all the negatives and concentrating on the one positive thing that had happened to her—him. "Sorry."

"Are you nervous?" When she shook her head, he frowned. "You're not afraid of me, are you?"

The conversation had sure gone sideways in the past few seconds. When her thoughts started spinning, he'd shifted into worry mode. She wanted him to back out of it. "I wouldn't want you with me if I were. Truth is, you make me feel safe…and other things."

He nodded but instead of leading her to the bed, he pulled her in close. "We're going to do this first. Get it out of the way so it's not hanging out there between us."

Before she could ask what he was talking about, he lowered his head and his mouth covered hers. The kiss seared through her from the start. Hot and full of need, it pulled her under. Heat enveloped them as his hands found her lower back and hers went to his shoulders. Fingers speared through his soft hair as their lips met again and again.

Something welled inside her. It felt like power and excitement. An intoxicating blend. She couldn't get close enough as her mouth traveled over his.

After a minute of touring and tasting each other, he broke away, panting. Heavy breaths blew through her hair as he rested his cheek against hers. "That may have been a mistake."

She could feel his erection press into the space between her legs. A fresh rush of warmth raced through her. "Felt pretty good to me."

"Too good." He stepped back, putting a few inches of air between them. "That's the point."

For a second she thought he was going to leave, but he leaned down and pulled the covers back. "Get in."

She didn't hesitate. She scurried inside, letting the soft sheets fall around her. She was about to say something to him, give him an out, when he slid in beside her. One turn and he lay behind her with an arm around her waist. His mouth lingered in her hair and a now familiar bulge pressed against her.

"You're safe with me." The words vibrated in his chest as he spoke them. "Always. You can count on that."

She knew what he was saying. He'd keep her safe but he also wouldn't make a move tonight. The last part both settled and unsettled her. Shane was asleep right outside the door, and the walls were on the thin side. Noises would carry. Then there was the harsh reality of bad timing and the fact that getting involved with Holt would amount to a huge mistake.

All the right answers and items in the "no" column. Still… "I like you holding me."

"Anytime." He laughed. A rich, gruff sound. "Does that sound cheesy?"

"The exact opposite."

She snuggled in, letting her muscles relax as she balanced against him. She should close her eyes and fall off to sleep. Let the poor guy grab a few minutes of rest. But even in the warm wrap of comfort a restlessness churned inside her. For the first time ever she felt the need to spill. To unburden herself.

She fought it off for minutes. Opened her mouth, then closed it and started to fight again.

"You can tell me about whatever has you fidgeting." He squeezed her tighter in a touch so comforting.

Two more minutes of quiet passed, then… "He took me there after the divorce, to New Foundations." The words tumbled out before she could stop them. "Mom got custody, but my father put me in a car during a visitation and drove me away. Stopped to pick up his brother and then we all kept going."

"How old were you?" There was no judgment or surprise in his voice.

"Seven." She kept her eyes open because closing them invited the mental images. "I remember the surroundings turning from sunshine and palm trees to miles without houses or stores."

She'd ridden in the backseat and listened to them talk. Put her hand against the window, and instead of feeling the usual heat, coldness greeted her. Then she saw snow on the ground. She'd begged them to call her mom, and that only agitated her dad more, which started her uncle yelling. He called her ungrateful and blamed her for their move.

The drive went from talk about this big adventure where she got a new name, any one she wanted, to yelling and threatening. Her crying only made it all worse. Her uncle Walt grew angrier the longer they drove, and every time he twisted in his seat to glare at her, she cowered more.

"New Foundations wasn't bad at first. There were other kids and all these people, and my dad kept insisting my mom would come there eventually." Insisted until the one day her uncle told her never to ask again or he'd kill her mom. She stopped talking for weeks then. "Back then it had a different name and really was a sort of commune."

"But it changed."

She guessed he knew most of the background. "Was that in your research?"

"Yeah."

She rubbed her hand over the arm banded around her stomach. Having him there, touching her, so close, settled her nerves. Made it possible to tell the story. "Things changed a few years in. My dad went from nervous and jumpy to paranoid. He was convinced the police were coming to take me away and made me practice all these drills. Learn how to shoot. My uncle seemed to encourage the mental decline and instability."

Holt placed a soft kiss on the side of her head. "Did something happen that caused the change?"

"Looking back now, I think it was gradual, or maybe he was never well. I'm not sure." She struggled to remember all he'd said, but in her young head it sounded wild and scary. Now she wondered if he suffered from delusions. It was as if he'd talked about being tracked and followed so many times that he started to believe it. "I'm not sure, but this new leader came in and the light feeling at the campground went away. I was probably twelve at the time."

That was when the fear started. Her father had told her years before about her mother dying. Showed her a clipping from the paper. The new leader made her yearn for her other life, the one before. Her father loved the guy, and soaked up every word, while her uncle hung back. It caused a rift between the brothers. One she never quite understood because she did everything to stay out of Uncle Walt's way.

"I tried to run away." Twice, but the second time resulted in her being thrown into a hole and guarded, and she had no wish to relive that in her memories. "The days got worse. People left and the guns rolled in."

"They've been up there for that long?"

She assumed that meant he had seen the storage facilities and all the weapons. "I was about fourteen when the amount of firepower started to register in my head. No one said what it was for. The adults likely knew, but I didn't."

"There's enough for a small army up there now. Weapons regular citizens shouldn't possess."

She shivered at the thought and he pulled her in tighter against his body, tucking her head under his chin. "I escaped before my fifteenth birthday. I was supposed to start learning new battle techniques. I had no idea what that meant, but I needed out. The kids rarely got to leave the camp back then."

"It's still the case. Adults can come and go with more ease."

"I hid in the back of a delivery truck. It was refrigerated and I almost froze by the time I got off the mountain and out of there." If she thought about it long enough, she could still feel the numbness in her fingers. "The older Sheriff Carver was up there all the time, so I knew not to run to him. I hitched and got far enough away where I could ask for help."

"That story makes me crazy." Holt blew out a harsh breath.

She could hear the anger in his voice but knew it wasn't aimed at her. "Why?"

"You were put in danger." His back moved as he blew out a long breath. "The police wherever you ended up didn't do anything to start an investigation at the campground?"

"I didn't contact the police. If I did, my father and

uncle would find me, or at least that's what I thought."
Her only goal back then had been to get out. She didn't
really have the life skills to do much else, but her survival instinct kept her going. "I found a woman, who
got me to another couple, who eventually got me to my
aunt."

"Your mom really was dead?"

"Yes." The biggest regret of Lindsey's life was not
getting out in time to let her mom know she was safe.
"I went with my aunt, who taught me what I needed to
know and changed my name and hid with me."

Aunt Chloe turned her life upside down for her without question. She made Lindsey promise not to go near
her father ever again. When Lindsey lost her last year
in a car accident, she'd lost her last ties to her extended
family.

"A few years ago, my father died in a raid about a
hundred miles away from here. The New Foundations
folks stood up for some guy engaged in a battle with the
FBI." Her aunt had delivered the news without emotion.
Lindsey tried to mourn but couldn't.

Holt leaned over and kissed the side of her head. "I'm
sorry."

The sweet touch sent a new spiral of warmth running
through her. That and the acceptance. She didn't hear
pity or disgust in his voice. Just a gentle understanding.
"Great gene pool, huh?"

"Don't let your father's actions define you." Holt's
hand slipped up higher, to just under her breast. "I think
you're pretty amazing."

"You know I want to turn over and face you, right?"

His breath grew heavier. "Go to sleep."

He was right and she tried not to grumble about it.
"Where will you be?"

"Right beside you."

She took that as a vow and let herself drift off.

ONCE SHE FINALLY fell asleep, the morning came fast. She woke up with her legs tangled with Holt's and his arms still around her. When he got up to shower, she turned and buried her face in his pillow. Smelled his scent on the sheets.

He'd left a few minutes ago to run some errands for what was supposed to be his job. He said some sort of memorial service was being planned for Grant and he had to do some things for it.

That left her alone with Shane. Not exactly a hardship, since he stood in the middle of her kitchen making her breakfast. There was no end to the talents of these Corcoran Team gentlemen.

She watched him move. He had the same easy control over his surroundings that Holt had. They both stood around six feet tall. Shane was broader and more muscular. Handsome, with his light brown hair and the scruffy start of a beard around his chin.

He had a bit of a boyish handsomeness about him. Not the dark and brooding look Holt possessed. She found Shane cute and easy to be around. Holt made her hot and jumpy and ready to replan her entire life to spend time with him.

Yeah, she was in trouble in the don't-get-attached department.

"Have a good night?" Shane glanced up at her as she took a chair at the small kitchen table. "You should see your face. It was a neutral question, I promise."

It felt more like a test. Since she guessed Shane was like Holt in that he believed in straight talk, she gave him some. "We're not sleeping together. Me and Holt, I mean."

One of Shane's eyebrows lifted. "Are you sure? Because I woke up by myself in the family room this morning."

She ignored his grin and the lift of amusement in his voice. "I meant sex."

He gave her a wink, then returned to the frying pan and cooking bacon. "Not my business."

She inhaled, enjoying the smell. Then she wondered where the groceries came from, as her idea of breakfast consisted of cereal eaten over the sink. But another more pressing question picked at her brain. "He wouldn't tell you?"

"Holt is my best friend."

Not the clearest answer, but then she guessed that might be her real answer. "I'll take that as a yes." Which raised another question. "Is he always so…bossy?"

Shane made a noise that sounded like a snort. "Absolutely."

Just as she feared. Having two of the same type under the same roof—and Shane might add a third—would make the next few days rough. "Wonderful."

He dumped the bacon on a rack and then turned back to her. A smile lit his face a second later. "Really, never play poker. You don't exactly hide your feelings well."

"Your best friend can be difficult." An understatement but not wrong.

Shane put a cup of coffee in front of her and pushed the milk container closer to her. "You should meet his sister."

Lindsey froze in the act of pouring. "I didn't know he had one."

"A baby sister. Makena." Shane got a strange look in his eyes. "She's…um."

*Well, well, well.* "Is the word you're looking for *hot*?"

"She's definitely that. Tall with long black hair." Shane wiped a hand over his mouth, then shook his head. "They share their Japanese mom's features and a raging case of stubbornness, which I blame on their tough career military dad."

Lindsey liked the insight into Holt and his personal life, but she got the very real sense Shane had pivoted into biographical data to keep from talking about Makena. A part of Lindsey would love to know what Holt thought about his best friend having an obvious thing for his baby sister.

Later she just might, but now she stuck with low-controversy subjects. "Sounds like a good way to grow up."

"Not really, but I'll let Holt tell you about it."

That grabbed her attention. After spilling about her past last night, she'd drifted off to sleep. Holt didn't offer up anything, but she really hadn't given him a chance. "I'm not sure he will."

Shane dumped food on her empty plate. "You don't see it?"

The aroma of eggs and bacon filled her head. She fought off the temptation to start eating before he took his share. "What?"

"How he looks at you."

Her appetite withered and she lowered her fork. "Like he wants to strangle me?"

Shane laughed. "Yeah, sometimes that, but I mean the other times."

She ran through the conversation and the things he'd

said last night after the deputy left, and she came to one conclusion. "Are you matchmaking?"

"Of course not." He dug his fork into the pile of eggs in front of him. "I'm a tough run-and-gun type."

But that twinkle in his eyes. Shane might be big, but he was also quite charming. She wondered if Makena had ever had all that attraction and cuteness aimed in her direction. The woman wouldn't stand a chance.

Shane swallowed and reached for his coffee mug. "I'm also the only one in this house sleeping alone. Just saying."

Lindsey thought about ignoring the comment but decided not to. "I don't trust many people."

"I get that, but if you're going to pick one person, Holt is the right one." Shane shoveled in another forkful of eggs and washed it down with more coffee. "And after that comment I need to go out and shoot something to get my commitment-phobic reputation back."

*Definitely matchmaking.* "Very reasonable."

This time he picked up bacon. "It'll give me something to do while Holt is out."

The way Shane said it clued her in. Holt had mentioned work and errands and things he needed to do, but it sounded as if Shane knew more. "Where is he?"

"The boss called him in for a one-on-one meeting."

"You mean that Connor guy who runs the Corcoran Team, right?" She hoped but she doubted.

Shane winced. "I mean his boss at the gun-running cult. Holt is pretending to be Hank at the moment."

Her stomach dropped and a spinning started in the center of her chest. She dropped her fork and it clanked against the side of the plate. "I notice you waited until now to tell me that part."

Shane looked at her plate, then at her face. "Did the stall work?"

It only prolonged the inevitable. Now she'd worry all afternoon until Holt walked in the door again. "Let me put it this way. Do you have a gun I can borrow for some of that shooting practice?"

Shane smiled. "I'll take that as a no."

"Right."

"I like you, Lindsey Pike." Shane reached for the coffeepot. "And I promise you Holt will be fine."

She decided to believe him. It was either that or storm up to the camp, and that couldn't happen...though she might make an exception for Holt. And that scared her to death.

## Chapter Nine

Simon leaned back in his chair and eyed up the man in front of him. He had the look of someone skating on the edge. Stayed in shape and scored off the charts on the shooting trials, but there was a certain something bubbling under the surface, as if he stood a step away from causing chaos. Simon liked that about him.

Without the Lindsey piece, Hank would be the ideal candidate to groom as second in command. But Lindsey's presence put that plan into serious question. Nothing new there. She had a tendency to ruin everything and everyone she touched. She would understand that soon enough.

"You've had a busy few days." Simon tapped his fingertips together as he quietly assessed and analyzed every move and reaction.

But Hank didn't give anything away. His expression never changed. His temper stayed even. When questioned about his shaky past, he insisted the day he fired on the collaterals in that Afghanistan village he was following orders and worried for the safety of his men. Instead of being honored or winning an award he got booted. Faced charges and had to start over.

Simon knew all about starting over. It took years but he'd worked his way up at New Foundations, taking every crappy job and learning how the camp operated. When he found the training subpar, he left and acquired the skills and contacts he needed.

He returned renewed and when a position of power opened, he went for it. He removed the people in his path and made a grab for what he wanted. And when the day came to take over and spin the camp's direction, he did not hesitate.

He sensed those same qualities in Hank. Simon just had to bring them out. Mold them to what he needed.

Hank continued to stand half at attention with his arms folded in front of him and legs apart. "I'm just trying to keep my head down and do my job."

"That didn't work." When Hank frowned at that, Simon explained. "My understanding is you recently ended up in the middle of a crime scene."

"That's not exactly what happened." Hank hesitated over each word as if wondering how much he should say.

"Tell me what did." Simon knew but he wanted to test Hank's ability to tell the truth. The man bucked authority since authority had jerked him around, but Simon demanded full obedience. It was one of the things missing from his predecessor's regime. The first thing Simon did after he cleaned out the members who would slow them down and try to tinker with his vision.

"My friend owns the property where Grant's body was found," Hank said.

A sanitized version. Simon appreciated that Hank could offer one, but he needed more. Mostly, he needed Hank to know all of his moves were being watched and accept it. "Lindsey Pike."

"Do you know her?"

"Of her." An understatement, but the answer worked for now and Simon was not ready to explain. But soon.

"The deputy sheriff has been asking questions about her and Grant."

Hank leaned in. A subtle move but noticeable if you watched closely, and Simon did. A potentially dangerous thing since jealousy and ridiculous talk of love had led to the downfall of more than one man.

"What do you mean?" Hank asked.

"Grant had a crush on Lindsey." Simon repeated the made-up tale. "He came over and you two kicked him off the property. Not to state the obvious issue but now he's dead. Even ignoring New Foundations' stated preference for its members not to draw attention, the timing is not ideal."

Hank returned to his expressionless stance, looking both rigid and disinterested. "You think I'm involved."

Simon dodged that question more to test Hank's reaction than anything else. "Surely, you can see where law enforcement would draw some conclusions."

"They're wrong."

The guy stayed solid. Didn't shake. Good to know. "I'm sure, but still we need to play this the right way."

"I don't know what you mean."

"Sit down." Simon gestured to the seat in front of him and waited until Hank, like the good soldier he was, obeyed. "You should come back to the bunkhouse. For now."

"I would prefer to stay with her." Before Simon could respond, Hank continued. "I have a friend in town and he's staying with me at Lindsey's house, as well. It would be awkward for him to be there while I'm not. She barely knows him."

Unexpected news. Simon hadn't planned ahead for another new player in town. Nothing in Hank's file pointed to him even having friends. "I had the impression after your military issues your support system disappeared."

"All but this guy. He was there and tried to testify for me." Hank remained as blank as ever. "I've actually been thinking about introducing him to you and the idea of the camp. He would appreciate what we do here."

Simon didn't care for the turn in the conversation. He'd learned from his short time in charge to be aware of tone and subtext. "Which is what? What do you think we do here?"

"Live our lives without hassles. No government interference. No rules except the ones agreed to long ago." Something close to a smile formed on Hank's mouth. "That's why I came here and why I stayed."

"And no one here is subjected to the government's idea of criminal charges." Simon believed in handling issues in-house, which explained Grant's current state.

"Exactly. I've had enough of those."

Simon liked that Hank didn't try to deny or explain. Not that he could do the former. They'd talked about his past in the very first interview. "That's why I think you should be a little careful with Ms. Pike."

"Is that a warning?" Hank asked in a voice suddenly filled with venom.

Simon matched Hank's attitude with some of his own. "Does it need to be?"

"I don't intend to stop seeing her."

*Interesting.* Simon still couldn't tell if that insistence made Hank an ally or an enemy, but it did set off an alarm that Simon would not ignore. "Of course not, but I am considering increasing your duties here. Moving you into Grant's position and providing you with more extensive training."

"I would appreciate that."

Of course he would. Anyone would, especially the type who came to the camp. Simon understood the need of men to belong and feel as if they were accomplishing something.

Up until now they'd been working behind the scenes. Fighting the government by supplying weapons to a militia here and providing men on the ground there against the ATF. For the next step to work, the promise of instability and the reorganization, New Foundations needed to move into the leadership role and not just be the might behind the fight.

Leading sometimes meant destroying and rebuilding. It was a general principle most people forgot these days. They threw money and people on the same problem over and over again. He would not make that mistake.

"The position requires, at times, taking on some difficult tasks," Simon said, laying the groundwork.

Hank nodded. "I'm fine with that."

"If Ms. Pike had something to do with Grant's death, your loyalties could be tested."

A stark silence pounded through the room. The clock on the edge of his desk ticked and the springs on his chair let out a slight squeak as he rocked back and forth.

It took a full minute for Hank to speak again. "If she did it, I'll drag her up here myself to atone for her crimes."

*Right answer.* "I knew I could count on you."

HOLT BARELY MADE it in the door before he heard Lindsey's heavy sigh.

She started walking toward him then jogged. She hit his chest with her arms wrapped around his neck. "You're home."

The relationship bounced around from on-the-verge-of-sex to trying to maintain control. After holding her last night, smelling her hair and touching her skin, Holt doubted he could go back to playing indifferent, so he didn't try.

His arms tightened around her and he placed a quick kiss on her lips. "I should leave more often."

Shane cleared his throat. Since he practically stood on top of them, it was hard to miss. "I was thinking the same thing."

A red flush stained Lindsey's cheeks and she tried to step back. "Sorry."

Holt didn't let her get far. He hated the idea of her being embarrassed or using the reaction this time as an excuse not to show him affection next time. He telegraphed all of that in a kiss, this one slower and a bit more lingering, before he let her go. "Don't be."

She stood there, fidgeting as she rubbed her hands together. "I just thought you could be in trouble. That—"

"It's okay." And it was…for now. He'd played the role of Hank without slipping even though he'd had to fight off the urge to smash a fist into Simon Falls's face the entire time they talked in his office.

"Is it?"

*Fear.* He got that from her voice and the relief in her eyes when he walked in. She worried for him and he did not hate the sensation of having someone care about him. "True, Simon Falls threatened. He worked that in along with trying to plant the seed you killed Grant."

She went from nervous to ticked off in two seconds. It was an amazing thing to see. She drew up, her shoulders stiffening, and a new determination washed over her. "What?"

Yeah, he knew that would get her attention. "After

that, Simon moved on to offering me Grant's job…
sort of."

Shane nodded. "So, your typical business meeting."

As if Holt knew. "Don't ask me. I've never had one."

"Go back." Lindsey stepped between them with a
hand on Holt's chest and another hovering in the air in
front of Shane. "He's blaming me?"

"He and Deputy Carver." That was the interesting
part for Holt. Simon made sure to mention law enforcement, which made little sense for a man like him. Sure,
he probably had to walk a fine line, but if he really did
want to start his own militia, cozying up to the sheriff
seemed like an odd course.

Shane shot her an I-told-you-so smirk. "Remember
my comment about the setup? Here you go. These are
the building blocks."

"This is sick." She touched a hand to her head.

Holt lowered it again so he could see her face. The
fact he kept holding on meant nothing. "What do you
know about Falls?"

"I've never seen or met him. He never leaves the
campground. I once tried to have someone smuggle out
a photo but it didn't work." She shrugged, clearly frustrated by the walls she kept hitting. "All my research
points to a guy who appeared on the scene out of nowhere and moved into the leadership role when the person above him died."

That all sounded familiar. "Us, too. This Falls char-
acter didn't exist before a few years ago."

"Right when the accident that wasn't occurred,"
Shane mumbled.

Her gaze shot to him. "What?"

Holt decided it was best she knew what they knew.

"We've reviewed the record and think someone tampered with the guy's car."

"You mean Simon Falls." She looked from one man to the other. "He killed the guy in power and took over."

"Simon did benefit from the death." Holt didn't have the proof. He also didn't have a doubt that was what happened, but he'd like some verification about Simon from people who lived there. "Do you have files on other people up there?"

"Yes." Lindsey launched right into offering help. Gone was the stalling and backtracking from when they first met. "I'd start with Todd."

"Lindsey, we need to talk to the people who got out. The intel we have doesn't show anyone escaping," Shane explained.

For the first time since they'd started talking about the camp she smiled. "You don't have the intel because I'm good."

"You made that happen? You engineered the escapes?" Shane asked, clearly impressed.

"I get them out. New Foundations lies in order to keep its 'no one ever wants to leave us' motto clean, but there are people who have escaped, those I've helped and probably more who got out before I stepped up."

If he hadn't been attracted to her before then that explanation would have done it. Holt admired her and genuinely liked her. He was also determined to protect her, and that meant digging into her private life and all of her accomplishments in uncomfortable ways. "You can get us a meeting?"

She bit her bottom lip but then nodded. "Yes."

"That's trusting." He liked it.

"Are you telling me you can't be trusted?" The words sounded tough but she said it in a joking voice.

"I'm telling you I'm the one man you need to believe in." And he wasn't kidding. He meant it to his soul.

She nodded. "Done."

WHILE LINDSEY GATHERED her intel and files and all the material she kept in coded folders that no one could read because they didn't make sense as written, Holt stepped outside. The weather had turned and a warm air blew over the porch.

He heard a noise but didn't have to turn around to check it out. He'd known Shane long enough to know he'd follow.

Shane took up the position next to Holt and stared out over the lawn. "So…"

That was just about as much as Holt wanted to hear. "Stop talking."

"Not going to happen." Shane turned and leaned against the post. The move put him face-to-face with Holt. "You still saying she's just a job?"

Holt wanted to say yes, but he couldn't force the word out. "No."

"That's progress."

He didn't even know how to explain it. He'd known her for a short time, but he'd been watching her for longer. Her looks knocked him flat, but there was something about her strength that reeled him in. Now that he had a window into her past and all the chances she'd taken, he couldn't help being in awe of her.

This was not a woman who ran or withered. She'd meet him head-on, not take his grumpiness personally. Question was whether she'd welcome him into her bed again. "She's…special."

"Agreed." Shane held up a hand as soon as he said

the word. "Don't look at me like that. I mean for you. I like you two together."

The anger welling up inside Holt died back down. Shane wasn't blind and Holt understood that, but Shane didn't quite get this point. "We're not."

"You gave up the couch last night. I know because I woke up and took it."

Yeah, there was no way to dodge that fact, so Holt didn't try. "She was upset."

Shane leaned his head back against the railing. "You are not really going to use that excuse for wanting her, are you?"

"I don't deny it." Holt had to give in. Blaming Lindsey amounted to being a coward on this score.

Truth was he'd walked into that room, knocked on that door, because he'd heard the faint tap of footsteps. He only picked up on that because he was attuned to everything about her and looking for any excuse to get her to open that door.

"You *can't* deny." Shane pointed at Holt's head. "It's obvious in the way you look at her and watch her move around the room."

That sounded kind of pathetic. Holt had seen Cam fall under Julia's spell. Had heard all about the others treading water as they met these certain women. Like her or not, want to sleep with her or not, Holt still didn't want to get sucked into that kind of mess.

"It's an attraction." That wasn't a lie, so he went with it.

"No, man. It's more than that."

Holt refused to bend on this. "I am not Cam or the other guys. I'm not looking to get all tripped up by a woman."

But the more he said it, the less he believed it. He tried

to work up his usual horror at the idea of being trapped and tied to one woman. Not that he slept around or liked to lead women on. He absolutely didn't. He lived by one simple creed when it came to women—treat them how he would want his sister treated. That meant with respect and honesty.

He always started off by making the parameters clear. Fun and nothing more. He tried to remember if he'd delivered that speech to Lindsey. They'd been racing on fast forward since they met. There had barely been room for any sort of understanding…and he couldn't bring himself to suggest whatever he had with her would be fleeting at best.

The woman was tying him up in knots and he couldn't get free. Now he had to figure out if he even wanted to.

"One thing?" Shane's tone suggested this could be a kick-to-the-gut type of thing.

Holt knew he should say no. Should walk away. Maybe get in the truck and go for a drive to clear his head. "What?"

"Tonight when you go into her room—and you will, so don't deny it—maybe test and see how deep that attraction goes."

Holt's mind zipped to the night and Lindsey in those near-see-through pajamas and his brain shut down. "You're giving me love-life advice?"

"I'm trying to save you from running around in circles like Cam just did."

Holt feared it might be too late. "That's not something I would do."

"Right." Shane pushed off from the railing. "You keep thinking that."

# *Chapter Ten*

Late that afternoon Holt's truck pulled into the driveway in front of what looked like an old barn. The inside had been converted. A brother and sister lived in there, watching over the camp from afar and feeding information to Lindsey whenever possible.

She'd helped them get out, but truth was they were about to run away from the place on their own. From time to time, she'd stumbled onto Kurt Noonan buying maps and stealing tips from the café she worked in. It had taken Lindsey forever to build up enough trust to move in and make contact. But she had and now Kurt and Kelly were out.

That's why Lindsey liked the café. Her aunt had left her with enough to be comfortable with her conservative money-spending lifestyle, but Lindsey needed to fit in and be able to gather intel, and working part-time at the café proved to be the perfect place for that.

She shut the truck door and came around to the front to stand next to Holt. Together they stared at the peeling red paint and what deceptively looked like a door half off its hinges. Grass grew wild and the tree branches inched closer to the house.

No one would ever guess about the technology setup

in there. That would teach Simon Falls to educate kids on computer warfare.

"Where's Shane?" she asked, thinking a third hand with a gun would not be a terrible idea.

Kurt and Kelly feared for their safety. Knowing two bodyguards stood watch might put them at ease.

"Doing a full-scale search of Roger's cabin with Cam. They have some equipment to detect explosives and are going to plot out the safe places to move around on the property."

The words fell flat inside her. "You mean they're over there searching for his body."

One of Holt's eyebrows lifted. "Did I say that?"

He could skip the defensiveness, because she got it. From the first time she saw that blood pool, she'd known. This was not a case of Roger faking his death. This time he was gone. She could feel it to her bones. "Didn't have to."

With Grant dead and her the lead suspect for some reason, Holt claimed reporting Roger missing would only shine the spotlight brighter on her. The decision not to run to Frank Jr. with this, too, eased some of the anxiety pinging around inside her.

She followed Holt's gaze. Watched him do his usual scan of the area. He stood always ready to protect and defend. It was one of the many things she liked about him.

He frowned at her. "I thought you told them we were coming."

As much as he seemed to enjoy the frowning thing, it annoyed her. She filed that away for later because she would tell him. "I did."

Holt leaned against the front of the truck. "Looks like no one's home."

"Always does." Lindsey was prepared to be worried about a lot right now but not this one thing. "That's part of the subterfuge."

"They're certain that someone from New Foundations is going to track them down and, what, drag them back?" The tone made the idea sound far-fetched. As if Simon Falls had better things to do with his time.

Lindsey knew better. "Kill them. The stockpile of weapons have some people up there twitchy, and that was before the newest round that you say is so dangerous was delivered."

"It's hard-core lethal."

That was the part Lindsey couldn't understand. Never did. They had the weapons and the ability to fire them. What then? Unless the guy planned to do battle with the next town over, the arsenal didn't make sense.

She joined him in leaning. Felt the heat of the engine seep through her clothes. "Is Simon Falls planning on blowing up the town of Justice?"

"I wish I knew. If someone is in on it, they're keeping it quiet."

That wasn't even a little hard to believe. "People up there thrive on secrets."

"True." He stood up and held out a warning hand to her. "Stay here."

As far as exits went, that was a good one. But it would not get him anywhere. They stood twenty feet away from the front door, and Lindsey doubted the Noonans would let them get more than a few inches closer without unleashing something. "They won't let you in."

"I get that, but I need to know it's safe for you to come with me." Holt kept walking, watching her but throwing glances in the direction of the building's front door.

When he breached what she knew Kurt considered

to be the final perimeter and nothing happened, something twisted inside her. She jumped away from the car. "Holt, wait."

He immediately stopped. Didn't question her warning, just obeyed. "What is it?"

"Something."

He gestured toward the truck with a flick of his chin as he hit a button on his watch. "Get back in."

"Too late." She didn't know, but she sensed that to be true. It was as if a huge ticking clock swung over her head and she could hear the ripping sound as it tore away, ready to crush her.

"Do not move." He held a hand out to her as if that would stop her.

She might listen, but he still didn't understand the people he was dealing with here. Kurt and Kelly were people with nothing left to lose because they'd lost everything, including the parents still inside whom they hadn't seen in two years. "I could be wrong and if I am they won't let you in."

He frowned at her. "Yes, they will."

She was all for confidence and a healthy shot of ego, but this was about safety. The idea of seeing him go down and watching the blood run out of his body nearly dropped her to her knees.

She had the sudden need to heave but bit it back. "They are trained, Holt. They will shoot you without question and not care how much I scream for them to stop. They might only be in their early twenties, but they spent most of their teen years being indoctrinated into a certain way of dealing with outsiders."

Something got through, because his demeanor changed and resignation set in. "Fine."

She was at his side a few steps later. Today she held

one of Shane's backup guns. It fit her hand and she'd practiced with it a few times, but she missed her own. The idea of it showing up somewhere connected to a crime scene sent a chill through her.

She still remembered racing into the house after Shane's dire warning that it would be gone. The safe in her nightstand had been broken into. The gun gone.

But that was days ago. Now she ignored the fear and the frustration and focused on the adrenaline. It pumped through her, sending her heart racing in a wild beat.

The closer they got to the door, the more the dread settled in. She instinctively knew something had happened. If they walked into another crime scene, complete with blood, she might just lose it for the first time in her life.

Holt turned before getting to the front door. He took them around the right side of the building. He looked up and around the walls, his gaze never stopping as they closed in.

She wanted to ask about the plan, but she wasn't sure there was one. But he had a destination in mind. Maybe he hoped to peek in a window, but that was not going to happen. The windows consisted of long slits, smaller than the size of a person and set up high. The Noonans had thought about everything when they converted this place.

As they slid along the side, Lindsey heard something. Faint and almost undecipherable. A noise, possibly the whistle of the breeze through the trees surrounding the building. Whatever it was. Holt must have picked it up, too, because he stopped. Froze and signaled for her to hold up.

Then she heard it again. An animal's cry maybe? So soft. So odd.

Holt watched each step as he started moving again. The pebbles crunched under their feet, but he somehow limited the noise.

By the time they got to the back corner of the building, her nerves buzzed. The quiet had her jumping and glancing around. She couldn't shake the sensation she was being watched. Stalked.

With his back to the wall, Holt looked around the corner. He shifted and then shifted back without making a sound. He stared at her and widened his eyes. She knew it was some sort of signal, but she didn't know for what. That was enough to keep her quiet and standing there at the ready.

Holt looked again. This time longer. He must have seen something, and curiosity had her turning to try to look over his shoulder. No sooner had her front touched his back than she heard the noise. This one clear.

The crunch of stones had her turning back to where they just came from. The man appeared out of thin air. One second she heard the footsteps and the next a guy was almost on top of her. Not Kurt or Kelly or anyone else she knew. A stranger with a feral grin and a shiny gun.

He slammed into her side, sending them both sprawling to the ground. Her gun bounced out of her hand as she made a grab for Holt. She felt only air as her body flew. She landed with a hard thud on the ground. She expected the attacker to fall on top of her, pin her down, but nothing happened.

When she opened her eyes again, she saw Holt grab the guy. The men grunted and thuds rang out as they each landed punches. In form and fighting style they appeared evenly matched.

The attacker smashed Holt's body into the wall, and

the wood cracked beneath him. Then Holt landed a knee to the stomach.

They fell and rolled. The world whipped around her as a blur of men and dark clothes passed in slow motion in front of her. She patted the ground and scanned the grass for her gun. If she could grab the weapon and separate one man from the other, at least in her mind, she might be able to get off a shot.

As she watched, the attacker gained the advantage. After a series of punches to Holt's side, the attacker threw him on the ground and straddled him. Slipped a knife out of a holder by his ankle and held it up over Holt.

Lindsey scrambled to find the weapon—any weapon. She needed to punch and kick. She'd made it to her knees, ready to jump on the guy and at least buy Holt time, when she saw a flash. Holt, looking defeated a second ago, lifted an arm. Got the gun between him and the attacker and fired.

The shot rang out. The attacker froze. The knife dropped as his hand went to his stomach. Red slipped through his fingers, and his eyes rolled back. Holt didn't wait for him to fall. He shoved the man to the side and rolled away.

Lindsey unfroze from her spot and took off on her knees. She crawled over to Holt's sprawled body. He had to be in pain and possibly on the verge of unconsciousness.

"Holt?" He said something in response, but she didn't hear it. She leaned in closer. "What are you saying?"

His eyes popped open, clear and filled with anger. "We need to find the Noonans."

He jackknifed into a sitting position. The move, so

quick and sudden, scared her. She waited for him to fall over. Instead, he jumped to his feet.

Then it hit her. The defensive position and all those groans as the attacker landed punches…all fake. "Are you hurt at all?"

"No, but the guy could hit."

Holt acted as though getting pummeled was no big deal. The other man had rammed his fist in Holt's side over and over. Any other man would have fallen down in defeat. Not Holt. He created a ruse and lured the guy in. Lindsey looked over at the attacker's still form and decided the right way to say it was that Holt lured him in and then killed him.

Without missing a beat, Holt checked the attacker for a pulse, then pocketed his weapon. Next he scooped up her gun and handed it to her. She stumbled around in a stupor. She hadn't even been able to get off her knees.

He held a hand down to her. "Let's go."

She took it and got up. Rounding the corner, she saw what he'd been staring at. The tall grass around the back of the house had been trampled down for a long stretch. The path led away from the building and toward a second, much smaller one, half a football field's length away.

Ducking down, Holt took off. He followed the path, walking beside it. She followed, keeping low. Her footing faltered when she glanced down at the crushed grass and saw blood. Not a tiny trickle. This was enough to leave a long smear.

Panic whirred to life inside her. Her emotions had been bouncing from relief to fear, teetering one minute to the next. Now they stayed locked on blinding fear.

Her fingers tapped against Holt's back to let him

know she was there. He treated her to a short nod and kept going, which was exactly what she wanted. The danger hadn't lapsed for the Noonans, people she considered both rescues and friends of a sort. Kindred spirits at least.

The storage shed sat away from the house. They kept everything in there from tissues to food. The shed housed their end-of-the-world supplies. They'd been so indoctrinated by Simon Falls that they couldn't shake the hoarding tendency loose.

Holt looked around with an expression filled with scorn. She thought he might circle the shed looking for windows and thought to warn him. She didn't have time. He lifted his leg and kicked the door in.

The wood shattered and the lock broke open with a crack. The door bounced, but Holt caught it with his shoulder. Going in first, he moved and hustled...then stopped.

Dread and sadness crashed over her in waves. "What is it?"

Holt didn't stop to answer. He flew across the room to where Kelly was tied to a chair. He felt for a pulse and cut her free. With gentle hands, he laid her down against the floor.

Lindsey almost missed it all because she was busy hovering over Kurt's lifeless form. He lay doubled over, almost in the fetal position. She checked for a pulse and couldn't find one. Convinced her emergency skills were on the fritz, she looked to Holt.

He was already moving. He slid in beside her and felt for a pulse. Then tried again. He turned Kurt over and blood drained from the injury in his shoulder, washing over Holt's hands to the floor.

He glanced up at her. "We need an ambulance, and

fast. I don't know what directions to give, so you'll have to."

As if she could remember at that moment. "Right."

"Here's my phone. Press number seven and say medical transport." He shook the phone. "Not 9-1-1 or anything else. Only number seven."

With her mind turned to mush, she struggled to understand his message. There were things in the house the police couldn't see. A treasure trove of intel on New Foundations ferreted out online. "But what about—"

"Connor will handle the rest."

She had no idea what that meant. Her brain raced to catch up but failed. All she could do was stare at him.

In the beat of hesitation, Holt grabbed her arm. Not hard but enough to kick her out of her stupor. "Now, Lindsey."

"Right." She reached for the cell and punched it in.

His hand slipped farther down her arm. "I get the worries, but you need to trust me on this."

She looked at Kelly, then Kurt. They'd been beaten and shot. Even now bruises formed. Kurt took the brunt, but Kelly had not been spared either. The attacker clearly didn't care that she was a young woman, which confirmed everything Lindsey already knew about the group.

"Number seven, then Deputy Carver." Holt nodded at her after issuing the order.

"Why him?"

"As hard as it's going to be, it's time to start flushing Falls out." Holt's expression grew even darker. "Before he attacks anyone else."

This time she didn't disagree or even blink. She just followed the instructions and hoped Holt knew what he was talking about. She wasn't one to trust and she was placing a lot in him and this Connor person she'd never even met.

By the time the ambulance arrived and the victims were loaded, she'd become convinced everything she knew and everything she cared about was about to blow up.

Holt stepped up beside her as the second ambulance took off. "You okay?"

"No." She couldn't even travel to the hospital with the Noonans. Not really.

Deputy Carver had acted exactly as Holt predicted. The deputy clearly assumed the Noonans had been loaded into normal medical transport. After all, the ambulance looked legitimate. But no. Holt arranged for something else.

He had ambulances on his payroll, or Corcoran's, that would take the couple somewhere safe. That meant she'd hear any new information relayed through Holt. While she hated losing control, under the current circumstances, she needed the help.

She rubbed her hands over her arms, but what she really wanted was him holding her. "I need to go home and pretend this day never happened."

He nodded without looking at her. "I agree."

That was a surprise. "No speech about how everything is going to be okay."

"I'll give that once I find the missing body."

The comment hit her like one more body blow. "What?"

"The attacker I shot? Gone."

She heard his anger, but the words got muffled. She turned them over in her head, trying to make sense of them. "Not possible."

"Looks like whatever militia Simon Falls is building

is coming after us." Holt finally looked at her. "Good news is I like our chances."

That made one of them.

*Chapter Eleven*

Simon stood with Deputy Carver near the main gate of New Foundations. A high fence outlined a portion of the hundreds of acres owned by them. The rest was set off with a shorter electrified fence, along with motion sensors and warning signs that promised a bullet for trespassing.

Guards watched the front, and people mingled inside the walls. No one knew about the danger lurking just outside. They'd heard about Grant and assumed a vagrant shot him. For now, Simon was content to let that story stand to all but the elite staff members who answered only to him and shared his vision.

Simon had listened to Frank Jr. talk about the attacks on a couple he described as random. Heard all about Lindsey and Hank being found there with the Noonans.

The job of framing Lindsey Pike just got easier and easier.

Simon moved in for the kill. "You no longer have a choice but to do something about her."

"I don't have any forensic evidence linking Lindsey to any crime." The deputy waved to a couple walking nearby. They didn't respond with anything other than by looking away. "I think it's more likely that Hank guy. He comes to Justice and people start dying."

"Interesting theory, but he's been up here with us."
And getting Hank arrested didn't serve any real purpose
for Simon. If anything, finding another man with those
skills and that temperament would take forever. So, no,
he'd need to remain free. "Lindsey is the one you need
to bring in."

"Possibly."

Simon decided to let it lie there. For now. He would
push later. Bring up some information Frank Jr. either
didn't know or did a good job of hiding. Simon would
be more impressed if the case were the latter, but he
suspected the former.

Buying his father off had been easy. A beloved sheriff
with a small pension and a big heart condition. Simon
stuck to Frank Sr.'s practical side and got a mountain of
assistance in return. No interference at the camp and a
free flow of information.

Now it was Frank Jr.'s turn, though he didn't seem to
realize it yet. But soon he would.

"What's the plan now?" Simon asked, trying to keep
the disgust out of his voice.

"Collect more evidence."

A response Simon couldn't control, which made it his
least favorite option. "What can I do for you?"

"I need everything you have on Hank."

Now Simon had a problem. He wanted to make a
scene and bring the deputy in line right now, but there
were too many people around. And some things needed
to be handled in privacy. That gave Frank Jr. a reprieve
for now. "I'll send it over."

"Appreciate it." The deputy nodded, then walked
away. Right past the guard and through the gate. Out
into a world where he could do nothing but cause trouble.

Todd appeared at Simon's side. He stood there but wisely did not say a word.

Simon wanted to break the man in two.

"Maybe you would like to tell me why you suddenly can't handle a simple job." Simon smiled and waved at the people he saw, but inside he seethed.

"Hank and Lindsey came in a beat too early." Todd scanned the area, never showing any outward sign of distress or blowback from what he had done. "Jeb panicked."

"And now he's dead." That counted two men dead. Simon hated losing anyone. The training needed to bring people up through the ranks proved daunting, but Simon had bigger concerns at the moment. "Jeb is a man who could trace back to me, who definitely traces back to New Foundations. It's only by pure luck he'd been doing survival training and hadn't met Hank."

"I took care of him." Todd cleared his throat and lowered his voice. "No one will find the body."

Simon wanted to argue about forensic evidence, but he let it drop. "I have a new job for you. This is your last chance to prove to me you can handle it."

"Yes, sir."

"Figure out how to take the deputy's attention off Hank." Simon thought about all he had planned for Lindsey and how none of that would happen if she left town in a panic. "And make it quick."

LINDSEY SLAMMED EVERY cabinet door in the kitchen. Holt knew because he stood right there listening to the drum show. They waited for Shane to return with news. Holt toyed with the idea of diverting her attention, but now, when her nerves rode the edge, was not the time for more kissing. Which was a damn shame.

Just when he thought he couldn't take the noise for one more second, Shane walked in. He hit the alarm code before it started screaming, then came into the kitchen.

Lindsey spun around. "Well?"

"Kelly is in stable condition." He stopped there.

Holt knew that was a bad sign. If Shane had good news he'd spill it, especially if he noticed the hope on Lindsey's face, which seemed hard to miss. But they needed everything out in the open, so Holt asked, "Kurt?"

"He didn't make it."

Lindsey sat down hard on the kitchen chair. Her mouth opened and her eyes filled. Her pain vibrated out of her and took over the entire room.

Holt wanted to go to her, and he would, but he needed to know where they were first. "Give me the full report."

Shane didn't need further coaxing. He launched right into it, even though his usually lighter tone had disappeared. "Cam and Connor are making arrangements to get Kelly to safety once she can travel."

Holt waited for Lindsey to pipe up. To say anything. Instead she just sat there, almost in a daze of sadness. With flat eyes and a pale face, she sat motionless. All the life and energy that usually buzzed around her had disappeared.

He reached over and grabbed the list Lindsey had compiled while they waited. "She saved six others. Most relocated outside of Oregon."

"I contacted them." Lindsey's voice cut through the quiet, sounding more mechanical than human.

As each minute passed he worried more about her and how she would cope. Losing Kurt, losing anyone she'd helped, would be a huge blow. Most people would shrivel and stop functioning. He hoped she would spin out of it.

"Connor helped." Holt could still hear Connor's calm voice as he worked with Lindsey to reassure everyone.

Shane nodded. "I just talked with him. He's dispatching Joel and a few others to get these people, relocate them and watch over them until we know what's going on."

The news brought relief. The tightening in Holt's chest finally eased.

"But Kurt is still dead and Roger is missing." Lindsey stood up. Went to the refrigerator and opened the door. Just stood there doing nothing as the cold air escaped.

"We're going to get these guys," Holt said, vowing to do just that.

She glanced at him over his shoulder. "After how many more people die?"

"Hopefully none." And Holt meant that. He couldn't promise everything would run smoothly and no one would get hurt, so he didn't try. But he could make a vow. One to protect and defend.

She shut the refrigerator door. "I'm going to bed."

That was all she said and then she walked out of the room. Down the hall. Holt waited to hear the soft click behind her.

Before he could say anything, Shane jumped in. "She's having a rough time."

"This sucks for her." People dead at her feet and attackers behind every door. It was too much for him, and he played this game every single day at work.

"Tonight when you go in there to help her sleep, throw everything at her to reassure her."

Holt wasn't even sure what tools he could bring to that. "Maybe she needs a break. Some alone time."

Shane shook his head. "If you think that, you still aren't getting it."

Holt had no idea what that meant, but he was a hundred percent sure Shane was right. "Any chance you're going to be out of the house tonight?"

A grin spread across Shane's mouth. "That's more like it. Give me ten minutes and I'll disappear. Check the grounds and watch from a distance so you won't need to guard your back."

"You have five minutes."

# Chapter Twelve

Lindsey wasn't in the mood to be coddled or placated. She wasn't a fragile doll, but she wasn't heartless either. She knew how a person could wither without affection and what it did to everything from your self-esteem to your outlook on life.

Someone she'd helped and nurtured and groomed to fit better into the real world was gone. At twenty-two. It amounted to a sick and horrible waste. She had no idea how Kelly would recover when the only support she'd ever had was her brother, now dead.

And then there was Roger…and Grant, whom she didn't know but who should still be mourned. The guy outside the Noonans' house. The bodies kept piling up until her insides shook with fear.

She sat on her bed, then stood up. When the nerves in her hands began to tremble, she rubbed her palms together. Was it really just a week ago when she was happy to lock and relock and check and triple-check her doors each night? That made her feel safe. Now she knew how naive that all was.

"Lindsey?"

She didn't hear a knock or the door. Nothing but Holt's

deep voice as it filled her room and moved through her head. "Do you need something?"

He stepped inside and closed the door behind him. "You."

She couldn't have heard that right. All the adrenaline and crackling of her nerves had her brain misfiring. She looked up and tried to read his expression but couldn't. "What did you just say?"

"Nothing."

"I don't think that's true."

His hand went back to the doorknob. "I can leave."

"No." She practically shouted the denial.

"Okay." He stepped farther into the room. Kept coming until he got to the bed. Then he sat down beside her.

The mattress dipped from his weight, and her body slid into his. "I can't seem to calm my nerves. I feel like I'm six seconds from flying apart."

His palm slipped over her thigh. "It's aftermath."

"It's pretty awful." She thought that qualified as the understatement of the century. "Do you always feel like this?"

"Just sometimes." He slid his hand over hers and their fingers entwined. "Your nerve endings are on fire. The danger and fear, the sadness and pain. It's all mixing and getting jammed up inside you."

"How do I get rid of it?" She flipped his hand over and studied his palm. Such a strong hand. Long fingers and the calluses of a man who engaged in physical labor on a regular basis.

"Different things work for different people." His thumb rubbed against the back of her hand. Slow, lazy circles that soothed her even as her insides continued to churn.

Bold had worked for her once before. She tried it again. "Any chance kissing does the trick?"

He froze for a second before resuming the intoxicating touching. "I am trying very hard not to be a jerk here."

She'd never thought of him that way. Stubborn, yes. The man could give classes in that. "You're not."

"Are you sure? Because it feels like I'm about to cross the boundary."

He'd lost her. "What do you mean?"

He shook his head, and his voice dipped even lower. "You're upset and I don't want to take advantage."

Wow, was he misreading the situation! The worry was sweet but misplaced. If anything, her mind wandered in the other direction. She'd made it clear she was interested. Even made a not-so-subtle offer in bed last night. He ignored it all.

She'd begun to think he could fight back his feelings for her without trouble, which was not the most flattering idea in the world. Also made her crazed with a mix of disappointment and sadness.

She knew that was ridiculous now. Energy whirled around him, but he kept it in check. He was so set on doing his job that he put being a man with needs aside. She wanted him to let loose. To trust her enough to take a chance.

But he needed to say it. She could not be alone in taking the risk. "Do you want me?"

"Since the first time I saw you in the café. Not a question and don't ever doubt it." There was no hesitation in his words or in his smile. "The way you looked and the way you carried yourself. The mix of strength and hotness had me forgetting about the assignment, and for the record, that never happens."

She wasn't sure what to say, so she went with the obvious. "Wow."

"You poured my coffee in the café and I was lost. And watching you walk?" He whistled. "Lost my mind."

For some reason the idea of that made her laugh. "I'm pretty good with coffee."

"I'd say."

She jumped right to the part that mattered. To the words spinning in her head that she was so desperate to say. "I want you, too."

He stared at her, with his gaze searching her face. His eyes softened and that sweet smile continued to play on his lips. "You sure?"

"Yes."

He mumbled something about timing. "Maybe we should wait until—"

*Absolutely not.* "What? Bodies stop dropping? I'm not sure when that will be."

He shifted a little, turned to face her head-on. "We're going to get this figured out and keep you safe."

With every sentence they emotionally moved further apart. He didn't get her concerns or where her mind had gone. "I'm not worried about me right now. I'm sick about what happened, but every second you sit here a new feeling inches its way in."

"Describe it."

The words wouldn't come. She couldn't think of one big enough. "Desire. I don't know what else you'd call it."

"Maybe I should just kiss you and we'll work on definitions later."

*About time.* "Yes."

She expected him to lean over and start with a gentle kiss. Not Holt. He lifted her, turned her. She moved through the air and when she landed she straddled his lap with a knee on either side of his hips.

Before she could catch her breath and before the room stopped spinning, his mouth covered hers. It was a kiss filled with hunger. A promise of the night to come. Her vision blurred and her fingers dug into his shoulders through his T-shirt. She held on as the world whipped around them.

His lips crossed over hers, coaxing and exploring. He'd deepen the kiss until her breathing kicked up and her heartbeat raced; then he'd gentle it. Every move and shift had her mentally begging for more. And when his mouth kissed in a trail down her neck, then up to that small dip at the base of her ear, her control evaporated.

Forget being smart. Forget the danger and the worries. She wanted this—him—right now. Just the two of them. Not about rescue or protection. About attraction flipping around wildly and out of control. About a welling inside her and a thirst that needed to be quenched.

The room tilted as his arm wrapped tighter around her and his palm balanced against her lower back. One minute she was on his lap, kissing as she felt his body reacting to her closeness. The next, her back hit the mattress and a hundred eighty pounds of pure hot male moved over her.

She welcomed his weight. From this position she could trace those pronounced cheekbones and see the bits of brown in those near-black eyes.

Her fingertips traveled over his shoulders. When she couldn't take even the small barrier of his clothes between them one more second, she reached down and stripped the tee off him. Up his torso and gone. Then her hands touched skin. She almost sighed.

Her fingers skimmed old scars. Battle wounds. She

learned every angle and line of his chest and back, and he didn't do anything to stop her. His groan cheered her on. And when her hands came to rest on the elastic waist of his boxers, he lifted his hips, as if urging her to go on.

She'd just decided to dive in when she felt his hands move. Fingers slipped up her waist, under her top. The flimsy cotton proved no match for his strong hands. He had the material bunched up around her neck and then off.

Then his mouth was on her. Licking and kissing. One breast, then the other. Every nerve ending snapped to life. With each pass of his tongue, her hips lifted higher off the mattress to flatten against his erection. He had her thrashing on the bed, her head shifting side to side.

The mix of his mouth and his hands set her whole body on fire. When his hand dipped into her pajama shorts, past her underwear to settle on her heat, she nearly jumped. He was an expert at everything, and this proved to be no exception.

He caressed and her legs tightened against his hips. She wanted him touching her, inside her. She slid her hand down the front of his briefs and cupped his erection. Her fingers moved over him, testing his length, and he groaned in response.

When he lifted off her, she grabbed for his arm, trying to pull him back. "Holt?"

"Condom." He didn't go far. Just to the dresser near the door.

She saw him pick something up. As he got closer, she recognized the packet. "You had it in my room?"

"In my hand when I came in." He shot her the sexiest smile. "I was hopeful."

Everything about him charmed her. "What about lucky? Do you feel lucky?"

As he ripped open the packet, she slid the elastic band of his briefs down. Rubbed the back of her hand against his erection, touching him until his eyes drifted shut. Then the briefs were off and nothing separated them except her shorts. She kicked them off before he could crawl back up the bed.

When his body slid over hers, the glorious friction had her gasping. Everywhere his body touched hers, something inside her popped to life. With him she felt sexy and free, a little wild and ready to explore.

She took his erection in her hand. Loved the feel of his skin and the warmth of him in her palm. She savored every noise he made, every grunt and every groan. She kept going, pumping her hand until she felt his fingers on her, in her, and her mind went blank. A mass of wild sensations bombarded her.

When he lifted her legs, pushing them farther apart as he moved up her body, she knew it was time to end the anticipation. Everything inside her had tightened and every cell begged for more. She hovered so close and was desperate for him to push her over.

The tip of his erection brushed over her. She didn't know when he got the condom on, but he did. Then he was pushing inside her. Plunging in and pulling out. The rhythm, each move causing her body to clench in anticipation. Something spun up inside her and she tightened her tiny inner muscles as a way of begging for some relief, and a heavy sigh escaped Holt's lips.

The sounds of their lovemaking filled the room. The steady click of the leg of the bed against the floor. The mix of their heavy breathing. Somehow she heard that over the hammering of her heart in her ears.

She'd turned into a bundle of cells and nerves, all begging for release. She called out his name as he pushed in deeper. When the tightening turned to pulses, she let go. Didn't fight it. Her back came off the bed, and her heels dug in. Control abandoned her as her neck strained and she said his name.

Nothing mattered and nothing could touch her. In that moment she was his and when her vision blanked out she let it be true. The strong arms, the warmth of his skin. She fell into it all as the thumping pulses racked her body.

When she finally came down again, she felt him stiffen. His shoulders froze and his hand slipped underneath her to her lower back. He held her tight against him as his body bucked.

They had been loud and sweaty, sexy and full of need. Now in the aftermath, they lay unmoving with her shouldering most of his weight. Not that she minded. The brush of his skin against hers felt better than anything she could imagine.

After a few minutes of quiet he pushed up on his elbows. "You okay?"

She tried to remember if she'd ever felt this good. "Except for the part where my muscles feel like mush and I can't move."

"Is that good?"

She skimmed her fingers over his shoulder. "Great, actually."

"Nice." He lifted his weight off her and moved to the side, taking her with him. "I'll take great as an answer."

Part of her wanted to ask what this meant, if anything. The rest wanted to savor the moment. She put a hand on his chest and snuggled into his side. In this relaxed state exhaustion overtook her.

She expected to drift off to sleep, but one question kept ringing in her head. "Is it always like this for you?"

"This is a first."

That woke her up. "Which part?"

"I don't sleep with women on my assignments. Ever. I'm not that type." She pushed up and looked down at him. Before she could say anything he started talking again. "You don't believe me."

"I was actually asking about the violence, but it's good to know I'm not a number." Something inside her stomach spun and danced at the idea of meaning more to him than a onetime thing.

"You are not a number. Consider that a guarantee."

She wanted to ask what she was to him, but she feared the answer and went with something safer. "Do you ever get scared?'

"There is fear on every job. The key is in controlling it." His fingers slipped through her hair. "Funneling that energy into something positive that will get the job done."

"The pounding in my head that started with the first attack still hasn't gone away." She'd had a constant migraine since everything started happening.

He rubbed a thumb over her temples. "Stress."

"You get that, too, I guess?'

"Stress? Yeah." He laughed. "I learned to deal with that early. My dad was a hard guy, career military. Nothing was ever good enough. He met my mom in Hawaii and set down the rules about what he expected and the perfection he demanded from day one."

She tried to imagine Holt growing up in that. It explained the stubbornness, the born leader type. "Sounds like a tough guy."

"Others had it much worse." He swept the hair back off her face. "You did."

"It's not a contest." And if it was, she didn't really want to win it.

"But it's a shot of perspective." He shrugged. "He made it clear he loved the military more than us. That we came second."

"You're not him." For some reason she needed to say that.

"I'd rather talk about you." His hand snaked down her back, then went lower.

"For the record, what you're doing there with your fingers is not really talking." When his hand cupped her butt she almost jumped. "But you should keep doing it."

"Does that mean I can stay in here tonight?"

She was prepared to offer him much more than that, but she knew he was a loner. He didn't have serious female relationships. So now was not the time. "For as long as you're in town, you should plan to be right here."

"Deal."

# Chapter Thirteen

The news hit the local paper the next morning. The facts were thin, but the story linked Grant's death to that of a brother and sister in a town a few hours away. A separate story on another page talked about a New Foundations member gone missing and believed drowned in a nearby lake. There wasn't a photo or any information, but Holt tagged the story, sure this explained the missing dead attacker outside the Noonans' home.

The paper failed to mention Kelly Noonan was actually alive, which was a good thing, since Connor made sure everyone thought she was dead. She'd been relocated and would soon be given a new identity. Her time in New Foundations would fade into memory, or so everyone at Corcoran hoped. Her time at the camp would only become general knowledge if she chose it, but she was in no condition to make any decision. Cam described her grief as profound.

Holt couldn't imagine what he'd do if something happened to his sister. Rip down buildings with his bare hands. Lose it completely. He would not accept being shipped off and handled, but then he'd be the type to seek revenge. The nasty type.

The people behind the story ached in very real ways, but the fact that a story existed wreaked havoc with the assignment. This was the kind of story sure to whip people into a frenzy. Get them panicked and create vigilantes. Especially the reference to Lindsey.

The story suggested she'd been questioned. The headline didn't blare final thoughts about her guilt, but there were enough dots to make a connection. She knew all three people. One died on her property and she discovered the other two. Pieces of her past, when pulled apart, appeared murky.

The story bore the faint touch of someone trying to smear her name. Careful and cautious, but the intended consequences weren't hard to guess.

Holt slowly lowered the newspaper to the kitchen table with shaking hands. He wanted to shred the thing. Hide the evidence and make sure Lindsey never saw it. She didn't need the hassle. Not on top of all she'd seen the past few days.

But reality stole that choice from him. She lived in this town. She served coffee to the residents. She chatted with them, lived among them. The gossip would ping from house to house until going anywhere would become difficult for her. She'd be "that" woman. The one people assumed did something wrong even if they couldn't pinpoint a logical reason why.

Holt wiped a hand through his hair. He tried to think of the right thing to say to encompass his fury and frustration, but nothing came to him.

The coffee cup thudded against the table as Shane put it down and leaned in. "I told you it was bad."

He had texted that he had news. He forgot to mention that this bordered on the apocalyptic type. "You undersold it."

"I figured reading it would be bad enough without me broadcasting the details from the car."

Holt wasn't so sure. A warning might have helped him prepare Lindsey. But that was just one regret he harbored. "I shouldn't have called in Carver to the Noonans."

Shane shook his head. "You needed to so we could have Kelly officially and publicly declared dead. Just as important, you needed to send a message to Simon Falls so that we could bring this showdown between him and Lindsey closer to happening."

She picked that minute to walk into the room from the small hallway. "Good morning." Her smile fell as she looked from one man to the other. "What's wrong?"

"Why do you assume something is?" Other than the fact a new crisis did seem to pop up every two seconds. Holt had been stomping out fires since the moment he arrived.

"Your expression, both of you." She turned on Holt. "The fact you just answered a question with a question, which seems like a stall tactic."

The woman did know how to read him. Holt didn't know if that was good or bad, but he knew he couldn't put this off. He shoved the newspaper in her general direction. "Here."

Shane shook his head. "You could warn her first."

"She can take it." Man, he hoped he was right about that. Holt had come to assume she could take anything. She listened to bad news and lived through attacks without so much as blinking. He had to hope this didn't derail her.

She scanned the page, then flipped to read the photo caption below the fold. The whole exercise took about two minutes. She glanced up with a stark look in her eyes. "I am being set up."

And she understood the facts without having them

spelled out to her. That made Holt's job easier, but the reality didn't change. Her life and all she knew were about to be turned upside down. "No question."

"I warned you," Shane said.

"Who would feed this information to the paper?" She crumpled the page in her hand as she waved it around.

"Someone at the camp, likely Simon Falls. Not on his own but through someone, so he had cover." The news might implicate others, but Holt knew the intel could be traced back to Simon. He'd keep his hands clean and his name away from the story, but he'd pulled the strings. People had been planting stories this way forever.

"It's rubbish." She threw the paper down and stalked around the table and headed for the cabinets. "Certainly people will know that."

Shane shot Holt a quick look of concern before answering, "People can be fickle in cases like this."

She turned around with an empty mug in her hands. Held it like a shield in front of her. "What exactly does that mean?"

Shane winced. "Expect the town to turn on you."

She had to know that was coming. She might not have been raised in the usual way, but small towns had an energy to them. When news spread, it raced around, hitting everyone and then circling back again with new details.

In a place as tiny as Justice, a story like this could feed the gossip mill for weeks. And as more details emerged, and Holt feared they would, the days would get longer and harder for her.

He wanted to spare her. To make things easier, but she deserved the truth. "We think he's trying to make it difficult for you to live and operate here."

Her fingers clenched around the sides of the mug. "Fine, I'll move a few towns away and do my work."

That might solve some of the immediate social pressure, but she still ignored the bigger picture. "Even without the law enforcement issues, which are very real but can be guided somewhat by Corcoran, I think it's deeper than that. Simon wants you to come to him."

She made a face as if she'd tasted something sour. "Why?"

"To stop you. To confront you." Those were only some of the angles. Holt could think of others. Worse ones. "I have no idea, but this is all too planned. It has the feel of him laying out bread crumbs and waiting for you to follow."

Shane snorted. "Only in this case the bread crumbs are dead bodies."

The comment brought the conversation to a slamming halt. Lindsey looked from Shane to Holt. "Is it wrong that part of me wants you guys to shoot this Simon Falls in the head and be done with this?"

Holt shook his head. "No."

"Not at all," Shane said at the same time.

Her grip on the mug eased and she set it down on the table. "That's why I like you two."

Some of the tension had left her voice, and her mouth no longer fell into a flat line. Holt hoped that meant they were moving in the right direction. Maybe flirting could push her the rest of the way. "Is that the only reason?"

"If so, that's kind of sad for you," Shane mumbled under his breath.

"That's enough of that discussion." She opened her mouth to say something else, but the ringing stopped her. With a sigh she reached for her cell. "The phone. And it's work. Why do I think this is bad news?"

Because she was smart. It was one of the many things

Holt liked about her. "This could be the start of a series of nasty calls. Be prepared."

"Let's see." She pushed the button and said hello.

The rest of the conversation consisted of her listening and frowning. She tried to break in a few times but seemed to get cut off. She ended with a "fine" and hung up. "Well, it was nasty all right. I just got fired."

"It's as if Simon has the bad guy handbook and is working his way through it," Shane said. "Of course, he skipped ahead with the whole multiple murders thing."

Holt watched, waiting to see if she would fold or at least scream. She'd earned the right to do so. When she just stood there gnawing on her lip, he asked the one question he hated but had to know the response to. "Any word from Roger?"

"None." She exhaled as she dropped down into the chair next to Holt. "What do we do now?"

He liked her spunk. She didn't suggest hiding or running. She wanted to dig in. All good thoughts, but Holt wanted her here, with a witness at all times, and no trouble. If someone was trying to set her up, giving him more opportunities to do so wasn't the answer.

He had another plan. One that might force Simon's hand. "You? Nothing. I'll take a shot."

Shane frowned. "At what?"

"Who. Maybe it's time I see if I can be of greater service to Simon." The guy hired him and had just given him the "guy" talk. Time to speed up the process and offer him more help than he expected.

"You can do that without breaking cover?" she asked.

Holt smiled at that. "Have some faith in my skills."

"Don't blame her," Shane said. "I was going to ask the same thing."

That one Holt ignored. "Give me a day and I'll handle it."

"How exactly?" She sounded wary as she asked, and her expression looked even more so.

The idea had hit Holt as soon as he saw the paper. Simon wanted to ratchet up the stakes. Then Holt would, as well. "I'm thinking a pretend breakup may be just the thing for our made-up relationship."

For a second no one said anything, and then the anxiety that had been pulsing off Lindsey disappeared. She didn't smile, but she did look amused.

"That makes me pretend sad," she said in a fake crying voice.

"Not half as sad as I am that you won't be serving me coffee anymore." Losing the opportunity to watch her walk around and see that bright welcoming grin made Holt want to kick Simon's butt even harder.

She wiggled her eyebrows at him. "I'm happy to make it for you here every morning."

"And serve it in bed?"

Shane shoved away from the table. His chair legs screeched across the floor as he stood up. "I'm clearly the only sane one left."

"Where?" she asked, clearly confused by Shane's abrupt change in conversation.

"On the Corcoran Team." Shane glared at Holt. "The rest of you lack self-control."

She frowned at Shane. "What does that mean?"

No way was Holt letting Shane answer that one. "Never mind."

SIMON GAVE THE approval for Deputy Carver to be brought to his office. He'd shown up at the gate, fighting angry and demanding access. Normally Simon would ignore the outburst and send Frank Jr. away as a lesson. Simon was tempted to do that, but he did need to talk with the younger man and the time may as well be now.

After the knock on the door and being welcomed in, Todd gestured for the deputy to step into the office. He did more than that. He walked right up to the other side of Simon's desk and stood there. Hovering.

Frank Jr.'s face turned red and he started pointing. "You interfered with my investigation. First, you blocked access so I couldn't ask about Grant. Now the story that raises suspicions about Lindsey. Why?"

The more frantic the deputy got, the more calm Simon became. This man he could handle, but he needed a lesson in discipline first. "As you can see, I'm working."

The deputy put his hands on his hips. "I don't think you understand how serious this is."

That fast, Simon reached his limit of tolerance. He gestured for Todd to step forward. "No, Frank. You are the one who's confused."

Without saying a word, Todd put the deputy in a chokehold. The position allowed him to take the deputy's gun and radio. He grabbed a few more things. Simon didn't pay attention. He didn't care. The point was to humiliate the man. Show him he was no longer in charge and never had been.

"How dare—" His words cut off when Todd aimed a gun at his head. "What are you doing?"

"Todd will hold your weapon and other items for you while we talk."

The deputy tried to look around, but Todd's gun was right there and his hulking figure loomed over the deputy's much smaller one. He froze and his gaze shot to Simon. "What's going on?"

"We're clarifying the ground rules." Simon closed

the file in front of him and folded his hands on top of it. "They've actually been in place this entire time, but you've been running around as if you have a say in anything that goes on in Justice. For the record, you do not."

Never did. Never would. Simon had seen to that with years of laying groundwork, of gathering the right evidence, of building contacts. He ran guns and weapons and whatever else militia groups needed. He supplied and planted the seeds to spread discontent. He caused the battles, then supplied the weapons to fight them.

It was quite a lucrative business, and a place like New Foundations, with the endless supply of bodies and shooters, had proven to be the perfect place to launch the operation. The freeloaders and communal types were long gone. He'd rushed the last ones out and taken care of the ones who refused to go. The leftovers were believers and he was their leader.

"You think you run the town?" The deputy spit out the words in what looked like a last bit of adrenaline-fueled strength. "Half the people don't know who you are and the other half think you're a cult leader."

Now that he had his say, wrong as it was, Simon would have his. "I am the person who gets things done. To do that I make deals, like the one I've had with your father for years."

"What are you talking about?"

Amazing what a well-placed bit of factual history could do to suck the life out of a man. Simon could actually see the deputy deflate as his shoulders fell. "Your father has been a very helpful silent partner in this venture. He understands that sometimes you need to look outside the law to get things done."

"That's not true."

Simon had no trouble lying, but he wasn't this time.

The senior Frank Carver was very much involved with the New Foundations operation. The real business, not the retreat. He'd financially benefitted over the years. And a few times when he needed evidence planted or someone to go away, Frank handled that, as well.

It was a mutually advantageous arrangement, one that would have gone on had the sheriff not gotten sick. With a bit of a leadership vacuum, Simon stepped in on his own. But the Carver family's responsibilities to the partnership had not ended. "With him sidelined, his partnership duties fall to you. I told him to tell you. Since it's obvious he has not done so yet, I am."

"I don't know what you're talking about."

Of course he didn't. One of the things that made Frank Sr. such a great partner was his ability to hold a secret. His life walking on the dark side appeared to be one of them. Until now.

But Simon had bigger concerns than an ill man working his way through rehab. "It's time for Lindsey Pike to meet with me."

The deputy's eyes were wide and wild with confusion. "Then ask her."

"She won't come on her own. She needs an… incentive." Killing Hank in front of her might do it, but Simon wanted to keep that man around for a while. Test him out. See if he was a better choice than Todd as an assistant.

The deputy moved and Todd grabbed his arm, holding him in place. Frank Jr. swallowed as he got the words out. "What do you plan to do to her?"

"Reason with her." And by that Simon meant make her remember.

"About?" The confusion was obvious in the younger man's voice.

"Not your concern." This was between him and Lindsey. No one else. She had set the terms for the battle. She just didn't know it yet.

The deputy's eyes narrowed. "And if she won't listen?"

Simon's patience for the deputy and his questions expired.

"She'll have something in common with poor Grant." When Frank Jr. flinched and looked ready to bolt, Simon held up his hand. "Nuh-uh. Stay still."

The deputy's chest rose and fell on hard breaths. "Why would I help you?"

That was simple. Simon would not give him a choice. "Because your family is in this. I have taken special care to make sure all the paperwork about the weapons leads back to your father, and by connection, you."

"Weapons." The deputy repeated the word two more times.

Todd laughed. "You are behind, aren't you?"

"You're insane." The deputy tried to look around, but Todd held him in place. "Both of you."

"Determined." Since he was done with this conversation and this man, Simon stood up. "Now you'll go with Todd here and fetch Ms. Pike."

"I won't do it."

And Simon would not play this game. "Then you will die where you stand. You have ten seconds to decide."

Because he had new prey to play with, and one way or another she would be here soon.

## Chapter Fourteen

Lindsey stepped out onto the porch a few hours later. She needed a rest from the questions and the tactics-and-strategy discussion between Shane and Holt. If she heard one more scenario where Simon tried to hold Holt and how he could break free, her head would explode.

She promised not to stray, which seemed ridiculous, as this was her house and her property. But she still couldn't look in the direction of the lake thanks to Grant's body being found there. It might take a lifetime for her to feel comfortable again, and she'd never felt fully at ease to begin with.

The right answer could be to sell and find another small town nearby. It made sense, but she couldn't take on one more thing at the moment.

She walked down the back porch steps and toward the small garden. Some of her vegetables were ready to be picked, and shocks of color from the flowers she planted not too long ago gave the backyard a homey glow. She bent down to touch a purple petal. One would never know so much death and danger lurked nearby.

As she thought it she heard footsteps off to her left, through the trees. She lifted her head, ready to tell Holt he could spare the lecture about how she needed to stay aware of her surroundings. Deputy Carver walked into view.

Instead of his usual cocky smile, hiding a heap of inexperience, he stared at her. His eyes were flat and his color seemed off. He almost looked a chalky gray. She thought about asking if he was okay, but she didn't want to say anything that might make him feel welcome, since he was not.

"What are you doing here?" If he'd come to arrest her she just might pass out.

She'd been through so much lately and had handled it all. She was strong and smart by nature, but having Holt as backup increased her confidence. Together, they could beat whatever Simon Falls threw at them.

"I need to take you in for questioning."

Fine, she'd grab Holt and Shane and drag them with her. Let the police or the sheriff or even the FBI deal with those two. But first she had a question of her own. "Are you the one who planted the false story in the news?"

"Lindsey, don't make this difficult."

He didn't deny it. That meant he was in on it and no way was she going anywhere with him without backup. "I want Hank with me."

She took a step toward the cottage and started to call out for help. A hand clamped over her mouth and a strong arm pulled her back until she slammed against a hard chest. A flash of a gun registered in her peripheral vision.

"Do not scream or you die right here." The familiar voice, all threats and rasp and anger, whispered into her ear.

The deputy took a quick look in the direction of her house. "I have this handled."

"One sound and her boyfriend will come running.

You do not want to face him in a battle. Trust me." Todd put his face close to hers. "Behave or I shoot the first man who walks out of that house, and I shoot to kill."

She nodded and the tight grip pressing bruises into her cheeks eased. She didn't expect much from Todd and men like Todd, but Frank Jr. should be different. "You're working with him?"

Todd hadn't bound her hands and she used them now. She put a hand on Todd's restraining forearm. With the other, she slipped her phone out of her pocket. If there was a panic button of some type on there, she didn't know about it. She counted on her other skills. She couldn't see to call, but she knew where the text button was and typed all the time on that without looking. This message would be for Holt.

Todd answered her question. "Law enforcement in this county answers to us, and Mr. Falls would like to see you."

The name sent an icy chill running through her. "Tell him to go to—"

The deputy held up both hands as he threw her a wild look. "Lindsey, stop."

She could match his panic with some of her own. But she could also fight, so she hit the last button, hoping she came close to making sense. "He will kill me. You get that, right? You are setting me up to die."

"I know." Frank Jr. reached for his gun.

Todd proved faster. His grip eased as he leaned forward. A knife appeared out of nowhere and the blade stabbed into the deputy.

Lindsey was about to run, to scream, but the sight in front of her riveted her to the spot. Frank Jr. sank to his knees as his hands clutched his stomach. Blood seeped through his fingers. He opened his mouth, but no sound came out, which meant the screaming she heard was echoing inside her head.

Before her muscles unlocked, Todd was on her again. He had her in a strangle hold with the gun right there. "You are a hard woman to get alone."

The menacing words sliced across her senses. She had to focus to stay coherent while terror ran rampant inside her.

"Holt...he will find you." She stumbled over the pronoun and hoped she saved herself in time.

"Do you mean Hank?" Todd clutched his arm tighter across her neck. "I hope so, since I owe him some pain from those fighting moves in your house a few days ago."

She grabbed for his arm as he choked off her breath. "You admit you broke in and attacked me?"

"Imagine what I plan to do to you next."

Sick laughter filled her ear. Just before everything went dark, she hit Send and dropped the phone.

HOLT WALKED BACK into the family room from the bathroom to find Shane sprawled on the couch. Legs up on the cushions and a stack of papers in his hand. Now that they knew about Lindsey's side business, she'd opened up her office, and with Joel's computer help at increasing her security, they had an easier line to Connor and the office.

The information flowed back and forth, as did Connor's warnings. He didn't like what he was finding on Simon Falls, which was nothing. The photos that Cam took showed large stores of weapons.

Other people might miss the signs; Connor didn't. He recognized boxes and specific weapon types. Grenade launchers and a surface-to-air missile. That was the truly scary one. All of that corroborated what Holt had seen up there.

This Simon Falls, whoever he was, had access to serious firepower. He could cause a lot of damage. If he was a true believer or someone bent on revenge, he likely would. Holt had to hope he was the militia no-government type, not looking for trouble, and not someone seriously delusional or looking to make a name for himself.

But then, Holt had never been the luckiest guy. He wondered if meeting Lindsey had changed all that. Danger and women did not mix. He'd seen his friends turned around and shoved deeper into risk over the decisions they'd made in the name of love.

After spending his entire life honing his skills, Holt couldn't imagine abandoning them for anyone. Of course, Lindsey wasn't just anyone. In a short period of time she'd turned into someone who mattered and he just didn't know how to process that potential vulnerability.

He'd learned the hard way not to trust. A person Holt thought was his friend picked dealing drugs in Afghanistan over him. Shot and left him for dead. But Holt instinctively knew Lindsey would never make that deal. She'd stand up beside him.

It was the same certainty that helped him learn to trust the team, that kept him so close to Shane and Makena. Now he had to figure out if he had room in that circle for Lindsey…if she even wanted to be included.

Shane waved a piece of paper in the air. "We got the intel back on Lindsey and her past. There's not much under that name, but Joel managed to pull a lot from the fingerprints I scanned and sent."

"What?" Holt looked around for her. Glanced out the window and saw her headed for the flower bed.

He'd give her five minutes before he went out there and dragged her back in. During that time he'd watch…once he figured out what Shane was saying.

Shane's sneakers hit the floor as he sat up. "You ordered that we do a full background check on her to be safe."

"I actually didn't." Holt specifically hadn't wanted to go down that road.

"Right." Shane shot him a side eye. "Maybe that was me trying to protect your butt."

Holt remembered the discussion and meant to circle back and stop Joel's digging. He'd even told Connor to put the brakes on. Looked as though the word never got back or Connor purposely ignored the request.

In their shoes Holt would have done the same thing—charged ahead. But that wasn't really the point.

Shane continued to hold up one piece of paper. "Did you get the part where it says Lindsey Pike isn't her real name?"

With one last look in Lindsey's direction and a second of watching her pick flowers or whatever she was doing out there, Holt went to the couch. "I knew that."

Shane's arms fell against his thighs. "Were you planning on sharing?"

"She was raised at the camp, escaped and took on a new identity." Holt glanced at the file and the photo in the abducted child report. A sunny girl with a big smile and missing tooth stared back at him. He saw the intelligence in her eyes but did think the glasses were a nice touch. "And look, apparently."

Shane cleared his throat. "You seem happy with the current version. Can't blame you. The woman is fine, and I mean that in an entirely clinical don't-punch-me kind of way."

An understatement on the looks. The fresh-faced attractiveness appealed to him. So did the smokin' body and smart mouth. If Holt was being truthful, everything worked for him except for maybe the stubbornness, and even that had its moments.

But there was more to it than that. He thought about her all the time, watched her when she was puttering around the house and even enjoyed her off-key humming. He'd never gotten this attached, this sucked in. Never dreamed he could feel secure and messed-up and vulnerable all at the same time over a woman.

So he went with the most natural response to his best friend's prying. "Shut up."

Holt didn't have much else, because he didn't seem capable of fighting this. Whenever he thought about finishing up the assignment and moving on, a tightness filled his chest. The idea of her dating someone else, sleeping with someone else, hit him like a sucker punch to the gut.

Forget the sensation of being dragged under. He was falling for this woman. At rapid speed and without a safety net. He thought back to how he made fun of Joel and Cam—all of them—and now he got it. This one woman walked into your world and everything else stopped. It was downright annoying.

Shane leaned back against the couch cushions. "You know that's your go-to response when I give you grief about being with her, right?"

Knew and planned it that way. "Your point?"

"It's lame."

Holt really couldn't argue with that, so he tried to turn the conversation. "So are your attempts to tick me off."

"We're taking bets, you know." Shane leaned over the coffee table and shuffled through a pile of papers.

Holt was so busy watching the photos and lines of writing flip by that he almost missed the comment. "What?"

"About how long it will be before you're on your knees, begging Lindsey to forgive you." Shane smiled as he said it, clearly enjoying this moment too much.

"For what?" Holt didn't doubt it, but he did want a heads-up if Shane knew something he didn't.

"Oh, there will be something." Shane separated the documents into stacks, using some system in his head.

One page grabbed Holt's attention. He put out a hand to stop others from burying it lower in the pile. "Hold up."

"What?" Shane brought the paper up to the top. "That's Walt Freeland, Lindsey's uncle. He died in a shoot-out with ATF."

Holt picked up the papers as wave after wave of anxiety washed over him. The photo was old, but the resemblance was unmistakable. The jawline. The mouth. The dark evil in the eyes. One thing was for certain—her uncle was not dead. "No, he didn't."

"What do you mean?"

Holt forced his memory to cover and compare every detail. He'd changed his appearance, likely on purpose. Only someone looking would know. Someone who faced the guy every day, or sat across a desk and answered questions.

"Different hair and he's lost a lot of weight, but this guy is definitely not dead."

Shane frowned. "How do you know?"

"He's my boss. Hank's boss." When Shane just stared, Holt tried again. "That's Simon Falls."

"Why didn't she recognize him?"

"She's never seen him in his role as Simon Falls. Few have. I've been up there, trying to figure out how to sneak a photo back to Connor and Joel and haven't been able to." Holt's mind immediately shot to Lindsey. He spun up off the couch and stalked toward the back door with Shane right behind.

Holt's gaze started at the last place he'd seen her and zipped across the yard. He looked for any sign of her as the panic started beating in his head.

"Lindsey?" Shane yelled her name, not being shy about being as loud as he could.

Dread gripped Holt. "Where is she?"

"Look." Shane took off before he explained. He ran toward the trees to a crumpled form lying in the leaves.

Holt recognized the uniform before he turned the deputy over. Blood pooled around him, and his eyes had gone glassy. He was alive but not for long.

"He's knifed." Holt ignored the ping of his cell in his back pocket letting him know he had a text and stayed focused. He ripped the bottom of his T-shirt and pressed it against the wound. "Where's Lindsey?"

"I'm sorry." The deputy's mouth barely opened.

"Later with that. Where is she?"

Shane scrambled in the grass toward something. He came back and dropped to his knees beside Holt. "Her cell."

Holt unlocked it with the code Lindsey had given him in case of an emergency. As Shane called for an ambulance on his own cell, Holt punched buttons on hers. He found the message without any trouble. Misspelled and almost incoherent, but he knew. Also knew what the text on his phone said. "Todd has her."

As Shane talked in the background the deputy tried

to nod as he forced out another string of words. "Took her to Simon…not sure where on the property."

"That's the easy part." Holt thought about the cell in his pocket and the app that would lead him straight to her. "I'll find her."

They would go and get her. Holt made a personal vow to make it happen and to take out whoever he had to in the process. But right now his entire world focused on the jumbled message filled with typos. He could make out the most important part—"hury, luv u."

# Chapter Fifteen

Holt got through the New Foundations front gate without trouble. He expected the guns to come out and Simon to appear. Something that matched the fierce grandness of Lindsey's abduction.

But the camp operated as usual. People carried on, did chores, rode in trucks to the gun range. If anyone knew an innocent woman had been grabbed and dragged up here, they didn't show it. It was possible they didn't care but more likely they didn't know.

The lack of knowledge worked to Holt's advantage. The tracker he had placed inside Lindsey's back jeans pocket, the same tracer he put on her every morning since moving into her house, showed her on the property. But that spread for miles. With Shane's help, Holt had narrowed down a location. An off-limits building on a part of the property used to store equipment.

According to the files Connor had collected, the place once operated as an employee rec room. Using Cam's aerial photos, they determined that because of the fencing and forest surrounding the area, there was only one easy way into the building. Through the front door.

Trying not to draw attention or pop up on one of the seemingly thousands of video cameras spread around the campus, Holt walked with a sense of calm. His insides had been diced raw, but he didn't let any of that pounding panic show on the outside. Lindsey needed him safe and strong. And she needed him now.

Walking along the lines of cabins closest to the dining hall, Holt passed right in front of the steps to Simon's office. It was the path Holt took every workday, and he did not stray now. Not when anyone could be watching. A quick turn and he slipped between delivery trucks and around a giant storage shed used for nonperishable items.

He had too far to go on foot for the little time he feared he had. Transportation proved tricky. Everyone had to sign out a vehicle to use it. Holt had left his truck in the parking lot per protocol. That left running or improvising. Holt chose lying.

He slipped into the camp's makeshift garage. He had a choice of two vehicles. Both would have GPS trackers and become unusable once he collected Lindsey. That was fine with Holt, since he had other transportation arrangements in mind for the getaway.

With his usual wave to the mechanic, Holt walked right up to the dispatch station. He grabbed the clipboard hanging there on the nail and started filling out the appropriate lines. Holt saw the guy working there almost every day on duty and hoped that counted for something.

The dispatch guy looked up. "I don't have you down for a vehicle today."

"We have some trees down over by the exercise yard." Steady and calm. Holt delivered the line with the dead accuracy of the truth.

The trees were fine, but the story proved easy to sell. The wind knocked things around here all the time. Holt had spent most of his first days cutting fallen branches and clearing paths.

Today he pretended to do the same even as the countdown clock started clanging in his head. He was running out of time and if this dragged on he'd have to turn to Plan B. That consisted of running and finding her and hoping not to get shot as he took off in the most overgrown direction.

Holt handed the clipboard back and waited. He'd know in two seconds if Simon had put out the call to stop him.

The dispatcher didn't miss a beat. He grabbed an extra set of keys and handed them to Holt. "We need this tomorrow for a supply pickup, so I need it back by the end of the shift."

Holt kept his relieved breath locked inside him. "No problem."

He got two steps toward the truck before the dispatcher called his name. Holt turned nice and slow as he conducted a mental inventory of the weapons he had on him. Last thing he wanted to do was kill this guy or injure any of the members who seemed to want quiet more than a battle.

Any except Todd. That guy had a bullet waiting for him.

The dispatcher pointed toward the sign above the checkout clipboard. "Don't forget to fill the tank."

"Will do." Holt felt the trapped air leave his lungs. He read that faded and peeling sign almost every day. Passed by it and followed the order, which wasn't tough, since there was a filling station not far from the garage.

Not waiting another second, Holt slipped out of the building and slid into the front seat of the truck. With every second he expected guards to swarm and guns to fire. But the big escape plan ran smoothly. No one tried to stop him. No one questioned his right to be in certain areas. He moved with confidence and they responded by giving him room to find what he wanted. In this case, space.

The drive took minutes but lasted an eternity in his head. The building looked worse than he remembered. Rotting wood lined the walls, and the roof tilted as if the whole thing could shift and fall any second. The door had a padlock, but the windows high on the walls of the two-story structure were smashed and broken.

He didn't go right up to the place. He parked and let the engine idle, figuring that might make anyone hiding out here come running.

When the day stayed quiet except for the brush of air over grass and leaves, he turned the engine off. This would not be his choice to hold someone in. In this day with internet videos and all the crime shows on television, the criminals had grown more savvy. This building looked hard to defend and easy to escape from. Just as Holt liked them.

He slipped to the front door and obvious entrance. A quick walk around the place uncovered few other options. Holt decided to go with the door where the ceiling looked the sturdiest.

He thought about what Lindsey's fear level must be, and his temper raged. She sat around here somewhere, alone and afraid. Possibly injured thanks to Todd's man-handling.

Holt vowed he would rip every building apart and question every person on campus if needed. He had to get her out no matter the cost.

After a quick visual check of the inside through the slim crack in the wall, Holt moved. He pushed on the door and the wood creaked. At least it moved. He could work with that.

Large boxes of equipment, now old and useless

thanks to the ever-present Oregon rain, blocked his path. He tried to ease his hand inside. He shoved and worked until he could move his fingers and raise a latch. Breaking in didn't matter to Holt, but this proved quieter and preserved the scene. If his calculations were off or the tracker misfired, Holt didn't want to leave a trail leading back to him.

He used his shoulder to move the door the rest of the way. The hinges squeaked but the door moved. Holt only needed a small space to slip inside. Once he had it, he disappeared into the building.

It took a second for his eyes to adjust to the fading light. The inside was open, with scaling walls and piles of debris in each corner. Dirty windows set up high blocked most of the light and made breaking in or out through them impossible.

The location did not make any sense. No way would Simon keep a valuable asset here. Not with the sorely lacking security.

Holt had walked a few steps before the wrongness of the situation hit him. The quiet bothered him. So did the potential of a tracker malfunction. He was about to turn around or back his way out when he saw the sliver of light. Barely identifiable right there in a small space where the walls supposedly met.

He visually traced the edges. Thought about the layout of the building and the possibility of a room being behind this one. Seemed like an odd choice, but then again nothing should surprise him. He'd been on a wild ride since he got to Oregon. Nothing went as expected and death fell all around him.

Holt went in to investigate. There were boxes stacked and blocking a better look. He lifted everything aside, all while making zero noise. Not an easy task, but he'd do just about anything for Lindsey.

He'd sell his soul for a promise of her safety right now. Anything to keep her from the inevitable confrontation with her uncle. The man who should be dead and if Holt had any say would be soon.

The transformation from sidekick to leader didn't make all that much sense. Usually a big thing had to happen for that sort of change. Holt made a mental note to see if there were any weapon dumps around that time. Somehow, somewhere, this guy caught everyone's attention. If most people never met him, that ruled out charismatic speaker. Very few other alternatives made sense.

Holt slipped his knife out of his pocket to match the gun in his other hand. He'd burst through the wall if he had to. Go in firing as soon as he located Lindsey's position and could account for her safety.

He ran his fingers over the wall, looking for any mechanism to open it. Nothing happened. When he finally ran the tips up and down the outside of the molding around the door, he found it. A small button. He clicked it and heard the grinding of gears. A ticking sound and a thunk and then the door in front of him opened.

Lindsey, behind a thick see-through partition, sitting in a cell that spanned about eight-by-eight. She sat there on the floor with her arms around her knees and her forehead resting on her arms. It took a second to realize she was unhurt. Holt didn't see blood or the signs of pain.

Just as he was about to call to her, her head shot up. She blinked a few times and her mouth dropped open.

That fast, the look of relief on her face turned to horror. She motioned and he started to turn, but it was too late. The unexpected elbow shot nailed him in the back and sent him to his knees.

The next one landed on the side of his head. Something hard and possibly metal. Holt tried to reason it out as he forced his body to keep from keeling over, but the room started to spin and bile ran up the back of his throat.

He forced his eyes open as he watched Lindsey, all panicked and jumpy, put her hand against the partition separating them. Then a blinding pain flashed across his temples and everything went black.

SIMON CLOSED DOWN his computer and removed the hard drive. He had numerous security measures in place. No one but him had computer access at the camp, so unwanted access to the outside world rarely was a problem for him.

He never left anything lying around that he didn't want found. Sometimes that was the best way to spread the word about some bit of news, like the leak about Grant and hints about Lindsey's involvement. Start the gossip and let the members spread it so he could rush in and console. Most times, he had information no one else needed to know.

Today he was in a rush to see Lindsey. She'd been on-site for an hour. Cameras carefully monitored her position. As soon as he had a word with Hank about the new expectations for his position, he would meet his honored guest.

Today was the day.

There was a knock at the door, but before he had a chance to say anything Todd came storming in. "We have a new problem."

Not one to bellyache without reason, Todd was the

type of guy who rarely showed nerves and when he did everyone got scared. But he wasn't privy to everything happening at the camp or with the people involved in the activities. More than likely he saw an expected entrance as a problem.

"I see Hank has arrived." Simon had watched it all on the monitors, then sat back and waited to see what Hank would do. He didn't show any signs of nerves or of wanting Lindsey back, which Simon found interesting. "Good. I'm in the mood for a demonstration of loyalty. It's his turn."

"That's just it. He's not Hank."

Something inside Simon crashed. He oversaw every careful plan, every perfectly placed domino. He could ill afford to have Hank be a wild card. "What?"

"Lindsey called him Holt."

More than likely Hank was short for Holt or some other name. They all sounded close, so Simon didn't worry about that. No, he had a much bigger concern and it dealt with ongoing incompetence. "How did they see each other? She is locked up and he is…where?"

Todd didn't hide or back down, despite the rise in Simon's voice at the end. "He is with her. Now. He came on the property and went straight to the barn. Didn't work or go to the lockers."

For Simon to believe that Hank or Holt just knew to go there would amount to a coincidence. Simon didn't believe in those. He would need to be open to those, and he wasn't. Not even a little. "You're certain?"

"He didn't draw any attention. Acted as if he was doing work, but he went out there." Todd shrugged. "You could see the guy's training."

Simon had seen some of that talent on the video screens and believed Hank, or whatever his name was,

was checking in just like any other day. But it sounded as if he'd switched to rescue mode and Simon didn't know how Hank would know where Lindsey was or that she needed help in the first place.

He rarely made mistakes but suddenly Simon questioned every piece of information he'd gathered on this Holt or Hank guy. "You followed, I assume."

Todd nodded. "Yes."

"Good work." Now Simon would rip down every wall until he got the truth out of Hank, which raised another issue. "You said Hank went to find Lindsey."

"Found her." Todd's mouth fell into a flat line. "He's locked in with Lindsey."

The cell. One door and a firm see-through bulletproof shield. Just what Simon needed for questioning. "Perfect. They can celebrate seeing each other for the last time."

"Who do you think he really is? I mean, come on. Those skills are impressive. I had the advantage of surprise on my side, but without it…" Todd shook his head. "I don't know."

Simon did. He knew his men could take on one dishonorably discharged military member and come out ahead.

"I'm more concerned that Hank knew about the location of the building. No one goes there." Simon made sure of it. He did some work on the structure, but no one ventured out that far. If they did they were told to stay away.

"It was like she led him there somehow."

"It would appear Hank or Holt or whatever he calls himself has a lot of explaining to do." And some secrets Simon wanted to uncover.

"Are you going to let him talk?" Todd sounded as though he'd prefer the answer to be no.

"Since I can teach him a lesson in the process, of course." One he wouldn't forget because he wouldn't live to talk about it.

Todd's eyes narrowed. "He's a dangerous guy to keep around."

Simon knew that all too well. "But he won't be once we kill him."

Todd actually smiled. "Good."

"And keep watch." This part got trickier. Holt alone was lethal. He could be a true threat if he banded with a friend or a team. "I remember him saying something about having a friend in town. They could be working together."

"If so?"

*An easy question.* "Lindsey will get to watch them both die."

# Chapter Sixteen

She willed him awake.

Lindsey sat on the floor of the cell Todd had thrown her in. With her legs stretched out in front of her, she waited with Holt's head in her lap, stroking his hair as she counted the minutes. He could have a concussion or worse. Could be dying.

The wound bled a lot, but she remembered reading somewhere that head wounds did that and not to panic. Most of the time the skull protected the brain from damage. Still, she used the towel Todd threw in with her to fix Holt up. She worried touching him might make whatever was keeping him unconscious even worse.

This was just one more test in a horrible few days of them. The past hour had been a roller-coaster ride of confusion. The rush of happiness she'd experienced in seeing Holt step up in front of her died when Todd stepped up behind him.

The hit. The way Holt's eyes rolled back into his head and his body crumpled. The horror show would play in her head forever.

She needed to get out of there and to safety. To check on her people and make sure the rest of her rescues were safe. But first she had to wake Holt up and be satisfied he was okay. In the five minutes since Todd left she'd tried saying Holt's name and singing to him. Kissing his hair and touching his back. Nothing brought him out of his stupor.

She was about to try shaking him when he stirred. He stiffened and then in a snap pushed up to a sitting position beside her. The move came too fast and his head lolled. She thought he might collapse or worse.

"Easy." She put a hand on his thigh and another on the back of his neck. "Are you injured?"

"I'm fine." He started to get up but fell back down hard.

She pulled him closer and leaned his body against hers. "Todd hit you three times in the head."

At least that was what she'd witnessed. There could have been more before Holt ever found her. She had no idea what was happening in the outside world. The small cell worked like an echo chamber, blocking out everything but the fear. That rattled around her until she had to fight off the urge to talk to herself.

"I hate that guy." Holt rubbed his head and hissed. A wince of pain came next.

For a smart guy he kept missing this pretty elementary issue. "My point was, you could have a serious concussion or something else equally awful."

"I'm good." He leaned his head against the wall and exhaled. "I made it seem worse than it was."

"Right. That's why you look ready to drop into a deep sleep."

He turned to look at her without lifting his head from the wall. "Once the first blow came, I knew I was in trouble."

"You're saying you tried to end up in here?" Because that didn't sound smart to her. He should run and get help...shouldn't he?

Yet part of her loved that he didn't leave. He didn't send in helpers. He was the hands-on guy who got things done. Since the wild attraction she felt for him continued to grow and expand, she added being able to count on him to the list of things she liked about him.

He reached over and took her hand in his. "I need to get you out of here."

She was fully on board with that plan, but… "No kidding, but I need you not to pass out."

"I'm not a fainter." He sounded appalled by the idea.

"Can you crawl through glass or whatever that is?" She pointed at the barrier separating them from the outside world. If tough guy wanted to take something apart, he could start with that.

"Cam and Shane are here."

The entire team. For some reason that gave her comfort. His ability to track her so easily should calm her but it didn't feel right. "How did you find me?"

He rubbed his thumb over the back of her hand. "I've been tracking you."

"Excuse me?" She willed her body not to react. Her usual response would have been to start barking questions. She let him come to her.

"It's a tiny dot." He made the symbol with his hand. "Not intrusive."

"I plan to get indignant about that tracking device later. Mostly about you hiding it from me." For some reason the fact that something like that existed made her twitchy.

He shrugged. "It worked."

"And that is why I will thank you. For now." She looked at his face and saw the strain there, tugging at the corners of his eyes and mouth. Every time he moved he let out a small gasp as if his body constantly fought off the pain. Not that he let her see that. No, he tried to bury it. "So, what's the plan? Are we going to sit around and wait to get rescued?"

Holt straightened his back even more. Pressed away from the wall and tried to turn his head side to side.

His eyes slammed shut. "Does that sound like me?"

His stubbornness was going to be the death of both of them. "No, but last I checked you couldn't walk through walls."

"So little faith."

Since they had nothing but time left to wait and see what this Simon Falls creature wanted with them, she kept babbling. "Come on, this has to be the worst situation for you so far."

She expected an agreement. She got a scoff.

He started to shake his head, then stopped. "Not even close."

She looked around at the walls. Air seemed to be pumped in from somewhere, making the spot extra cold, but there were no windows and there was very little hope here. "How is that possible? We're trapped in here, just waiting for our turn to die."

The last part of the sentence ripped out of her. The words scratched against her tongue. She refused to believe this was her day to die, but the evidence kept pointing her to that conclusion.

That was why she wrote and sent that text. She hoped it said what she wanted it to. She didn't throw the word *love* around easily or decorate her mail with little hearts, but there was no question each day she fell a little further in love with him.

"I've been left for dead. That was much worse than this." Using the wall for balance, he slid up until his back was plastered to the wall, and his face went pale. His body seemed to close in, as if the memories proved too much to handle more than in small pieces.

She knew pain when she saw it. The squinting of his eyes and the weight of it pushing on his shoulders. She wanted to rush in and comfort, but she didn't understand his comment. "What are you talking about?"

At first he didn't say anything. His eyes half closed as he stood there. His palms flattened against the wall behind him. She couldn't tell if he was holding his body up or stopping to rest.

Just as she was about to ask, he started talking. His rich, deep voice rang out in the small cell. "In Afghanistan. I figured out a friend, not Shane, was dealing drugs over there. Getting some of our men high at dangerous times. Selling to the locals. Basically, making a lot of money."

He stated the facts in an almost remote voice. As if he'd separated what happened from his real life. She guessed this was a defense mechanism or a way of releasing the poison, but she wanted the thinking and feeling parts of him. Dealing with awful things by using both was the only way to move on.

"I have a feeling I know where this is going." And she feared the story was not going to end with this random guy, whatever his name, remaining one of Holt's lifetime friends. At least she hoped not or she might have to go find him and punch him.

"We were friends, so I gave him a chance to come clean." Holt lifted a hand and pinched the bridge of his nose and then rubbed his eyes. Did the whole uncomfortable guy routine. "I'd missed the drugs and felt responsible. I couldn't help thinking if I'd seen it coming I could have stopped the train."

"I don't think it works that way."

"When confronted with two options—turn yourself in or go home—he picked a third option." Something in Holt's eyes said he was reliving the entire thing as he described it. "He decided to shoot me instead. Left me to bleed out in the desert."

The words shocked her. Everyone read and heard about the horror of war in a distant way. This was personal. A painful memory that appeared to plague him. "How did you survive?"

"I crawled to a hiding place. Kept pressure on the wound." Holt made a noise akin to a short hum. "It's under my hairline, by the way."

He acted as if everyone possessed his survival skills. As if people got shot at and moved around without help for hours all the time. The idea of him making it out alive made her shake her head in awe.

But none of that compared to the betrayal that lingered in every one of his words. "Your friend actually shot you in the head in order to save himself?"

"Yes, it quickly became clear he was looking for a more permanent solution to my refusal to mind my own business."

"Where is he now?" She hoped locked up somewhere and feeling the weight of his guilt.

"Prison."

Finally some good news after swimming through a sea of bad. "Military, or did he come back and get in trouble?"

"Sort of both but it's military."

"No wonder you don't trust anyone." All the pieces clicked together in her head. The anti-commitment thing.

He connected with certain people, likely people he knew before the incident in Afghanistan, but not others.

But now he'd closed his feelings off and buried them down deep. Locked emotions away. Or he claimed to have done so until he'd made love with her. She hadn't seen any signs of him wanting to be somewhere other than her bed that night.

"Do you talk to him?" She couldn't imagine that. Facing down the person who tried to take your life. She didn't even get what the conversation could be unless it included an apology.

"Never. He blames me."

Of course he did. That type would.

"That's ridiculous." Kind of made her want to punch the guy on Holt's behalf.

He gave her eye contact. The type that made it feel as if there was no one else in the state. "And for the record, I trust you."

The words echoed in her brain and she rushed to say the one thing she might not be able to say once Todd got through with them. "Did you get my text?"

"Yes. Very smart."

Yeah, she was not talking strategy here. "I meant—"

"You're awake."

At the sound of Todd's voice, she jumped to her feet. Tried to put her body in front of Holt's, but he held her against his side.

Some of the haze had cleared from his eyes. He still moved half a beat slower than usual and seemed to be holding his head so it did not move much, but the big fierce protector was not far under the surface. She felt him hovering right there, ready to fight.

Todd gestured with his gun for them both to move

toward the door. "That's good, since we have a surprise for you."

"What?" Holt asked.

"Apparently it's time to prove yourself." Todd's gaze traveled over both of them. "The boss is ready to see you guys now."

# Chapter Seventeen

With each step, some of the fuzz muddling Holt's brain cleared. It still hurt to move too fast or even keep his eyes open for long periods of time, but he was snapping out of it. A few more minutes of rebooting and he would be ready to go.

The point was, he needed to protect Lindsey. Yes, she could handle most situations. But this one was too horrible for her to face, and he didn't want it rolling out in front of her the way he feared it would.

Simon Falls was a psychopath. He'd destroyed people and killed to get to his position. He hid his identity under false names and documents. Lindsey used a cover for safety and to help others. Not this guy. And now he wanted Lindsey. Holt didn't know exactly why, but he guessed it centered on some sick mix of revenge and reunion.

As they walked out of their cell and into the larger building that contained it, they stayed next to each other into the main room of the old rec center, her fingers brushing his. Knowing it was unwise to hold her hand but desperate to show her how much she meant to him, he touched the back of his against hers. He knew she noticed when she glanced at him out of the corner of her eye.

He spent the rest of the time getting to know his surroundings. He'd been all over the campground. Even got close to the weapons storage. The inside of this place was new. Made him wonder what else he'd missed.

They stopped in the middle of the long rectangular room. Junk and old supplies littered the floor. There was an odd musty smell that suggested the place hadn't been opened in years. The high-tech cell suggested Simon had lots of contacts with the outside world. He clearly did not limit himself to the camp and refuse all worldly possessions, hypocrite that he was.

Todd stood behind them with his gun trained on Lindsey. Smart move. With her in the firing line Holt would not lunge. If it was a matter of him catching a bullet during a fight, fine. But he wouldn't risk her life that way.

So they stood. They waited in silence for what Holt guessed was the big entrance scene from Simon. Holt wanted to lean over and whisper the man's secret to take some sting out of his entry. Holt hadn't gotten the chance to warn her earlier and was about to do so now, but the megalomaniac in question walked in.

He wore casual clothes and had his hair styled so one side swooped over to cover a spot before reaching the other side of his head. He had an assault weapon strapped to his chest and carried a handgun. For a second Holt thought he'd walked into the middle of some stupid coup.

He knew the second Lindsey recognized the man she secretly viewed as her enemy. "It can't be." Her voice trailed off but the surprise lingered.

"Lindsey Pike, or should I call you Beth?"

"Walt?"

He shrugged. "It's Simon now."

Her mouth dropped open and it took a few tries to get it closed again. "You died."

With each shocked sentence Holt felt worse for her. The need to block her from all this struck him hard. He wanted to tuck her away and never let this nutcase or his campground touch her life again.

But he couldn't protect her from this truth. This one walked and talked and threatened. Simon Falls didn't think twice of pulling his niece into his schemes and scaring her for no reason. That made him one dangerous man. And one that Holt would likely need to kill.

"What's the plan here, Walt?" Everything Holt did now was just a stall for time. Shane and Cam had to either fight their way into the camp or wind around and come through the lush greenery and over the huge fence. Since Holt didn't hear gunfire, he assumed they were trying the non-bloodshed method. That meant Holt had more time to waste before reinforcements arrived.

"It sounds as if we all know each other's real names." Simon's smile turned feral. "Isn't that right, Holt? Or should I call you Agent Holt?"

The man was guessing, assuming Holt has a government agent of some sort. This guy did not have the skills to break through Joel's encryptions and multilevel securities and built-in redundancies and fake covers. Holt had faith in all of that…and he wasn't actually an agent. Not in the sense Simon meant.

Simon put a hand behind his ear. "What? No smart reply for that?"

Lindsey took a small step forward. The move put her slightly ahead of Holt. "You want me. Let him go."

Simon shook his head. "That is not going to happen."

"Holt didn't do anything."

That was enough poking. Holt pulled even with her

and tugged on the bottom of her shirt again to let her know to keep the other man calm. Fighting and threatening would only ratchet up whatever was wrong with him. He would react and everything would blow up.

"Don't waste your breath. He wants us both, don't you, Walt?" Holt asked.

"Call me Simon. I ceased being Walt years ago after I realized that the weakness gene in our family could be exorcised out."

That sounded crazy to Holt. From the severe frown on Lindsey's face, he assumed she didn't get it either.

"Our family is not weak." And she sounded every bit strong and proud as she said it.

"My brother could not quiet the voices. You run away and then scurry back." Simon shook his head. "I'd like to think this means you missed the discipline and structure of the camp. Have you kept up with your lessons in weaponry? Because that's what we do. Move around and sell them. Provide backup, when needed. It's a very lucrative business. Much more so than yoga, or whatever the hell was happening here before."

*Bingo.* Exactly what Holt suspected. Not that he cared about being right or the mission with Todd waving a gun around somewhere behind them.

"This is insane." Lindsey hesitated over each word as if she couldn't believe she had to say them. "How did you even know who I was?"

"Your friend Roger." Simon tilted his head to the side and threw her a sympathetic look. "In the end he was not very loyal, I'm afraid. Pain will do that to a person."

An angry flush covered her cheeks. "What did you do to him?"

"Lindsey." Holt tugged on her shirt again. Her losing

her control would hand Simon the victory he craved. No way could she do that.

"He worked for me," Simon said in a voice filled with pride.

Lindsey started to shake her head and didn't stop. "He left."

"And came back. That's the point."

Breath hiccupped out of her. "You're lying."

But Holt feared Simon was telling the truth on that one. Part of Holt always thought the crime scene seemed staged. Then there was the issue with no body. Every other body got dumped right near Lindsey. Why not Roger's?

Holt hated for the betrayal to be true. He knew how deep that sort of pain cut. You wrestled with it for years, turning over every conversation and decision until it slowly drove you insane. It certainly robbed you of normalcy.

"This man betrayed you," Simon said, as if he genuinely needed her to understand. "He came to me with the information about your identity and your secret campaign to steal away my members."

"I thought they were always free to leave," she said.

"That's PR nonsense. People need to stay and be grateful." Simon's careful facade crumpled. "End of story."

"I don't believe you about Roger." She glanced around. "If he's on your payroll, bring him out here. Let him tell me."

"I would, but he is no longer with us." Simon actually smiled as he said it. Looked at Todd and he joined in, too.

The color leached from her face. "You killed him."

"He had an accident, but I can show you his files and the communications going back and forth between us."

Simon waved all the words off as soon as he said them. "But we have more pressing issues right now."

Lindsey's body visibly shook. "What?"

"Cleaning up your mess with Holt here."

Holt had expected the threat. Knew it was coming and started the mental countdown to shoving hard against Todd as they wrestled for the gun. Holt had to hope any shot the other man got off would go wide.

This time she did step in front of him. "Do not touch him."

Holt put his hands on her forearms and dragged her back against him. His mouth went to her hair and he whispered, "It's going to be okay."

Like that, some of the tension eased from her body.

"I do believe you've come to care for him. That's a shame, really." Simon spared Holt a glance but not a long one. "He is not who he says he is. I'm digging into that because I want to know who is meddling in my business. I like the idea of making Holt here an example and having him pay a steep price to persuade others not to."

"He is my boyfriend." Her voice rang out loud and clear with that one.

At any other time, Holt would have smiled. Now he had to hold it in and save it for later.

Simon shrugged. "I think we both know you could do better, Beth."

"That's not my name anymore." She exhaled as she stared at her uncle in confusion. "But what happened to you? You were poor and angry. When did you become the leader? Or should I say how? I don't doubt that you eliminated everyone in front of you."

"Beth will always be who you are, just as this place is part of your legacy." Simon skipped over most of her accusations and anger. He went right for one point and stuck there.

"I don't want anything to do with New Foundations."

"Of course you do." Simon used his arm to gesture around him. "I've created this."

Holt wondered if Simon knew he was pointing to a falling-down building in the middle of nowhere as the example for his success. To Holt, Simon's bigger claim was those weapons. He sat on a pile of firepower, which did give him a certain status. Would also make him a target of other people in the business. Holt didn't spare one second of pity for Simon on that score.

"If I end up with this place, I'll turn it into a cat sanctuary or something." She glared at Simon as if she dared him to contradict her.

Simon's mouth fell into a straight line. "I will not dignify that."

Holt thought the idea had potential. "I like it."

The comment earned him a shove from behind by Todd. Holt had almost forgotten about the man and how he hovered. He clearly viewed himself as the second in command to Simon. It was a match made in hell as far as Holt could see.

"I'm going to make you a deal. It's better than I've ever given anyone else."

Lindsey shuddered. She looked ready to heave. "No."

Simon talked right over her. Acted as if she'd never spoken and didn't get to say her mind. "I will allow you to make it up to me for running away and leading your life in ways that do not follow the camp's guidance."

Her frustrated expression mirrored the anger in her voice. "Stop pretending as if I had a choice."

Holt knew the story. The one thing the men in her family had never given her was a chance. They didn't respect her or appreciate her. Holt vowed not to make her suffer from the same thing from him.

"You have a choice now." Simon unclipped one of the guns from his belt and handed it to her.

She stared at his palm and the weapon but didn't take it.

Holt didn't have the patience for this. He jumped in while Lindsey stood there staring in stunned silence. "What is this about?"

Simon's smile grew. "If Lindsey kills you, she gets to live."

## Chapter Eighteen

The words echoed in Lindsey's brain. Her uncle, the man she despised and the same one who had scared her so much growing up, actually thought she would choose him. Take money over integrity and happiness.

"Prove to me you are as strong and independent as you claim." Simon continued to push the gun in her general direction.

Holt stared at the gun with an intensity that suggested he thought this whole barbaric exercise was real. Somehow her idiot uncle thought she could be bought and brought back into the sick family fold with the equivalent of a fancy watch.

"It's him or you, Lindsey." Simon's hand stayed steady.

"I won't do it." She couldn't do it. She couldn't kill another human being in cold blood. The heartlessness and sheer depravity of that act tore at her. If he'd offered this deal before to other people, members new and old, that meant others died, and she couldn't think about that.

Beyond all that was one very simple fact. She loved Holt. She didn't know how or why it had happened. It had started out with attraction and she thought it would always simmer there. He'd come into town and eventually move on. Instead, he'd stayed and lured her in.

Even as she'd waited in that cell for death to come,

she'd thought about him and the pain subsided. There were so many facets to him. Pieces she kept learning that helped explain the man.

He was stubborn and good, handsome and gruffly charming. He made her knees weak and her head spin. And if she managed to get out of here, she would say it. Somehow.

But no matter what Simon promised or how much he egged her on, she would not capitulate. She would not kill Holt.

That was when it hit her. Not Holt. The choice became so clear then. She would die first.

"This is your last chance." Simon nodded in Holt's direction. "You kill him or I will."

Only if he came through her. "I said no."

"Lindsey, do it." Holt's voice carried over Simon's shouting.

Her gaze flipped to him and she shook her head. Her heart flipped inside out as every cell ached for him. She knew he meant the words. He'd made her a promise and was willing to ride it into death. The idea of losing him, of living in this world without him, sent a numbness spreading through her. She couldn't feel or taste or think.

But one thing was absolutely clear. She would not be the second person he cared about—and she was pretty sure he did care—to shoot him and leave him to die. No way. He'd survived once. There was no telling if he could survive a second time. And even if he could she couldn't. It would be a move she'd see for the rest of her life.

Shooting him to save her. Never going to happen.

"Be a smart girl and listen to your boyfriend."

Simon was an idiot in every conceivable way. She thought it back then and thought it now. "I'm a woman, not a girl."

"If it's between me and you, you live." Holt's voice, sharp and focused, bounced through the open room and back at her. "I need you to live."

*No, no, no.* This was not a sacrifice she would allow him to make. "And I want you with me."

"Lindsey, please." The begging in his tone slapped at her.

"I…" She could not make the admission among all this hate. She loved him, but that was between them. Private. "I care about you. I can't lose you."

"You won't."

She didn't know what that meant. Desperation filled her as she tried to ferret out the clues and figure out a safe way through this for both of them. Because her life dragged them to this place. Her vile past. The shocking sight of her uncle. This was all on her.

"You are weak." Simon shook the hand with the gun sitting in it. "Prove to me you understand what's happening here and end this. One bullet to…what do you call him, Holt? To Holt's brain and we restart. All will be forgiven."

Her uncle's sickness spewed out and covered everything. Wallowing in it made her long for a bath. "I don't need your forgiveness."

"Lindsey, be careful," Holt said in a tone she'd heard so many times over the past few days. Not preachy or demanding but concerned.

Simon's face was a mask of pure fury. Red and blotchy with teeth snapping. "Yes, he's right. There is such a thing as respect, and you are not showing any."

He could not possibly think she owed him anything. He and her dad had kidnapped her and stolen her life. The stress killed her mother. That sealed their relationship and guaranteed that the only thing she would ever feel for the man with many names who claimed to be her uncle was hate. "Not for you. Never for you."

"I flipped my world upside down for you."

She listened as he turned it all around and took on the role of savior. She gagged on the thought. "I never asked for it. I was happy with my mom."

"Do not talk to me about that stupid cow."

"Lindsey, no." Holt yelled and reached for her.

She was already moving. She grabbed the gun and pointed it right at Simon's chest. She fired once and then a second time. The gun kept clicking, but it didn't fire any bullets.

Holt blew out a long breath. "It wasn't loaded."

She had no idea how he knew. Her whole body shook as the unspent adrenaline coursed through her. After a few seconds she looked up into her uncle's evil eyes.

"You will pay for that betrayal," he said.

He'd offered her the out and now that she took it he held her accountable. If he wanted to play games, she would. "Now give mc one with bullets."

Simon stared at her for long minutes. The hatred pummeled her as the disdain dripped from his lips. When he finally spoke she almost wished he hadn't. "Now it's my turn to fire the gun."

# Chapter Nineteen

Holt knew they were officially out of time. Simon had played this out and put Lindsey through the wringer. He planned every minute in order to suck the life out of her. Now she stood there looking devastated with her energy draining into a puddle on the floor.

He got it. She'd been fighting with this man, hiding, for years. In her position, he probably would have taken the shot. But he'd known the gun was empty. It was the reason he didn't tackle the guy and steal the gun. That personality type, narcissistic and unbound by social conventions, Simon thrived on the chaos. He liked to create fear.

He was sick and Holt had no idea how someone as special as Lindsey had come out of a household that included Simon.

"Get on your knees." Simon gave the order as he waved the gun around.

It was a novice move and it worried Holt more than all the threats. "I'll stand."

If Simon wanted to kill him, he could look him in the eye and do it in front of his face. Holt intended to hold firm but then, with a simple nod of his head, Simon issued the one argument Holt could not counteract. Todd stepped up and put the gun right against Lindsey's head.

In other circumstances with family members, Holt might not be so ready to agree one family member would go through with killing another. But Simon's logic had gotten all twisted up. He lived in a place where belief in something should matter, but he seemed utterly devoid of any sort of personal code. His motivation turned out to be simple and timeless—greed.

Holt looked over and saw the fear in Lindsey's eyes and the gun right behind her head, and his knees started to buckle. He would not lose her to pride.

"Very good." Simon turned to Lindsey. "Now you."

She didn't hesitate. She hit her knees, kneeling close enough that their shoulders touched. Her fingers tangled with his. Holt gave in to a second to enjoy the touch. Her hand had turned ice-cold and he took that hesitation to try to warm them.

But he had no plans to die today.

No way was he allowing any harm to come to her, and this was not his time. He always thought he'd know. When he lay bleeding in that sand, convinced that was the end, his mind had rebelled. Just as he'd accepted his fate, he found a new burst of energy. This was how they would get through this time, too.

He might only have one shot. If Cam and Shane had infiltrated the camp and this building, all would be well. They'd unleash firepower from above and take Simon and Todd right out. There would be others in camp they'd need to interview and possibly remove, but Simon was the key. Take him out of the equation and the whole thing might unravel.

Holt tried to think of a way to clue in Lindsey. They would need to go together. Both duck and roll. Both move and keep going until the shooting stopped. Holt just wished he had a gun. Todd had taken his, but he'd missed the knife. Big mistake.

Simon pointed the gun first at Holt. "You will die for thinking you could infiltrate my camp without consequences." The barrel moved to Lindsey. "You will die for failing me."

"Do it," Todd egged his boss on as he stood over them with a weapon of his own.

Holt gave Lindsey's hand a squeeze as he prepared to go. He started the mental countdown.

Since Simon seemed to be dragging this out and enjoying every minute, Holt didn't know how much time he really had, so he took one more shot. "All this is over money."

"I am able to do something others failed to do." Simon's ego took over. He shifted focus from the weapon to his perceived brilliance.

Just as Holt had hoped. "You move weapons around. It's not that hard."

"There are causes that need support. A silent partner, of sorts."

Holt had heard this speech from so many men. All of them twisted by the endless race for money. "You don't care about ideals. You're about collecting cash."

"Are you trying to get me to kill you first?" Simon smiled. "No worries. That is the plan. Lindsey should see the man she thinks is so strong and perfect bleed out at her feet. Watch the life drain right out of him."

Holt hit his maximum. There would never be a better time, what with Simon half pontificating and his weapon slightly lowered. Holt gave Lindsey's hand a final squeeze and started moving.

He plowed into Simon's legs as shots rang out over his head. He heard screaming, a woman's voice, as wood and glass splintered above. The room broke into a volley of gunfire and banging sounds.

The dive had Simon falling back and his gun skittering across the floor. Holt heard thuds and crashes and wanted to look around and check on Lindsey, but all his focus stayed on Simon. She needed him gone. The world needed him gone.

But Simon wasn't the type to go out without a fight. His knee caught Holt in the chin, making his teeth rattle. The older man's legs flailed as he kicked out. Between the punching and shifting, Simon scooted across the floor on his backside with Holt right there chasing him.

When Simon got close to the wall, he flipped over to his hands and knees and crawled, quick and determined like a spider. Holt caught him in the back right before he lunged for the dropped gun. He kicked one of Simon's legs out from under him and leaped onto his back. The move flattened Simon against the floor. He continued to thrash and rear back, but Holt refused to let go. He had his knife out and was about to deliver a slicing cut when shoes appeared in front of them. Boots to be exact.

Simon looked up and Holt followed his gaze. Shane stood there with a gun aimed right at Simon's head.

Shane did not blink as his finger sat on the trigger. "I dare you to keep fighting."

Holt didn't realize he was breathing heavily until he rolled off Simon. The dropped gun wedged under his thigh. His side hit the floor and he conducted a frantic visual search for Lindsey. She sat a few feet away and when he nodded at her, she scrambled to her knees and fell against his chest. With one arm, he pulled her in tight. The other held the knife.

A quick glance around the room showed chaos in every corner. The walls and what little furniture was in there had been torn up and destroyed by gunshots. Todd lay on his back with a small round hole in the middle of his forehead.

Simon survived. That meant he would face charges. Not a perfect ending, but an ending of sorts, which was what Lindsey needed.

And Holt needed her.

Simon was babbling about something. Talking and arguing. Holt ignored it all. He was too busy with the woman in his arms and the thoughts bombarded his brain.

Then it hit him. Where they were and the weapons load nearby, and his brain snapped into action. "We have to get out of here."

He was about to get up when Simon moved. Went from still, as Shane started to slip the zip ties on, to a fighting rage.

Simon came up off the floor yelling. Shane aimed his gun, but he was a beat too late. Holt grabbed Simon's own gun and nailed him in the chest with a bullet. His eyes widened and his breaths came out in a wheeze. It only took a few seconds for him to slide to the floor in a motionless heap.

"This time check his pulse," Cam called out from the other side of the room.

Shane said something back, but Holt missed it. He looked down at the woman in his arms. Her heartbeat thundered so hard he could feel it. A tremble moved through her every few seconds and he knew she'd need some time to work out what had happened today.

"Lindsey?" He wasn't sure what to ask or how to help.

Those wide eyes stared up at him. "Take me home."

# Chapter Twenty

Lindsey gasped for breath as Holt pushed into her again. She lay sprawled on her big bed with Holt on top of her, tucked into the V between her legs. It had been this way for hours. They came home, showered and crawled right into bed. They hadn't been out or without each other since.

The bed shook and her fingers curled into the sheets. She tried to regain control of her muscles but couldn't. Her thighs trembled from the force of the pressure against his hips. The way he moved, plunged. He had her grabbing on to his back and not letting go.

She couldn't take another second. She pinched his shoulder to let him know he needed to push her over the edge. No more sensual play. No more making her want him until it choked her.

"Now, Holt." She scraped her fingernails against his lower back to let him know she was serious.

His rhythm stayed steady and he pressed in deep. With each movement he brought her in tight. Held her hips steady so she could feel every inch. But when his fingers dipped below her waist and dragged through her heat, something exploded inside her. Need washed through her as her hips lifted off the mattress.

She exhaled as the tension clamping down inside her

released. Her hips moved and her body bucked as the pulses pounded through her. She held on to him through it all. Feeling his body stiffen as the pleasure became too much. The release hit him right as she finished, their bodies in sync until the end.

When she finally came up for air again, she saw daylight outside her window. Birds sang and the rain from the night before lingered in the air, giving everything that fresh scent.

Not that she wanted to be outside. The mix of sheets and his warm body felt so much better. She knew that sooner or later she'd need to get up and face the world. There were questions and documents. The media kept calling. Corcoran Team members called and checked in with Holt to make sure he was okay after his injuries.

That was a lot of reality for her to handle right now. She already had the aftermath of being abducted and stepping so close to death. In her mind, her uncle had been dead for years. Then he was alive. Now he was dead again. She knew she should mourn in some way, but the tears refused to fall.

That wasn't the case for Deputy Frank or Roger. She mentally added both names to the already long list of casualties and felt their losses. And Justice was awash in law enforcement officials. Holt told her ATF, FBI and others had swarmed over the campground. She hoped that meant an end to New Foundations, but only time would tell on that issue.

She rolled over, groaning from all the aches and pains. "I could sleep for a month."

"Do you mean sleep or have sex?" His voice carried an early morning husky grumble. "Because I'll need vitamins if it's the latter."

She kind of doubted that. The man had amazing stamina. Amazing everything.

She threw her arm across his chest and prepared to stay there all day. "We should eat something."

"I'd rather not fly without eating."

The comments had her eyes popping back open. He didn't move, which figured. She sat up and glared at him because he'd earned it.

Finally one of his eyes inched open. He looked startled to see her there hovering. "What?"

"Plane?" Right now she was ticked off at having the information dropped on her like that, but she could easily move through a few more emotions depending on what else he had to say.

He slipped an arm behind his head. "I have to get back for a check-in with Connor and debrief."

"I barely know what any of that means." It all sounded official and work-like. It made sense that he needed to give the information while it was all fresh. She'd had to answer what felt like a thousand questions before she could leave the campground yesterday.

He smiled up at her. "Basically—"

"I don't care."

The smile faded as quickly as it came. "Okay."

He couldn't possibly think she cared about the intricacy of a crime scene and the aftermath. She'd be dealing with her own emotional fallout on this one. Likely for weeks, maybe more. There had been so many shocks and such horror. All that death.

The one bright spot—some days the only one—had been him. He made the terrible bearable. He warmed her heart and set her bed on fire.

She didn't know what kinds of relationships he'd had before. Not serious, from the sound of them. But she knew what this one wasn't—ordinary and forgettable. This transcended. At least it had for her.

But if he could pack up and leave and not spend two minutes thinking about her, then she had more than aftermath ahead of her. She had a blinding heartbreak that would leave her raw and aching. Just thinking about losing him touched off a pain in her stomach.

She wanted him to just know what to do next, but she needed things spelled out. "Are you coming back?"

He had the nerve to frown at her. "When?"

She sat up, dragging the sheet along with her. "You cannot be this slow."

Wariness fell over him as tension thickened the room. "What are you talking about?"

"There's something between us." It took much for her to admit that out loud. To go out on that limb and hold the risk by herself.

"I agree."

Relief zinged through her. "The question is what we're going to do about it."

Slow and deliberate he sat up. Not the whole way. Just balancing on his elbows as he surveyed her. Studied her as he might a map. "I don't know."

For a second she wasn't sure what question he was answering. The response seemed so vague and so dull. One of those things men said while walking out the door even though they never planned on calling again.

And she couldn't wrap her head around that at all. They sparked in the bedroom and worked everywhere else. When she gave him a peek into her feelings, he seemed to agree. Now she was getting the "we'll see" type of response.

She had to get out of the bed. An hour ago she would have said she'd stay in those sheets with him for days if he'd just ask. But that was the problem. He never asked. He probably never would.

With the sheet held tight against her breasts, she swung her legs over the side and looked around for a shirt. She snagged his T-shirt and slipped it over her head. Feeling more in control and less ready to be sucker punched, she stood up.

He tugged on the sheet and it fell loose from her body. "Where are you going?"

"Food." That was all she could get out.

Words crammed in her throat and she tried to swallow them back. Part of her knew this reaction wasn't fair. They hadn't made promises or had a deal. She was trying to drag them into something serious, and he didn't do serious. Shane had told her that.

"Wait a second." Holt sat up the whole way this time. "Did I say something?"

"Nothing." That was the point.

"Lindsey."

The pleading in his tone had her spinning around in the doorway to face him. She thought about saying something clever or making a joke. Anything to ease the tension.

"I've fallen for you." Not at all what she wanted to say. Embarrassment welled inside her, and her stomach did this strange bouncing thing. But she couldn't take it back now. Really didn't want to, because it was true.

He smiled at her, all warm and sexy-like. "I like you, too."

They were not saying the same thing, and the reality of that difference slammed into her like being hit with a bat. Yeah, they were not saying the same thing at all. She was invested and hopeful and looking to the future. He was enjoying the sex. That was what it came down to.

She had no doubt he enjoyed her company. She could see it in his eyes when he looked at her. But the idea of talking about anything bigger seemed to send him running. All the way back to Annapolis this time. She didn't know where it would be next time, but she had no intention of waiting around to find out.

The ball was in his court. Now she needed to make him see it. "I'm going to make you breakfast and then we'll get you packed."

He leaned back against the pillows as if now was the time to get comfortable. "I don't need to leave yet."

His cluelessness actually gave her hope. He wasn't dumping her or giving her the let's-be-friends speech. "Yes, you do."

His eyes narrowed and some of that casual comfortableness eased away. "Why?"

"Because this isn't a hotel." Maybe that hit a little lower than she intended, but it felt good to say that.

This time he climbed out of bed and walked over to stand beside her. "What the hell is that about?"

"You like me."

"Yes." He put his hands on her arms and pulled her in closer.

He clearly missed the part where she had hers folded across her chest. "Fine."

But something got through, because his body switched to high alert and it showed in every muscle. "What's happening here?"

"If you figure out what you feel is more than like— because that's how you feel about a neighbor's cat and not a woman—call me."

"My neighbor has a dog."

He had to be messing with her now. "Fabulous."

"Lindsey, I really don't understand this."

"Right." That was the problem, and for a smart man he was fumbling his way through it. "When you do get it, let me know."

HOLT MADE IT to the private airstrip in record time. He actually got there two hours before their scheduled departure. He had planned to hang around the house, go back to bed. Spend more time with Lindsey.

He didn't want to say goodbye. Didn't even want to leave. He thought things were going fine, and then the questions started. He panicked and then he was in the rental car.

At least they could get moving, since they were all there. Cam was in the process of walking around the plane, performing a safety check. Shane sat on a duffel, using it as a chair as he played with his phone.

Holt did not want to be here. He had no idea what had happened. The day started out so promising. A hot woman and a warm bed. He'd been all over her all night. He knew that wasn't the problem, because a woman didn't beg like that if she lacked interest.

No, the problem came with the talking. Always the talking.

Cam glanced up and stopped working. "Why are you here?"

Holt knew that was a bad sign of the conversations to come. It didn't help that Cam and Shane kept looking at each other, talking some language that they spoke and he didn't seem to.

So he went with the obvious answer. "I lead the team."

"I meant, why aren't you in bed with Lindsey?" Cam asked.

"I would be," Shane said at the same time.

That was just about enough of that. "We need to get home for the debrief."

Holt said it even though he sort of dreaded it this time around. Walking into the apartment meant stepping into a place without her. Her house smelled good, like a mix of her shampoo and something cooking on the stove. He generally ordered takeout when not out on the job.

Man, he really was a confirmed bachelor.

"Wait, does that mean you blew it already?" Shane asked as he stood up and came over to join them on the tarmac.

Cam nodded. "I think so."

Okay, Holt officially hated that conclusion. "No."

Cam leaned against the plane. "Does she think you blew it?"

All of a sudden the guy was a dating expert. Though Holt had to admit he kind of was. He was in a committed relationship. They talked about a future. Holt thought about a future and felt everything inside him clench. Well, it used to. Not lately, but he was sure the sensation of being strangled would come back.

Until then he had a much bigger problem. "I don't know what she wants."

"Oh, boy." Cam dropped his clipboard on the ground.

Again with the looks between Shane and Cam. They glanced and smiled, almost laughed. Holt wasn't loving the byplay. That sort of thing was much more fun when he wasn't the victim. "Okay, enough. What is it?"

Cam shrugged. "You missed a cue. That's almost always it."

Holt didn't even know what those words meant in the context of a woman. "Speak slower."

Shane rolled his eyes. "What did she say she wanted?"

This was downright embarrassing. Holt wasn't accustomed to spilling his guts about a woman. Some things a guy should keep to himself and just handle.

Then he remembered the look on Lindsey's face. A mix of hurt and anger, and he tried to put the ego aside. "I don't know. More time together."

"And what did you say?" Cam asked.

"I like her." He almost shouted the phrase as a plane passed overhead.

They both stared at him and not in a good way.

Cam bit his upper lip. "Wow."

Shane shook his head. "That's terrible."

Tough talk coming from a guy with an awful divorce in his recent past. Holt wanted to point that out, but it seemed like a jerk move, so he let it pass. "Like you would be better."

Shane snorted. "A puppy would do better."

Holt refused to debate based on the animal kingdom. "What do I do?"

"Do you love her?" Cam asked.

The question made him twitchy. Holt got that Cam had figured this relationship stuff out and was happy for him. Holt thought about love and the future and mortgages and felt something inside him go haywire. "It's too soon."

Cam looked at Shane. "I didn't hear a no."

The last thing Holt needed was these two bonding together on this topic. He was just looking for a little advice here. Simple stuff…stuff that he sucked at. "I care about her."

Shane shook his head. "Stop saying that before she kills you."

Holt was two seconds from going out and asking a cat or dog for advice. "You two aren't helping."

"Here's my suggestion." Cam pointed at the bag near

Holt's feet. "Take your bag, go back there and tell her what you really feel. Inside. The hard stuff."

That sounded both easy and really hard. Holt didn't like the downside risk. "Are you messing with me?"

"I'm trying to help you get your woman back before you lose her."

The thought of that knocked out any concern about talking about his feelings. He'd open up all day if it stopped her from giving up on him. Holt hated that idea. "I don't want that."

"Then go tell her." Shane and Cam said it at the same time.

So, they agreed with each other on that one. Holt took that as a good sign.

# Chapter Twenty-One

Lindsey sat on her front porch with a glass of lemonade between her palms. The ice cubes chilled her, but she didn't put it down. She couldn't really move. She was too busy sitting and staring and doing nothing.

Getting dressed took a lot of effort. So did the mandatory check-in with all the law enforcement agencies, which she promised she would do. People came by and others called. The newspaper said something about printing a follow-up making it clear she wasn't a suspect. Nice of them, since she wasn't one.

After so much everything, nothing felt good. Well, not really. She couldn't actually feel anything. Watching Holt leave had numbed her inside. She felt hollowed-out and raw. She didn't want to eat and seriously considered burning her mattress. Too many reminders there.

She kept thinking Holt would turn around. Get a mile down the road and realize he'd lost his mind and come back and help put them back together. But no. She didn't wear a watch because then she'd know the exact time he took off, and that was too hard to take on top of everything else.

And this town. She didn't have anything keeping her here now. The people she'd helped could live in the open, free. The memorial services would be set for the others.

She didn't know if she could stay in a place made up of so much pain.

She had just decided to take a sip of the lemonade when a truck rattled up her driveway. Not just a truck. *The* truck. His rental truck.

She started to wonder how long she'd been sitting here. By her calculation it had been an hour, but that didn't make sense. Not if he was back. It was what she had wished for but so out of context that she couldn't make the timing work in her head.

The truck stopped and he sat there for a second with the engine on, leaning on the steering wheel and staring at her. She officially had no idea what was happening, and when that tiny bit of hope flickered inside her again, she knew she should tamp it down.

More seconds passed. He must have had the radio on, because at first she heard music but now none.

Finally, after what felt like an eternity, the door opened and he got out. Jeans and a gray T-shirt. Yep, same outfit, so she hadn't lost her mind or a bunch of days. He'd driven to the airport and driven back. Again, not much sense there, but she guessed she'd have to wait and see what he said…if he actually said anything. He wasn't always the best at explaining.

He disappeared again for a second when he leaned across the bench seat. He had something in his hand and he was dragging it. When he came around the front of the truck she got a good look. His duffel bag. The one that had been sitting in her bedroom. The same one he'd packed to leave.

And now it was back. That meant something. It had to.

The hope started doing more than flickering. It danced and bounced. Some of the anger and sadness that had been weighing her down since he'd left lifted. She took a big gulp of lemonade to make sure she wasn't dreaming. The pucker told her she wasn't.

She didn't know when she'd stood up, but she had. She had a glass dangling from her hand and her heart right out there for everyone to see. It was kind of embarrassing how much she loved this man. So few days had passed and yet she felt as if her life had become tied to his.

Without thinking about it or remembering a thing, she met him at the steps to the porch. She wasn't sure what that meant, so she didn't pick at it too much. She stood one above him, which put them face-to-face. She could look into those dark eyes. Wariness lingered there. She sure got that.

It seemed to her that he should be the first to say something. But when his gaze toured her face but he stayed quiet, she jumped in. "What are you doing here?"

"This is where I want to be." He shuffled his weight back and forth. Not really something he did. He never fidgeted. If anything, he could hold still for what felt like hours. It always struck her as a bit freaky, but the wounded puppy look was sure charming.

And that was such a better answer than the ones he'd given her before. It didn't make her want to scream or strangle him. Both good signs. "You said you have to go home. Something about briefings."

She didn't remember all the other stuff. Basically he talked about flying out and her brain shut down. Maryland meant going across the country without her. She hated everything about that plan.

"I should, yeah. But I'd rather be here with you. Anywhere with you." He shrugged. "I mean you can come home with me if you want. So long as we're in the same house and same bed, I'm good."

The responses just kept getting better and better. This one shot off the charts.

Here she sat trying to figure out where and how she fit in. Then in a few words he'd made her an offer. Quick and to the point. He wasn't a guy who lingered over facts and details.

She knew when he put it out there he meant it. She could count on it. And she just might.

But she tried not to get too excited, because he looked more shell-shocked than in love. His skin had an odd dullness to it and he looked as though he should consider sitting down. "Why the change?"

"Cam and Shane basically told me I'm an idiot."

She smiled as she set the glass down on the porch and out of kicking range. After spending a few days with Shane she could almost hear the conversation. "I like them."

"Don't be fooled. They're idiots, too." Holt matched her and dropped his bag. Didn't put it on the ground or near the car. No, he walked up two steps and put it on the porch and then returned to where he was standing below her.

For some reason that struck her as significant. It would be better if he put it in her bedroom or loaded her stuff in his truck to leave. Both worked for her.

She had a home and a life here, but she could shift. She could anchor herself to him. After all these years obsessing over the same thing, it might be good to find a new hobby. Find new work and another passion. Though her passion for him did consume her at the moment.

The warm sun pounded down on them. The temperature had turned and the unseasonably cool weather had moved out, leaving a bright blue sky behind. Summer in Oregon was a beautiful thing. The water close by and the towering trees lining the mountains. Between the fresh air and the good food, she could almost forget all the killing.

Almost.

Neither of them said anything for a minute. She was content to stand there and look at him. The temptation to brush back his hair. All that touching in the bedroom. She wanted that feeling of intimacy no matter where they were together.

The bag and sweet words already told her what she needed to know about his commitment. None of this came easy to him, but he was trying. This was hard for him, but he pushed through and she knew he did it all for her. Maybe because his friends gave him a hard time, but she could accept that.

She was about to take pity on him when he started talking. "When I said I cared for you I meant it."

"I know." But the lukewarm phrase made her back teeth slam together. Instinctively, she knew it was a lot for him to say. That it was a big deal. But she wanted more. After a lifetime of settling and helping others, she was ready to grab something for herself. And she wanted it to be him.

He took one of her hands in both of his. Played with her fingers and caressed her palm. The gentle touches had her nerve endings screaming for more. "I will never lie to you."

"I get that, too."

"I'm going to mess up." He peeked up at her. "A lot. This relationship stuff doesn't come naturally to me, and the strength of my feelings for you scares me. They knock me sideways and that's never happened before."

She loved every word.

"I see you and I want to strip your clothes off." He threw her a lopsided smile. "It was that way from day one. Something very primal and instinctive."

But she wanted this—no, needed this—to be about more than sex. She had already said the words, and she'd stopped short. He needed to make part of the journey now. "Tell me what you really want from me. I know what I want from you, but what are you looking for?"

"Everything."

"Holt..."

"I've had a messed-up life. A weird relationship with my dad and nearly dying." He shrugged. "Those aren't excuses for anything. More like explanations."

"I get it." She did. "The past shapes us. I mean, really. Look at my life and my obsession." So much of who she was and how she reacted to things came from back then. She'd set her entire adult life around a place she professed to hate.

For her, New Foundations and everything that had happened this week were about closure and moving on. For the first time she felt as if she had the power and strength to make it happen.

"Any chance you're looking for a new one?"

She missed the comment, but she caught the smile. It was infectious. When he opened up and let his feelings shine through, he was even more attractive. She loved the brooding side. The darkness and his need to control and protect. Those were all parts of him and together they made up this beautiful, complex, wonderful man.

His comment finally registered. "Wait, what did you say?"

"Obsession. If you're looking for one I'd be happy to volunteer." He started ticking off points on his fingers.

"I don't smoke. Not a big drinker except for a beer with football. I can cut firewood and take you to dinner."

The words hit her and that hope turned into a raging bonfire. He stood there handing her everything. Stuff she'd always dreamed of and things she didn't even know she wanted until they came in a package that included him.

She wrapped her arms around his neck. The poor thing looked lost and ready to be sent away. But she wouldn't do that. She hadn't wanted to do it earlier, but the decision to stay had to be his.

But pushing him out. That was not going to happen again. From now on she'd make him stick around and fight. About work and home and friends and even what was for dinner. If they were going to try this, going to make it work, they had to be a partnership, and sometimes that was a rocky thing.

"Are you volunteering for this obsession position?"

He rubbed his hands up and down her back. "Since I'm half in love with you I thought it might be good if you decided you couldn't live without me. You know, be tied to me and not want to let me go."

And there she went. Totally, fully in love with him. No partway. No think about it. No waiting to see. It was right there in front of her and she grabbed it.

But they had to backtrack a bit. They'd jumped over the simple steps like getting to know each other and spending time together. They could circle back to those. For now, she was fine with the rest moving at top speed. They'd fill in the blanks, from simple things like meeting his sister to the more complicated, like where to live.

He sighed into her hair. "I'm not great at this, but—"

"Wrong. You might be a slow starter, but you're pretty great at it." She kissed his cheek and then his neck. "At so many things. At most things, actually. Come to think of it, you're not going to be easy to live with."

"I already listed the pros."

She gave in to the temptation and ran a hand through his hair. "All very impressive."

"Does this mean I can stay?"

She dropped a quick kiss on his mouth. "Just try to leave me again."

"That's exactly what a man likes to hear." He picked her up and her legs wrapped around his. They stood there in the sunshine with the warmth pouring over them. "The debrief can wait. Let's go check out that bed again. I think I left a bit too early this morning, but we can fix that."

He was full of great ideas all of a sudden. She didn't know who she should thank, Cam or Shane or both, for the nudge in the right direction, but she would. Because right now she'd never been happier. Never stood on the cusp of getting everything she wanted. And she loved the sensation. "Only if you promise we'll stay in there all day."

He smiled. "Deal."

*Chapter Twenty-Two*

Cam read the text from Holt. Read it a second time just so he could enjoy it. Looked as though the big man had found the right words to win Lindsey over. Either that or she'd taken pity on him and let him stay. Either way, Holt won.

Lindsey was a good woman. Right for him. Strong and smart, beautiful and able to handle Holt's personality. They fit together. Cam had noticed the sparks right away.

Cam knew how it felt. Since he'd been with Julia, everything felt right. The danger worried him. Not for him but for her. He'd lived his entire life on the edge. He didn't question it, but he'd feared it would drive them apart, but she insisted she went into the relationship knowing about his background and need for danger.

He'd gone from "no, thank you" on commitments to craving one. He even had the ring picked out...not that Julia knew that. Only Joel knew and Connor, since Cam didn't know a thing about rings and Connor was already married.

Technically, it was too early. Not by Cam's standards. He'd known after day four that Julia was the one. But he was willing to wait a respectable amount of time, however much she needed. He just hoped that didn't extend past six months, because a guy could only take so much. When he decided he wanted to see his bride walk down the aisle, he wanted it to happen now.

With Holt partnering up, that left one single guy on the team. Shane wasn't easy to pin down. Well, for others to pin down. The identity of the right woman was not really a mystery. He just had to get out of his own way long enough to give her a chance. Not make such a big deal of the little problems between them. Let go of his past once and for all.

If the rest of them shunned commitment, Shane was openly hostile to it. Divorce would do that to a guy, and his was of the nasty variety.

But people changed. The rest of the team had. One by one they'd paired up. They'd found stability and women and a home to go to. None of them were ever party types. Their jobs didn't allow that, because they had to be packed and ready to go on short notice. Being drunk would be a hindrance to that.

Seven down, one to go. As soon as Cam filled the office in on Holt's chosen vacation destination, the pressure would be on Shane. Good thing the guy could handle it. Could handle anything...except Makena Kingston.

Cam slipped his phone into his back pocket. "It's just the two of us on this ride. Holt decided to wait here for a few days."

A stupid grin split across Shane's face. "A few? I guess that means he's staying or we're going to have to move her to him. Either way you know we'll end up helping, right?"

"Wouldn't you stay if you were him? Pretty woman he's falling for and a warm bed." It was a test and Cam had a feeling Shane was about to fail.

"You're asking the wrong guy. The staying thing is not for me. Not now and not ever. If you don't believe me, ask my divorce lawyer. I'm still paying his bill." Shane loaded the bags into the plane's cargo area. They had their personal items plus a few boxes of intel about the campground. Another few about the weapons.

Cam decided to ignore the divorce because that was too tough to operate around. "You notice you're the only one around here not paired up."

After dropping a few hints about the woman involved in this case and Holt's interest in her, the Annapolis office decided he was taken. They were already talking about Shane being next, and last, and poor Holt was still in the getting-to-know-you phase.

Shane kept loading. Kept his head down. Ignored most of the conversation and stuck to short answers. In other words, the usual.

After a few minutes of quiet he finally piped up. "You've all lost your minds. Never seen guys go from confirmed bachelors to husbands so fast. Half of you are in relationships that are right on the verge of ending with a ring."

Cam couldn't argue. "It's your turn next."

The reply came fast and sharp. "Nope. No to the serious dating and definitely not to anything that will lead to a ring. I've already done that. In fact, I think that means you guys are behind me."

"You never know who you'll meet. Maybe it's someone you already know." But Cam knew about the panic that set in when the others paired off. He'd been there. Breezed through the dating stages with Julia and hit the denial part pretty hard.

But there's that one woman. The one who turns your

head and gets you thinking about things you never dreamed about.

Cam had found that with Julia. All the guys now had it. All but Shane.

"Again, I've been married," Shane pointed out. "I know all about the realities, and you can't sell the institution to me."

Since the topic of Shane's divorce never led to a good conversation, Cam tried to come at this from another direction. "Looks like we'll have a few days off."

"Sounds good to me." Shane loaded the last box and shut the door. "I can't remember the last time I've been home."

The guy walked right into the trap. "Right about the time Shane's sister moved down the road."

Shane's shoulders froze for a second. Then he went back to work. "Yep."

Shane had it bad for Makena. It was one of those attractions you could see. Well, everyone but the two people trying hard not to be in the relationship. Makena denied it. Shane denied it. Holt ignored it. It was an interesting trifecta of dysfunction.

But that didn't change the fact that Shane watched Makena move and eat. They talked in groups and shut down around each other when it was just the two of them. It wasn't always that way...but then Makena had grown up.

"She's still around, right?"

Shane snorted. "You know where Makena is. Stop matchmaking."

Easier said than done when the wives were involved and poking around. "I was wondering if you did."

"She's off-limits."

"Right." The whole baby sister of Holt thing. Dating

the boss's sister was problematic. Adding in the fact that her brother and Shane were best friends just complicated things.

"I'm serious." And Shane growled that out as if to make sure Cam got it. "Don't help me."

"We'll see."

\* \* \* \* \*

*Don't miss the heart-stopping conclusion of
HelenKay Dimon's miniseries*
CORCORAN TEAM:
BULLETPROOF BACHELORS
*when TAMED goes on sale next month.*

## "I'm not a callous jerk, no matter what kind of first impression I gave you."

She patted his hand, which still rested on the table in front of her. "You still have a chance to redeem yourself."

By the time the waiter brought the check, Graham felt almost comfortable with her. He debated asking her out for a real date, but decided to wait. He'd be sure to see her again; the case gave him a good excuse to do so.

He walked her to her Jeep and lingered while she found her keys and unlocked the car door. "Here's my personal cell." He wrote the number on the back of his business card and handed it to her. "Call me anytime."

"About the case—or just to talk?" Her tone was teasing.

"Either. Maybe you'd like to give me your number?"

She smiled and opened her purse. But she never had a chance to write down her number. The loud crack of gunshots shattered the afternoon silence. Her screams rang in Graham's ears as he pushed her to the ground.

# LAWMAN PROTECTION

## BY
## CINDI MYERS

MILLS & BOON

Published in Great Britain 2015
by Mills & Boon, an imprint of Harlequin (UK) Limited,
Eton House, 18-24 Paradise Road, Richmond, Surrey, TW9 1SR

© 2015 Cynthia Myers

ISBN: 978-0-263-25312-2

46-0715

Harlequin (UK) Limited's policy is to use papers that are natural, renewable and recyclable products and made from wood grown in sustainable forests. The logging and manufacturing processes conform to the legal environmental regulations of the country of origin.

Printed and bound in Spain
by CPI, Barcelona

**Cindi Myers** is an author of more than fifty novels. When she's not crafting new romance plots, she enjoys skiing, gardening, cooking, crafting and daydreaming. A lover of small-town life, she lives with her husband and two spoiled dogs in the Colorado mountains.

**For Mike**

# Chapter One

"Would you rather face down half a dozen reporters at a press conference, or shoot it out with drug runners in the backcountry?"

FBI Captain Graham Ellison gave his questioner, Montrose County sheriff's deputy Lance Carpenter, a sour look. "Is that a trick question? At least with the drug runners I've got a fair chance. It doesn't matter what I say at these press conferences. The media puts the spin on it they want."

"If the questions get too tough, just look menacing and tell them the safety of local citizens is your primary concern." Carpenter clapped Graham on the back. "You'll do great."

Graham eyed the crowd of reporters, cameramen and news trucks waiting in the parking lot outside the trailer that served as headquarters for The Ranger Brigade— the nickname given to an interagency task force addressing crime on public lands in southwest Colorado. "The safety of citizens *is* my primary concern," he said. "Or one of them. I have a lot of concerns—and I don't need reporters telling me how to do my job, or wasting my time listing all the ways I'm doing it wrong."

"I don't think you've got any choice in the matter

this time." Lance studied the gathering over Graham's shoulder. "Prentice and Senator Mattheson forced your hand."

Graham let out a low growl and shifted his focus to the newspaper that lay open on his desk. Twin headlines summed up his predicament: Mattheson Calls for Dismantling Task Force read one. Prentice Readies for Battle declared the other. Peter Mattheson, senator from Colorado, was on a crusade to "get the feds out of local law enforcement business" and "stop wasting money on federal boondoggles."

Richard Prentice, a billionaire who'd made a career out of buying up environmentally or historically valuable properties, then blackmailing the federal government into paying top dollar to save the parcels, had filed a lawsuit to force local authorities to allow him to develop property he owned at the entrance to the Black Canyon of the Gunnison National Park.

Graham's bosses in Washington had "suggested" he hold a press conference to address both these issues. "We'd better get out there before they start making stuff up," Graham said. He straightened his shoulders, opened the door and stepped out into a hail of shouted questions.

"Captain Ellison, have you spoken with Richard Prentice?"

"Captain Ellison, has the death of Raul Meredes slowed drug trafficking in the area?"

"Captain Ellison, how do you respond to Senator Mattheson's criticisms of the task force?"

Graham stood on the top step of the trailer and glowered at the gathered media. Flashes around him let him know his scowling face would be in newspapers all over the region tomorrow. More than one news account had described him as "a big bear of a man." He hoped this time they'd look at him and think "grizzly." He scanned the crowd for a familiar face, some reporter he knew who'd let him ease into the grilling with a softball question.

A cameraman moved to one side, adjusting his angle, and a woman took advantage of the opening to step forward. Digital recorder in one hand, notebook in the other, she was clearly a reporter, but not one Graham had seen before. He wouldn't forget a figure like hers. She was tall, with a generous chest and curvy hips, a wild tumble of strawberry blond hair and full lips in a perfect pink bow of a mouth. Her eyes were hidden by fashionably large sunglasses, but he had no doubt she was looking right at him. And frankly, he couldn't stop staring at her. Forget the fragile, stick-figure women so popular in magazines and on television—here was a real-live, flesh-and-blood goddess. Here was a woman he could embrace without crushing, one he could kiss without getting a crick in his back, one…

"Captain Ellison, what are you doing about the disappearance of Lauren Starling?" the woman asked, her voice husky and deep, carrying easily even in the crowd.

At her words, his fantasy vanished like a puff of smoke. She wasn't the perfect woman—she was a reporter. And judging from the frown on her face, she didn't think much of him. "So far it has not been determined that Ms. Starling is a missing person, or that she is, in fact, missing in our territory. We are working with the Denver police to try to determine her whereabouts."

"You don't think finding her car abandoned in the National Park, not a half mile from where we're standing right now, points to some connection between her failing to show up for work two weeks ago and 'your territory?'"

Lauren Starling was the popular nightly news anchor at Denver's number two news station. Three weeks ago, she'd failed to return from a few days' vacation and park rangers had discovered her car abandoned at an overlook in Black Canyon of the Gunnison National Park. "Denver police are in charge of that investigation and they are keeping us apprised," Graham said. What he wished he could say was that, for all he or anyone else knew, Lauren Starling was in Mexico with a secret boyfriend. "At this point we have no evidence of foul play."

Twin lines, like the number eleven, formed between the woman's eyes and her mouth turned down in disapproval. Clearly, she didn't think much of his answer. Too bad. He had bigger things to worry about than one woman who the Denver cops had hinted was more than a little flighty. His officers were keeping their eyes open for any sign of Ms. Starling, but he wasn't losing sleep over her.

"Captain, did the death of Raul Meredes put an end to drug trafficking on public lands?" A reedy man Graham recognized as being from the local county paper asked the question. Meredes had been in charge of a large marijuana-growing and human-trafficking operation based in the National Park. Identifying him as a key figure in the recent crime spree had been the task force's biggest achievement thus far. Unfortunately, Meredes had been murdered before they could question him. The crime rate in the area had dipped following his demise, but Graham sensed the lull represented only a marshaling of resources, in preparation for another surge.

"Mr. Meredes played a major role in the crimes going on in this area," Graham said. "But we don't believe he was the one supplying the money and man power for the operation. We're still trying to track down that individual."

"Do you think Richard Prentice has any connection to criminal activity in the park?"

Graham wasn't sure who asked that question; it came from the back of the crowd. Had someone leaked the task force's suspicions, or had Prentice himself sent someone to test how much the Rangers knew?

"We have no reason to believe Mr. Prentice has anything to do with the crimes in the park," he said. Prentice was a jerk and a thorn in the side of federal and state officials in general, but being nasty and unpleasant didn't make a man a criminal. Which didn't mean the task force wasn't watching him very closely. But Prentice had a lot of money, and a lot of lawyers, so they had to tread carefully, which meant not airing their suspicions to the press.

"What do you think of his plans to build a housing development at the entrance to the park?" asked the stringer for the Telluride paper.

"I don't think my opinion on the matter is relevant," Graham said. "I have bigger things to focus on at the moment than Mr. Prentice's battle for public opinion." He glanced at his watch; he'd been standing up here only five minutes. How much longer before he could make his escape?

"What do you have to say to Senator Mattheson's charges that a multi-agency task force is an ineffective and expensive way to address problems better handled by local law enforcement?" The question came from the female reporter. She'd removed her sunglasses to reveal hazel eyes fringed with long, dark lashes. But there was no warmth in those eyes for him.

"I would remind Senator Mattheson that local law enforcement requested help from the federal government in addressing the multiple crimes that seemed to be originating from federal lands," Graham said. "Law enforcement on public land has always been the purview of federal park rangers and the various federal agencies who oversee various federal regulations, from ATF to Border Patrol. This task force brings members of those agencies together to pool resources and provide a more focused approach to addressing crime in a vast and largely unpoliced area."

"But in three months you've only made one arrest, and you're no closer to identifying the person responsible for this crime wave," she said.

"Real life isn't like television, where every case is wrapped up in an hour," he said, barely reining in his annoyance.

"And you don't think Lauren Starling's disappearance has any connection to the other crimes within the park?" she asked, recorder extended toward him.

"I believe I've addressed the question already." He turned away, aware of her gaze boring into him.

"Captain?"

He turned and found Lance, cell phone in hand. "I think you'd better take this call," the deputy said. He handed the phone to Graham, then stepped forward to address the reporters. "We're going to have to wrap this up now," he said. "Thank you all for coming."

At first, Graham thought the sheriff's deputy had manufactured the call, as a ruse to end the press conference early. *Points for him*, Graham thought as he turned his back to the reporters and spoke into the phone. "Ellison here."

"Captain, Randall here." Randall Knightbridge was the Bureau of Land Management's representative on the team. His voice was strained, putting Graham on alert; this was no fake call.

"What is it, Randall?"

"Marco and I were patrolling in the Curecanti Recreation Area and we came upon a plane wreck. It looks recent—within the last day or so." Marco Cruz was with the DEA, probably the best tracker on the task force—well, the best, except for Randall's dog, Lotte. "A Beechcraft Bonanza," Randall continued. "One casualty—the pilot."

"Give me your coordinates and I'll send a team right away." Graham pulled a notepad and pen from the front pocket of his uniform shirt.

Randall rattled off the GPS coordinates. "You probably want to come with the team," he said.

Graham tucked the notebook back into his pocket and glanced over his shoulder at the departing press. The curvy blonde was trailing the pack, headed toward a red SUV parked at the far end of the lot. For a moment he was transfixed on the tantalizing sway of her backside as she moved away from him. Too bad she was a reporter...

"Captain?" Randall's voice recalled him from his fantasies.

"I'm here. What were you saying?"

"I said, there's some interesting cargo here you're definitely going to want to see."

EMMA WADE STARED at the captain's back through the windshield of her Jeep Wrangler—broad shoulders, muscular arms and yes, a very nice rear end. In other circumstances, he was exactly the kind of guy she'd go for—big enough that she wouldn't feel like an elephant next to him. Strong. Intelligent. Too bad he was a jerk.

He finished one call and immediately made two more, then barked something at the sheriff's deputy at his side. She was too far away to hear the words, but the tension in his expression and body language made her sit up straighter. Something was up.

Graham Ellison and the deputy headed for a black-and-white FJ Cruiser parked on the side of the task force trailer. Emma fastened her seat belt and started her vehicle. The press conference had been a bust as far as gathering any new information, but she didn't have to go home empty-handed. Wherever the captain was headed, maybe there was a story there.

He could refuse to answer her questions at the news conference, but he couldn't keep her off public land. Fresh anger rose at the memory of his easy dismissal of the idea that Lauren Starling might be a concern of his precious task force. The police had had the same attitude ten years ago, when Sherry had turned up missing. The next thing Emma knew, she'd been attending her sister's funeral. She gripped the steering wheel of the Jeep until her knuckles ached. Captain Ellison might think he'd heard the last from her about Lauren, but he was wrong. She wouldn't let another family suffer the way hers had if she could help it.

She eased off the accelerator, letting the Cruiser get farther ahead. Unpaved roads made following easy— she could track the plume of dust that rose behind the speeding vehicle, her own vehicle hidden by the dirty cloud.

When the Cruiser's tracks turned off the road, headed across the prairie, she hesitated only a fraction of a second before following. The Jeep bounced over the rough terrain, rattling her teeth, and she prayed she wouldn't blow a tire. They were headed away from the canyon that gave the park its name, across an expanse of rocky ground pocked with sagebrush and piñon trees, deep into the roadless wilderness area where few people ventured. All that largely unpatrolled public land had proved attractive to the criminals who'd taken advantage of sheltered canyons and abandoned ranch buildings to plant marijuana, manufacture methamphetamine and smuggle people and illegal goods. Hence the need for the task force, though public opinion wasn't convinced that the influx of law enforcement had been much of a crime deterrent.

The dust was beginning to settle around two black-and-white Cruisers by the time Emma parked the Jeep a few yards behind them. As she climbed out of her vehicle, she focused on the mass of wreckage behind the cops: the tail and one wing of a small plane pointed skyward, the nose crumpled against the prairie. She took a couple of pictures with her digital camera then, aware of at least two cops glaring at her, strode forward with all the confidence of a journalist who knows she has every right to be where these men didn't want her.

"Stop right there, ma'am." A rangy officer in a long-sleeved brown shirt, khakis and a buff Stetson stepped out to meet her. A blond-and-black police dog stalked at his side, golden eyes fixed on her.

"Hello, Officer. I'm Emma Wade, from the *Denver Post*."

"You need to turn around and leave, Ms. Wade. This is a crime scene."

"Oh?" She directed her gaze over his shoulder, to where the captain and two other officers were huddled at the door of the crashed plane. "What kind of crime? Was the plane carrying drugs? Illegal aliens? Some other contraband? Did anyone survive the crash? Do you know who the plane belongs to?" She took out her reporter's notebook, pen poised. She didn't really expect him to answer any of her queries, but sometimes interrogating men who were more used to assuming the role of interrogator yielded interesting results.

He glanced over his shoulder toward the plane, then back at her, his expression tense. "No comment," he said.

"Then I'd better talk to someone else." She started forward, but he put out his arm to stop her.

"You really need to leave," he said.

"After I've driven all the way out here?" She folded her arms across her chest. "I'll stay."

"Then you'll have to wait over there." He motioned in the direction of her Jeep.

Clearly, he wasn't going to let her any closer. Better to wait him out. "All right." She replaced the notebook in her purse. "Tell Captain Ellison I have some questions for him when he's finished."

She turned and walked back to her vehicle, not in any hurry. Once there, she rummaged in the glove compartment until she found a pair of binoculars. She leaned against the Jeep and trained the binocs on the wreckage.

Debris littered the area around the crash—chunks of fiberglass and metal, a tire, a plastic cup, the remains of a wooden crate. She focused in on the crate and made out the words *Fragile* and *Property of*— Property of whom?

She scanned to the right of the crate and froze when she found herself looking into a pair of eyes the color of hot fudge, underneath craggy brows.

Angry brown eyes, she corrected herself, that belonged to Captain Graham Ellison. He glared directly at her and she gasped and drew back as he stalked toward her.

By the time he reached her Jeep, she'd lowered the binoculars and was doing her best not to look intimidated, though the site of the big bear of a man glaring at her was enough to make a guilty person tremble.

But she hadn't done anything wrong, she reminded herself. "Hello, Captain," she said. "What can you tell me about this plane crash?"

"Why did you follow me out here?" he asked.

"I'm a reporter. It's what I do— I track down stories." She took out her notebook and pen. "When do you think the plane crashed? It looks recent, considering the broken tree limbs are still green, and the scar in the earth looks fresh."

"So now you're an expert?" Irritation radiated from him like heat, but she was no longer nervous or afraid. His intensity excited her, both professionally and—she wasn't going to analyze this now, only note that it was true—personally. Being attracted to Captain Ellison might complicate things a little, but it didn't mean she couldn't do her job.

"Not an expert," she said. "But I've been a crime reporter for a while now. Who does the plane belong to? Do you know?"

"Whoever he is, he's dead."

"Oh." Her pen faltered, leaving a scribble on the notebook. "I suppose it would be difficult for anyone to survive a crash like that."

"Oh, he survived," Ellison said. "Then someone put a bullet in him."

She swallowed hard. She didn't like this aspect of her work, dealing with violence. But finding justice for victims often began with exposing the particulars of the crime. "How was he killed?"

"He was shot. In the chest."

"Do you know who he is?"

"Who do you work for, again?"

"The *Denver Post*. I'm with the Western Slope Bureau." She *was* the Western Slope Bureau. While she wrote stories about everything from local festivals to water rights, she specialized in crime reporting. The attempted arrest and subsequent murder of Raul Meredes had focused her attention on The Ranger Brigade—a romantic name for a disparate collection of officers from all the federal law enforcement agencies.

"If you're so interested in this story, maybe you'd like a closer look." He took her arm and pulled her toward the plane.

She didn't protest. Clearly, he wanted to shock her, to frighten her even, but she'd seen death before. Whatever that plane held, she'd study it objectively and write about it later. She'd show the captain she was tougher than he thought. She wouldn't be bullied or intimidated just because he didn't like the job she was doing.

The pilot slumped sideways in his seat, safety belt still fastened, his shirt stained brown with dried blood. Flies buzzed around him, and she swallowed hard against the sickly stench that rose to greet her. "Recognize him?" the captain asked. He still held on to her arm, as if he feared she might bolt.

She started to look away, to shake her head, but that was what he wanted, wasn't it? For her to be horrified and repulsed. She straightened her shoulders and forced herself to lean closer, to study the dead man, whose face was turned away from her. When she did so, true horror washed over her. She fought to breathe, and tears stung her eyes.

"What is it?" the captain shook her. "You're not going to be sick, are you?"

She shook her head and wrenched away from him. "I...I do know him," she gasped, then covered her mouth with her hand, fighting nausea.

"Who is he?" Ellison demanded.

"His name is Bobby Pace. I... He... We were dating. I went out with him two nights ago."

# Chapter Two

The stricken look on Emma Wade's face made Graham feel like the lowest form of jerk. He'd been furious with her for nosing her way into his investigation, but that didn't give him the right to treat her so cruelly. "Come on." He put his arm around her and turned her away from the sight of the dead man. "I'll take you back to headquarters and we can talk there."

"I'll be fine." She tried to rally, but fresh tears streamed down her face.

"I'll have one of the officers bring your Jeep," he said. "You come with me."

She didn't protest as he helped her into the Cruiser. "Bring her Jeep with you when you come back to headquarters," he told Randall, then he climbed into the driver's seat.

Neither of them said a word as the vehicle bounced over the rough terrain. He kept stealing glances at her. She'd stopped crying, and was staring out the windshield with the look of someone who wasn't seeing what was right in front of her. Even in her grief, she was beautiful; he fought against the desire to hold and comfort her. She was a reporter, and a potential witness in his case. He needed to fight his attraction to her and keep his distance.

At headquarters, he led her into his cramped office at the back of the trailer and moved a stack of binders to make room for her in one of the two folding chairs in front of his desk. The administrative assistant who helped deal with the mountains of paperwork the job entailed was off today, so they had the building to themselves, at least until the rest of the team got back from the crash site. He opened a bottle of water from the case that sat in the corner and handed it to her, then pulled the other folding chair alongside her. "First, I apologize for being such a jerk back there," he said. "I get a little...*intense*, sometimes."

"And you don't like the press." Her eyes met his over the top of the water bottle. They were the green-gold of dragonflies, he thought, fringed with gold-tipped lashes.

*Focus*, he reminded himself. "The press sometimes makes my job more difficult."

"And men like you make *my* job more difficult." Amusement glinted in those beautiful eyes, and he had to look away.

"What can you tell me about the man in the plane?" he asked. "Was he the pilot?"

"Bobby was a pilot. I never saw his plane, but I know he owned a Bonanza."

"You and he had been dating?" Some emotion he didn't want to look at too closely—jealousy?—pinched at him and he pushed it away. "For how long?"

"We only went out a few times. We weren't lovers, just friends. He was having a hard time and needed someone to talk to."

"What do you mean, having a hard time?"

"His little boy is sick, and needs a lot of expensive care. Bobby was worried about money—that's the reason he took the job with Richard Prentice, even though he couldn't stand the guy."

"He worked for Richard Prentice?"

She nodded. "That's how we met. I wrote a profile of Prentice for the *Post* last year. Bobby was kind of like a chauffeur—he piloted his Bonanza, or sometimes he flew a plane Prentice owned. He was on call to take Prentice wherever he needed to go."

"When you saw him two nights ago, did he say anything about doing a job for Prentice the next day, or the next?"

"No. We didn't talk about work. And he didn't just fly for Prentice. He worked for anybody who wanted to hire his plane. He taught flying lessons, too." She set the still-full water bottle on the desk and leaned toward him. "What happened? Did the plane crash because he was shot, or did that happen after they were on the ground?"

"We don't know, though someone would have to be pretty stupid to shoot the pilot while they were still in the air."

"You're sure there was a passenger?"

"We're not sure about anything. But someone shot your friend, and someone took the cargo that was in the plane. And we found fresh tracks that looked like a truck or another big vehicle pulled up alongside the wreckage." He clamped his mouth shut. He was telling her too much.

"I saw the busted-up crate," she said. "What was in it?"

"We don't know that, either." Though Marco Cruz,

the DEA agent who'd been patrolling with Randall, had recognized the markings on the crate.

"Do you think this is connected with Richard Prentice?" she asked. "Is he running a smuggling operation?"

"We don't know. How well do you know him? You said you wrote a profile for the paper?"

"I spent two weeks visiting his home and shadowing him as he conducted business. He was charming. Arrogant, but when you have as much money as he does, maybe it comes with the territory."

So she thought Prentice was charming? The idea annoyed him, probably more than it should, but he wasn't going to waste any more time playing the polite card. "I'll need you to tell me everything you know about Richard Prentice. And I want to see all your notes, recordings and any other material you collected while researching your article."

"I'm not one of your officers who you can boss around, Captain," she said. "If you really want that information, you can get a subpoena." She stood, her face flushed, eyes practically snapping with fury. "And if you want to know about Richard Prentice, read the article." She stalked out of his office, slamming the door hard behind her.

He stared after her, stomach churning. So much for his attempt to not be a jerk around her. But the thought of her and that arrogant billionaire...

"Captain! Wait 'til you hear this." Marco Cruz, trailed by Randall Knightbridge, burst into the headquarters trailer. Lean and muscular, with skin the color of honey, Marco was the epitome of the strong, silent type. But at the moment, his face was more animated than Graham could remember ever seeing it.

"What's up?" he asked, rising to meet them.

"I made some calls to some people I know," Marco said. "I think my hunch about what was in that crate was right."

"So what was in it?" Graham had no patience for top secret time-wasting, not when the agencies were supposed to be working together.

"I thought the crate looked just like the ones the military uses to ship Hellfire missiles. My sources in the army tell me they've had a few come up missing the last couple of years."

"What, they just lost track?" Graham asked.

"That's what I said," Randall said. "But I guess people steal them to sell on the black market."

"So what was a Hellfire missile doing in that plane?" Graham asked. "Provided that's what was really in that box."

"Hellfire missiles are what they use to arm unmanned drones," Marco said.

The hairs on the back of Graham's neck stood up. "Anybody with enough money can buy a drone from a private company. It's not illegal."

"But only someone with a Hellfire missile can arm that drone," Marco said.

"Who around here owns a drone?" Graham asked.

Marco nodded. "That's what we need to find out. And fast."

FORGET GRAHAM ELLISON, Emma told herself as she unlocked the door to her house in a quiet suburb on Montrose's south side. She didn't need him to get to the bottom of this story. Safely inside, she dumped her purse and the day's mail on the kitchen table.

"Meow!" A silver-gray tabby emerged from the bedroom and leaned against her ankles.

"Hello, Janey, darling." Emma bent and scooped the cat into her arms. As she rubbed a finger beneath the furry chin Janey—for Jane Austen—purred loudly.

"How was your day?" Emma asked. "I had to deal with the most frustrating man."

"Meow!" Janey said—though whether in sympathy, or simply because she wanted to be fed, Emma couldn't say.

But she opened a can of Salmon Supreme and dumped it into Janey's dish, then poured herself a glass of wine and sat at the table to try to organize her notes. She didn't have that much, but she had enough to write a story about the plane crash. For a painful moment the image of Bobby's lifeless body slumped in the pilot's seat of his destroyed plane flashed into her mind and she felt a sharp pang of grief for her friend.

She swallowed her tears and opened her notebook. All the more reason to do everything she could to find his killer. Bobby had been a great guy—not a man she could fall in love with, but a good friend, and he deserved better.

Her doorbell rang, the loud chimes startling her. She hurried to the door and checked the peephole, and sucked in a breath when she saw Graham Ellison standing there. He was still in uniform, but he held a large bouquet of flowers in his hand, wrapped in green tissue paper.

She unlocked the door and opened it. "Captain, what are you doing here?" she asked.

"It seems like I'm always apologizing to you," he said. "We got off on the wrong foot. Can we try again?"

She regarded him warily, trying hard not to notice how he towered over her, or how his shoulders were almost wide enough to fill the doorway. A man who made her feel dainty was a rarity, and she usually liked to savor the experience. But she had trouble relaxing around Captain Ellison. "Why should I give you another chance?" she asked.

"Because we both want to find out who killed your friend."

It was the one answer that was sure to sway her. She held the door open wider. "Come in."

He moved past her into the foyer, and handed her the flowers. "Peace offering," he said.

"Come in here." She led the way into the kitchen, and motioned to the table. "I was just going over my notes." She found a vase in a cabinet and filled it at the sink.

"I'm not going to make the mistake of asking to see them."

She flushed. "I don't like being ordered around. Also— I have my own system for organizing my research material. It's messy and it probably wouldn't make sense to anyone else."

"I shouldn't have barked at you like you were one of my junior officers."

She arranged the flowers in the vase and set it on the counter, then looked him in the eye, ignoring the way her heart sped up when she did so. "What is it about me you don't like?" she asked. "Is it just because I'm a reporter? Because we're on the same side here. I want to know who killed Bobby, and I want to see them brought to justice."

He grimaced, as if in pain. "You've got it all wrong.

Our problems aren't because I don't like you—they're because I'm so attracted to you."

Now her heart was really racing, and she felt as if she'd swallowed battling hummingbirds. So she wasn't the only one who'd noticed the heat between them. "I'm intrigued. Tell me more."

He looked around the apartment, everywhere but at her. His gaze finally focused on the cat, who had finished eating and was meticulously grooming herself. "When I saw you in that crowd of reporters, I had a hard time not staring." He hazarded a glance her way. "Is this going to get me into trouble?"

"That depends on your definition of trouble."

He shoved both hands in his pockets. "We're both professionals. Maybe we should keep it that way."

"Or maybe we should be more honest." She stepped out from behind the kitchen counter, moving toward him. "I'm an adult. I think I can handle my job and my personal life without ruining either."

"What are you saying?"

"I'm saying I'm attracted to you, too, Captain. It takes a special man to appreciate a woman like me."

His gaze swept over her like a caress. "Then those other men are fools."

She laughed. "Maybe. But some men don't know how to handle a woman who's five-eleven and probably outweighs them. I'm no delicate flower."

"I'm not interested in flowers." His gaze drifted to her cleavage. She had plenty of that. And an ample backside. He wouldn't be the first guy to appreciate her killer curves, even if the women in fashion magazines never looked like her.

"So did you come here this afternoon to ask me out?" she asked.

"No. I came to ask for your help. You know a lot more about Richard Prentice than I do. Maybe you can give me some insight."

"Richard Prentice?" The mention of the billionaire surprised her. "Do you think he's behind Bobby's death?"

"We don't know. Your friend worked for him, so that seems the most logical place to start our investigation."

He still wouldn't look her in the eye, a sure sign he was holding something back. "You're not telling me everything," she said. "Why focus on Prentice? Do you think he's connected to other crimes in the park?"

"I'd rather you tell me what you think—and what you know—about Prentice."

She considered the question for a moment, sorting through her impressions of the billionaire. "He pretty much hates the federal government, but you already know that," she said. "He's made a career of forcing the government's hand and of trying to circumvent regulations he sees as controlling and unjust. But he's never broken the law."

"Never that anyone can prove."

"But you think he has now? Why? How?"

Graham shook his head. "I have no proof that Mr. Prentice has anything to do with any crime—his only connection is that the dead pilot was known to have worked for him."

"But you have your suspicions."

His silence was as good as a confirmation. "I understand why you won't say anything more," she said. "And I wouldn't write anything about Mr. Prentice without a lot of proof to back it up—he can afford very good lawyers and we both know he's not afraid to use them. But anything you can tell me I'll keep in confidence until it's appropriate to write about it."

The line of his jaw tightened, but he gave a single nod. "I can't tell you everything I know about the case," he said. "But I will say—off the record—that the cargo we think was in that plane could be very dangerous, and it's definitely illegal."

"Will you tell me more when you can?"

He hesitated. "When I can, yes."

"Then I'll tell you what I know about Richard Prentice, even though I don't see how it can help."

He took his hands out of his pockets, and some of the tension went out of his shoulders. "Good. Why don't we discuss this over dinner?"

"Is this a date?"

He flushed. "No. Yes. Why don't we call it dinner and see what happens after that?"

EMMA INSISTED ON driving her Jeep to the restaurant, with Graham following in his Cruiser. He'd do whatever it took to put her at ease, though he wasn't used to yielding control. The little Italian bistro occupied an old house off a side street, and at this time of day they were the only customers, but the owners seemed to know Emma and greeted her warmly. "I just took some lasagna out of the oven," the woman, who looked more like Sophia Loren than an Italian grandmother, said.

"And we have a new wine you should try," her husband, a short, burly man added.

Emma looked at Graham. "Does that sound good to you?"

His stomach growled, and he realized he hadn't had anything but coffee since breakfast. "It sounds great."

The couple left them alone in a secluded booth and Graham studied Emma across the table, vowing that he wouldn't press her for information, even though he was dying to know her impressions of Richard Prentice— and what her relationship with the billionaire might have been. She'd insisted on changing before they went out, and instead of the jeans and boots she'd worn earlier, she'd put on a long dress made out of some light fabric that clung to her curves. A colorful scarf around her shoulders brought out the green in her eyes. She looked soft and sexy and too distracting for him to be comfortable. He still wasn't sure how he felt about her suggestion that they explore their mutual attraction. Getting involved with a reporter struck him as one of the worst ideas he'd ever had.

But if the reporter was a beautiful woman...

"My editor at the *Post* wanted a story on Richard Prentice after his run-in with the county officials here over his attempts to force the federal government to buy the land he owns near the park entrance," she said after their host, Ray, brought their wine. "I approached Prentice with the angle that this would be a chance for him to tell his side of the story. He ended up inviting me to visit his ranch and shadow him for a couple of weeks."

"Maybe he wanted you close, where he could keep an eye on you." His fingers tightened on the stem of the wineglass as he thought of how close Prentice had probably wanted to be to her. As close as Graham himself wanted to be.

"Maybe. But it worked in my favor. I met the people who worked for him, saw how he lived."

"What did you think?"

A smile tugged at the corners of her mouth. "You really should read the article."

"I will, but give me your impressions now."

"All right." She spread her hands flat on the table in front of her. She wore rings on one thumb and three fingers of each hand. Her nails were polished a shell pink, the manicure fresh. "First of all, he's smarter than you probably think. A genius, even. He can rattle off phone numbers of almost everyone he's ever called, remember minute details about things that happened years ago—he practically has a photographic memory."

"Smart people can still do dumb things."

"Yes. And he does have a weakness—because he's very smart, he views everyone else as dumb. That kind of arrogance leads him to underestimate his opponents sometimes."

The woman, Lola, brought two plates loaded with thick slabs of fragrant lasagna, accompanied by buttered and seasoned zucchini. "This looks amazing," Graham said as he spread a napkin in his lap.

"It is." Lola beamed. "My special recipe."

"It really is divine," Emma said. She slid a forkful into her mouth and moaned softly.

The sound made Graham's mouth go dry. He shifted to accommodate his sudden arousal, and took a long sip of wine. When was the last time a woman had affected him this way? Maybe when he was a teenager—twenty years ago. "What kind of people does Prentice hang out with?" he asked. *Focus on the case.*

"All kinds. Politicians. Foreign businesspeople. Fashion models. Celebrities. Lobbyists. People who want favors. People he can order around. He's not the kind of man who has close friends, though, just a lot of contacts and acquaintances."

"Any romantic interests?"

She shook her head. "He's been photographed with a lot of beautiful women at various events, but he treats them like accessories—necessary to his image, but there's no real attachment there. He likes women, but they're not an obsession. And in case you're wondering, he was a perfect gentleman around me."

Neither *perfect* nor *gentleman* fit his impression of Prentice, but he was relieved to know the man hadn't taken a personal interest in Emma. "How did he get all that money he has?"

"He was vague about that. Some of it he inherited. He owns a lot of different companies. He's sort of known for running competitors out of business, and for buying up marginal concerns and selling off their assets. As you might have gathered, he has no qualms about using people or situations for his own gain."

"He clearly enjoys sticking it to the government."

"Definitely. Believe it or not, he sees himself as a kind of champion, fighting against the feds. And there are people who look up to him for that."

"Even if it means destroying historic landmarks or using public land for private gain?"

She nodded. "I met some of his fans—everybody from property rights lobbyists to extremist groups who believe everything the government does is wrong."

"So if he wanted to do something illegal, he could probably find people to help him."

"I'm sure. And they don't have to be fans of his—he

has enough money to pay anyone to do what he wants. For some people that's enough."

He had enough money to buy a drone and a black-market missile to arm it. And people who'd cheer him on as he did so. "I'll probably have more questions for you later, but right now, let's change the subject to something less grim," he said. "Why did you decide to be a reporter?"

She laughed, and the sound sent a tremor through his middle. "You don't have to sound so disgusted. I'm not an ax murderer."

He winced. "Sorry. Let's just say a lot of my interactions with the press haven't been positive."

"I can't imagine." Suppressed laughter again.

Point taken. "So I'm not Mr. Personality. But I really do want to know what drew you to journalism."

She sat back and took a deep breath, as if bracing herself for an ordeal. "All right, I'll tell you. When I was nineteen, a freshman in college, my older sister disappeared. She was a nurse, working nights at a hospital. She got off her shift early one morning and was never seen or heard from again."

He felt the pain behind her words, despite her calm demeanor. "How awful for your family," he said, the words completely inadequate.

She nodded. "Sherry had left once before without telling the rest of us—she'd run off to Vegas with a guy she was dating for a wild weekend. At first the police suspected a repeat of that caper. We tried to tell them that this time was different, but they wouldn't listen. They didn't take the case seriously until we went to the newspapers. A reporter took an interest in the case and helped us. Eventually, the police found her body, not far from the hospital. She'd been murdered. They never found her killer."

He reached across the table and took her hand. "I'm sorry."

"Thank you." She withdrew her hand and sipped wine. "Anyway, that reporter inspired me. I wanted to help others the way she helped our family. Sometimes that means riding the police—reminding them to do their job."

"Those questions you asked about Lauren Starling." Understanding dawned.

She nodded. "She's another woman who's gone missing, and no one is doing anything about it."

"We are keeping our eyes open for any sign of her. But we don't have anything else to go on."

"I'm still trying to find out more about her and the case," she said.

"If you learn anything, let me know," he said. "I'm not a callous jerk, no matter what kind of first impression I gave you."

She patted his hand, which still rested on the table in front of her. "You still have a chance to redeem yourself."

They finished the meal over espresso and small talk about each other's background. He told her about growing up in a military family, playing football, then joining the marines and eventually moving into law enforcement with the FBI. "No wife or family?" she asked.

"I was married once, but it didn't work out. I guess I'm one of those men who's married to his work. No kids. What about you?"

She shook her head. "I was engaged once, but we both thought better of it."

By the time Ray brought the check, Graham felt almost comfortable with her. He debated asking her out for a real date, but decided to wait. He'd be sure to see her again; the case gave him a good excuse to do so. No need to rush things and risk screwing up.

He walked her to her Jeep and lingered while she found her keys and unlocked the car door. "Here's my personal cell." He wrote the number on the back of his business card and handed it to her. "Call me anytime."

"About the case—or just to talk?" Her tone was teasing.

"Either. Maybe you'd like to give me your number?"

"I could make you work for it. I'll bet the FBI could find it out."

"I probably could, but I'd rather you gave it to me voluntarily."

She smiled and opened her purse. But she never had a chance to write down her number. The loud *crack!* of gunshots shattered the afternoon silence. Her screams rang in Graham's ears as he pushed her to the ground.

# Chapter Three

Emma might have fantasized about Graham on top of her, but not like this. Gravel dug into her back, she couldn't breathe and her ears rang from the sound of gunshots. The smells of cordite and hot steel stung her nose, and she realized he had drawn a weapon and was firing. A car door slammed and then a revving engine and the squeal of tires signaled their assailant's escape.

Graham rolled off her, then took her hand and pulled her to her feet. "Are you all right?" he asked.

She brushed dirt from her skirt, and tried to nod, but she'd always been a lousy liar. Her legs felt like jelly and she was in danger of being sick to her stomach. "I think I need to sit down."

Ray and Lola emerged from the restaurant and crowded around them, followed by most of the wait-staff and half a dozen customers. "We called 911," Lola said. "What happened?"

"Someone shot at us." Graham put his arm around Emma. She leaned on him and let him lead her back inside. The reality of what had happened was beginning to sink in. They could have been killed—but why? "Can you bring us some brandy?" he asked.

Ray left and returned with a snifter of brandy. Graham held it to Emma's lips. "Drink this."

She did as he asked, then pushed the glass away, coughing, even as warmth flooded her. "I don't even like brandy," she gasped.

Graham handed her a handkerchief. It was clean, white linen and smelled of lemon and starch. She wiped her watery eyes, leaving a smear of black mascara on the pristine cloth. "If this is a typical date with you, I think I'm going to quit while I'm ahead."

She tried to return the handkerchief, but he waved it away. "You keep it. I promise you, this isn't typical."

"Did you see anything?" she asked. "The shooter, or their car?"

"A man dressed in black, wearing a ski mask and a watch cap. He drove a dark sedan, no license plate."

"I'm impressed you saw that much—I didn't see a thing."

"I make it a habit to notice things. The car was parked at the corner, waiting for us."

"So this was planned—not a random drive-by." She searched his face, hoping for some reassurance, but his expression was grave. Worried.

"I don't think so, no. Do you know anyone who might want you dead?"

The question brought another fit of coughing. "Don't sugarcoat it, okay?" she said when she could talk again. "What do you mean, does someone want me dead? What kind of a question is that?"

He patted her shoulder, his hand warm and reassuring. But these definitely weren't the circumstances in which she wanted to be bonding with a guy. "Can you think of any reason someone would want to shoot at you?" he asked.

The idea was as unsettling as the shots themselves. "No. I'm just a writer. And a nice person. I don't have enemies."

"Are you sure? Maybe you've written a story that's upset someone."

She shook her head. "No."

"What about Richard Prentice? What did he think of the profile you wrote about him?"

"He said he liked it—that I'd made him sympathetic. I mean, that's not what I set out to do, but that's how he took it."

"You said you've been a crime reporter. Has your reporting been responsible for putting any violent criminals away—people who might have vowed revenge?"

"I've reported on all kinds of crimes, but no one's ever threatened me, or even sent me angry letters." She knotted the handkerchief in her hand. "I thought that kind of thing only happened on television."

He squeezed her shoulder, and she fought the urge to lean into him and close her eyes. No, she had to be strong. "Tonight, when you've had time to think about it, I want you to make me a list of every story you've reported on that led—directly or indirectly—to the conviction of someone," he said. "We can run a check to see if any of them are out of prison. I'll work with the local police to determine if any of those people have been seen in the area."

"Shouldn't you leave this to the local police entirely? I thought your territory was the public lands."

He frowned. "It is. But when someone shoots at me, I take a personal interest."

"So maybe this isn't even about me." The idea flooded her with relief. "Maybe the shooter was after you."

"That's possible."

"Maybe whoever shot Bobby decided to go after you."

"That's taking a big risk, considering we have no leads in that case."

"Maybe the person responsible doesn't know that."

He nodded. "Maybe not."

"Sir?" A uniformed police officer stepped into the alcove where they were sitting. "I'm Officer Evans, with the Montrose police."

"Captain Graham Ellison, FBI. And this is Emma Wade."

"I'll need a statement from each of you about what happened," Evans said.

"Of course."

A female officer joined them and led Emma away to question her about what had happened. Emma kept her answers brief; everything had happened so quickly she had few details to share. "What were you and Captain Ellison doing before the attack?" the officer asked.

"We were having dinner."

"You two are dating?"

The dinner had been like a first date. But not. "I'm a reporter and I was questioning him about a case he's working on."

"What case is that?"

"The Rangers found a downed plane in Curecanti Recreation Area today. The pilot had been shot."

The cop's eyes widened. "Murder?"

"It looks that way."

The officer shook her head. "When I joined the force,

we might have had one violent death a year. In the past eighteen months we've had half a dozen. This task force doesn't seem to be doing much to slow things down."

Emma opened her mouth to defend Graham but stopped. Hadn't she had the same criticism of the task force? Knowing and liking Graham didn't change that opinion, did it?

"Did you see the shooter, or get a glimpse of the car?" the officer asked.

"No. Captain Ellison pushed me down as soon as we heard the first shot."

"And you have no idea who would want to shoot at you?"

"No. Maybe it's just one of those random things," she said. "Or a case of mistaken identity or something."

"Maybe so." The officer put away her pen and paper. "We'll do our best to find the person responsible. In the meantime, be careful."

The officer left and Graham rejoined her. "Let's go back to your place," he said.

She nodded. All she wanted was a hot bath and a cup of tea, and maybe a movie to distract her from all the horrors of today—first Bobby's death, then someone trying to kill her. It was too much.

When they reached her Jeep, Graham held out his hand. "I'll drive."

She started to argue—to tell him he was bossy and point out it was her car. "What about your Cruiser?" she asked.

"I can get it later."

Weariness won over stubbornness and she handed over the keys without another word.

Neither of them spoke on the drive to her house. She

was still too numb for words, and he appeared lost in his own thoughts. But he swore as he pulled the Jeep to a stop in her driveway. She sat up straighter, heart pounding. "What is it? What's wrong?"

"You didn't leave your front door standing open when we left, did you?" he asked.

She stared at the entrance to her house, registering that the door was open. Then she was out of the car before she even realized what she was doing, running up the steps. "Janey!" she shouted. "Oh, Janey!"

JANEY THE CAT turned out to be fine, though she was clearly upset. They found her hiding under Emma's bed—a king-size affair with a puffy floral comforter and at least a dozen pillows. It looked feminine and soft and sexy—and it annoyed Graham that he could think these things while in the midst of a serious investigation.

"Is anything missing?" he asked as he followed Emma through the house, which looked undisturbed.

"I don't know. I don't think so. I was so worried about Janey I didn't even look." She cradled the cat to her chest and he felt a stab of envy. Yeah, he had it bad for this woman. *Focus*, he reminded himself.

"Then let's look together."

They checked the spare bedroom, living room and dining room. Everything was neat and orderly, nothing out of place. When they got to the kitchen she stopped. "My papers," she said.

"What papers?"

She pointed to the kitchen table, where a half-empty wineglass and a pen sat. "I was going over the notes I took today—at the press conference and at the crash site. They're gone."

She set down the cat and hurried back into the living room and through a door to what turned out to be her office. "My laptop is gone," she said. She opened the accordion doors leading to a walk-in closet. "My files are gone, too."

"Which ones?"

"All of them." She pointed to the floor of the closet. "There was a rolling cart here, with two file drawers. It's gone."

"What was in the files?"

"Notes about articles I've written. Transcripts of interviews. Some photos."

"Everything?"

"The last couple of years' material. Anything older than that is in storage."

"You'll need to report this to the police," he said. "Then you can't stay here."

There he went, being bossy again. "Excuse me, but this is my home and I'll stay here if I want," she said.

"It's not safe." He turned away, as if that were the final declaration on the subject.

She grabbed his arm and pulled him back toward her. "Wait just a minute. We don't know if this is connected to the shooting or if the people who took my files mean me any harm."

"And we don't know that they don't. Do you want to take that chance?"

Of course she didn't. But she didn't want him thinking he could step in and rearrange her whole life for her. "I'm not leaving. I'll change the locks and I'll be careful, but I'm not leaving. Besides, where would I go?"

He pressed his lips together, as if debating his response. She crossed her arms over her chest and glared at him. "At least stay away for tonight," he said. "The police will want to come in and take photos, dust for prints. You can go to a hotel. While you're gone you can have someone in to change the locks."

He'd softened his tone—less bossy, more concerned. Her stomach knotted with indecision. She looked around and spotted Janey in the armchair where she liked to nap, busily grooming herself. "A hotel won't let me bring my cat and I won't leave her," she said. "Not when she's had such a terrifying day."

"Then stay with me. Janey can come, too." At her stunned look, he added, "I have a guest room. And a security system. No one will bother you."

"Fine." She was too tired—and yes, too scared—to argue anymore. "And thank you," she added.

She called the police and half an hour later found herself telling her story to an officer. While she dealt with the officers, Graham stepped out and made several calls. Every time she looked up she could see him out the window, pacing back and forth across her front lawn, phone to his ear. She had the feeling if she hadn't agreed to come with him tonight he would have insisted on staying and standing guard. She wavered between being touched by his kindness and concern, and annoyed at his overprotectiveness.

When the police told her she was free to go, she coaxed Janey into her carrier, packed an overnight bag and stowed everything in her Jeep. One of the officers had driven Graham back to the restaurant to retrieve his Cruiser, and she followed it out of town, toward the

National Park to an upscale neighborhood of large lots and lovely homes.

Graham turned out to live in a cedar-sided cabin with large windows providing a view of open prairie and the distant lights of town. He helped her carry in her and Janey's things, stopping to punch a code into an alarm panel as soon as they entered. Then he led the way into a high-ceilinged great room. "Let me show you your room," he said.

The guest room was Spartan but adequate, with a queen-size bed, an armchair and a large bath across the hall. Without asking, he helped her set up Janey's litter box and bed, and filled the cat's water dish in the bathroom and brought it back. "Do you have any pets?" she asked.

"I had a cat at my last posting, but my schedule makes it tough on a pet, so I decided not to get another one after Buster died." He ran his hand along Janey's flank and she responded with a loud purr. "That's a pretty girl," he cooed, and Emma felt a flutter in her stomach, as if she were the one he was stroking.

He looked up at her. "How about if I fix us a drink?"

She nodded. "That sounds like a good idea."

She shut the door to the bedroom to give Janey time to settle in, then followed him into the living room. Though it was well into June, the night was cool, and he turned up the flame on a gas fireplace. "This is a gorgeous place," she said, accepting the glass of wine he offered.

"I can't claim any credit. A Realtor found it for me. Let's sit down." He motioned to the sofa.

She sat at one end of the leather couch; he settled at the other end, close enough that she could see the pulse beat at the base of his throat. She had a sudden memory of the feel of his body on hers, a heavy shield from danger.

"I'm sorry if I came across a little gruff earlier," he said. "I'm used to giving orders all day, and when I see a problem, my natural approach is to try to fix it."

"Except sometimes it's not your problem to fix." She sipped the wine and watched him over the rim of the glass. The apology had surprised her. She admired a man who could admit when he was wrong.

"Since I was with you when those shots were fired, my instinct has been to protect you. Call it sexist if you want, but that's how I feel."

"I've gotten used to looking after myself," she said. "But I appreciate everything you've done. If I'd been alone, I'm not sure I would have reacted so quickly to those shots." She shuddered, and set aside the glass.

"Hey, you did great." He set aside his own glass and slid over to her. "You kept your cool under pressure. That's one of the things I admire about you."

"Oh." Her eyes met his. "What else do you admire about me?"

"Would you think I was superficial if I said you have a beautiful body?" He caressed the side of her neck and brushed his lips across her cheek.

"Superficial can be good." She turned her head and he covered her lips with his own. The kiss was hot and insistent. So much for holding back on their mutual attraction.

She slipped her arms around him and pressed against him, deepening the kiss. His body was big and powerful, and the need she sensed in him made her feel powerful, too. Maybe this was just what she needed, this physical distraction…

The strains of an Adele song jangled in the evening stillness. Graham raised his head and looked around. "My phone," she said, and reached for her purse.

*Unknown number* flashed on the screen, and she clicked the icon to answer, prepared to give a phone solicitor a piece of her mind. "Hello?"

"You need to stop now, before you get hurt," said a flat, accentless male voice.

"What are you talking about? Who is this?"

"If I'd wanted to kill you this evening, I would have," the voice said. "Next time, I won't miss."

The line went dead. Emma stared at the phone.

Graham took the device from her hand and set it aside. "I heard," he said. "Who has access to this number?"

"Lots of people," she said. "I mean, it's not listed, but it's on my business cards. People at the *Post* have it. Friends. Business contacts." She rubbed her hands up and down her arms, suddenly cold. "Maybe this is just a prank. Somebody trying to unsettle me." She gave a shaky laugh, perilously close to hysterical tears. "And they're doing a good job of it."

Graham stood and pulled out his own phone. "I'll have someone trace the call, though I doubt it will do much good. It was probably made from a throwaway." His eyes met hers, and the hard look she found there frightened her all over again. "This isn't a joke, Emma," he said. "I think you're in real danger."

# Chapter Four

Though Emma couldn't think of a safer place to be than Graham's spare bedroom, sleep still eluded her. Every time she closed her eyes, visions of what might have happened at the restaurant and the memory of that flat, menacing voice on the phone kept slumber at bay until the early hours.

Graham tapped on her door and awakened her a little after seven. "I wanted to let you sleep, but I have to get to the office," he said when she answered his knock. "I wasn't comfortable leaving you sleeping and alone."

His gaze drifted over her, and she was aware of her disheveled hair and the open robe over her nightgown. He wasn't leering or anything so crass, but she had the feeling if she'd suggested it, he wouldn't have hesitated to remove the crisp uniform he wore and join her back in bed.

She resolutely shoved aside the thought, tempting as it was. As much as her body might have enjoyed the release, her mind wasn't ready for that kind of involvement with the intense captain. "Thanks for the coffee," she said, accepting the steaming cup he held out to her. "Do I have time for a shower?"

"Take all the time you need. I'll be in the kitchen."

By the time she'd finished the coffee, showered and dressed, she felt she had a better grip on her emotions. Janey curled up on a pillow and watched as Emma brushed out her hair and completed her makeup. Unlike her mistress, the cat had seemed perfectly content with their temporary quarters. "I'll agree the curmudgeonly captain has a certain charm," Emma said as she slipped on a pair of gold hoop earrings. "I just haven't decided if that makes up for the fact that he doesn't approve of what I do for a living." Though he'd probably never admit it, she was sure Graham still viewed journalists as his adversaries.

Janey followed her into the kitchen, where they found Graham serving up eggs and toast. "It's nothing fancy," he said, and set a plate in front of her.

"It looks great. Thanks."

He refilled her coffee, then set a bowl of water and another of food on the floor by the sink. "I opened up one of the cans of cat food you brought over."

Janey rubbed against his ankles, her purr audible across the room. "She never gets quite that enthusiastic when I feed her," Emma said, amused.

"I get along with most animals." He took the seat across from her.

"Just not most people," she said.

The corners of his mouth quirked up in acknowledgment of the gibe. He had nice lips, full and expressive. Her memory flashed to the kiss they'd shared last night, before the threatening phone call had destroyed the mood. What would have happened if the phone hadn't rung? Would she have spent the night in Graham's bed? And then what? They weren't exactly on the same side of things right now. Yes, she'd agreed to help him as much as she could, but she wasn't naive enough to believe he'd be even half as open with her. She'd have to dig and fight for information as much as ever. It didn't strike her as a good formula for a healthy relationship.

"Were you able to trace the call to my phone last night?" she asked.

He shook his head. "No luck. Anyone who watches television these days knows to use a cheap throwaway phone that can't be traced. And if the caller really was the same person who shot at us yesterday afternoon, he's a professional."

"I still don't get why I'm a target all of a sudden," she said.

"What was in those notes that were stolen from your house?"

"Nothing that wasn't in the articles I wrote."

He took a bite of toast and crunched, a thoughtful look on his face. "You must take notes on some things that don't make it into the articles," he said after he'd swallowed.

"Oh sure—little details, background information— but nothing important."

"Were the notes you took during the weeks you spent with Richard Prentice in those files?"

"They were. Along with notes for a lot of stories. Everything I'd managed to pull together about Lauren Starling and her disappearance was in the file on the table. But why would they take everything?"

"Because they weren't certain what they were looking for? Or maybe they wanted to disguise their focus— take everything so it wouldn't be obvious what they were really interested in." He mopped egg from his plate with a triangle of toast and popped it into his mouth.

"It's not as if taking my notes would stop me from writing a story," she said. "I still have my memory, and my recorder—that was in my purse. I could even go back and interview people again."

"What are you working on right now?" he asked.

"I have to turn in a piece about your press conference yesterday."

He made a scoffing sound. "You couldn't have gotten much out of that."

"I'll have a few inches of copy, by the time I lay out the background behind the conference—Senator Mattheson's challenge and Richard Prentice's lawsuit."

"I can't see anything threatening in a story like that."

"I'm also providing background for a story on the plane crash and Bobby's murder, though because of my relationship to him, my editor is assigning another reporter to write the main article."

"Anything else?"

"I'm trying to find out everything I can about Lauren Starling and her disappearance."

"If it is a disappearance." He held up a hand to forestall the objection he must have known she'd have. "I'm not saying she isn't legitimately missing—only that we don't have proof of that yet. And she does have a history of erratic behavior."

"She didn't show up for work."

"At a job where she was rumored to be on her way out."

The sharp look he sent her told her he knew she'd underestimated him. "I guess you've been doing your homework," she said.

"I have. And everyone on the team has been on the

lookout for any sign of Ms. Starling. Despite what you may think, we are taking this very seriously."

"That's good to know," she said. "And thank you for telling me. I know you didn't have to."

He nodded. "Back to the problem of whoever threatened you. Maybe there's something in your notes that you don't realize is important, but whoever took them does. Maybe something you noticed about Richard Prentice that he doesn't want someone to find out."

"Do you really think Richard Prentice is behind this, or is it just that the man has made himself such a thorn in your side?" she asked.

He stabbed at the last bite of egg on his plate. "I already told you, I don't have any proof that he's done anything wrong. I just have a feeling in my gut that he's up to something."

"Raul Meredes was operating near Prentice's estate, wasn't he?" The criminal with ties to a Mexican drug cartel had been killed while attempting to take a college student who was conducting research in the area hostage, but law enforcement officers at the scene swore they hadn't fired the shot that had ended his life. He'd been done in by a sniper, who fled as soon as Meredes was dead. The task force had linked Meredes to the deaths of several illegal immigrants in the park, who they suspected were part of a marijuana-growing operation and human-trafficking ring operating on public lands. If he'd lived to testify, he might have identified the person in charge of the operation.

"He would have had to cross Prentice's land to get to his operations," Graham said. "I don't believe for a minute that Prentice didn't know what was going on. The man has guards and cameras all over that place."

"Maybe he thought it wasn't his responsibility to report it," she said. "He'd say he shouldn't have to do law enforcement's job for them."

"He would say that, wouldn't he?" Graham's face twisted in an expression of disgust.

"Even if you're right and he's responsible for the crimes you're trying to control, why target me?" she asked. "I was with him for hours at a time for two weeks and he never showed the slightest hostility. And that was months ago. Why suddenly decide I'm a threat?"

"I don't know. Maybe it has something to do with the pilot who died."

"Bobby?" A dull pain centered in her chest at the memory of Bobby's lifeless body slumped in the seat of his plane. "We were just friends. We'd get together to talk, mainly. It wasn't anything serious."

"Maybe Prentice doesn't know that. He might have heard you two were dating and feared Bobby told you something he shouldn't have. Like what that plane was carrying, and who the cargo was intended for."

"What was the cargo?"

His expression grew wary. "We're still looking into that." He drank the last of his coffee. "If you're done with breakfast, we'd better go. I need to get to work."

"So do I." She carried her plate and cup to the sink. "I can wash up."

"Leave it. I have a woman who cleans for me. She'll take care of them. You're welcome to stay here as long as you like, though."

"No, I'll head back to my place. I'm sure the police have finished there by now."

He turned toward her, his big body filling the doorway, effectively blocking her in the kitchen. "I don't think it's a good idea for you to go there alone," he said. "Whoever attacked before could be waiting for you."

"He already took my notes and warned me off. He's not going to waste any more time with me." But she sounded more confident than she felt.

"Let me send someone with you. One of my men—"

"No! I do not need a babysitter." She told herself he was merely concerned, not being deliberately overbearing, and she softened her voice, trying to appear less angry at his suggestion. "I appreciate your concern, but I'll be fine," she said. "I promise I'll be careful."

"I don't like it."

"This isn't about what you like and don't like. I'm not your responsibility."

He opened his mouth as if to argue this point, too, but thought better of it. "Call me when you get to your place," he said. "Let me know you're okay." He hesitated, then added, "Please."

She wondered how much effort it took for him to add that last word. "I'll call you," she said. "I'm sure I'll be fine."

He stepped aside to let her pass and she retrieved her bag from the guest room. He helped her load it and the cat supplies into her Jeep. "Thanks for taking me in last night," she said. "I think I would have been a lot more upset if I'd been alone when I got that call." Though she resisted his overprotectiveness, she had to admit his strong, calm presence last night had made her feel safe. She hadn't worried about anyone getting past him to get to her.

"I hope I'll see you again under better circumstances." He put a hand on her arm, his gaze focused on her mouth, as if debating the wisdom of another kiss.

She made the decision for him, leaning in to kiss him. The contact was brief, but intense, heat and awareness spreading through her. His grip tightened on her arm, but he didn't resist when she pulled away. "I'd better go," she said.

"Call me," he reminded.

"I will." And in the meantime, she'd try to figure out exactly what she felt for Captain Graham Ellison, and what she wanted to do about those feelings.


"SO THIS CRATE definitely contained a Hellfire missile?" Graham studied the debris they'd collected from the crash site, each piece tagged and cataloged, lined up on folding tables or set against the wall in a room in the trailer that had formerly been used to store supplies. The charred bits of wood and twisted scraps of metal told a story, though it was up to the task force to put that story together in the right order.

"According to the investigator the army sent over from Fort Carson, it did." Marco consulted a notepad. "They even know the serial number, a partial of which was stenciled on the box. If we find the missile, the numbers on the tail fin should match."

"Where did the missile come from?" Michael Dance, a tall, dark-haired lieutenant with the Border Patrol, asked. The newest member of the task force, he was also recently engaged to the woman who'd been instrumental in helping them find and target Raul Meredes. Abby was finishing up her masters in botany from the University of Colorado.

"Originally, from a shipment of Hellfires destined for Afghanistan," Marco said. "But a number of them disappeared along the way, probably to the black market in the Middle East and Africa."

"So, how did it end up here?" Carmen Redhorse, the sole female member of the task force, with the Colorado Bureau of Investigations, asked.

"Anyone with enough money can buy anything," Lance said.

"How much do you think one of these would sell for?" Michael nodded toward the busted crate.

Marco shrugged. "Half a mil? Maybe not that much, if you knew the right people."

Lance leaned against the door frame, arms crossed over his chest. "So who do we know around here with that kind of smack?" he asked.

"Being able to afford a missile doesn't mean Richard Prentice bought one," Carmen said.

"But the fact that the missile was on a plane flown by a man who was known to work for Prentice gives us reason to question him," Graham said. He turned to Lance. "What did you find out about Bobby Pace?"

Lance uncrossed his arms and stood up straight. "He keeps his plane in a hangar at Montrose Regional Airport. The Fixed Base Operations manager saw him there three days ago, checking out his plane, but Bobby said he didn't have a flight scheduled. I asked if he seemed nervous or anything, but the man I talked to " he checked his notebook "—Eddie Silvada, said Bobby always seemed nervous lately. Jumpy. Silvada thought it was just because he'd been having financial problems. His kid has cancer and even with insurance, the treatments are expensive."

Graham nodded. This fit with what Emma had told him.

"Does he have other family in the area?" Carmen asked. "A wife?"

"Ex-wife," Lance said. "Susan Pace. They've been

divorced a year and she says they don't talk much—just about the kid. She doesn't know what he was up to."

"A guy in that situation might be willing to fly an illegal cargo for a big payoff," Carmen said.

"When was the last time he filed a flight plan?" Graham asked.

"Last week," Lance said. "He flew an oil company photographer over a drilling site so he could get some aerial photos."

"When was the last time he flew for Prentice?" Michael asked.

"June 10. Almost two weeks ago. Before that he was flying him at least once a week, sometimes twice—to Denver and Salt Lake and other places where Prentice has business interests."

"Was Prentice using another pilot?" Carmen asked. "Did he and Pace have a falling out?"

"Or were they planning for Pace to pick up this missile and Prentice wanted to put some separation between them and provide himself with an alibi?" Graham asked.

"Do we know where Prentice was when Bobby was shot?" Lance asked.

"When was he shot?" Michael asked.

"The coroner thinks it was early Monday morning," Graham said. "Five or six hours before we found him."

"So what was Pace up to between Thursday and Monday?" Marco asked.

"And who was in that cockpit with him?" Michael asked. "Who shot him?"

"Someone could have met the plane at the crash site and shot him there," Carmen said. "The angle of the gunshot wound doesn't preclude that."

"We've got a couple of unidentified prints in the cockpit," Lance said. "Maybe a passenger."

Marco consulted his notes. "He was shot with a .38 caliber. A handgun, at close range."

"So someone was in the cockpit with him," Michael said. "They either flew in with him, or met him at the site and climbed in and shot him."

"The plane crashed on landing," Marco said. "The FAA and NTSB investigators are still sifting through the evidence, but something definitely went wrong in the air."

"Someone could have been following the plane on the ground," Lance said.

"Tough to do at night, with no roads," Michael said.

"Tough, but not impossible." Marco closed his notebook and stuffed it back into his pocket. "What next, boss?"

"I want you and Michael to go back to the airport," Graham said. "Talk to everyone at Fixed Base Operations—airport personnel, other pilots, anyone who might have seen Pace or talked to him. Find out if his plane was there on Friday or Saturday. Check the surrounding airports, too. Maybe he went to one of them to lay low for a few days."

"We'll get right on it." Michael said.

"Lance, you dig in to Pace's background. Look at his bank accounts, talk to his neighbors and his ex-wife, any friends."

"What do you want me to do?" Carmen asked.

"You're coming with me," Graham said. "It's time we paid another visit to Richard Prentice."

# Chapter Five

Before she went home, Emma stopped at an office supply superstore and purchased a laptop to replace the one that had been stolen. She intended to get right to work, restoring her files and reconstructing as much of the missing notes as possible. But when she unlocked the front door and saw the state of her apartment, she formulated a plan B. She needed order and peace before she could focus on work.

She spent her first hour home cleaning up after the crime scene investigators. A lemon-scented spray vanquished fingerprint powder and smudges. If only it could wipe away this sense she had of being violated. Satisfied that order was restored, she made a cup of tea and set up the new laptop on the kitchen table. Though she had a home office, she preferred this bright, sunny room, with the teakettle close by and Janey stationed in her favorite perch on the windowsill overlooking the side yard, with its flower beds and bird feeder.

Thanks to online backup, she was able to restore most of her files within minutes. The articles she was working on, as well as those she'd written in the past, were available once more. Though she'd lost the handwritten notes she hadn't bothered to transcribe and some secondary sources, such as brochures and copies of reports, she had most of the stolen material here on her computer. If she read through it all, would she be able to figure out what the thief had been after?

She finished up the story of the press conference for the *Post*, along with information about Bobby and his death that the editor would incorporate into a story another reporter was already working on. Then she turned her attention to her notes on the missing woman, Lauren Starling.

Despite her best efforts, she didn't have much to go on in the case. The police in Denver had provided polite but unrevealing answers to her questions. The television station where Lauren worked had downplayed her disappearance, at first saying they weren't concerned then, when Emma had pressed, saying Miss Starling had a history of "health problems" that had forced her once before to take an extended leave of absence.

More digging had uncovered a three-week period the year before when Lauren had been absent from her job as one of the evening news anchors for Channel 9, but that hadn't turned up any further information, either. The woman wasn't married or in a serious relationship, and her only relative seemed to be a sister in Wisconsin, who hadn't returned Emma's calls.

"I don't see anything here that would lead anyone to warn me off," she said out loud to the cat. Talking out loud helped her organize her thoughts, and Janey pricked up her ears and tilted her head as if everything Emma said was fascinating. "So if it's not the story about Lauren Starling, what is it that's got this guy so riled?"

She ran her cursor over the lists of stories in her files

and stopped when she came to her profile of Richard Prentice. She couldn't mesh the image of the intelligent, polite and sometimes charming host she'd written about with the criminal overlord Graham suspected him of being. Yes, Prentice held a grudge against the government, though she'd never been able to determine its source. He'd made a name for himself by fighting government regulation, government intervention and government restrictions, a stance that had made him a hero to many.

He was a ruthless businessman, someone who went after what he wanted with a single-mindedness few could match. But while some might justifiably charge that Prentice sometimes acted unethically, ethics weren't legislated in this country. What some people called immoral was simply good business tactics to others.

If he thought a story Emma was working on would get in his way, would Richard Prentice hire someone to threaten her, in order to make her stop? Maybe.

Would he hire a gunman to take a shot at her? She shook her head. Prentice was driven, but he wasn't insane.

But Graham didn't strike her as a man who jumped to conclusions. He'd been in law enforcement a long time. He'd seen crime in all its manifestations. If he suspected someone of wrongdoing, she had to seriously consider the suggestion.

Which meant that if Graham was right, and Prentice had been Raul Meredes's boss—and thus responsible for the death of half a dozen illegal immigrants—then he was a man who wouldn't blink at ordering someone to shoot at a woman he wanted out of the way. Breaking into her apartment and taking a computer and some files paled in comparison to the crimes he'd already committed—or rather, had people commit at his behest. Prentice had the kind of money that insured he never had to get his hands dirty.

She read through the profile she'd written. Richard Prentice had been the middle child in a family with three children. He had an older brother and a younger sister, whom he saw rarely. He had an undistinguished educational career and had married young, only to divorce two years later, with no children. He started out in real estate, buying up old apartment buildings, renovating them and raising the rent.

From there, he'd expanded to other investments— everything from small factories to office parks and even amusement parks. He had a Midas touch when it came to making money in real estate and soon his millions multiplied to billions.

The public knew him best for the transactions that pitted him against the federal government. He had a genius for discovering private property near or surrounded by federal lands. He'd threaten to build an eyesore on the property, to destroy historical artifacts or to construct a noxious business such as a paper mill or a commercial pig farm. He used the press to his advantage, willing to paint himself as the blackest villain in order to stir up public sentiment. Before long, the government would be agreeing to a trade—his precious tract for even more acreage elsewhere, or a large sum of money most grumbled was well over the actual market value of the property.

He'd used the same methods three times successfully. But when he purchased the large tract adjacent to the Black Canyon of the Gunnison National Park, he'd met a group of government officials who'd had enough. They refused to pay the price he demanded for the land, and quickly enacted enough restrictions to prevent any plans he had to exploit the property.

Emma suspected this was the source of much of his animosity toward local officials and The Ranger Brigade Task Force. He made a lot of speeches about the sanctity of private property rights and the oppression of parks that charged fees and were supported by taxpayer money. But Emma sensed the true cause of the undercurrent of rage he directed toward the Rangers was rooted in his frustration with being thwarted.

Which still didn't make him guilty of a crime.

"Was Bobby working for Prentice when he was killed in that plane?" she asked. Janey's answer was a yawn and a luxuriant stretch. "Who killed him, and why? And what was the mysterious cargo that Graham was so closed-mouthed about?"

Bobby had told her he liked working for Prentice. Or at least, he liked the generous paycheck the work generated. Robert Pace, Junior, who went by the nickname Robby, was on his second round of treatments for leukemia and the divorce decree stated that Bobby was responsible for all the medical bills not covered by insurance, which he also paid for.

Had Prentice—or someone—paid Bobby to smuggle drugs up from Mexico or South America? He wouldn't be the first pilot who'd make extra cash smuggling. Now that Colorado had legalized and regulated the production and sale of both recreational and medical marijuana, he might not even have seen what he was doing as so wrong. But bringing drugs—including marijuana— across state lines was still a serious federal crime.

Or maybe he'd been carrying cocaine or heroin or some other illegal substance. Graham knew, she was sure, and though she understood why he wouldn't want to blab the story to the press, it still stung that he didn't trust her.

She closed the file and rested her chin in her hands, brow furrowed in thought. Maybe whoever had killed Bobby thought she'd seen something at the crash site. Or maybe he thought if she kept digging, she'd uncover something he didn't want anyone to know.

She sat up straighter, her heart beating a little faster. "That has to be it, Janey." The man on the phone had warned her to stop what she was doing. What she did was investigate news stories—and the story of Bobby Pace's death was at the top of her list. She had a reputation as being good at getting to the truth of the matter, and in this case, Bobby's killer had a very good motivation for not wanting her to find him out.

She grabbed a notebook and began jotting down ideas and questions. Bobby was the key. She needed to find out what he'd been doing in that plane when it crashed—where he'd been, where he was headed, what he was carrying and who had hired him.

To find out, she'd start with the person who knew him best—the mother of his son and the woman who had been married to him for twelve years.

Susan Pace wore her bright pink hair in a pixie cut. Full-sleeve tattoos and multiple piercings in her ears, nose, eyebrows and lips gave the impression of a tough chick no one should mess with. But when Emma slid into the diner booth across from Susan and her son, Robby, she noticed the dark circles beneath the other woman's eyes, and the way she kept stroking and patting the boy, as if to reassure herself that he was still here. Susan might be tough, but she was also exhausted, frightened and hurting—a mother fighting for her child's life against an enemy that couldn't be intimidated by metal studs or tattoo ink.

"Thanks for agreeing to meet with me," Emma said, when they'd ordered coffee, and a milk shake for Robby. "I know you've got a lot on your plate right now."

"I was glad to get out of the house for a while." She smiled at the boy. "Robby's having a good day today, aren't you?"

Robby nodded. "I didn't throw up today," he said.

Emma's heart broke a little at that statement, said the way some boys might have announced that they'd hit a home run or gotten an A on a spelling test. Robby looked like his father, with Bobby's dark eyes, and the same dimple in his chin. She turned her attention back to Susan. "How are you doing?"

Susan shrugged. "Okay. The police were around, questioning me yesterday. About Bobby. I figure that's what you want to talk to me about, too."

Emma glanced at Robby. Susan sighed and reached into the pocket of her jeans and pulled out a handful of quarters. "Want to play video games, Robby?"

The boy's face lit up. "Yeah!"

"Here you go, then." She handed over the quarters and he scurried away. Both women watched him all the way across the room. He had to stand on tiptoe to reach the machine, but soon he was engrossed in the game.

"So, what did you want to ask me?" Susan asked.

"Someone broke into my house and stole all my notes. And I've received threatening phone calls. I think whoever killed Bobby is trying to stop me from writing about it."

Susan's eyes widened. "So what are you doing here now? If this person is a killer, why aren't you taking their advice?"

"Because I'm not that kind of person. I want to find out who they are—and why they killed Bobby."

Susan looked around nervously. "I don't have any idea what Bobby was up to," she said. "We didn't talk about his work. What if this person who's been threatening you followed you here and sees you with me? I've got enough problems right now—I don't need some killer following me."

Emma took hold of the younger woman's wrist. "It's okay," she said. "Nobody is following me. We're just two friends having coffee."

Susan looked into her eyes, then nodded and pulled her hand away. She sipped her coffee. "Sorry," she said. "I'm just a little on edge. Bobby and I were divorced, but having him die like that—it really shook me up."

"How is Robby handling it?"

"I don't think he really understands what happened. I tried to explain to him about Daddy being in heaven now, but he knows Bobby flew planes. He'd been up with him a few times. So sometimes he talks about his dad flying to heaven—as if he's going to come back. The doctors were worried it might affect his treatment, but so far it hasn't."

"I know Bobby was paying the medical bills. Is that going to be a problem now? I could write an article for the paper…"

Susan shook her head. "You don't have to do that. With Bobby gone, Robby's eligible for Social Security and health insurance through the state. Is that twisted or what? Poor Bobby busted his butt to pay those bills, and now the government's picking up the tab."

"I'm glad you don't have to worry about that, at least," Emma said. "So, Bobby never talked about his work with you?"

"We had other things to talk about. More important things. He was a lousy husband, but he was a pretty good dad." She turned the teaspoon over and over on the table. "I know he'd been working a lot. And when I saw him a few days before…before he died, he told me he'd have enough money to pay most of the doctor bills soon. I figured that meant he had a new client, but I didn't ask about it. I didn't care how he got the money, as long as the bills were paid and Robby could get his treatments."

"Did you know he'd been flying for Richard Prentice?"

"The gazillionaire?" She nodded. "Yeah. He did a lot of work for him, and I guess that paid pretty well."

"Did he say where he and Prentice went?"

"I told you, I didn't care about that." She sat back and stared out the window, at the parking lot where the sun glinted on the rows of cars and traffic zipped by on the highway. "I know one time he flew Prentice and some other people all the way to South America. He was gone for a few days and had to miss one of Robby's chemo appointments." She glanced back at Emma. "He always tried to be there on chemo day."

"When was this—the South America trip?" Emma pulled out her reporter's notebook.

"I told the police this. It was maybe a month ago."

"Do you think he was working for Prentice on this last flight?"

"How would I know?" She sounded annoyed, but Emma was used to people being annoyed at her questions.

"Think. What, exactly, did he say about how he was getting the money to pay off the bills? Did he mention a man or a woman? A particular destination? Anything at all."

She furrowed her brow, and looked back over her shoulder to where Robby remained absorbed in the video game, his thumbs furiously flicking over the controls. "I think it was a woman," she said.

"You think the client was a woman?"

Susan nodded. "Before he told me about the money, he said he'd met this woman. I thought he was talking about a new girlfriend, but now I'm thinking maybe he didn't mean that at all."

"Bobby talked to you about the women he dated?" Had he told Susan about the times he and Emma had gone out?

"No, he wasn't like that. I mean, I knew he dated. We were divorced, so he was a single guy with a plane—women like that. I liked that, once upon a time." Her expression hinted at a smile. "So I was a little annoyed when he started talking about this woman. I thought he was bragging or something. He said he'd try to get me an autograph—like she was someone famous or something. I thought he was just trying to be mean—letting me know what I was missing, or something. But it makes more sense if he was talking about a client."

"Did you tell the police any of this?"

"No. I just thought of it."

"What, exactly, did he say?"

"That he'd met a woman and they'd hit it off. They were supposed to meet again the next day and he'd try to get her autograph for me."

"Anything else?"

She made a face. "I wasn't very nice. I told him what he could do with that autograph. So then he told me he'd have the money for the bills soon."

"But you think this woman—this celebrity—was going to hire him to do a job?"

"Maybe. Or maybe it was just a date. But Bobby never bragged about women that way. I even wondered after he left if he'd been drinking or something, but that wasn't like him, either. Still, having a sick kid can make you do all kinds of crazy things. I know."

"So he didn't say anything else about who this woman might be? I'm sorry I keep picking at this, but it's really important."

"I wish I could help you, but he didn't say anything else." She sat up straighter, a bright smile transforming her features. "Did you have a good time?"

Robby crawled into the booth beside her and laid his head against his shoulder. "I did, but I'm tired now. Can we go home?"

"We can." Susan hugged him close, then took her car keys from her pocket. "Thanks for the coffee," she said. "But we have to leave."

"Sure. Thanks for talking with me."

They left and the waitress refilled Emma's cup. She sat for a long time, sipping coffee and replaying the conversation over and over. She felt a little sick over what she'd discovered. She could think of only one female celebrity who could have been in Montrose in the days before Bobby's death.

But what was Bobby Pace doing with Lauren Starling?

# Chapter Six

Imposing stone pillars and a massive iron gate marked the entrance to Richard Prentice's land, which he referred to as a ranch or an estate, depending on whom he was talking to. Though the road across the ranch had once been a public thoroughfare, Prentice had recently obtained a court order allowing him to close the road, hence the locked gate that confronted Graham and Carmen when they arrived.

He frowned up at the camera mounted on one of the pillars. "What now?" Carmen asked.

"He has guards, and I'm sure one of them is watching us."

"They could decide to ignore us."

"They could," he agreed. "But by now he's heard Bobby Pace is dead, and though he can deny a connection all he wants, there is one. If he doesn't at least pretend to cooperate with us, I can have him brought in for questioning."

"Someone's coming." She nodded toward an approaching cloud of dust.

The black Jeep skidded to a halt on the other side of the gate and two men in desert camo fatigues climbed out. The one on the passenger side carried an automatic rifle, its barrel pointed toward the ground. Graham recognized the driver from his last visit to the ranch, the day Raul Meredes died at the hands of an unknown sniper just as the task force was about to arrest him and bring him in for questioning. The shooting had occurred on national park land, within sight of the boundary to Prentice's holdings.

"We're here to see Mr. Prentice," Graham said, holding up the leather folder that contained his credentials.

"Any communication with law enforcement must go through Mr. Prentice's attorney," the young man said. "I can give you his contact information."

"I don't need it. I'm here to talk to Prentice."

The guard's expression remained impassive. "What is this in reference to?"

"One of his employees was caught red-handed with illegal goods."

"Who is the employee?"

"If Mr. Prentice wants you to know that, he can tell you."

The guard said nothing, but turned and walked back to the Jeep. A moment later, he and the man with the gun had driven away.

"What if he refuses to talk to us?" Carmen asked.

"Prentice likes to talk. I think he enjoys sparring with anyone in authority. But if he passes up this opportunity to play his favorite game, I can arrange with the lawyers to question him as a possible accessory to a crime."

"We don't have any proof that Bobby Pace was working for him at the time of the crash."

"We don't have any proof that he wasn't, either."

The Jeep returned ten minutes later. "He probably

drove out of sight and made a phone call, then kept us waiting a few minutes longer for show," Graham said.

The guard didn't bother getting out of the Jeep this time. "You can follow us," he said.

He turned the Jeep around and the gate swung open behind him. Graham put the Cruiser in gear and followed him up the gravel road. Five minutes later, a massive three-story house built of gray stone loomed over them. With its flanking towers and expansive wings it resembled a castle, or a fortress.

"So this is what too much money will buy you," Carmen said.

"Can you have too much money?"

"I think so, yes."

Another camo-clad guard ushered them into the house, into a front room filled with bookshelves and comfortable chairs. Richard Prentice didn't keep them waiting. He strode into the room with the air of a much larger man, though he was well under six feet tall and rather delicate-looking. Still, he carried himself like a man who wielded great power. Having billions of dollars made up for a lot of shortcomings, Graham supposed.

"I'm a busy man, and I don't have time for small talk," he said by way of greeting. "What is this about an employee of mine smuggling something?"

"Bobby Pace flew for you," Graham said.

Prentice's eyes narrowed. "Pace was a private pilot I hired sometimes. Not lately, though."

"When was the last time he worked for you?"

"Two weeks ago? Maybe more."

"Have you spoken to him since then?"

"No."

"Are you sure?"

Graham could feel the anger radiating from the man, but Prentice kept his voice even, enunciating his words as if explaining a simple concept to a recalcitrant child. "I hired the man from time to time to do a job. We weren't friends."

No, Prentice would not be friends with someone like Bobby Pace. "Were you aware that Mr. Pace has a young son who is being treated for cancer?" Graham asked.

"I was not. What does this have to do with me? What does any of this have to do with me?"

"Where were you from Sunday night through Monday morning of this week?"

Prentice stiffened. "Why are you asking me these questions?"

"Answer the question please." Graham kept his voice pleasant.

"I was here."

"Can anyone verify that?"

"Everyone who works for me, I imagine. The guards at the gate, for a start."

"Do the guards know where you keep your drone?" Carmen asked.

Prentice didn't miss a beat. "What drone?"

She shrugged. "I heard a rumor that you'd purchased a drone."

"What would I want with a drone?"

"Some people use them for security," she said. "You can patrol a large area—like this ranch—with only a single operator and a camera attached to the drone."

"Interesting. Maybe I'll look into it."

"Maybe you should."

He turned back to Graham. "You've wasted enough of my time. You'd better go."

Graham thought about staying longer, if only to annoy the man. But Prentice wasn't the only busy person in the room. "We'll be in touch," he said, and led the way back to the Cruiser.

"Why do I feel I've just poked a stick in a very big fire ant bed?" Carmen asked as they pulled away from the house. "We annoyed him and didn't learn anything useful."

"I wouldn't say that." Graham checked his rearview mirror. The Jeep with the two guards had fallen in behind them, escorting them to the main road.

"What do you mean?" Carmen asked.

"He wanted to know why I was questioning him about an employee smuggling something. But I never used the word *smuggling*. I said the employee had been caught with illegal goods."

"Do you think it means anything?" she asked.

"He knows more than he wants us to believe. I think he's hiding something."

"Maybe that drone," she said.

"Or a Hellfire missile. Or maybe something even bigger. Whatever it is, I'm going to find it."

"IF YOU LIKE, MA'AM, I can tell the captain you were here and ask him to call you." The Ranger, a young man with closely cropped blond hair and a nametag that read Sgt. Carpenter, hovered near her as she walked around the room in the trailer that served as Ranger headquarters. He reminded her of an Australian shepherd, ready to herd her away from anything that was off-limits. In fact, he looked as if he wanted to herd her right out of the office.

"I don't mind waiting for Graham to return." She took a seat in one of the gray metal folding chairs arranged around an equally utilitarian folding table and crossed her legs, her skirt riding up—just a little—on her thigh. Along with the gray pencil skirt she wore a scoop-necked knit blouse and four-inch red high heels. She might be here on serious business, but she wanted to make sure she held Graham's attention. Sergeant Carpenter looked even more nervous.

"He might not be back for a while," he said.

"I've got time." She smiled at him, the picture of the calm, collected journalist prepared to wait all night, if necessary. Though really, she felt ready to jump out of her skin. She needed to talk to Graham—in person. The things she'd learned from Susan Pace could change his whole investigation. Graham thought Bobby's murder wasn't connected to Lauren's disappearance, but now she was sure they were related. Maybe this was the break they needed to find the missing woman. Maybe it wasn't too late to save her.

"I guess that's all right, if it's what you want," Carpenter said, though he looked doubtful. He probably realized he didn't have a choice but to accept her presence. He'd have a tough time dragging her out of there by himself. He took up a position across the room, leaning against the wall, arms folded, eyes fixed on her.

"I don't mean to keep you, Sergeant," she said. She took out her phone and pretended to read something on the screen. "You can return to whatever you were doing. I'll entertain myself."

"I don't think the captain would like it if I left you here alone," he said.

Which she translated to mean he wasn't about to give her the opportunity to snoop around. That did sound like Graham. He might open his home to a woman in distress, but he wasn't going to trust a reporter.

For the next twenty minutes, she scrolled through messages on her phone while Sergeant Carpenter held up the wall and scowled at her. She debated telephoning Graham and telling him she was waiting for him, but she didn't want to give him the opportunity to put her off. If she was sitting here in his office when he returned, he'd have to listen to her.

The pop of gravel beneath the tires of a vehicle made her sit up straighter. Carpenter peered between the blinds on the window beside him. "He's here," he announced.

Emma was on her feet and halfway to the door when Graham strode in. She caught her breath at the sight of him. How had she forgotten how impressive he was? He exuded strength and command...and sex appeal. The speech she'd rehearsed went right out of her head as she remembered the kiss they'd shared last night.

"Emma! What are you doing here? Is everything all right?" He closed the gap between them in two strides and grasped her shoulders. "Has something else happened? Another threat?"

His obvious concern for her made her a little weak in the knees, but she rallied and shook her head. "Nothing like that. I'm fine." Gently, she stepped out of his grasp. "But I've learned something important. Something about Bobby."

"Come into my office." One hand at her back, he guided her into a small room to the side and closed the door behind them. He motioned her to another folding chair, and took a seat behind his desk. "What is it? Did you remember something about Pace?"

"I talked with his ex-wife this afternoon. Susan."

A deep V formed between his eyebrows. "We've already interviewed her."

"I'm sure you did, but sometimes another woman—someone who isn't in law enforcement—can learn things you can't."

"What did you learn?"

"She talked to Bobby a few days before he died. He mentioned a woman—a celebrity—he was seeing, and that he'd have the money soon to pay off his son's medical bills. I think he was talking about Lauren Starling. I think she hired Bobby to fly for her."

"Susan Pace said that Bobby was working for Lauren Starling?"

"She didn't say the name—only that he talked about a woman he'd met, that she was famous and he'd try to get Susan an autograph."

She expected him to be excited about this breakthrough, or to at least show some interest. Instead, he blew out a breath, impatient. "Emma, he was probably talking about you," he said. "You two were dating, and you're a well-known journalist."

Under less serious circumstances, she would have laughed. "Graham, I'm not famous!" she said. "Bobby certainly didn't think of me that way."

"Your byline is in the paper all the time. People know you."

"That's not celebrity. Not like Lauren Starling, whose gorgeous face was on television every night."

He pressed his lips into a thin line, as if he was

trying not to say everything he thought. "Susan Pace never mentioned any of this to my team when they interviewed her," he said. "She said she had no idea who Bobby was working for or what he was doing."

"And that's true." Emma sat on the edge of the chair and leaned toward him. "She didn't think this woman was important. But when I pressed her, she remembered her."

"I still think he was talking about you."

"And I'm sure he wasn't." It was her turn to be impatient with him. "Journalists aren't celebrities. No one wants our autograph. Besides, Susan told me Bobby didn't brag about the women he dated. So this wasn't a date—it was a client. It had to be Lauren. There's a connection you need to check out."

"Nothing we've found indicates any link between Bobby Pace and Lauren Starling," he said. "No one we've talked to has reported seeing them together. None of the evidence from the crash points to her."

"But Susan—"

"Doesn't know the name of this woman and can't even say whether her husband was talking about a client or a date." He shook his head. "I'm sorry, Emma, but at this point, it doesn't help."

"So you don't believe there's any connection between Lauren and Bobby?"

"It's not about what I believe. What matters is what I can prove. Investigations aren't built on hunches, they're based on evidence."

"So you're not going to look into this further?"

"There's nothing to look into." The edge in his voice was sharp enough to cut flesh.

She stood, swallowing hard to keep from telling him

exactly what she thought of him and his disregard for what she saw as vital information. "If you were willing to unbend enough to at least consider the possibility that Lauren is involved in this case, you might find your precious evidence."

He sighed, a long-suffering, patronizing sigh that made her want to scratch his eyes out. "Emma," he began.

"Don't say it," she said between clenched teeth.

"Don't say what?"

"Whatever patronizing, dismissive thing you were going to say. I already get the message. I won't bother you anymore."

"Emma! Wait!" He rose, but she turned and headed toward the door. She had to get out of there before he tried to talk her into staying. She couldn't let her physical attraction to the man overcome her loathing for someone who wouldn't listen to her.

# Chapter Seven

Graham stared after Emma, seething. Of all the unreasonable, pigheaded, unjustified shortsighted...

Lance tapped on the door frame. "Everything okay?" he asked.

"Fine." Graham bit off the word.

"Ms. Wade didn't look too happy," Lance said.

Graham grunted.

"Looks like she has a temper to match her hair." Lance lowered himself into the chair Emma had just vacated. "What did she want?"

"She wanted me to investigate the connection between Bobby Pace and Lauren Starling. Except there is no connection—no evidence that points to one except Emma's obsession with this Starling woman."

"She thinks the two of them know each other?"

"She's leaping to conclusions." Graham began opening and shutting desk drawers. If he still smoked, this would be the time for a cigarette, but he'd given up the habit five years ago. "Pace's ex said he mentioned seeing a woman who was a celebrity. On the basis of that, Emma has developed a whole theory that Starling hired Pace to fly her somewhere."

"It does sound a little thin. Want me to check it out?"

"There's nothing to check. We already interviewed everyone connected with Pace, and no one mentioned a woman—celebrity or otherwise."

"So we talk to them again. Sometimes people remember things better when you ask a second time."

"No. Don't waste your time. I'm more concerned with Pace's connection to Richard Prentice. Any luck there?"

"I've got copies of the flight plans he filed with the local airport. Lots of trips with Prentice, once a week or so for about four months, then nothing. I can't find where Prentice was flying with anyone else at that time, but he may have been using another airport."

Graham massaged the bridge of his nose, grimacing.

"Headache?" Lance asked.

"This day's been nothing but one big headache." He shoved up from his desk. "I'm calling it a day. It's after five, anyway, and I'm not getting anything accomplished."

"See you tomorrow," Lance said. "Maybe we'll catch a break."

"Maybe."

Graham drove home in a dark mood. When he walked in the door, the first thing he smelled was Emma's perfume. Maybe he was imagining it—after all, the cleaning lady had been in that day. The place ought to smell like the lemon-scented stuff she used on the counters and floors. Instead, the soft aroma of roses surrounded him.

He walked to the kitchen and pulled a beer from the refrigerator. When he opened the trash can to drop in the bottle cap, he spied the cat food can where he'd fed her cat, Janey. Maybe he should get another cat. It would beat coming home to an empty house.

Restless, he wandered the house. He should change

into workout gear and go for a run. That would clear his head. But on the way to his bedroom, he stopped outside the open door to the guest room. The cleaner had stripped the sheets, but he could imagine Emma standing before the mirror on the dresser, brushing out those red-gold locks.

With a groan, he turned away.

Five miles later he was sweating and tired, sure that a shower and a good night's sleep would set him right. But sleep eluded him. He spent the dark hours replaying their conversation, wondering what he could have said or done to make things come out differently.

He rose early the next morning and, after strong coffee and a bagel, headed for the airport. The Montrose Regional Airport was a small airfield that served a mix of commercial and private planes. Fixed Base Operations, headquartered in a low square building among the private hangars, was a buzz of activity in the early morning. Graham found a trio of pilots gathered in the lounge, drinking coffee, consulting charts, waiting for their turn to take off. When he walked in, several took in his uniform and soon they all fell silent, watching him.

"Did any of you know Bobby Pace?" he asked.

They exchanged glances. One of them, a younger man with sunglasses pushed to the top of his head and a red-and-blue plaid shirt open over a stained white T-shirt, said. "A lot of us knew Bobby. Shame about what happened to him."

"I'm trying to find whoever shot him," Graham said. "But I'm running into a wall. No one seems to know who he was flying for when he was killed."

"Can't help you there," the young man said. "Last

time I saw Bobby was maybe a week ago. He wasn't flying that day, just hanging around, shooting the breeze, hoping somebody might walk in and want his services."

"He was always looking for work." Another man, thin and hunched with lines carving a face like a walnut, spoke up. "We knew he had a sick kid, so we tried to help him."

"Do people wander in here looking for a pilot that often?" Graham asked.

"Now and then," the old guy said. "Tourists, or folks in a hurry to get somewhere. If they got the money and it ain't illegal, I'll fly 'em."

"Do people sometimes want illegal things?" Graham asked.

The old man made a snorting sound. "I stay away from any of that."

"What about Bobby? Did he stay away from the illegal stuff?"

Again, they traded glances. "Bobby was desperate," the young man said. "He might look the other way if the money was right."

"What kinds of things did he do?" Graham asked.

"I don't like to speak ill of the dead." The young guy looked nervous.

"Nothing big." The older guy took up the conversation. "Maybe he'd file a flight plan for a certain route and deviate from the route a little to drop off a passenger who didn't want everybody to know where he was going. Little things like that."

"We haven't been able to find the flight plan he filed for the day he was killed," Graham said.

"He probably didn't file one," the old man said.

"I don't think he flew from here that day," the younger man said.

"Why do you say that?" Graham said.

"I don't remember seeing his plane for a few days before that. I thought he was out of town."

"Where did he keep his plane?" Graham asked.

"He parked it out past the northwest runway. I keep my plane out there, too."

"Not in a hangar?"

"Hangar space is more expensive," the old man said.

"Did any of you ever see him out here with a woman?" Graham asked. "Did he have any women clients?"

"He had a female student for a while." The third man, short, balding and middle-aged, spoke for the first time. "Sheila or Sherry or something like that. She was a student over at Western State. But that was a while ago. Maybe six months back."

"What happened to her?" Graham asked.

"She moved, I think," the young guy said. "Anyway, she stopped coming around."

"No other women clients you know about?" Graham asked.

All three shook their heads.

"What about girlfriends? Did he ever bring them out here?"

"I never saw him with anybody," the old guy said.

"I got the impression he didn't date much," the young guy said. "I think he still carried a torch for his wife."

"He might have had a woman over by his plane a few days ago," the middle-aged guy said. "But I don't know if it was a girlfriend or a client. He and whoever this was were in his plane, and they were arguing about something. I thought the other person's voice was kind of high-pitched, but I couldn't see who it was. All I heard was raised voices, so I steered clear."

"When was this?"

The man squinted, as if examining an imaginary calendar. "Monday a week ago, I think."

"Did either of you hear or see anything?" Graham asked the other two.

They shook their heads. "Sorry we can't help you," the younger man said. "I hope you find who killed him. That's kind of scary, you know?"

They began to move away. Graham thought about pressing, but he thought it unlikely he'd get any more information out of them. He spent the rest of the morning talking to the FBO manager, a secretary and a mechanic who looked after the planes. All of them were sorry Bobby was gone, but they didn't know who he was working for, and none of them had seen him with a woman.

So, was Emma right? Had Bobby had a mysterious—famous—female client in the week before he died? Or was Graham right and the woman was Emma herself? She'd said she and Bobby were just good friends, but did the relationship go deeper? Was she hiding something from him? Had they argued and she was reluctant to admit it, either because it implicated her somehow, or simply because she didn't want to speak ill of the dead?

By the time he arrived at Ranger headquarters in the park, he had decided he'd have to speak to Emma again, to question her more about her relationship with Bobby Pace. He wasn't looking forward to what he was sure would be a tense conversation, but it had to be done, and he wasn't going to put it off on another member of the team. He wanted to hear the truth himself from

Emma's lips. She was already angry with him, so what did it matter if he upset her more? Though the thought twisted his stomach into knots.

Carmen met him at the door to the office, her normally serene face a mask of worry. "We've been trying to reach you all morning," she said.

"I had my phone off." He hadn't wanted to be interrupted while he was at the airport, then in his turmoil over Emma, he'd forgotten to turn it back on. He switched it on now, and in a few moments, message alerts began scrolling across the screen. "What's up?" he asked.

"In your office. There're some papers there you need to see."

"I'm not going to like whatever it is, am I?" he asked.

She shook her head. "Sorry. No."

The thick, legal-size stack of papers in the center of the blotter on his desk didn't hold the promise of anything good. Carmen and Randall Knightbridge followed him into the office and watched as he picked up the sheaf of documents and scanned them.

"Richard Prentice is *suing* us?" The words came out as a roar. He felt like punching something, but of course, that wasn't how a commander behaved, so he settled for dropping the papers back onto the desk and began to pace. "He says we're harassing him—am I reading that right?"

"That's what I got out of all that legalese," Randall said. "He accuses us of trespassing on his property, harassing his employees and him, and making false accusations against him."

"We've had legitimate reasons to question him every time we've done so," Graham said.

"He thinks we're picking on him because he's rich," Carmen said.

Graham pulled out his phone.

"Who are you calling?" Randall asked.

"Not Prentice. No sense adding fuel to the fire." A moment later, Graham connected with a federal attorney in Denver. Yes, he had received copies of the lawsuit. No, he didn't think Prentice had grounds for legal action, but they needed to tread carefully. After ten minutes, Graham disconnected the call, feeling no calmer, but somewhat resigned.

"Well?" Randall asked.

"That was our lawyer. He says to back off Prentice for now and see how this plays out." He sank into his chair and checked the clock. Only eleven. He still had a long day to get through. "Let's get back to work." He needed to type up the notes from the morning's interviews, and come up with a list of questions to ask Emma. Emma again—why couldn't he get her out of his thoughts for even half an hour? The woman was seriously messing with his head. He rubbed the bridge of his nose and tried to remember where in his desk he'd stashed a bottle of aspirin.

When he looked up, Carmen and Randall were still standing there, eyeing him nervously.

"What is it?" he asked. He looked around. "And where is everyone else? What's going on?"

"There's something else you need to see." Carmen gestured toward the desk. "Under the legal papers."

"Where is everyone else?" Graham asked again.

"They went out." Randall looked as if he didn't feel very well.

Understanding dawned. "You two got the short

straw," he said. "You had to stay here with me and deliver the bad news."

"Something like that," Carmen said.

He sighed. Whatever it was, it couldn't be much worse than the lawsuit. He set aside the legal documents and looked down at this morning's edition of the *Denver Post*. The headline was about the latest fracas in the Middle East. "What am I supposed to be so upset about?" he asked.

"Turn the paper over," Carmen said. "Below the fold."

He flipped the paper and read the bold lettering splashed across the bottom third of the paper. At first, the words didn't quite register, then his vision dimmed, his brain fogging with disbelief and rage. He blinked and read the words again. *Link Between Starling Disappearance and Pilot's Murder Goes Unexplored By Law Enforcement.*

He didn't have to check the byline to know who had written the story, but he did, anyway. *By Emma Wade, Post Western Slope Bureau.*

# Chapter Eight

Emma spent the morning in her home office waiting for Graham. She didn't know whether he'd call to chew her out, or show up in person, but she was sure he'd have some response to the article in this morning's paper. She hadn't said anything in there that wasn't true; she didn't claim to have proof, only a suspicion, and had spent much of the piece pleading for the mysterious female client to come forth, if it was someone other than Lauren Starling.

But she hadn't pulled any punches, either. She'd found someone from the television station to say that they thought local authorities should be investigating every possible sighting of Ms. Starling, while someone else told how people often asked Lauren for her autograph. "She was—is—glamorous and beautiful and we all thought of her as a celebrity," the coworker said.

In case Graham showed up in person, Emma dressed carefully, in a formfitting gray pencil skirt, red V-neck sweater and the confidence-inspiring red heels. Maybe he hated her now, but it wouldn't hurt to remind him what he was missing by making her his enemy.

By eleven o'clock she wondered if he'd decided to ignore her. She hadn't figured the captain would play things cool, but maybe she'd read him wrong. Maybe goading him this way hadn't been the best approach to getting him moving.

When the doorbell rang at eleven thirty, she jumped, heart pounding. The sight of Graham's big profile—and scowling face—made her debate retreating to the bedroom and pretending not to be home. But she wasn't a coward. She took a deep, steadying breath, and opened the door. "What took you so long?" she said, before he could speak.

He moved forward, giving her no choice but to back up or be run over. "You did this deliberately," he said, his voice low and ragged, eyes burning with rage.

"You wouldn't even listen to me yesterday," she said. "You treated me like some crackpot off the street with a story I'd made up out of whole cloth. This was the only way I knew to get you to pay attention."

"You embarrassed me and my team in front of the whole state," he said. "You couldn't trust me to do my job."

"You weren't doing your job." Her voice broke on the last word, and she cursed the lapse. She needed to stay cool and detached, to not let him get to her.

"I spent the morning at the airport, talking to people who knew Bobby Pace," he said. "Trying to find this mysterious woman. I know how to do my job."

She swallowed. *Uh-oh.* "I… The way you acted yesterday, I didn't think you took me seriously."

"Just because others before me didn't listen to you, doesn't mean I'd make the same mistake." He took another step toward her, forcing her to move farther into the house. He was breathing hard, his face flushed, hands clenched at his sides. She ought to be terrified, but he didn't frighten her. A sense of anticipation, of wondering what would happen next, made her a little unsteady on her feet, but determined to hold her ground.

"I'm sorry," she whispered. "I never meant to hurt you."

He moved closer, crowding her against the wall. In her heels, they were almost the same height; she looked him right in the eye and what she saw there made her insides feel molten. Graham Ellison wanted her, as fiercely as she wanted him. She moistened her suddenly dry lips, his eyes tracking the movement of her tongue.

"You're driving me crazy, did you know that?" he said, his voice almost a growl, the low cadence vibrating through her, like a physical touch.

"There's definitely a…connection," she said, more breathily than she would have liked. She'd always prided herself on being able to hide her emotions from other people, a talent that came in handy as an investigative reporter. But with Graham she felt defenseless, stripped bare.

"Why you?" he asked. "Why have I got it so bad for a woman who will bring me nothing but trouble?"

"I'm not your enemy," she said. "We both want a murderer brought to justice and a missing woman to be found safe."

"But I've got the law on my side. You're just a loose cannon." His gaze raked her, settling on the hint of cleavage at the neckline of her top.

She pressed her shoulders against the wall and tilted her pelvis forward, brushing against him. "I think the wildness in me is part of the attraction," she said. "You wouldn't want a tame pet you could control."

In answer he put his hands on her hips and dragged

her to him. His mouth crushed against her, fierce and demanding. She arched against him, a thrill racing through her at his strength and power. She slid her arms around his neck and slanted her lips more firmly against his, deepening the kiss. His heart hammered against her—or maybe that was the driving pulse in her own arteries.

Still holding her against him, he abandoned her mouth and dipped his head to trace his tongue along the curve of her cleavage. "What are we going to do about these feelings we have for each other?" she asked.

"I want to take you to bed and make love to you until we're both too exhausted to think about it." He nuzzled at the side of her neck.

"That…that sounds like a good plan."

He slid down the zipper at the side of her skirt and began pushing it down her hips. She grabbed his wrist. "Let's go into the bedroom, where we'll both be more comfortable."

Holding the skirt with one hand and him with the other, she led him into her room. She released him long enough to scoop Janey off the pillow and toss her gently in the hallway. She shut the door and faced him again. His eyes still burned with desire, but some of the earlier caution had returned. "Are you sure this is a good idea?" he asked.

"I think if we don't do this, neither one of us is going to think about anything else when we're together."

He nodded. "So, you're just trying to get me out of your system."

"I don't think shaking you is going to be as easy as all that." She moved closer and undid the top button of his uniform shirt. "It will probably take a lot of effort and practice. Months." She kissed the triangle of chest now exposed. "Even years."

She worked her way down his chest, unbuttoning and kissing, until she reached his navel, and the barrier of his utility belt. "I'll take it from here," he said, and pulled her up to kiss her once more, as his hands fumbled with the belt and trousers.

She broke the kiss and pushed away. "Where are you going?" he asked.

"Not far." She slipped into the bathroom and returned a moment later with a condom, which she placed on the nightstand. "When you're ready," she said.

"Oh, I'm ready all right." He pushed down his pants and she saw how ready.

"Captain, I'd say you were armed and dangerous." She finished unzipping the skirt and let it drop, then pulled off her blouse, so that she stood in front of him in her underwear and the red heels.

He grinned and reached for her. "Better than my best fantasies," he said.

She wasn't the flat-stomached, thin-thighed, cellulite-free version of a woman popular with magazines and television shows, but the look in Graham's eyes—and the eager movements of his stroking hands and caressing lips—told her he liked what he saw just fine. She'd vowed years ago to stop apologizing for her body and to focus on enjoying it. Graham made that vow easy to keep. In his arms she felt as sexy and womanly as she ever had.

When they were both naked, they lay back on her bed. "When I saw that article in the *Post*, I was so angry," he said.

"So I gathered." She suppressed a giggle.

"What's so funny?" he asked.

"When I opened my door and saw you standing there, you looked like a bull ready to charge." She flattened her palm against his chest and pushed him back against the mattress. "You were magnificent. I wanted to tear your clothes off right there in the doorway."

"Oh, you did?" He smoothed his hand along the curve of her hip. "Part of me was glad about the article, too. Because it gave me an excuse to come over and see you." He kissed her, long and deep, until she was dizzy and out of breath. He cupped his hand between her thighs and she moaned, a fresh wave of need and longing engulfing her.

He rolled her over, until she was pinned beneath him, then he lavished attention on first one breast, then the other, all while his fingers played between her legs.

She writhed beneath him, incoherent with desire. She could feel his erection pressed against her thigh, hot and heavy. He planted his knee firmly between her thighs. "You are a wild one, aren't you?"

She stared up at him, unspeaking, waiting to see what he would do. He took the condom from the nightstand and ripped open the packet, then slowly rolled it on. "Ready?" he asked.

"I've been ready." She wrapped her hand around him, guiding him toward her. "Stop wasting time."

He laughed and entered her, filling her, his laughter vibrating through her. He was always such a serious man—that he could laugh while making love to her made her feel a sudden tenderness for him, even as the passion between them began to build once more. She tightened around him, gratified by the glazed look that came into his eyes, and the long sigh that escaped from his lips. They moved together, meeting each other stroke for stroke, and she wanted to shout for the joy of it.

She did shout when her climax overtook her, and wrapped her legs around him, holding him to her as he found his own release. She reveled in the strength of his muscles moving against her, and the hard pounding of their hearts, almost in unison. She continued to hold him as he gently slid from her and lay beside her. Eyes closed, he breathed heavily, his face pressed against her neck.

"That was pretty incredible," he said after a while.

"Mmm." She closed her eyes, the afterglow of great sex humming through her. "It was." And Graham Ellison was pretty incredible, too. Handsome, strong, sexy—also stubborn, opinionated and too harsh in his judgment of the press. But she wasn't going to think about that right now. She wasn't going to think about anything but how right it felt to be with him in this moment, however fleeting the sensation might last.

GRAHAM CRADLED EMMA'S head on his shoulder, eyes closed, half dozing. He couldn't believe his luck, ending up with this gorgeous, sexy woman. And she was right—he wouldn't be as happy with a woman with no spirit. He liked that she stood up to him, no matter how much she aggravated him at times.

He leaned over and buried his nose in her hair, inhaling the sweet scent of roses and vanilla.

And smoke.

The acrid stench of burning wood and wiring brought him fully awake. He shook Emma. "Get up! The house is on fire!" Smoke curled around the bedroom door, a gray ghost of horror.

"Wh-what?" She sat up, hair tousled, clutching at the sheets.

"The house is on fire. We have to get out of here." He found his pants on the floor by the bed and began putting them on.

Emma stumbled out of bed and pulled on her robe. She looked around, frantic.

"Shoes," Graham instructed, shoving his sockless feet into his boots. He moved to the door and pressed his palm against it. It wasn't hot. A peek into the hallway showed the fire hadn't yet reached this far, though the glow of orange flame and the crackle of collapsing wood told him the front room was ablaze.

He returned to Emma and grabbed her hand. "Come on," he said. "We've got to get out of here."

Wordlessly, she followed him to the kitchen. Though smoke filled the room, it was flame-free and he was able to lead them to the back door. With his free hand, he felt in his pocket for his phone. As soon as they were both in the clear, he'd call for help. He jerked open the door, cool air bathing them like a soothing balm.

They were almost down the back steps when Emma jerked from his grasp. "Janey!" she cried. "I have to get Janey!" She turned and raced back into the house, back into the smoke and flames.

# Chapter Nine

"Emma, no!" Graham lunged for her, but she slipped from his grasp. He raced after her, but got only as far as the kitchen door before smoke and heat forced him back. His eyes stung and his lungs burned as he tried to see through the dense black smoke. "Emma!" he shouted, but could barely hear his own voice over the pop and crackle of the flames.

Had she headed back to the bedroom, or to the front room? He had no way of knowing, and both rooms appeared to be a wall of smoke and flame. Reluctantly, he retreated to the back door, driven back by the ferocity of the blaze. As he stumbled down the steps, sirens wailed in the distance; a neighbor or passerby must have seen the fire and called it in.

Someone grasped him by his shoulders: a balding man in glasses and wide, frightened eyes. "Are you all right?" the man asked.

Graham nodded and coughed. "There's a woman still inside."

"Emma?"

"Yes." Through eyes still stinging from smoke, he stared at the burning house, now fully engulfed in flames.

The man looked even more frightened. "I don't think anyone's coming out of there," he said.

The idea enraged Graham. Why had he let her go? Why hadn't he held on and insisted she come with him? He scanned the back of the house and found the bedroom window. If she'd gone that way, maybe he could reach her.

He shoved to his feet, jogged to the window and tried to pull it up, but it refused to yield. He looked around and spotted a large ceramic flowerpot. He jerked up the heavy pot and hurled it through the window, then stuck his head inside. "Emma!"

"Graham?" Her voice was faint and choked.

"Emma! I'm at the window."

A moment later, she emerged from the blackness, and thrust a bundle into his hands. "Take Janey," she commanded.

He took the cat, which was wrapped in a towel, and tucked it into the crook of one arm, then reached for Emma with the other. She tumbled out the window, onto the ground beside him, her face streaked with smoke, her robe scorched from cinders.

He half carried her, half dragged her farther from the burning building. "If I weren't so happy to see you, I'd wring your neck," he said, kneeling beside her and cradling her face in his hand.

"I had to get Janey." She stroked the cat, who had poked her head out of the towel and was looking around, unharmed. "She was right outside the bedroom door, crying for me."

"I'm just glad you're okay." Graham felt drained.

Emma's gaze shifted to the house, which was fully engulfed now. "Thank God, you woke up when you did," she said. "What happened? I hadn't been cooking or anything when you arrived."

"I don't think this was an ordinary cooking fire." The blaze had been too intense, and had spread too quickly. He studied the burning house, then his gaze shifted to a trio of gas cans on the sidewalk in front of the house. "Those cans weren't there before," he said. As distracted and angry as he had been when he'd arrived, he would have noticed something that obvious.

Emma struggled to sit. He helped her, and transferred the cat to her lap. Despite her ordeal, her mind remained sharp. "Someone left those cans there after they started the fire," she said. "They wanted me to know it was deliberate."

"I think you're right," he said. "And I've been so stupid. I never should have let you return to the house after the first threat." His grip tightened around her shoulder. "You could have been killed."

"We could have both been killed. Whoever did this probably knew you were with me." She nodded to his Cruiser, parked at the curb. "He—or she—was sending you a message, too."

"I'm sorry, Emma. I should have done a better job of protecting you."

"It's not your job to protect me," she said. "And I'm okay, really." She brushed her hair back out of her eyes. "Losing my home is upsetting, of course, but I'm okay. And you're okay and Janey's okay. Everything else can be replaced."

He wouldn't argue the point, but he should have protected her. "I'm going to find who did this," he said.

"I'd say you're not the only one who was ticked off by my article," she said.

He nodded. The article in the paper did seem the most likely trigger. "The phone caller told you to stop digging into the story, and this is his way of letting you know how serious he is."

"But it also tells me I hit a nerve," she said. "If there really was no connection between Lauren Starling and Bobby Pace, I'd think whoever is behind all this would want me to pursue that angle and ignore whatever was really going on. Instead, they send me this clear indication that I'm getting too close to something they don't want the public to know."

The wail of sirens made further conversation impossible as a trio of fire trucks, followed by an ambulance, screamed onto the street. Firefighters poured out of the vehicles and swarmed the house, while a pair of paramedics headed across the lawn toward Graham and Emma.

"Is there anyone else in the house?" one of the paramedics asked.

Graham shook his head. "But you'd better check Ms. Wade. She was in the smoke for quite a while."

"I'm fine," Emma protested, but a coughing fit proved otherwise.

"We'd better check you out, and give you some oxygen to help you breathe." The pair helped her to her feet. One looked back at Graham as they escorted Emma toward the ambulance. "You come with us, sir."

He headed after them, but veered away when he saw an older man in full bunker gear examining the trio of gas cans on the walk. The man looked up at Graham's approach. "Is this your house?" he asked, taking in Graham's half-dressed state.

"It belongs to a friend of mine," he said. No need

to elaborate on his relationship with Emma; he wasn't even sure how to define it. They were lovers, certainly, but they needed more time to work out what else they were to each other. He nodded to the gas cans. "Those weren't here when I arrived this morning."

The fireman held out his hand. "Captain Will Straither," he said.

"Captain Graham Ellison, FBI." Graham shook his hand.

Straither arched one brow. "Have you made any enemies recently, Captain?"

"Then you agree the fire was likely arson?"

"We'll test for accelerants, but I'd say arson is likely. Someone wanted you to know they did this."

"Let me know what you find."

"I'd ask the same of you, Captain."

Graham nodded and headed to the ambulance, where he found both Emma and Janey inhaling oxygen, the cat with a child-size mask held to her face by one of the paramedics. "They're both going to be fine," the paramedic said as Graham approached. "We're just giving them a little oxygen to help clear their lungs."

"What about you, sir?" the second paramedic asked.

"I'm fine." Physically, he was well, at least. His mind churned with questions about what had happened, and his emotions were in turmoil.

"Then you won't mind if I check you out," the medic said.

Graham submitted to having his pulse and blood pressure checked and his lungs listened to. "You're in good shape," the paramedic said.

Emma removed her oxygen mask. Graham was glad the paramedic didn't have a stethoscope to his chest at

that moment—the sight of her smiling at him definitely
made his heart speed up. With her hair tousled, her face
streaked with soot and her robe reduced to a dirty rag
sashed over her ample frame, she was still beautiful.
"I saw you talking to the fireman," she said. "What did
you find out?"

"He thinks the fire was arson. They'll try to find
out who did it, but I'm sure the cans won't have any
prints. If we get lucky, someone might have seen a car
or someone lurking around the house."

"They took a lot of risk, setting the fire during the
day."

He glanced down the street, at the rows of empty
driveways and curbs. "Neighborhoods like this probably have fewer people around during the day than in
the evening."

"True." She leaned back against the side of the ambulance and stared at the ceiling. "What do we do now?"

"I think you and Janey should move back in with
me. At least for now."

He braced himself for an argument; she was nothing if not independent. But she merely nodded. "All
right. But what do we do about the case? Do you agree
that someone is worried about the link I made between
Bobby and Lauren?"

"I agree it's a possibility."

The dimples on either side of her mouth deepened.
"I shouldn't rub it in, but I can't tell you how good it
feels to have you admit you were wrong."

He bit back a sharp retort. Maybe he deserved some
of her ire. "I told you I spent the morning at the airport," he said.

"Yes." She leaned forward and clasped both his

hands in hers, her expression grave. "Now it's my turn to apologize for doubting you. I should have trusted you to do your job. I'm sorry."

He squeezed her hands. "I think we're two people who don't trust easily. It's going to take us time."

"I'm willing to give you time."

At that moment, he wanted more than anything to lean forward and kiss her, but he was aware of all the people around them, watching. Instead, he squeezed her hand again and leaned in, lowering his voice. "While I was at the airport, I found a pilot who says he heard Bobby arguing with someone who was in his plane with him. The pilot thinks it was a woman. He couldn't hear what they were saying, but they were both angry."

"When was this?"

"Last Monday, he thinks. And no one had seen Bobby's plane at the Montrose airport since Tuesday."

"And he was killed on Thursday."

"We're going to check some of the other airports around here, see if he flew from there between Tuesday and Thursday."

"And see if Lauren was with him."

"She may have been the woman he was arguing with at the airport Monday," Graham said. "We don't know. But I can't see how she fits into the picture. With the cargo he was carrying when he died, there was only room for one passenger. If it was Lauren, where is she now?"

"What was this mysterious cargo?" she asked.

"I can't tell you." Her expression grew stubborn, and he knew she was about to object, so he cut her off. "I really can't. It's classified."

"But whatever it is, you don't think Lauren was connected to it."

"Not unless she'd decided on a new career dealing in black-market arms—and you didn't hear that from me."

Her eyes widened. "Okay."

"If Lauren did meet with Bobby, I'm not sure that has any connection to his death the following Monday," Graham said.

"Except whoever burned down my house seems to think there's enough of a connection to warn me off. Lauren's a TV personality, but she's also a journalist. Maybe she heard about this mysterious cargo and was investigating. That led her to Bobby."

"If she got involved with the people who killed him, I'm not holding out much hope that she's still alive," he said.

"No, that doesn't seem likely. But we still need to find out what happened to her." She straightened. "I think I'll pay a visit to Richard Prentice."

The mention of the billionaire struck a jarring note. "Why would you want to talk to him?" Graham asked.

"He has connections all over the world. He might have heard something—a rumor or a hint of scandal."

"Or he might be deeply involved in all of this and going to see him could put you in even more danger," Graham said.

"I'm just going to talk to him. I can say the paper wants a follow-up story." She smiled. "You can come with me, if you like."

"He'd love that. He's suing the Rangers for harassment."

"He is? Since when?"

"Since this morning. It's another reason I was in such a foul mood when I showed up at your door."

"Then that's perfect," she said.

"How is it perfect?"

"I can say I want to talk to him about the lawsuit. But it probably wouldn't be a good idea for you to come with me."

"I don't want you going there by yourself."

"I'll be fine. I'll make sure he's aware that you and everyone at the paper know what my plans are for the day."

"Emma, I think this is a very bad idea."

Her expression sobered, and she met him with her direct, take-no-prisoners gaze. "Graham, I'm going to talk to him," she said. "You can't stop me."

## Chapter Ten

The sun painted the sky in shades of gold and pink by the time the firefighters, paramedics and local police left the charred remains of Emma's home. Graham, who had spent the past hour on the phone with his team, bundled her and Janey into his Cruiser and headed for his home near the canyon. With Janey in her arms, Emma gratefully followed him inside. She set the cat on the sofa, then stretched her arms over her head. "I want a bath, clean clothes and a glass of wine—not necessarily in that order," she said.

Still shirtless, his uniform pants streaked with soot, he looked around, everywhere but at her. "We can handle all that. The big question is, where do you want to stay?"

"That depends," she said. "Where do you want me?"

His eyes met hers at last, and she felt the same, warm thrill his looks always sent through her. "I want you in my bed, but I don't want to push you. I know you like your independence."

"You're learning, Captain." She smoothed her hands down his chest, enjoying the sensation of hard muscles beneath supple flesh. She hadn't minded a bit watching him walk around shirtless most of the afternoon.

"Why don't I set up Janey's things in the guest room and use it for changing, but I'll spend the nights with you."

"Sounds like a plan."

They indulged in a long, slow kiss that could have led to more, but the ringing doorbell interrupted them.

Muttering what might have been curses under his breath, Graham checked the door, then opened it.

"I got everything you asked for." Carmen Redhorse stepped into the room, her petite frame weighed down by two large shopping bags. One of the calls Graham had made was to pass along Emma's sizes and preferences and ask that Carmen make an emergency run to the store.

"Thank you so much." Emma rushed forward to take the bags, stopping to peek at the contents—underwear, shoes, tops and pants, as well as makeup and hair care products. "I pretty much got out of the house with nothing."

Carmen took in Emma's bare feet and the scorched robe cinched around her waist. She looked at her boss, who was still shirtless, her expression carefully neutral. "Do you need anything, boss?"

"Thank you, Carmen, that will be all."

She nodded and stepped back. "I'll see you later, then." She betrayed no emotion, but Emma had no doubt there would be plenty of talk back at Ranger headquarters about the captain and the reporter being caught literally with their pants down.

Carmen had also brought litter, food and other supplies for Janey. Once Emma had the cat comfortably set up in the guest room, she showered, did her hair and makeup, and put on the new clothing. Carmen had good taste, at least, and Emma felt almost human. She avoided thinking about everything she'd lost in the fire—not just clothing and jewelry and furniture, but books and pictures and other items that could never be replaced. Later on, she had no doubt the loss would hit her hard. But she couldn't let that distract her now.

She went looking for Graham and found him in his home office, seated in front of the computer at his desk. He'd showered and shaved, and wore jeans and a soft blue polo with leather moccasins. "I'm reading the article you wrote on Richard Prentice," he said.

She settled into the armchair to one side of the desk and tucked her feet up. "And?"

"You made him sound a lot more sympathetic than I would have." He swiveled the chair toward her. "I don't understand all these people who see him as some kind of hero."

"Just as many people are ready to list him as public enemy number one," she said.

"Do people admire him just because he has money?" Graham asked.

"Some of them do, and some hate him for the same reason. I think some people admire him because he flaunts authority."

"What did you think of him—really?" he asked.

She shifted. Graham wanted her to say she disliked Richard Prentice as much as he did, but she couldn't say that. "He was polite and cooperative and a gracious host," she said.

"So you liked him?" Graham asked.

"I didn't dislike him." She leaned toward him, teasing. "Are you jealous?"

His answer was a grunt. "My take is he's good at manipulating people. He saw your article as a benefit to him, so he turned on the charm. If he sees you as a threat, he could be dangerous. He may already be dangerous."

"I'm not going to be threatening," she said. "I'm going to be the reporter who wrote a wonderful profile of him and who is still on his side, while all you government types continue to persecute him."

Graham's face reddened, but he took a deep breath and relaxed a little. "I know you're just teasing me, but I don't like it."

"That's because no one ever dares to tease you," she said. "I like getting you all riled up, Captain."

"Oh, you do?" He stood and moved toward her.

She stood to meet his embrace. "Oh, I do," she said.

His kiss was more tender than she would have expected, his embrace almost gentle. She pulled back and looked into his eyes. "Hey, what is it?" she asked.

"I could have lost you." He closed his eyes and rested his forehead against hers.

"Yeah. We could have lost each other." Before they ever had a chance to find out how great they could be together. She kissed the side of his face. "Don't worry. I'm not going anywhere."

"Except into my bedroom." He took her hand and tugged her toward the door.

"I hope you've got plenty of condoms," she said.

"Guess what else Carmen bought while she was out shopping?"

"Graham, she didn't!" She wasn't one to blush, but right now her face felt as if it was on fire.

He grinned. "I'm not sure what kind of message she was trying to send, but I'll be sure to thank her tomorrow."

"You have no shame."

"Not one bit." He pulled her with him down the hall. "And right now I'm ready to pick up where we left off, before we were interrupted by that fire."

"Sleeping?"

"Just recharging. Now I'm ready to go."

"Mmm, so you are."

EMMA HAD TO use all her persuasive powers to convince Richard Prentice to grant her another interview. "Now isn't a good time," he said. "I'm very busy."

"So I've heard. I heard you're accusing The Ranger Brigade of harassment. I'd really like to hear your side of the story."

"My lawyers would advise me not to talk to you." She pictured him seated at his ultramodern glass-and-mahogany desk, in his home office that overlooked one end of the Black Canyon. Far different from the worn oak model in Graham's office, which she sat behind the morning after the fire, her second new computer of the week open in front of her.

"You've always been a man who followed his own counsel," she said.

He liked that; she could hear it in his voice. "Still, I think this time the attorneys may be right."

"Do you really want the public thinking you've done something wrong?" she asked.

"I haven't done anything wrong."

"Of course not, but if the Rangers are focusing their investigations on you…"

"I heard you were spending a lot of time with the Ranger captain—Ellison? The FBI guy?"

So Prentice knew about that? Should that surprise her? She and Graham hadn't exactly made a secret of their affair, so she supposed word could have gotten back to Prentice through any number of channels. Or had he been paying special attention to Graham—or to her?

"We've had a little fun together," she said. "But you know me—I'm my own woman. I like to make up my own mind about things. I really want to hear your side of the story—and so do my readers."

"Ellison isn't sending you here to spy on me, is he?"

"No man tells me what to do." Graham might try, sometimes, but he recognized the effort was futile. "I'm a reporter. I report on stories that are newsworthy. And you are always newsworthy."

"Why now more than any other time?" he asked. Give the man credit; he wanted to know all the facts before he made a decision.

"The lawsuit is one reason, but I'd also like to know what you have to say about Bobby Pace's death. I know he flew for you sometimes."

"Pace hadn't made a flight for me for some time." The chill had definitely returned to his voice.

"Then you need to let people know that, because I've even heard rumors some people think you might have had something to do with his murder."

"Where did you hear that?"

As if she would ever reveal a source. "Oh, you know how pilots are—they sit around between flights drinking coffee and spinning wild theories."

He fell silent and she let him stew, fingers crossed that his desire to defend himself in the press would outweigh the advice of his lawyers to keep quiet. "All right, I can give you an hour or so," he said. "Tomorrow morning. Be here at ten. I'll leave your name with the guards."

"Thank you so much. You won't regret this, I'm sure."

She dressed carefully for her meeting with the billionaire the next morning, pulling out all the stops, with new sexy red heels and a formfitting red-and-gray dress in the retro bombshell style she favored. She looked professional and sexy, a combination she was sure appealed to a man like Prentice. With Graham occupied at Ranger headquarters, she was able to make a quick getaway, driving the rental car her insurance company had provided, since her vehicle had been destroyed in the fire that consumed her house and garage.

"It's good to see you again, Ms. Wade." The guard at the ranch gate greeted her with a grin. During her many visits to the ranch while she was writing her profile of Prentice, she'd gotten to know all of the guards.

"How are you, Jack?" She gave him her brightest smile. "It's good to see you again, too."

"Mr. Prentice said to bring you on up."

She followed Jack to the front of the house where another bodyguard—a new guy whose name she didn't know—showed her into the library where Prentice liked to greet visitors.

He kept her waiting ten minutes, about what she'd expected. He liked to drive home the point that he was a busy man who was doing his visitors a great favor by making time for them. She was happy to play along, and greeted him warmly. "Mr. Prentice, thank you so much for taking time out of your busy schedule to speak with me," she said. "I really appreciate it."

He took both her hands in his and kissed her lightly

on the cheek. "Only for you, Emma." He motioned to twin armchairs before the unlit fireplace. "Would you like some coffee?"

"That would be lovely."

He picked up a phone and ordered the coffee, then they settled into the chairs. If he'd been under any kind of additional strain these past few weeks, she couldn't see it in his face, which, if anything, was more relaxed than she remembered. Had he had plastic surgery? "You look happy," she said.

"I do? I suppose I am happy."

"Any special reason?"

"Do I need a reason? I mean, why wouldn't I be happy with all of this?" He spread his arms to indicate the wealth and luxury that surrounded them.

"I don't know. Forgive me for being forward, but you almost look like a man in love."

He laughed—not a mocking sound, but one of genuine contentment. "You're very perceptive," he said. "But I'm not prepared to talk about my private life today."

"Not even a hint?"

"You can say that I'm happy. That should be enough."

The coffee arrived and she waited while Richard poured and added cream and sugar to her cup—just the way she liked it. She decided to broach the subject of real interest to her. "You certainly don't look like a man who had anything to do with a murder," she said.

His expression sobered. "I was shocked to learn of Bobby's death, but as I told you on the phone, he hasn't worked for me for several weeks."

"Why is that? I assume you still need a pilot."

"Bobby was very stressed by some personal issues—his son's illness, the aftermath of his divorce. Unfortunately, that led to some behaviors that made me less willing to trust him as my pilot."

"What kind of behaviors?"

"He drank more than he should. Understandable, but drinking and flying definitely don't mix."

She'd never seen Bobby indulge in more than a couple of beers, but she couldn't claim to have known him really well. And he was under the kind of stress that drove a lot of people to self-medicate with drugs or alcohol. "Do you have any idea who he was working for when he died?" she asked.

"None. We hadn't been in contact since I told him I'd have to let him go."

"I know you're a man who has his finger on the pulse of many things. I was hoping you'd heard a rumor or gossip, maybe about someone who was looking for a pilot who would be willing to do a job that wasn't necessarily legal."

"Why do you think I would know about illegal activities?" he asked.

She smiled her most disarming smile. "Some of the people who admire you the most do so because they see you as a rebel protesting against unjust laws. Though you might not break the law yourself, some of them do, and they might tell you things, or even try to pull you into their illegal schemes, perhaps as a way of gaining cachet for their activities."

"You overestimate any contact I have with those types of 'fans'," he said. "I abhor extremism in any form."

"So you hadn't heard any rumors about Bobby."

"Everyone knew he was desperate for money. That's probably all anyone who was looking for a pilot needed to know. But I hadn't heard of anyone in particular who needed such a pilot."

"How did Bobby take the news that you wouldn't be using him anymore?" she asked.

"He was upset, but he understood. I wished him well."

"Poor Bobby. I never knew anybody with such hard luck."

"You knew him?" Prentice's eyebrow twitched—a nervous tic she'd noted before.

"We went out a few times." She shrugged. "It was just as you said—he had a lot of personal problems, the kind of thing that leads people to drink too much. But he was a great guy. I was really wishing he'd catch a break."

"I felt the same way." He set aside his still-full coffee cup. "I've set up a fund for his boy. At least the child and his mother won't have to worry anymore about those medical bills Bobby was always struggling to pay."

"You did that for him?" She was touched, though she didn't want to show it.

He nodded. "It was the least I could do. After all, he did work for me at one time, and I make it a point to take care of my own."

"I'll be sure our readers know that." She set aside her own cup and picked up her notebook. Even though she'd set her digital recorder on the table between them, she liked to have written backup in case the electronics failed her. "So, on to this lawsuit. What have the Rangers been doing that you feel is harassment?"

"It would be easier to ask what they haven't been doing. They've come to my house several times, questioning me. Every time a crime occurs within the park, they seem to consider me as their number one suspect. They drive by my gates at all hours and fly over my property. I'm sure they have me under surveillance. Tell me, would you want to live that way?"

"No one would. Of course, that is a public road in front of your ranch gate—one that leads to the Ranger headquarters. And can you be sure the planes that fly over are theirs?"

He scowled. "Are you saying you don't believe me?"

"Not at all. But it's important for me to preserve my position as an unbiased reporter. I have to ask the tough questions and play devil's advocate, even when I don't want to." Most of the time, truth be told, she relished the role, but he didn't need to know that.

He relaxed a little. "I think it's enough to say that I have sufficient proof of harassment to justify my lawsuit."

They talked for a few more minutes, about his business interests and his long-held views against restrictions on public land and government interference in private property rights. All things she'd heard before, but she let him ramble, looking for any indication that he'd become more radical or unstable. But he seemed the same rational, if arrogant and stubborn, man she'd profiled months before.

After fifty minutes, he made a show of checking his watch. "I'm afraid we're going to have to wrap this up," he said. "I have another appointment."

"Of course. I just have a few more questions. Do you know Lauren Starling?"

He studied her, his gaze intent. "Who?"

But she was sure he'd heard her clearly. "Lauren Starling. She's the prime-time news anchor for Channel 9 in Denver. I thought you might have met her at a charity or political function. She's blonde, blue eyes—very beautiful."

"I've seen her on television. I might have met her once or twice. It's hard to keep up. But why are you asking me about her?"

"She's missing. Her car was found several weeks ago, abandoned in Black Canyon of the Gunnison National Park. I was hoping you might have seen or heard something about her."

"I haven't heard anything. There's been nothing in the papers."

"Only a couple of smaller articles I've written." Had he really missed the front page article in which she'd theorized a connection between Lauren and Bobby? Or was he lying? "The police aren't taking her disappearance seriously. They think she might have decided to lay low for a while, or run away with a lover or something."

He smiled, though what about this news he found amusing, she couldn't imagine. "Maybe she has. The press spends too much time trying to manufacture news where there is none, and like the government, too much time prying into people's private lives." He stood. "And on that note, I really must go."

She closed her notebook and shut off her tape recorder, refusing to be baited by his rudeness. "That's all the questions I have. I think it's going to be a great article."

"Then I'll see you out."

"If you don't mind, could I use your ladies' room? It's a long way back to town."

"Of course. Down the hall and to your left."

More than a standard powder room, this bathroom

featured double sinks, a steam shower and a soaking tub. A second door, which was locked, apparently led to a ground-floor guest room. Convenient if you had a guest who couldn't handle stairs, she supposed. Or maybe the locked room was a home gym and Prentice didn't like having to go all the way upstairs to shower after his workout.

She used the facilities then, telling herself it was her duty as a reporter to snoop, she checked behind the cabinet doors. She found towels, cleaning supplies and extra toilet paper in three of the cabinets, but the fourth was locked.

She stared at the lock for a long moment, then reached over and turned the water on full blast, to cover any noise she might make, and pulled a penknife from her purse. A few seconds later, she'd popped the lock and was staring at an impressive array of hairstyling products, perfume bottles and women's cosmetics, everything neatly organized in matching quilted travel bags. A carton to one side held feminine hygiene products. Emma knelt and was reaching into the cabinet to pull out one of the bags when Prentice knocked on the door. "Are you all right?" he asked.

"I'm fine. I just, uh, spilled liquid soap on my skirt and was washing it off." She pulled out her phone, snapped a picture of the contents of the cabinet, then shut the door, turned off the water and walked out to meet him.

"Sorry about that," she said.

He looked down at her skirt. "Your skirt's dry."

"I know." She smoothed her hand down her thigh. "This fabric is amazing."

He took her arm and escorted her to the door. "Goodbye, Emma." No kiss this time, only intense scrutiny, as if he was looking for some flaw in her face.

"Goodbye, Mr. Prentice. I'm sure we'll talk soon."

She climbed into her car, a little surprised that Jack or one of the other guards wasn't waiting to escort her back to the gate. But maybe Prentice figured she'd been here so many times she knew the way, and he trusted her not to stray.

She started driving, her mind a whirl. She couldn't wait to hear what Graham made of all the feminine accessories stashed in Prentice's guest bathroom. Did they belong to the mysterious new love he didn't want to talk about? That seemed the most likely explanation—and she couldn't blame the man for wanting to keep his private life private.

Still, the reporter in her wished for something a little juicier. Maybe Prentice was a secret cross-dresser—though the feminine hygiene products didn't fit with that scenario. Maybe he had a secret mad wife in the attic—or in this case, stashed in the guest bedroom?

She shook her head, and laughed at her own wild imagination. No, the stuff probably belonged to his girlfriend, whoever she was.

She rounded a bend in the road, the house out of sight now, and pulled out her phone. She'd promised Graham she'd call to let him know she was okay. It was sweet, really, how he worried about her, though there was no need. Sure, a lot of strange things had happened in the past few days, but she was sure Richard Prentice wasn't behind them. The man had too many other things on his mind to waste his time with her.

She slowed and punched the button for Graham's

number, then a hand reached around and grabbed the phone. Another hand clamped over her mouth, and then the world went black.

## Chapter Eleven

"Emma? Emma!"

Graham hadn't realized he'd been shouting until Randall and Marco rushed into his office. "Something wrong, Captain?" Randall asked, amusement dancing in his hazel eyes. Ever since Carmen had reported on Graham's and Emma's nearly naked state in the middle of the afternoon—and her joke gift of a large box of condoms—Ranger headquarters had echoed with good-natured gibes at Graham's expense. "I don't think Ms. Wade is here," Randall added.

"Something's gone wrong," Graham said. "Something's happened to Emma." One minute he'd picked up the phone, elated and relieved to see her number on the screen. The next, he'd heard her low, anguished moan and a sound like screeching brakes. Then—nothing. He sank into his desk chair. He'd never admit it to his men, but his legs shook too much to hold him. If anything happened to Emma...

No. He wouldn't even think it. He had to pull himself together and help her. "She had an appointment with Richard Prentice this morning," he said, his voice steadier. "She'd agreed to call me when the interview was over. That was the call, but all I heard was a moan, then the phone went dead."

"Maybe it was just a bad connection," Randall said. "Have you tried calling her back?"

Graham snatched the phone from where he'd let it drop on his desk. He punched in Emma's number and waited for the ring. "I'm sorry, the person you are try-ing to reach is not available, or out of area. If you wish to leave a voice mail…"

He shoved the phone in his pocket and moved out from behind the desk. "I'm going out there," he said.

Marco grabbed him, the DEA agent's grip like an iron vise. "Not a good idea," he said.

"He already thinks we're harassing him," Randall said. "If you show up out there and Emma's all right, you'll only be adding fuel to his lawsuit."

"And if she's not all right, you won't be doing her any favors barging in on him." Marco's expression was grim.

Much as he wanted to run to Emma's rescue, he rec-ognized the sense in his men's advice. The first rule of a hostage situation was to step back and make an as-sessment. Charging the scene was a recipe for disaster, especially if you weren't sure where the hostage was or what had happened. He didn't know if Emma was a hostage or not, but he wouldn't help her by rushing to her rescue without a plan.

"Is Carmen here?" he asked.

"I'm here." She must have been listening right out-side the door. She joined the three men in Graham's of-fice. "What can I do to help?"

"Call Richard Prentice and ask to speak to Emma. Tell anyone who answers that you're a girlfriend and the two of you were supposed to meet for lunch, but now you can't reach her by phone. You knew she had the interview scheduled and you need to get a message to her that you're running late."

"You want me to use my phone or yours?" she asked.

"Use one of those throwaways we keep around."

"Roger." She left the room and returned a moment later with one of the disposable pay-as-you-go phones they used when they didn't want to be easily tracked. Lotte, Randall's Belgian Malinois, followed her into the room and went to sit beside Randall, ears alert.

"She knows something's up," Randall said, smoothing his hand along the dog's side.

Carmen made the call, adding a bubbly, upbeat note to her voice that Graham hadn't heard before. In different circumstances, he would have been amused at this image of Carmen as the carefree coed, only interested in lunch and shopping. But the half of the conversation he could hear left him anything but amused.

"She's not? Are you sure? Because she definitely said she had an interview with Mr. Prentice. She was really excited about it...So her car's not there or anything...All right. Thank you. I can't imagine where she's gotten to."

She disconnected the call and met the others' worried gazes. "The guy on the phone—I think he must have been one of the bodyguards—says Emma never showed up for the interview. Mr. Prentice is very upset that she wasted his time this way."

"He's lying," Graham said. "The interview was scheduled for ten, and was supposed to last an hour. Emma called me at..." He picked up his phone and scrolled through the call log. "At eleven oh three."

"So you think whatever happened, happened as she was leaving Prentice's ranch," Randall said.

"Maybe she had a car accident," Carmen said. "Talking on the phone, a deer jumps out..." The scenario was more common than Graham wanted to admit. The combination of distracted driving and unpredictable and abundant wildlife was a recipe for numerous collisions.

"I'm going to drive out there." He started for the door once more. Emma might be lying in a ditch, unnoticed by a passerby.

"There's a quicker way to locate her," Marco said.

Graham stopped and turned to the taciturn agent. "How?"

"She was driving a rental car, right?" Marco asked.

"Yes. Her car burned up in the fire."

"What agency?" Marco pulled out his task force issued phone. "Most rentals are fitted out with LoJack, or some other locator service, in the case of an accident or theft."

"I don't know the agency, but there can't be many in a town the size of Montrose."

"When my sister's car was in the shop, her insurance company used Corporate Rentals," Carmen said.

"I'll try there first," Marco said.

He dialed the number, and put the phone on speaker, so they could all hear the conversation. Marco explained who he was and what he wanted to the young woman on the other end of the line, gave Emma's name and was transferred to a man who must have been the boss. "Come to our office at the Montrose Airport and I'll have that information for you," the man said. "I'll need to see some credentials, of course."

Graham didn't wait for more. He headed for the door, the others hurrying after him.

Marco slid into the passenger seat of Graham's Cruiser and Randall and Carmen, with Lotte in the backseat, followed in Randall's vehicle. Graham resisted the urge to head to the airport with lights and sirens, knowing this was the quickest way to pick up a trail of followers, including the press. He forced himself to keep within reasonable range of the speed limit as he raced toward town.

The manager of Corporate Rentals was waiting at the front desk with a computer printout. His already pasty face grew a shade whiter at the sight of four officers practically storming the office, but after glancing at Graham's badge, he slid the single sheet of paper across the counter. "Those are the GPS coordinates where the car has been parked for the last thirty minutes," he said.

Marco pulled out a handheld GPS unit and punched in the numbers. He angled the screen toward Graham. "That's on public land. In the Curecanti Recreation Area." The recreation area occupied forty-three thousand acres on the west side of Black Canyon of the Gunnison National Park.

"It's about a mile from Prentice's property line," Marco confirmed.

"There aren't any roads in that area," Carmen said.

The manager frowned. "The rental contract prohibits taking the vehicle off-roading," he said.

"She didn't go off-roading," Graham said. "Not voluntarily."

No one said anything as Graham steered the Cruiser cross-country, detouring around gullies and mountains, following barely discernible trails in the rough terrain. They'd left the rental agency forty minutes before and had encountered no one since leaving the pavement. "We should be close," Marco said, consulting the hand-held GPS unit.

Graham leaned forward, scanning the landscape for anything out of place. He didn't spot the car until they were almost on it. Dust coated the once shiny red sedan, and a spiderweb of cracks spread out across the front windshield. Two tires were flat, and one front fender bowed inward.

"Looks like a rough ride," Randall said, as he and Carmen joined Graham and Marco at the front of the car.

Graham wrenched open the driver's door. The keys dangled from the ignition, and Emma's purse spilled its contents onto the passenger side floorboard. "Her phone's gone," he said, checking the contents. "So's her recorder and notebook. Her wallet's still here."

Randall let Lotte sniff the wallet. *"Sich,"* he ordered.

The dog sniffed around the car, then began following a trail, but stopped after a few dozen yards. She sat and looked back over her shoulder at Randall, whining softly.

"She got into another car and they drove away," Randall said, pointing to the faint tire tracks visible among the rocks and cacti.

"She didn't walk." Marco pointed to twin lines in the sand. "Those are drag marks. The kind that would be made by a woman's high heels."

Graham remembered the sexy red heels Emma had insisted on buying when she'd gone shopping for an outfit to wear to her interview with Prentice. "We need to get Lotte onto Prentice's ranch to look for Emma," he said. "If he took her, he's probably hiding her there."

"He'll never let us on his property," Randall said. "Not without a court order."

"He's got enough judges in his pocket that getting such an order won't be easy," Carmen said.

"We don't have time for that," Graham said.

"We could go in the back way," Marco said. "Cross-country."

"The place is crawling with guards," Carmen said. "He's practically got his own paramilitary force."

"We go in at night." Marco offered a rare grin. "With Lotte, we'll know they're there before they spot us." He nodded at the tire tracks in the dirt. "We can follow these tracks all the way to her."

Graham checked his watch. It was just after noon. "Another seven hours before dark," he said.

"That'll give us time to prepare," Marco said.

Graham only prayed they had the time, and that Emma wasn't already dead, her beautiful spirit silenced, the way Bobby Pace had been silenced. Forever.

EMMA WOKE TO a darkness so intense she thought at first she still slept, her eyes not yet open. But her other senses told her she was awake to an aching in her arms and shoulders, and a heavy throbbing in her head. The smell of earth and rocks surrounded her, with an undercurrent of a more acrid, ammonia odor. The darkness pressed in on her, frightening in its intensity. This wasn't merely nighttime, but the absence of light.

*Don't panic.* She repeated the words over and over, a mantra to keep the loss of control at bay. Think. What had happened? She'd been driving, talking on the phone with Graham… No, she'd been calling Graham, but she hadn't talked to him yet. Then…nothing. She had no memory beyond picking up her phone.

She was lying on a hard surface—rock hard. Her hands and feet were bound, her arms stretched painfully behind her. Carefully, she bent her knees and arched her back, trying to get a sense of the space she was in. Her feet brushed something solid—a wall, the surface uneven and hard. The source of the ammonia odor came to her—the smell of bat guano. She was in a cave, or maybe a mine. Old shafts and exploration tunnels riddled this part of the state, a remnant of the nineteenth century gold and silver rushes.

She struggled into a sitting position, the effort making her head spin. *I must have been drugged*, she thought, as she fought a wave of nausea. She pressed her head back against a sharp protrusion of rock, welcoming the distraction of the pain.

As her head cleared, she struggled to hear any sound beyond the rasp of her own breathing. Nothing—not a drip of water or traffic noise or anything at all.

"Help!" Her shout echoed back to her, fading away into the limitless blackness. This was bad. Was someone coming back for her, or had she been left here to die?

She shuddered at the thought and struggled to stand, bracing her back against the rock and slowly, agonizingly, inching to her feet. The rock tore at her clothing and scraped her skin, but this gave her an idea. She dragged her bound wrists along the rock until the zip tie holding her caught on a jagged edge. Ignoring the pain in her shoulders, she dragged the tough nylon tie back and forth across the rock until it gave with a satisfying snap!

"Yes!" The shout rang off the rocks. She rubbed feeling back into her painful wrists and lowered herself to a sitting position once more. The ache in her swollen fingers brought tears to her eyes, but she blinked them away. She didn't have time for crying; she had to get out of here.

When she could move her fingers without crying out, she went to work undoing the bindings around her ankles. Her captors had used duct tape here, and she spent many long minutes unpicking it layer by layer.

Free at last, she stood. Being surrounded by darkness fostered a sense of vertigo, and she put out a hand to steady herself. By following the wall around, she was able to trace the outline of the chamber where she was trapped. The square room was maybe eight feet on a side. Not a cave, then, but a shaft of some kind. The walls, though rough, were slippery. Even if she took off her heels, she didn't think she could climb them, especially if she couldn't see where she was going.

She sat down again and tried not to think about how hungry and thirsty she was. Focus on the positive. She wasn't tied up anymore, and a steady current of fresh air reassured her she wasn't going to suffocate. Graham would look for her when she didn't come home. He knew she'd been going to Prentice's ranch this morning.

Had Prentice arranged for her to disappear? Had he sent one of his men after her, with instructions to shut her up? But why? She'd learned nothing in her interview that connected him to Lauren Starling's disappearance or to Bobby Pace's death. She reviewed what she could remember of their conversation, but nothing stood out. He hadn't appeared upset or concerned about any of the questions she'd asked.

Maybe someone else had attacked her after she left Prentice's home. Someone who'd followed her to the ranch and been waiting. If only she could think, but the pounding headache and painfully dry mouth interfered with her concentration.

After a while she lay on her side on the dirt floor of her prison, curled into a fetal position. She tried to sleep. Someone would come for her. She wouldn't give up hope.

# Chapter Twelve

Shortly after 9:00 p.m. when the sun had fully set, Graham, Dancc, Marco, Randall and Lotte set out to track Emma across the rugged terrain of the Curecanti Recreation Area. The most heavily trafficked areas of the preserve attracted hikers, campers, ATV and snowmobile riders, and fishermen. The interior land remained largely unvisited, making it the perfect place to hide illegal activity.

The Rangers wore night-vision goggles, which gave everything the eerie green glow of a video game. But this was no game. Marco led the way, keeping a shielded light fixed on the ground, following the faint impressions made by tires on the crumbly, dry surface of the prairie. Though Marco didn't have Lotte's keen sense of smell, he was the best visual tracker Graham had ever seen. He somehow picked out the subtle differences in broken grass stems and barely disturbed ground. Even now, Graham couldn't see the tracks until Marco stopped and pointed them out to them.

Randall held the GPS. "We just crossed onto Prentice's land," he said softly.

They stopped, alert for sounds of dogs or guards. A chill breeze stirred the needles of the stunted piñons and sagebrush that dotted the ground, bringing with it the odors of dry earth and pine. An owl hooted and Graham turned in time to see the night-hunting predator lift off from the branch of a piñon on silent wings.

Marco started walking again and the others followed. Clouds obscured a quarter moon much of the time. Graham prayed he wouldn't step on a snake, then wished he hadn't thought of that.

Lotte froze, ears forward, one paw up in a pointer pose. "She's found something," Randall said. "Go on, girl. Find her." He unclipped her leash and she started off, nose to the ground. The three men followed closely, Randall taking the lead this time, just behind his dog.

Piles of rock and pieces of broken metal littered the ground around them. "Mine waste," Marco said, shining his light on a pile of bent metal strapping stained orange-red by rust.

Just ahead of them, Lotte stopped, then sat. Her excited whines sounded loud in the still darkness. "Good girl," Randall said. "What have you found?"

He stumbled on the rough ground and almost fell into what turned out to be a large hole. "Whoa!" He knelt beside the hole and looked down into it. "She's telling me there's something here, but I can't see it." He shone his light into the hole, but the darkness swallowed up the tiny beam before it penetrated the depths. "I think it's a mine tunnel."

"Not a tunnel, a ventilation shaft." Marco beamed his light onto the remains of a metal frame around the opening, then onto a massive metal grate just behind the frame. "That frame isn't as old as the rest of the metal around here. It was added later, probably as a safety precaution."

"So who moved it?" Randall shoved to his feet. "And why?"

"It would be a good place to dump a body," Graham said, fighting the cold dread growing in his stomach.

"Lotte's signaling a live find," Randall said.

Graham glanced at the dog, her gaze riveted to the shaft, tongue lolling, eyes bright. He'd heard some search and rescue dogs became depressed after finding dead bodies. Lotte didn't look depressed.

He knelt beside the shaft and cupped his hands on either side of his mouth. "Emma!" he shouted.

The cry echoed against the rock walls of the shaft. "Emma!" he called again.

"Graham? Is that you?" Emma's voice floated up to him. "Please tell me I'm not dreaming."

"You're not dreaming." He shone his light down, frustrated by his inability to see more than a few yards down. "Are you okay?"

"I'm all right. You're going to get me out of here, aren't you?"

"I'll get you out." The big question was how? They had no rope to toss down to her, no vehicle to help pull her up, no ladder to climb down.

"This shaft provides ventilation for the mine tunnels," Marco said. "The mine entrance is around here somewhere. Maybe we can reach her that way."

"You and Randall look for the entrance," Graham said. "I'll stay here with Emma." He called down to her. "Hang on. We'll get you out as soon as we can."

"Do you have any water?" she asked. "I'm really thirsty."

He pulled a bottle of water from his pack. "How far down are you? The light won't reach."

"A long way," she said. "I can't see you, either."

"I'm going to toss down a bottle, but I don't want to hit you."

"There's an opening to one side where I can stand. I think it might be the entrance to a tunnel."

"Okay. Here comes the water."

He dropped the bottle and listened for it to hit bottom, counting one-Mississippi, two-Mississippi… Before he'd counted two seconds he heard the bottle strike the rock below. "I got it!" Emma called up. "Thank you!"

"It didn't break?" he asked.

"It's a little dented, but okay."

"I think you're down about sixty feet," he said, after he worked out the math. "Are you sure you're okay?"

"A little sore, but no broken bones or bleeding. I think I was pretty out of it when whoever it was tossed me in here."

"What happened?"

"I don't know. I think I was drugged."

Hurried footsteps scuffed through the rock, coming toward him. "Randall and Marco are coming back," he said. "They must have found something."

He stood and turned to face the Rangers, but the new arrivals weren't Marco and Randall, but two strangers dressed in black. One punched Graham in the stomach and when he doubled over, the other pounded a fist on the back of his head, driving him to his knees. One good shove and he was falling, scrabbling for a hold on the sides of the shaft, the rock floor of the shaft rising up to slam into him.

GRAHAM LANDED HEAVILY at the bottom of the shaft, a single, low grunt the only sound escaping him. Emma screamed and ran to him. In the faint glow of moonlight she could just make out his form, lying awkwardly on one side, so still and silent she was afraid he was dead. "Graham." She shook him. "Graham, please."

"Emma." He opened his eyes. "Are you all right?"

"I'm fine. Better now that you're here. Are you all right?"

He grimaced, and shoved into a sitting position. "I banged up my shoulder on the way down. Maybe cracked some ribs."

"Who attacked you?" she asked.

"I don't know." He looked up and she followed his gaze to the opening of the shaft. Dark shapes appeared, blocking out what little light filtered down from the moon.

"You were warned to stay out of this!" one of the shadowy figures shouted. "You should have listened."

A narrow beam of light from a flashlight swept down into the shaft, but couldn't penetrate more than a few feet of the darkness. Graham put a finger to his lips and motioned that they should move against the wall. Emma nodded, and crawled toward the opening where a passage split off from the main shaft. She didn't want to be in the line of fire if whoever was up there started dropping rocks on them—or firing bullets.

Footsteps scuffled on the rocks far overhead, then an automobile engine roared to life. Metal clanged, and the ground shook. A horrible, screeching sound, like something heavy being dragged across rock, made her cover her ears. Then the world went black once more.

Emma gasped, and clung to Graham. Only his solid, warm presence kept her grounded in that sudden, disorienting absence of light. He put one arm around her. "They've dragged the cover back over the hole," he said.

"We're trapped." Emma shut her eyes tightly, and pressed her face against his chest. "We're buried alive."

"Don't panic." His fingers dug into her arm. "That's what they want—for us to feel helpless. We're not helpless."

He might not be helpless, but that's exactly how she felt. She was at the bottom of a mine shaft, underground in pitch-darkness with no light or food. She'd even lost the water Graham had tossed to her. The only thing keeping her from losing her mind was the man beside her, solid and strong and calm despite the impossibility of their situation.

"I think they're gone now," he said.

"So we're alone." The words added to her despair.

"The rest of the team will look for us." He took his arm from around her and she started to protest. "I'm just taking off my pack," he said. A few seconds later, light surrounded them. She blinked in the brightness. Graham handed her the mini Maglite. "You take this. I've got another one."

She shone the flashlight around her prison. "It's not as bad as I feared," she said. No slime covered the walls, and they were alone in the chamber, with no spiders or rats or other creepy-crawlies for company. She retrieved the bottle of water from the floor and drank. "What do we do now?" she asked.

"When was the last time you ate?" he asked.

"This morning." Her stomach growled. "Yesterday morning, I guess."

"Eat this." He pressed a wrapped sandwich into her hand. "I hope you like peanut butter."

"I love peanut butter." She took a bite and almost moaned with relief.

"What happened this morning?" he asked. "At Prentice's."

"Everything was fine," she said between bites of the sandwich. "I showed up for the interview, we talked. He was his usual self, polite and businesslike. He said he stopped using Bobby as a pilot weeks ago because Bobby was drinking too much and he was worried about safety."

"Was Bobby drinking too much?"

"Not when he was with me, but we only saw each other a few times. He certainly had a lot on his mind, worries about Robby and money problems—the kind of problems that might drive a person to drink."

"And of course, Prentice didn't know anything about what Bobby had been up to since then."

"Not a thing. He did tell me he'd started a fund to pay for Robby's medical bills. I thought that was really generous of him."

"Oh, he's generous, all right." Graham shifted, and stifled a grunt.

"Are you okay?" she asked.

"I'll be fine. What happened when you got ready to leave?"

"Nothing, really. I got in my car and started driving toward the gate. I did think it was a little unusual that he didn't have one of the guards escort me—that's the way it's always worked before. No one goes anywhere on the ranch without an escort. But I just figured they were busy, and since I'd visited so many times, Richard trusted me to see myself out."

"I answered your call, but all I heard was a cry and

a sound like squealing brakes." The memory made him sick to his stomach.

"I don't remember much about the next part. I think someone in the backseat of the car grabbed me, then knocked me out—maybe with chloroform or something. I felt pretty sick when I first woke up."

"You woke up down here?"

"Yes. I was tied up, hands and feet, but I managed to cut the ties. I still felt pretty bad, so I lay down and slept, until you showed up. Thank God you did."

"I knew you had the appointment with Prentice, and I was betting the call came while you were still here. The rental company was able to track the location of your car."

"Where was it?"

"In a gully in the Curecanti Recreation Area. A long way from any road, but not too far from Prentice's ranch. From there, Randall Knightbridge and his dog, Lotte, were able to track you to where another vehicle must have picked you up. We came back after dark and followed the tracks of that vehicle to here."

"You didn't come by yourself, I hope," she said.

"No, Randall, Michael Dance, Lotte and Marco Cruz were with me."

"What happened to them?" she asked.

"I don't know. I sent them to search for the main entrance to the mine while I waited with you." He looked up toward the ceiling. "They haven't come back yet. That's not a good sign." If the people who had thrown him and Emma down here and left them to die had killed members of his team, too, they wouldn't want to be alive when Graham got out of here.

"Maybe they're okay," she said. "Maybe they got away and went for help."

"Maybe so." He couldn't afford to dwell on what might have happened. He had to focus on right now, and what he and Emma needed to do to survive.

She finished the last of the sandwich. "What else do you have in that magic pack?" she asked. "Maybe a phone to call for help?"

"It didn't survive the fall." He held up the phone, its screen shattered, bits of plastic hanging off it. He dropped it back into the pack and took out a flat plastic box. "I'll need you to help me fashion a sling for my shoulder and wrap my ribs. There are some bandages and gauze in this first aid kit."

She brushed crumbs from her hands. "All right. But just so you know—I never did get my first-aid badge in Girl Scouts."

"There's a booklet with diagrams in with the supplies." He began unbuttoning his shirt. "Do the ribs first."

She helped him out of the shirt, but even though she tried to be gentle, she didn't miss the sharp hiss of breath through clenched teeth as she slipped it off his injured shoulder. "Do you think it's dislocated?" she asked.

He shook his head. "Just separated. Take the gauze and wrap it as tightly as you can around my ribs."

Getting the gauze tight was easier said than done, but after several false starts she managed to encase several inches of his torso in gauze. She pressed her lips to his chest, just above the white line of gauze, and breathed deeply of his clean, masculine scent. "Thank you for coming after me," she said. "I knew you would."

He wrapped his free arm around her. "Kiss me," he said.

"You do love to give orders, don't you, Captain?" But she kissed him, a deep, lingering kiss meant to communicate better than words how thankful she was that he was here with her.

They might have done more than kiss, but the sharp edges of the rock walls made sitting, standing and lying down uncomfortable. And Graham still needed his shoulder tended to. Reluctantly, she broke off the kiss and reached for the triangular bandage and the first aid book. "Let's see if I can figure this out," she said. "There's some ibuprofen in here, too. You should take that."

After he had washed down two ibuprofen with water, she helped him back into his shirt, then unfolded the bandage and managed to fashion a descent sling. She sat back on her heels to admire her handiwork. "Feel better?" she asked.

He nodded. "When we're out of here, I'll show you just how much I appreciate your help."

"Are we going to get out of here?" She hated the wobble in her voice, hated the panic that clawed at the back of her throat like a wild animal waiting for the chance to tear down the fragile wall of self-control she'd managed to construct. She'd always thought of herself as a strong woman, one who wasn't timid or afraid of anything.

But she'd never been in a situation like this before, attacked and buried underground by an enemy she didn't know or understand.

"We're going to get out of here." Graham sounded strong, and confident. "This shaft was dug to provide fresh air for a mine tunnel," he said. "All we have to do is find the main entrance to the mine."

And hope it wasn't blocked by rock or a steel plate, she thought, but she didn't say that. "There's a tunnel leading off from this shaft," she said.

"Then we'll start there." He slipped the strap of the pack onto his uninjured shoulder. "I'll lead the way. You can keep that light, but switch it off to save the battery. Stay close to me."

As if she needed to be told the latter. She wasn't going to let him out of touching range.

The tunnel leading away from the shaft was tall enough to walk upright for the first hundred feet or so, then narrowed so that they had to crouch, then crawl. Emma's knees ached and the rock scraped her hands, but she bit her lip and kept going. Graham wasn't complaining, so neither would she.

"I can feel air flowing past," he said. "We're on the right track."

Suddenly, crawling didn't hurt so much. She increased her speed; when she got out of this she was never going into a cave again. She might even have to avoid basements.

Graham stopped so abruptly, she bumped into him. "What is it?" she asked.

"There's a side passage here."

"Is that where we need to go?" she asked.

"It looks like someone's been using it for storage. There are a bunch of boxes and stuff."

"Has someone been using it recently?" she asked. "That could be a good sign that the entrance is still open."

"Very recently." He turned into the passage, and she followed. The tunnel opened into a rock chamber, the ceiling high enough they could stand upright once more. She massaged her aching knees and looked around, following the beam of Graham's flashlight. On first glance, it looked as if someone had been using this side tunnel as a trash dump. Rusting tin cans, old glass Coke bottles and discarded mining tools filled one corner. But as the beam of the flashlight arced across the space, Emma realized the trash had been swept aside to make room for the wooden crates and plastic tubs with lids that lined one side of the chamber, along with half a dozen red plastic gas cans. She squinted at the stenciling on the side of one of the crates. It appeared to be in a foreign language—was that Russian, or maybe Arabic?

Graham let out a low whistle. "I don't believe it," he said.

"Believe what?"

"Take a look at this."

She moved to his side and stared at the object spotlighted by his flashlight. "Is it a bomb?" It lay on its side, a six-foot-long bullet shape with four metal fins at one end.

He played the light along the sinister black shape. "I'm pretty sure it's the missing Hellfire missile we've been looking for."

# Chapter Thirteen

Graham studied the missile, the pain in his shoulder and side momentarily forgotten. His hunch had been right—the cargo that had cost Bobby Pace his life had been destined for Prentice's ranch. This discovery busted his case wide-open. He'd caught the billionaire practically red-handed. No way would he be able to wriggle off the hook this time.

"Is this the mysterious cargo Bobby was carrying in his plane when he died?" Emma asked.

"This is it." He moved closer to the missile, and directed the light onto the numbers embossed on one of the tail fins. "The crate was damaged on impact, but we still have the pieces. The numbers on it should match the numbers here—and the ones in the army's records."

"Richard Prentice stole this from the army?"

"Not directly. The missile apparently went missing some time ago. He probably purchased it on the black market."

"But…why? Is he a collector or something?"

"It's more sinister than that, I'm afraid. Rumor is, he's purchased an unmanned drone. With this missile, he can arm the drone."

"Does he plan to start his own war?"

"He already has, at least if what we believe is true—that he's the power behind the crime wave in the area. His billions have funded the meth labs and illegal grow operations, the human trafficking and artifact destruction and murders, thefts and other crimes."

"But...he's made so much money legitimately—through real estate and the companies he owns. Why risk all of that to do something illegal?"

"So he can make even more money? Crime on the scale he's operating definitely pays. Or maybe it's just an extension of his desire to gain power and defy the laws of the government he hates."

"It's unbelievable," she said.

"Not many people have wanted to believe it," he said. "But with this proof, they'll have to." He looked around the chamber. "I wish I had my phone. I'd like to take some pictures."

"Speaking of pictures, I took some interesting photos at Prentice's house." Emma rubbed her forehead. "I'd forgotten until just now."

"Pictures of what?"

"You're going to think it's silly, but at the time it seemed important."

"If you thought it was important, I'm sure it was."

"I had to use the bathroom before I left the house—we'd been drinking a lot of coffee. While I was in there, I snooped in the cabinets. Everything was normal, except one cabinet was locked, which I thought was strange."

"What was in the cabinet?"

"How do you know I opened it?" She attempted—but failed—to look indignant.

"I don't think you'd bother taking pictures of a locked bathroom cabinet."

"All right, I opened it. It was a cheap lock and it popped with no trouble."

"What was inside?"

"Makeup. Hair products. Tampons."

Definitely not the answer he'd expected. "So he has a girlfriend?"

"That's the thing—when I first arrived, I was struck by how happy and relaxed he looked. I even teased him about being in love. He didn't deny it, but he refused to say anything more."

"Maybe he likes to keep his private life private."

"But what woman locks up all her personal stuff—and in a downstairs guest bathroom?" She shook her head. "It just seemed weird to me. And what's so special about this woman? And why does no one know about her? I read everything about the man to prepare for my initial interview with him. Except for a seven-year marriage when he was much younger, which ended in divorce, he's remained acutely single. He's photographed from time to time with various socialites or the daughters of foreign dignitaries, but there's never even a hint of a woman—or man—he might be seriously dating. I even asked him about it and he said it was because he was married to his job."

"The kind of money he has can buy the attention of almost any woman he wants, and the discretion to keep relationships silent."

"But why be so secretive?"

"It's a little strange, but it's not a crime."

"I know, but I took the pictures, anyway. And I was in there so long he knocked on the door and asked if I was all right. I wonder if, after I left, he went in there and found the broken lock. He'd have known I did it. If he was trying to hide something, he might have sent someone after me to make sure I stayed quiet."

"That's going a little far to protect the identity of a girlfriend," Graham said.

"Maybe she's married. Or famous. Or both."

"Or maybe this has nothing to do with a girlfriend." He turned back to the missile. "We've got evidence of a much bigger crime right here."

"Then why toss me down here with all this evidence?" she asked.

"Because he didn't think you'd ever get out," Graham said.

She wrapped her arms around him and laid her head on his shoulder. "If you hadn't showed up, I might have died down here."

"I don't believe that," he said. "You're too strong to merely give up. You'd have eventually made your way to the entrance." He patted her shoulder. "Which we still have to find. Come on. Let's get out of here."

Crawling through the tunnel was an agonizing process. His knees, ribs and shoulders protested with every movement. But he could still feel a strong flow of fresh air from the air shaft behind them toward some opening ahead.

After another half hour of crawling, the tunnel widened and became taller. Graham struggled to his feet, then turned to help Emma.

"I see an opening!" she cried, and pointed ahead, where pale light streamed through a gap between the rocks.

They raced toward the opening and began clambering up a pile of rubble that half blocked the mine entrance. Emma had almost reached the top, ready to run outside, when Graham grabbed her and pulled her back, just as bullets slammed into the rocks near where her head had been seconds before.

In the ringing silence that followed, she clung to him, breathing hard. "Did you see anyone?"

"No. I just had a feeling. If I'd dumped two people in here, but I wasn't sure of their condition, I'd station a gunman outside, to pick them off when they emerged."

"That's sick."

"Does that really surprise you?"

She glanced up at the opening, longing on her face. "I guess not. So what do we do?"

He withdrew his service weapon from the holster at his side. "I can create a distraction while you make a break for it."

"But where would I go? There might be half a dozen of them out there, waiting to grab me. Besides, if I leave, you'll be stranded."

He removed his hand from the gun. "You're right. We need to get a better idea of how many people are out there, and where they are."

"How are we going to do that?"

"I'm going to try to see out, without them seeing me." He put on the night-vision goggles, then took off the pack and dropped it at her feet. "You stay down here. I'll be right back." Keeping low, he crawled up the cascade of rubble that had either fallen, or been dumped into the mine entrance. He kept to the side of the opening, out of the moonlight, but opposite the direction from which he thought the gunfire had come. He doubted Prentice or whoever was behind this would send more than two people to babysit the cave opening, but he couldn't take the chance that he was wrong.

He lay on his stomach at the top of the opening and drew the pistol once more. Extending his arm, he squeezed off three shots in rapid succession. Then he threw himself farther to the side, out of reach of the barrage of gunfire that immediately answered his challenge. He picked up at rock and fired a fastball toward the shooters, drawing another round of fire.

He slid back down the rubble to where Emma waited, arms folded across her chest. "Since you seem to be all right, I won't waste my breath lecturing you on the foolishness of risking your life," she said.

"There's two of them, and they're both positioned under one of those pop-up shade shelters, next to a Jeep, to one side of the mine entrance. They've got a perfect view of the opening, and at that close range, even in the dark they'd mow us down with no trouble at all."

"Then why do you sound so cheerful?" she asked.

"Because—since they assume they have all the advantages, they've gotten lazy. They've positioned themselves too close to the entrance, they've lit a lantern and both of them are together, instead of spread out."

"So you're going to shoot them before they shoot you?" She shifted her gaze to the pistol.

He shook his head. "I couldn't get a good aim without presenting myself as a clear target, and they could too easily see me first and duck down behind the Jeep."

"Then what are you going to do?"

"I'm going to give them a bigger problem to think about than the two of us." He started back down the tunnel, retreating the way they'd come.

"Where are you going?" she cried, hurrying to follow him.

"I just need to retrieve a couple of things." Now that he knew where he was going, the trip down the narrow corridor didn't seem to take as long. He dragged himself along, ignoring the pain, focused on his plan. If this didn't work, he and Emma would probably both end up dead. Maybe the smart thing was to wait for help to arrive. By now the other Rangers must be looking for them.

But any moment now, the two guards under the shade canopy might grow bored with waiting and decide to come in after them. He and Emma and his pistol stood little chance against the two guards and their AR-15s. Better to risk escape while they still had a chance.

He stopped at the entrance to the storage tunnel that held the missile and began unbuttoning his shirt. "Not that I don't love the sight of you naked, Captain, but now doesn't quite seem the time," she said.

"I don't want to bother taking off the sling." He extended one arm to her. "See if you can start a tear and rip most of the shirt off me."

"This is sounding more interesting all the time. What are you planning?"

"I need the torn fabric to make a fuse."

She didn't ask "a fuse for what?" Instead, she grasped the hem of the shirt and bit at it, then ripped at the resulting small tear, splitting the shirt in half. She slid it off his shoulder and held it out to him.

"Could you tear it into strips, about an inch and a half to two inches wide?"

While she worked on the cloth, he ducked into the storage chamber and fished two glass Coke bottles from the pile of trash. Then he headed for the gas cans stashed in the corner. Grasping the nearest one, he heard the satisfying slosh of the contents. Quickly, he filled both bottles two-thirds full, then he made his way back to Emma, careful not to spill the gas.

She wrinkled her nose as he approached. "Do I smell gasoline?"

"You do." He knelt and stuffed a long strip of rag into each bottle.

"Molotov cocktails?" she asked.

"Exactly. How's your pitching arm?" he asked.

"I throw like a girl. But I was on a pretty good interleague softball team two summers ago and I held my own."

"Do you think you could throw one of these about thirty feet?"

"I could probably manage that. What am I aiming for?"

"Their Jeep. I'm going to try to pitch the other one into their shade canopy. While they're dealing with the resultant fire and explosions, we make a break for it."

"Do you have a lighter?"

"I do." He reached into his pack. "Once these are lit, we have to get rid of them fast. And be careful not to spill any gasoline on you on your way over the rubble."

"We're not in a big hurry to get up there, right?" she said. "I'll crawl carefully. And here. I'd better ditch these." She slipped off the red high heels and stuffed them into the pack. "I might want them later, but for now I'll do better without them."

He slipped the pack over his shoulder once more and, each holding a bottle, they crept back up the tunnel to the mine entrance. "You'll need to stand up to get the best trajectory," he said. "The moment right before you release the bottle is the most dangerous, when they might see you and fire. So I'll go first."

"How chivalrous."

"It's not just chivalry. I can throw harder and farther, so I don't have to move as far forward into the opening." None of that played into his reasoning, of course. But in order to protect Emma, he needed to appeal to her sense of independence and fair play. She'd appreciate logic and facts more than emotions.

"I don't know whether to be insulted or impressed that with one arm in a sling you still think you can throw farther and harder than me."

"Emma, this isn't up for debate. I'll throw my bomb, then you throw yours."

"I wasn't objecting to your orders, merely your reasoning." She stepped forward and kissed his cheek, her lips a soft caress, unexpected in the tension of the moment. "Thanks for trying to distract me," she said. "And for not getting mushy. I don't think I could take that."

"I'll save the mush for later." He stared into her eyes. If these were his last moments on earth, he couldn't think of a better last image to take with him. "We're going to get out of this," he said.

She nodded. "I trust you."

He angled his hip toward her. "The lighter's in my pocket. You're going to have to ignite the fuses."

She fished out the lighter, fumbling a little. "Sorry," she said. "My hands are shaking."

"You're doing fine. Light mine, and as soon as I've launched it, light yours, throw it and run like hell. Head right, as far away from them as you can."

"Okay." She took a deep breath. "Are you ready?"

"Ready."

The lighter flared, and she held the flame to the end of the cloth fuse. It smoldered, then caught. "Step back," he said as he raised his arm for his windup.

The bomb sailed in a perfect arc and landed on top of the shade canopy, where it exploded, raining fire down onto the two guards beneath. Graham stepped to one side and Emma moved up. She tossed underhand, but her aim was just as effective. The bomb exploded in the front seat of the Jeep.

"Run!" he shouted, and took off.

EMMA WOULD HAVE given a month's worth of chocolate for a pair of tennis shoes just then. Sharp rocks cut into her feet, and she repeatedly stumbled on the uneven ground, stubbing her toes and twisting her ankles. But terror was a powerful anesthetic, and she scarcely felt the pain as she followed Graham on an undulating course through the rock and scrub. She struggled for breath and clutched at the stitch in her side. Tears streamed down her face and one knee began to throb. But still she ran, too afraid to stop, or even to risk a look back.

After what felt like an hour, but was probably only ten minutes or so, Graham slowed and dropped down behind a large boulder. "Let's...rest...a minute," he panted.

She collapsed beside him and rested her forehead on her drawn-up knees. "What's happening back there?" she asked. "Can you see?"

"I can see the glow from the fire. They're probably trying to put it out. It doesn't look like they're following."

"But they probably will follow, eventually," she said.

"We won't be that difficult to track." She looked down at her bruised, bleeding feet. "And I won't be able to go much farther without shoes," she said.

He rummaged in the backpack and pulled out a pair of thick wool socks. "Put these on. They won't help much, but they're better than nothing."

She slid on the socks. "What else do you have in that magic pack of yours?" she asked. "Any chocolate?"

"No chocolate. A space blanket, duct tape, a whistle, a mirror and fire starters. Basic survival gear."

"Socks."

"Wet feet or blisters will slow you down faster than almost anything."

"Well, I'm glad you have them. I think they'll help some."

"If things get too bad, I'll carry you," he said.

The image of Graham trying to lug her five-eleven, well-padded frame across the prairie surprised a laugh from her. "You will do no such thing. I'd be more likely to be able to carry you."

"Don't test me, Emma. A fireman's carry can be pretty uncomfortable, but effective. Don't think I won't sling you over my shoulder if I have to."

"You won't have to." She wouldn't make another complaint, and she would keep up, even if her feet fell off.

"Are you about ready to move on?" he asked. "We shouldn't stay in one place too long."

"All right." She shoved to her feet, biting her lip to keep from crying out.

"We don't have to run." He took her hand. "We can walk."

Even walking was painful, though she forced herself

to keep putting one foot in front of the other without complaint. They stayed in the cover of trees and rocks as much as possible, but the added darkness made walking that much more difficult. She kept tripping over rocks and roots and she felt bruised all over. That last drink of water in the mine was a fond memory. "Where are we going?" she asked.

"We're headed for the highway. Once there, we should be able to flag someone down and call headquarters."

"How do you know which way to go?"

"I have a good sense of direction."

Of course he did. Not that she wasn't glad he was so competent, but being in a relationship with a superhero was just a little intimidating. She wasn't used to having someone who was so capable of looking after her. After so many years of relying only on herself, the idea that someone else was looking out for her unsettled her. Not that she couldn't get used to it. A little more time in his arms and she might willingly let him carry her—or at least try.

A low droning, like the buzzing of a large bee, vibrated the air around her. She looked around, but saw nothing. "What is that?" she asked.

Graham stopped and listened. "I don't know." He looked around them, then pulled her into the shelter of a group of piñons. The buzzing noise grew louder.

"Is it a glider, or something?" Emma pointed at a light in the sky. The glowing light gradually grew larger, the buzzing louder. "I know—it's one of those remote-controlled planes," she said. "My neighbor used to belong to a club for people who met every weekend to fly their planes, some of which cost thousands of dollars.

Someone must have driven out here to practice their hobby. Maybe he has a phone." She started to move out from the cover of the trees, but Graham pulled her back.

"No one's going to be out here in the middle of the night flying a hobby plane." He'd fished a pair of binoculars from the pack and had them focused on the light. "Though you're right that it's remote-controlled, after a fashion." He handed her the glasses.

She studied the gray, futuristic-looking craft. She'd seen photographs in the newspaper, but surely this couldn't be. Did thirst make people hallucinate? She swallowed hard, and forced the words past her parched lips. "Is that a drone?"

# Chapter Fourteen

Graham restowed the binoculars in the pack. "It's a drone," he said. More proof that Prentice was behind this. Who else in the area could afford such an exotic toy? "Instead of sending men to look for us, Prentice sent out his drone. He can use it to pinpoint our position, then send someone out to pick us off."

The drone buzzed slowly over the copse of trees that shielded them. "Can it see us down here?" Emma asked.

"Probably not, if it's just equipped with a camera. An infrared scanner could spot us, though."

"Prentice can afford all the hottest technology toys," she said. "I'm betting he sprang for the infrared."

"Whether or not it can see us, as soon as we can, we should move on," he said. "We need to find a good place to hide, and to make a stand if they come for us."

"I'm not going to cower behind some rock and let them kill me." Anger brought a flush to her pale cheeks and glittered in her eyes. "I'm sick of these people seeing me as a victim—someone they can pick off at will. I'm going to show them I'll fight back with everything I have."

"You were never a victim." He pulled her close. "You're one of the strongest women I know."

"So you're not going to tell me if I had minded my own business and let the police do their work unhampered by my badgering, I wouldn't be in this fix—and you wouldn't, either, for that matter?"

"I'd as soon try to tell water to run uphill."

"That's not how you acted when we first met. You made it plain I was the enemy."

He wanted to deny the charge, but Emma would see through the lie. "I might have thought that when we first met, but no more. You were right to push for more information, and though I didn't always agree with your methods, it's clear you've struck a nerve. Thanks to your prodding, Prentice has showed his hand. I think this case is about to break wide-open, and I owe part of the credit to you."

"You're not the only one who's big enough to admit to a change of opinion," she said. "I've seen how hard you work, and how good you are at your job. You would have solved this case without me. I only sped things up a bit."

The buzzing of the drone increased as it made another pass. "We haven't solved anything yet," Graham said. "I'm more sure of my suspicions, but I don't have proof. But as soon as we're safe again, I'll set about getting it. Prentice and his expensive lawyers won't slip away this time."

The drone passed overhead, then headed west, away from them. Graham took his arm from around Emma. "We'd better go," he said.

He kept their course toward the road, moving as quickly as they could. Emma limped along, grim faced and in obvious pain, but uncomplaining. Her fashionable dress was streaked with dirt from the mine, the hem undone on one side and her hair a wild tangle. Most of her makeup had worn off. But her spirit and determination struck him as more beautiful than any physical perfection.

After this was all over, he'd ask her to go on vacation with him. To the beach, or a lake, where they could be alone and truly get to know each other better. Somewhere far away from drug runners and drones.

"Do you see any place to hide and make our stand?" she asked.

"No." Unfortunately, the closer they got to the main highway, the more open the terrain. The ground sloped gradually toward a valley, the coarse, gravelly soil pocked with clumps of sage and bunchgrass and the occasional spiky prickly pear. If there had ever been trees here, they'd been cut down a generation ago to build fences, houses and corrals for the ranchers who had once homesteaded the land. The almost full moon shone down like a spotlight, making him and Emma visible to anyone who might be searching for them. Their only hope was to reach the highway, and help, before their enemies found them.

"Then I think we're in trouble," Emma said. She sounded calm, but when he turned to look back at her, she'd turned sickly pale. She pointed behind her. "Someone's coming, and they're in a hurry."

Two headlights headed directly toward them. Within minutes, the vehicle would be on them, but long before that, they'd be in range of a rifle.

"Get behind me." Graham pulled her behind his back and drew his gun. If a gunman in the Jeep decided to pick them off they'd both be dead within seconds, but if their goal was to take the two of them prisoner, he might have a chance, at least, to do some damage before they were taken.

Emma's fingers dug into his unhurt shoulder. "Should we surrender?" she asked. "Ask for mercy?"

"These people haven't shown a lot of mercy so far." He tightened his grip on the weapon. "When they get closer, run," he said. "I'll hold them off as long as I can."

"Graham, that's suicide."

"Then at least I'll have died protecting someone I love." It was the closest he could come to professing his feelings for her. He hoped she didn't think the words sounded forced or phony. He meant them with all his heart, even if he would have chosen a better time to say them.

In answer, she squeezed harder and pressed her face against his back, saying nothing.

The vehicle was close enough now that he could make out that it was similar to the ones Prentice's guards drove. The glare of the headlights prevented him from seeing much, though he thought he saw the silhouette of two men, a passenger and a driver. At least one of the men was armed, the butt of the weapon braced on his thigh. Graham took careful aim. A few more seconds, and they'd be within range.

# Chapter Fifteen

The vehicle skidded to a halt, just out of range of Graham's pistol. "Captain, don't shoot!" the passenger called. "It's us—we've come to save you."

"Oh my gosh!" Emma moved out from behind him. "It's Lieutenant Dance and Sergeant Cruz."

Graham holstered his weapon and followed Emma toward the Jeep. The driver—Marco Cruz—started the vehicle and met them before they'd walked more than a dozen feet. "We're sure glad to see you two," Michael said.

"This is one of Prentice's Jeeps, isn't it?" Emma asked. "And those uniforms—how—?"

"Get in and we'll explain later," Marco said. "We have to get out of here."

Emma and Graham piled in the backseat. Graham didn't need to know how these two had found him or why they were masquerading as Prentice's guards. Not now. He sagged against the seat and closed his eyes, aware for the first time in hours of a dragging fatigue.

"Are you okay, Captain?" Michael shoved a bottle of water into Graham's hand and nodded to the sling. "Should I radio ahead for an ambulance?"

"Yes," Emma said. She twisted the cap off her own water bottle and drank greedily.

"I'm not going to the hospital," Graham said.

"He's got broken ribs and a separated shoulder," she said. "He needs to be checked out."

"What about you, ma'am?" Michael asked, clearly trying not to stare at her ruined dress and wild hair.

"My feet are one big blister and I'm exhausted, but it's nothing a long bath and a good night's sleep won't help. The captain is the one I'm worried about."

"You don't need to worry about me," he said.

She patted his arm. "Humor me."

Now that the danger was past, she was back to being her bossy, independent self. But he couldn't say he didn't like it.

"How did you find us?" she asked Michael.

"We've been driving around, looking for you," Michael said. "We figured once you left the mine, you'd head for the road, so we've been searching a grid. We got lucky."

"The luck is all ours," Emma said. "I don't know how much longer we'd have lasted out there by ourselves."

"Marco, what happened after you left me at the ventilation shaft?" Graham asked.

"We got into a firefight with a couple of guards who were stationed at the mine entrance. We didn't like leaving you there, but they didn't give us much of a choice. Randall took a bullet in the arm, but he'll be okay."

"Is Lotte okay?" Graham asked.

"Yes, sir. We put together a team to try to go in again and rescue you, but by the time we got there, the place was deserted—no guards and the mine was empty. That's when we set out searching for you."

"But the Jeep and the uniforms," Emma asked. "Are they Prentice's?"

"Nah," Michael said. "We borrowed the Jeep from the sheriff's department, and the uniforms are from the local army surplus story. We figured if we were going to be driving around near Prentice's place it would be a good idea to blend in."

"Did you see anyone else while you were searching for us?" Graham asked.

"Not a soul," Michael said. "The mine looked as if no one had been near it in decades."

"Too clean." Marco spoke for the first time. "They practically sanitized the place."

"Did you see the drone?" Emma asked.

"Is that what that was?" Michael asked. "We saw something, but it was so far away, we weren't sure."

"Was it armed?" Marco asked.

"No," Graham said. "He doesn't have the missile yet. Or at least, he doesn't have it with the drone. It's stashed in a side tunnel of the mine where we were trapped." He leaned forward in the seat. "Who else is out looking for us?"

"Carmen and Simon have a Jeep like this one," Marco said.

"We need to call and let them know we've found you okay." Michael picked up the radio.

"Give me that," Graham said. "I want them to watch the mine. As soon as I can get patched up and Emma's safe, we need to go back and stake out the location. They won't want to leave the missile there, now that they know we must have spotted it."

"I'll go with you," Emma said.

"No. It's too dangerous." And he couldn't focus on his job while he was worried about her.

"You've heard of embedded reporters? I'm your embedded reporter." She glared at him, chin up, arms crossed, eyes blazing. "I haven't been through all of this to miss out on the story of my career. I promise I'll stay out of your way, but I want to be there."

Though Michael and Marco faced forward, Graham knew they were taking in every word of this conversation. He didn't want to fight with Emma, not when they'd suffered so much already. And she'd proved she could keep her head in tense situations. "You can come," he said. "But you have to stay in a vehicle until I say it's safe for you to come out."

"I love it when you try to give me orders." Her tone was teasing and sexy, sending a shiver of desire through him. She was the most aggravating, challenging, confusing woman he'd ever met.

And he didn't know how he'd made it this far without her.

WHILE THE PARAMEDICS tended to Graham, Michael found camo pants and a shirt to replace Emma's ruined dress. Marco contributed a pair of boots; he and Emma wore the same size. With blisters bandaged and fresh socks she felt, if not 100 percent, at least ready to face whatever came next. When she joined the others in the conference room, the sun was just showing over the horizon. Graham had changed into a new uniform, and a fresh black sling supported his arm. "How are you feeling?" he asked.

"I'm not up to running a marathon, but that wasn't on my to-do list for today, anyway. What about you?"

"I'm fine." He turned to the others. "Carmen and Simon report no one's returned to the mine yet, but we know they will. They can't leave the missile there now that we know about it."

"They'll probably wait until it's dark again," Michael said. "Moving it in the daylight would be risky."

"Maybe." Graham walked to the whiteboard on the wall behind him and began sketching. Emma recognized a map of the mine interior. "We want to be in place, hidden and waiting for them," he said.

"You'll go back into the mine?" Emma's stomach rolled at the thought.

"The mine is the best place to hide, to catch them with the missile," he said. "I don't want anyone later claiming they didn't know it was there."

She pressed her lips together, wanting to object, but knowing she had no right. She didn't want Graham telling her how to do her job, so she wouldn't tell him how to do his. She crossed her arms and glared at him, hoping he'd read the message in her eyes, even if she couldn't say the words. A man with busted ribs and the use of only one arm had no business going down into a hole in the ground to face people who wanted to kill him.

"Marco, I want you and Michael stationed in the mine, in the chamber with the missile." He indicated the niche along the corridor that connected the air shaft and the mine entrance. "I'll put Carmen and Simon near the entrance."

"Where will you be?" Michael asked.

"I'll be parked here, behind these rocks." He sketched in a pile of boulders, to one side of the entrance. "Emma, you'll be with me."

She let out the breath she hadn't even realized she'd been holding. As long as she was with Graham, they'd both be all right. A silly superstition maybe, but one she believed.

EMMA WAS ABLE to catch a few hours' sleep on a cot in a back room at Ranger headquarters. Graham refused to go home to sleep, so she stayed also, though she tossed and turned, worried about the night ahead. Going anywhere near Richard Prentice again frightened her, but they couldn't let him get away with whatever he had planned for that missile.

At seven, the team began gathering at headquarters. Graham briefed them again on their assignments for the evening. Rather than watch Graham as he spoke, Emma studied the faces of the team. They trusted the captain with their lives; their confidence in him showed in their attention to his words and in the determined expressions on their faces. Emma knew she could trust him, too.

Everything happened very quickly after that. They all put on body armor; after some scrambling, they unearthed a Kevlar vest that left Emma's breasts only somewhat squashed. A heavy helmet with visor was guaranteed to give her a headache, but she didn't dare complain. When Marco began handing out weapons she started to ask for one, then stopped herself. She probably couldn't hit the side of a barn, even if she could figure out how to fire a gun. Instead, she asked for the one weapon with which she was truly proficient. "I need a notebook and a pen," she said.

"What for?" Graham asked.

"I need to record everything that happens."

"So you can write about it for the paper?" He didn't look pleased with the idea.

"Yes. But think how handy an eyewitness report by a civilian might be in court later."

"Michael, there's a notebook and pens in my desk."

Thus armed, she followed the others out to the Cruisers. Graham said nothing as he drove along the paved park road, headed for Curecanti Recreation Area. Emma followed his lead and kept silent, and tried not to think of the danger that lay ahead. Instead, she focused on Richard Prentice. Was he really behind all of this? The idea of him with a gun, killing anyone, was so out of place with his businessman's image.

Then again, maybe he never actually pulled a trigger. Instead, he paid others to do his dirty work.

After half an hour, they reached the turnoff from the paved highway onto the dirt track that led across Curecanti Recreation area to the mine. They sped across the rough ground, the ride jarring and even painful, but Emma held on and said nothing. She wouldn't give Graham a reason to regret including her. Near the mine, the team split up. Michael and Marco headed across the desert, while Graham maneuvered the Cruiser behind the boulders, until it was hidden from anyone who approached the mine entrance.

He unbuckled his seat belt and Emma did the same, then they sat in silence, listening to the ping of the cooling engine. In spite of the cooling night air within seconds she was sweating under the body armor. The helmet hurt her head and her feet ached. Graham had to be feeling even worse, but he didn't show it.

"What do we do now?" she asked.

"We wait."

The silence closed around them once more. She shifted in her seat and glanced at Graham, his face impassive, gaze focused on the horizon. Did he even remember she was here? They had so much they could talk about. Where was their relationship going? Could they really make it together? Did he still see her as the enemy reporter, or had his feelings changed?

But she already knew he wasn't a talker. Under duress, he'd admitted he loved her. That would have to be enough.

The radio crackled. "We're in place in the tunnel," Cruz said. "But there's a problem."

Graham keyed the mic. "Go ahead."

"We're in the passage between the entrance and the air shaft. It's like you described it, a storage area, with boxes and gas cans. But no missile."

"Could you repeat that? I didn't copy."

"The missile's gone, Captain. They got here ahead of us."

# Chapter Sixteen

Graham might have stayed at the mine all night while evidence techs combed over the tunnels and the surrounding areas, searching for any clue to the missile's whereabouts. But Emma persuaded him to take her home. He might not admit that he himself was worn-out, but he'd given in for her sake.

Janey greeted them at the door to his house, her indignant yowls letting Emma know she was not pleased by her empty supper dish. "Yes, you're so neglected," Emma cooed, cuddling the cat to her. She smiled at Graham over the top of the cat's head. "As soon as she's fed, all I want is a hot shower, a glass of wine and a bowl of soup," she said.

"You get your shower first," he said. "I'll open the wine."

"I like the way you think." As soon as Janey was purring over a bowl of Seafood Deluxe, she headed for the bedroom, stripping on her way to the shower, where she stood under the spray with her eyes closed, letting the hot water pummel away all the pain and fear of the past thirty-six hours.

She emerged from the bathroom a half hour later, hair freshly washed and blow-dried, her body shaved and moisturized and smelling of vanilla and lavender. Graham sat on the edge of the bed, a glass of wine in his hand, which he offered to her.

"You're a saint," she said as she took the wine. "My favorite person, next to whoever invented indoor plumbing. There's nothing like a hot shower for making me feel human again." She sat on the bed next to him and sipped the cold, crisp wine.

"I'll have to settle for a bath," he said. "I'm supposed to keep these bandages dry."

She caressed his uninjured shoulder. "Want some help?"

"I don't want you to think you have to play nurse."

"Who said anything about nurse?" She slid one hand beneath the open collar of his uniform shirt. "I was thinking I'd offer to scrub your back."

"I'm probably too tired for anything else."

"So am I. This will just be a nice, relaxing bath."

He slid his fingers into her hair at the back of her head. "I can't say I wouldn't enjoy the company."

The master bathroom featured an oversize soaking tub in addition to the steam shower. Emma started the water, then helped Graham out of the sling and his clothes. Bandages swathed his upper torso and wrapped one shoulder. "Does it hurt much?" she asked, kissing the white cotton over his heart.

"I'll live."

She shut off the water when it reached his waist, then climbed in after him and picked up a washcloth and a bar of soap. "No fair," he said. "I didn't get to wash you," he said.

"Maybe next time. Now close your eyes and relax."

He submitted to her ministrations, but he kept his

eyes open, his gaze as intense as a touch, caressing her bare breasts and shoulders. She washed his shoulders, arms and upper back, then transferred her attention to his stomach and hips, deliberately skipping over his very obvious erection. She set aside the washcloth in favor of her hands, caressing and stroking every inch of him, enjoying the sensuality of warm water and silken soap, and the slow burn of building desire.

He grabbed her wrist and guided her hand to his arousal. "You're forgetting something," he said.

She stroked him, watching the passion flare in his eyes. "I thought you were tired," she teased.

"I am. Exhausted. And you still turn me on." He pulled her close, pressing her breasts against his chest, and kissed her, his mouth urgent, tongue probing. His eagerness banished her own weariness, as desire surged within her, almost overwhelming in its intensity. Water sloshed, and the soap disappeared somewhere beneath them.

"Let's get out of this tub," she said.

He stood, pulling her to her feet with him. She grabbed a towel for herself and one for him, and followed him into the bedroom. Fifteen minutes before, she'd been certain she'd fall asleep as soon as her head hit the pillow, but the reality of the man beside her trumped any dreams sleep might conjure.

They made love gently, avoiding bruises and bandages, the necessity to take things more slowly adding sweetness and tension. Graham lay back against the pillows and she straddled him, his free hand caressing the small of her back while he kissed and suckled first one breast, then another. She arched against the base of his shaft, but he pushed her away, just enough to insert one finger into her, then another, while his thumb traced lazy circles around her arousal.

She moaned, gasping for breath on the edge of control. "Do you like that?" he asked, increasing the pressure of his thumb.

"Y-yes."

Then she lost the ability to talk as he increased his tempo, his mouth returning to pull hard on one breast, and then the other. She screamed his name as her climax ripped through her, then before she had time to recover he coaxed her to raise up enough that he could slide into her, filling her and starting the spiral of desire over again.

She couldn't have said how long she rode that wave of passion, crashing to shore only to climb again. When Graham finally cried out his release along with her she was utterly spent and utterly filled. She slid alongside him and laid her head on his uninjured shoulder, his arm tight around her.

"You're supposed to be hurt," she said. "I've been so worried. I'm not used to having to think about anybody but myself and Janey, and suddenly I can't stop thinking about you. That almost feels more dangerous to me than gunfire. Do you think I'm crazy?"

When he didn't answer, she lifted her head and studied his slack face, eyes closed, lips slightly parted. He breathed slowly and evenly, lost to the world—and to her—in sleep. She kissed his cheek and lay down once more. Maybe she was crazy. Or maybe—for the first time in a long time, or maybe forever—she was in love.

THIS IS WHAT *is must feel like to have been hit by a truck*, Graham thought. He lay in bed with his eyes closed, taking inventory of his aches and pains. Head, ribs, shoulder, legs—yep, pretty much everything hurt.

Then the scent of lavender and vanilla drifted to him, and he smiled in spite of the pain. Not everything had been bad. The end of the day had been pretty spectacular, in fact. Emma had moved him yesterday, both with her strength and bravery, and with her tenderness and passion. He'd never met another woman like her, and when he thought he'd lost her he'd felt bereft in a way he never thought possible. He wanted to show her, every moment he could, how much she'd come to mean to him.

He opened his eyes and rolled toward her, only to find her half of the bed empty. He checked the clock, which showed half past nine. He couldn't remember the last time he'd slept this late, but then again, he couldn't remember another day as eventful as yesterday. He rose and pulled on his robe, then went in search of Emma.

The aroma of coffee and the sound of tapping keys led him to his office, where he found Emma at his desk, laptop open in front of her. "Good morning," she said. Dressed in a blue silk top and jeans, her hair curling around her shoulders, she looked relaxed and content, nothing like a woman who had been knocked out, kidnapped, trapped in an abandoned mine and shot at by fleeing criminals.

"Good morning." He bent to kiss her, a long, slow embrace he hoped would persuade her to come back to bed.

She broke the contact, gently but firmly pushing him away. "You have to see what I've found," she said.

He recognized the determined gleam in her eyes. She was in work mode and there'd be no distracting her. He might as well shift gears, too. "Let me put on some clothes and grab some coffee and you can share your discovery."

"All right, but hurry. This is too good to keep to myself long."

Ten minutes later he was back at her side, dressed and caffeinated, feeling slightly less stiff and sore. He pulled a chair alongside her. "What have you got?"

"I've been researching the women in Richard Prentice's life," she said.

"You're looking for the owner of the cosmetics and other stuff in his guest bathroom."

She nodded. "It bugs me that he had the stuff locked away. And when I asked about romantic interests, he was so coy."

"I get that you're curious, but does this have anything to do with what happened yesterday?" he asked.

"Maybe. I might have ended up at the bottom of that air shaft because Prentice knew I'd found the things locked away in the bathroom. Or, I might have found another angle to explore. Take a look at this." She indicated a document on the computer screen. "This is the article from a late May issue of the *Denver Post*. Check out the photo."

The photograph that accompanied the article showed the billionaire, dressed in black tie and tails, with his arm around a slender, dark-haired beauty in a red designer gown that left little of her figure to the imagination. "Who is she?" Graham asked.

"Her name is Valentina Ferrari. According to various gossip columnists, she and Prentice were together a lot after that party."

"All right. But why should I be interested?"

"Her father is Jorge Ferrari, Venezuelan ambassador to the United States, appointed just a few months ago. For some time before that, Venezuela and the US didn't exchange ambassadors, due to strained relations. Ferrari's arrival was seen as a step forward in our relations with a country that is said to be sympathetic to terrorists. Another article I read said that Ferrari had pledged his government's cooperation in fighting suspected terrorists."

A cold chill swept through Graham. "Terrorists would love to get their hands on a Hellfire missile." He studied the photograph of Valentina, Prentice's arm around her, holding her close. "Maybe Valentina, or her father, has a connection to that missile and Prentice may or may not be in the clear."

"She could be serious about him, or she could be using him as a cover," Emma said. "Or we could be completely wrong."

"I'll put some feelers out and see if anyone in the Bureau has intel on Valentina and her dad."

"Do you have any indication Prentice is involved with the terrorists, too?" She frowned. "He didn't strike me as the type to link up with extremists. He likes to run his own show and, despite all the railing he does against government intrusion, he sees himself as a patriot."

"So do some of these jihadists. What else do you know about Valentina? Is there anything in her background to suggest she has extremist views?"

"Not really. Her mother died several years ago, so she's served as her father's official hostess. She's a part-time fashion model and has a degree in political science from NYU."

He tapped the screen. "Print me a copy of this. It may be nothing, but we'll check it out."

"It gets even more interesting." She scrolled down the page and enlarged a section of text. "Lauren Starling was at this same party. Her name is on a list of other guests, down near the bottom of the article. But it proves Prentice knew her, too."

"Maybe. Though it's possible they were both at the party and never met."

"Lauren strikes me as the type who would seek out a news-making billionaire, even if he'd somehow managed to overlook her," Emma said. "And admit it— Lauren isn't a woman many men would overlook."

The blue-eyed, blonde anchor woman would definitely turn heads, which made her disappearance all the more troubling. She wasn't the kind of woman who would easily blend into the background.

"I hadn't thought of questioning women Prentice might have associated with," he said. "It's a good idea. They would know things about him we don't. Anybody else we should look into?"

"I didn't find mention of anyone else since Valentina came onto the scene, but I did find this." She shrank the news article about the embassy gala and brought up another article, this one a small mention in the local paper. "Jorge Ferrari is coming to Colorado today—and not to Denver, but here, to Montrose."

"Why is the ambassador from Venezuela coming here?" The relatively small town wasn't a center of industry, government or education.

"The paper says he's here 'on business.' I suppose it's possible a local company has some sort of trade agreement or something with the Venezuelan government."

Graham frowned. "Is his daughter coming with him?"

"The paper doesn't mention it. Here, I printed you a copy of that article, too." She handed him a sheaf of papers, then pushed back her chair. "I think I'll head out to the airport and ask the ambassador a few questions."

"That's not a good idea," he said. "Until we know who attacked you, and why, you should stay here." He wanted her safe and out of sight.

"I'll be careful." She stood and slung her purse over one shoulder. "I had the rental car company drop off a new ride for me this morning. I'm going to stop in town and get a new phone and I'll be all set."

He rose, also. "Emma, don't be foolish," he said. "We still don't know who kidnapped you. You could still be in danger."

She set her mouth in a stubborn line he was all too familiar with. "Whoever attacked me yesterday wants me to be timid and afraid," she said. "If I stay here, hiding, I'm doing what they want. I can't let them have that kind of power over me."

"Emma, please." He tried to reign in his exasperation, but couldn't keep the edge from his voice. "I can't do my job if I'm worried about you. Whatever you have to do, it can wait until we've cleared this case and you're out of danger."

"I can't put my life on hold until you decide it's safe for me to go out!"

"And I can't let you risk your life foolishly." His voice rose to match hers.

"You can't stop me, either." She headed for the door.

"Emma, wait!"

"No, Graham. I won't wait. And you don't have any

right to ask me to." She left, slamming the door behind her.

He glared at the closed door, wanting to run after her and drag her back, but knowing that would only make her angrier. Maybe he didn't have a right to ask her to stay here, where she'd be safe. But didn't the love they shared entitle him to some consideration? Was she so independent that she couldn't consider his feelings at all? Or was being independent more important than her feelings for him?

# Chapter Seventeen

Fighting with Graham made Emma feel sick to her stomach. He wasn't the type to cower inside when someone was after him, so why should he expect that of her? Even if he only wanted to protect her, the best way to do that was for both of them to work toward finding out who was responsible for harassing her. Since the only two stories she'd been working on when the threats started were Bobby's Pace's murder and Lauren Starling's disappearance, solving those two mysteries should give them the answers they needed.

After a quick stop to buy a new cell phone and restore all her contacts, she drove to the airport, checking her mirrors often to make sure no one was following her. She saw nothing suspicious, and by the time she reached the airport, most of her usual confidence had returned. She'd purposely arrived earlier than the ambassador, in order to stake out a prime location and to do a little background research. She headed for Fixed Base Operations and greeted the group of men gathered in the pilot's lounge. "I hope you gentlemen can help me," she said.

"Yes, ma'am." A stocky older man stepped out from behind the counter at one end of the room and offered his hand. "Eddie Silvada, Fixed Base Operations. What can we do for you?"

"She was talking to us, Eddie," a wiry man at the table said.

"I'm sure you can all help." She took the photo of Valentina from the paper and laid it on the table. "Have any of you seen this woman here at the airport in the last week or two? Or anytime, really?"

They passed the picture around, most shaking their heads. "I think I'd remember her," the wiry man said.

"I don't remember her," Eddie said.

The man at the far end of the table, his gray hair pulled back in a ponytail, took a pair of glasses from his shirt pocket and slipped them on. He scrutinized the picture. "She wasn't this dressed up when I saw her, but I'm pretty sure it's the same woman. She was in here a couple of weeks ago. She wanted to hire a pilot."

Emma's heart sped up. "Did she give you a name?"

"She called herself Val. Sounded foreign, maybe Mexican or Spanish? She offered to pay cash, so I didn't ask too many questions."

"Why didn't you tell the police about this when they were here?" she asked.

"They wanted to know about Bobby Pace," he said. "Nobody asked if a gorgeous woman stopped by, wanting to hire a pilot."

"Where was I when this was going on?" Eddie asked.

"I don't know," he said. "Maybe you were in the bathroom."

"Did she hire Bobby Pace?" Emma asked.

"No," the man with the ponytail said. "She hired Fred Gaskin."

So much for thinking she finally had the answer she needed. "Who's Fred Gaskin?" she asked.

"He was here a little while ago." Eddie looked around, as if Fred might pop out from behind the vending machines.

"I think he's out by his plane." A younger man turned in his chair and pointed out the window, toward the airfield. "Look for a red-and-white Beechcraft, parked on the west side. Fred's got red hair—you can't miss him."

She thanked them, and hurried out the door and across the tarmac toward the line of small planes tethered a short distance from the runway. The red-and-white Beechcraft was third in line, and a lanky man with fading red hair looked up from the engine cowling at her approach. "Can I help you?" he asked.

"Are you Fred?" She offered her hand. "I'm Emma."

He wiped his hand on his jeans before shaking hers. "What can I do for you?"

"I understand this woman hired you to fly her a couple of weeks ago." She showed him the picture of Valentina.

He studied the picture, then shook his head. "No, ma'am. You must have the wrong guy. I've never seen her before."

"But a man in there, with a gray ponytail, said she hired you." Why hadn't she stopped to get the man's name?

"Tony said that?"

"He said she came by, looking for a pilot, and he referred her to you."

He bobbed his head up and down. "I remember now. I never actually saw her—she called me on the phone. Said she needed somebody to fly her to Rhode Island for a quick trip. The plan was to stop there overnight, then come back here. You a friend of hers?"

"More of an acquaintance. When was this?"

"Hang on and I'll tell you." He walked around to the other side of the plane, leaned into the cockpit and pulled out a brown vinyl-covered day planner. He flipped through the dog-eared pages. "I talked to her on Thursday. We were supposed to fly out Saturday and come back the next day, the twentieth."

The coroner had estimated that Bobby had died on the twenty-first. If he and Val had left Montrose as planned, on Saturday the nineteenth, it was possible they'd been delayed in Newport. Or maybe they hadn't flown out until Sunday. "You said 'supposed to.' Did things not work out that way?"

"I ended up in the hospital on Friday with acute appendicitis." He made a rueful face. "I sure hated to miss out on the money, but no way could I make the trip."

"How much was she offering to pay you?"

He rubbed his hand across his jaw. "I don't know if I should say."

"Why not?"

"It might put me in a bad light. Let's just say it was a lot. More than I usually get from tourists who want a quick look around, or businessmen who need to get from one place to another in a hurry. What's it to you, anyway?"

"I'm trying to find her, that's all. Was it enough money that you thought maybe she was doing something illegal?"

"The thought did cross my mind. She said we'd be picking up a crate with some tractor parts her cousin in Durango needed right away."

"But you didn't really think it was tractor parts?"

He shrugged. "Who offers ten thousand dollars plus expenses to fly tractor parts? Then again, what else are you gonna buy in Rhode Island?"

The smallest state in the union didn't strike Emma as a hotbed of terrorist activity, but Rhode Island was home to a major port. "When your appendix went bad, what did you do?" she asked.

"I called the number she'd given me and told her the trip was a no go. She was pretty upset. She rattled off a bunch of words in Spanish and from her tone of voice I gathered some of them weren't that nice. I gave her the numbers of some other pilots she could call who might do the work, though."

"Did one of those numbers belong to Bobby Pace?"

"Yeah." He let out a sigh. "When I heard Bobby had been shot, I wondered if it had anything to do with her."

"Why didn't you go to the police?" If he had, he might have saved them all a lot of trouble and heartache.

He held up both hands in a defensive gesture. "It wasn't really any of my business. Besides, if she was cold-blooded enough to shoot Bobby, she wouldn't think too long and hard about coming after me if she thought I'd betrayed her."

Plus, he might not get any more lucrative but possibly illegal flying jobs if word got around that he went running to the cops. "What was this woman's name?"

"All I know is Val. And before you ask, I threw away the number she gave me. Who are you, anyway? Are you a cop?"

"No. I'm a writer." But she knew a cop who would be very interested in talking to Fred. "I may need to make a quick trip to Denver soon," she said. "Do you have a card so I can get in touch with you about flying down there?"

He hesitated, then pulled a card from a pocket in the front of the day planner. "Call me. I'll give you a good rate."

"Thanks, Fred. I—"

But the rest of her words were cut off by the arrival of a sleek jet. The gleaming white fuselage dwarfed the two- and four-seat private planes tethered in sight of the runway, like an elite racing greyhound mingling with mongrels. The aircraft taxied to the end of the runway and came to a halt in front of the terminal. "Somebody with money," Fred said, raising his voice to be heard above the whine of the jet's engines. "Foreign, from the looks of that emblem on the tail."

Emma squinted at the red, blue and gold flag on the tail of the jet. She was no expert on foreign geography, but she was pretty sure the emblem indicated the plane was from Venezuela. A door to the rear of the aircraft opened and lowered to form steps leading to the tarmac. A swarthy man in a crisp navy suit and blue tie stepped out, followed by a red-faced, balding man Emma recognized from many television news stories and press conferences.

She grabbed her recorder and her notebook from her purse and raced toward the arriving dignitaries. "Ambassador Ferrari, why are you in Montrose?" she asked the darker man.

The ambassador looked down his long nose at her. "Who are you?"

"Emma Wade, with the *Denver Post*." She waved her library card in his direction. Her legitimate press pass had been destroyed in the fire at her house, but the library had been happy to issue her a new card on the spot yesterday morning when she stopped by on her way to Richard Prentice's ranch. "Do you have business locally?"

"The ambassador's business is none of your business." Senator Peter Mattheson stepped up as if to block the ambassador from Emma's view.

"Why are you traveling with the ambassador, Senator?" Emma asked.

"That's none of your business, either."

Fine. She didn't care about the blowhard senator, anyway. She turned once more to his finely dressed companion. "Ambassador Ferrari, can you tell me about your daughter's relationship with Mr. Prentice?"

"My daughter's affairs are her own concern," Ferrari said.

"Will you be seeing Mr. Prentice while you're here in Colorado?"

"I will be seeing many people while I visit your state." His smile was suave, polite and cold as ice.

"Mr. Prentice, as a concerned citizen, was kind enough to offer us any assistance he may provide while the ambassador is in Colorado," Mattheson said.

"Will Valentina Ferrari be staying at the Prentice ranch, also?" Emma asked.

"My daughter is a model," Ferrari said, cutting off Mattheson, who had opened his mouth to declaim some more. "She has a very busy schedule. I do not expect to see her during my short visit."

"But she is involved with Mr. Prentice?" Emma asked, pen poised over her notebook.

"No more questions." Ferrari moved past her, head erect and shoulders stiff.

"What about Lauren Starling?" Emma called after him. "Is she a friend of your daughter's or of Richard Prentice?"

He ignored her. Mattheson glared at her, then followed the ambassador toward the terminal.

That hadn't given her much, except to confirm that the ambassador knew Prentice and Mattheson. And the senator and the billionaire were well-known to be working together to try to disband The Ranger Brigade. But Emma couldn't see how this tied in with either Bobby Pace's murder or Lauren Starling's disappearance.

She hurried to the parking lot and slid behind the wheel of her rental in time to fall in behind the black Lexus that carried Mattheson and Ferrari. She didn't have anywhere in particular she had to be, so she might as well follow them for a while. Maybe she'd find out what Ferrari's mysterious business was. He'd probably come to Montrose, Colorado, to sample the sweet corn or something like that. Sure—and Emma was going to take a cue from his daughter and be a fashion model in her next career.

By the time the Lexus turned onto the highway headed out of town, Emma was sure the senator and the ambassador were headed toward Richard Prentice's ranch. Either that, or the ambassador had a desire to see the Black Canyon of the Gunnison. They had to be aware she was behind them, but she wasn't breaking any laws, traveling on a public highway. As it happened, she had to go this way, anyway, to get to Graham's house, though she had no intention of turning off before the Lexus did.

She pulled out her new cell phone and punched the button for the camera. When the Lexus did make a move, she wanted a picture. When she called Richard Prentice to ask why the Venezuelan ambassador paid him a visit, she didn't want him to try to deny that the ambassador had been there.

The Lexus signaled a turn onto the road leading to the park, and Emma prepared to follow. But the car swerved as she made the turn, so that she had to fight to keep it on the road. Heart pounding, she guided it to the side of the road. A check of the mirrors showed the coast was clear, so she got out and checked the tires. Sure enough, the front passenger side was flat. Sighing, she pulled out her phone to call AAA. But before she could make the connection, a familiar black-and-white Cruiser slid in behind her.

Randall Knightbridge exited the Cruiser, leaving the engine running. "Car trouble?" he asked.

"A flat." She motioned to the tire.

He frowned. "Looks like a bad one. Do you have a spare?"

"I have no idea. This is a rental. They dropped it off this morning."

"Pop the trunk and let's take a look."

She opened the trunk and he took out the spare tire and tools. "This shouldn't take long," he said, rolling up his sleeves.

"Are you sure about this?" she asked. "I heard you were shot."

"Nothing serious." He indicated the bandage on his right forearm, just below a tattoo of crossed lacrosse sticks. "It was just a scratch."

"Were you following me?" she asked, as he knelt and positioned the jack under the car's frame.

"I was headed back to headquarters." He looked up. "Why would you think I was following you?"

"Graham wasn't too happy when I left the house this morning. He thought I should stay out of sight and safe. I thought he might have asked one of you to keep an eye on me."

"No offense, ma'am, but we've got too much work to do to follow you around—even if the chief had asked. Which he didn't." He pumped the jack and the car began to rise. "What were you doing, anyway?"

"I tried to interview the ambassador from Venezuela about why he's visiting Colorado, but he didn't have much to say. Have you seen Graham this morning?"

"I saw him for a few minutes. He wasn't in a good mood." He hefted the old tire off the axle and rotated it slowly. "There's the problem." He fingered a slash in the sidewall. "Big enough to do real damage, but small enough you wouldn't discover it right away."

She leaned over him, frowning at the gash. "What caused that?"

"If I had to guess, I'd say either a pocketknife or a screwdriver. Jam it in quick, pull it out and be on your way." His eyes met hers. "The G-man's right. Someone is still out to hurt you."

She ignored the cold knot that had formed in her stomach. "This didn't hurt me. It just annoyed me."

"What if I hadn't come along right away?" He looked around them. "There's not a lot of traffic out here. Someone else could have driven up and grabbed you. Maybe that was even their plan."

She swallowed the bitter taste of fear. "I see your point. Are you going to tell Graham? It'll just make him more upset."

"I think you should be the one to tell him, not me."

"I can't let whoever is making these threats silence me," she said. "I can't let them frighten me into changing who I am."

He shoved the spare into place and began tightening the lug nuts. "I get that."

"I'm not sure Graham does."

"He's a smart guy. He'll figure it out."

"I hope so." She cared about him enough to be patient. But she couldn't keep fighting the same battle with him. She had to remain independent, to fight for what she believed in, no matter how anyone—including the man she loved—tried to stop her.

# Chapter Eighteen

Graham's head ached, but he welcomed the distraction from the different kind of pain in his heart. Better not think about Emma right now; he had to focus on work. "What did we turn up at the mine yesterday?" he asked.

"Not much," Carmen said. She handed out copies of a spreadsheet. "This is an inventory of all the evidence we have that may or may not be related to Bobby Pace's death, as well as everything we've managed to compile from the fire at Emma's house and her kidnapping yesterday."

Graham frowned at the slim list under the heading *Emma*. "Not much," he said. "Not enough." The evidence in Pace's murder wasn't much better—a single thumbprint and a few partial fingerprints from the cockpit that they hadn't been able to link to Pace or anyone he knew, the spent bullet that had lodged in his chest, the busted crate from the missile and his incomplete logbook, plus lots of photographs of the body, the wrecked plane and the surrounding terrain. At the mine, they had a few mostly generic tire tracks, Emma and Graham's statements, the bullet that had wounded Lance and more photographs.

"The FAA and NTSB ruled Pace's plane crashed due to pilot error," Carmen said. "He miscalculated his approach."

"Maybe he was distracted," Michael said. "By, say, someone with a gun to his head."

"Check for a print match with a Valentina Ferrari," Graham said. "She's a Venezuelan fashion model, the daughter of the ambassador to the US."

"I'll see if I can find anything." Carmen made a note. "How does she know Bobby Pace?"

"She knows Richard Prentice. It's a long shot, but I want it checked."

The front door opened and Lotte trotted into the room, followed by Randall and Emma. Face flushed, hair windblown, she greeted him with a smile warm enough to melt a glacier. Graham wanted to pull her close and tell her how glad he was to see her but, aware of his team watching, he settled for a brief smile and a nod.

"Am I interrupting?" she asked, looking around the table.

"We're almost done." Graham motioned her toward the table. "Did you speak to Ambassador Ferrari?"

"The ambassador from Venezuela flew into Montrose this morning," she explained to the others. "I met his plane and asked questions, most of which he refused to answer. But I learned he does know Richard Prentice. In fact, I think that's who he's here to see."

"Was his daughter with him?" Graham asked.

"No, but state senator Peter Mattheson was."

The mention of the agitating senator made Graham clench his jaw. The lawmaker had made it his personal crusade to do away with The Ranger Brigade Task

Force, and spouted off about it in the press at every opportunity. "What did Mattheson have to say?"

"Not much. The whole interview was pretty much a bust." She pulled out an empty folding chair beside Graham and sat. "But my visit to the airport wasn't completely wasted. Before Ferrari and Mattheson arrived, I talked to some of the private pilots. I showed them Valentina's picture and one of them recognized her. She called herself Val and tried to hire a pilot to fly her to Rhode Island about the time Bobby was murdered."

She definitely had the attention of everyone in the room now. "Did she hire Pace?" Randall asked.

"She originally hired a man named Fred Gaskin, but he came down with appendicitis the day before they were supposed to fly out. So he gave her Bobby's name."

"What would she be doing in Rhode Island?" Carmen asked.

"She told Fred she needed to pick up tractor parts for a cousin in Durango," Emma said. "So she planned to bring something back with her."

"Providence, Rhode Island, is a major port on the Atlantic," Michael said. "She could have been collecting something that had been smuggled into the country."

"Like a stolen Hellfire missile," Graham said.

"But who was the missile for?" Carmen asked. "Did Richard Prentice want to arm that drone he supposedly bought?"

"What good would it do him if he did?" Randall asked. "If he drops that anywhere, he'll attract all the wrong kind of attention and end up in a federal prison for the rest of his life."

"He's not a hothead," Emma said. "And he's definitely not stupid."

"But he has the money to buy a black-market missile," Michael said. "Maybe he's planning to frame one of the militia groups who are such fans of his. Or maybe he owes one of them a favor and this is the payback they're collecting."

"Or maybe we're looking at this all wrong," Emma said.

"What do you mean?" Graham asked.

"We know Venezuela is on the US watch list as a possible source of terrorists," she said. "What if Valentina and her father have contacts with those terrorists? Maybe they're even sympathizers?"

"And Prentice knows this and has exploited it to acquire the missile?" Michael asked.

Emma shook her head. "No. Maybe it's the other way around. Valentina is taking advantage of any feelings Prentice may have for her by persuading him to buy the missile for her."

"Most women settle for a big diamond," Carmen said.

"We don't know why she wants the missile," Emma said. "Maybe she's a true believer in the cause, or maybe she owes someone a big favor, or she's being threatened. Whatever the reason, she gets Prentice to pay for the missile, which she plans to pick up and deliver to the terrorists back in Venezuela."

"But the plane crash delayed delivery and she had to hide it in that cave," Carmen said.

"Then we found it, and she had to move it," Graham said.

"And now her father is here to pick it up and make

the delivery," Michael said. "No one's going to stop and search a diplomat's plane."

"Is Ferrari with Prentice now?" Graham asked.

"I don't know," Emma said. "I was following him, but my car had a flat before I could see where they turned. Officer Knightbridge stopped to change the tire for me."

"A flat?" Graham asked, all his old worries about her safety surging forward again.

"The car with Ferrari and Mattheson turned down the road that leads to the park and to Prentice's ranch," Randall said.

Emma refused to meet Graham's gaze; he'd have to question her later. He forced his attention back to the matter at hand. "Chances are, Ferrari is at Prentice's ranch now," he said. "And I'd lay odds the missile is there, too."

"He probably wouldn't risk hiding it at the house," Carmen said.

"He put it in a mine before," Michael said. "There are plenty of those to choose from around here."

Graham turned to the large topo map tacked to the wall behind him. The others stood and joined him around the map, studying the symbols and letters identifying features of the park and surrounding lands, including the Prentice ranch.

"There." Randall pointed to the crossed pickax symbol for a mine. "This one is closest to the ranch house. They could even have extended one of the tunnels under the house." He traced a likely path between the mine and the house with one finger.

"We need to get in there and take a look," Graham said.

"Can you get a warrant?" Cruz asked.

"Now that we have a possible terrorist connection, I think I can," Graham said. "We've got to get that missile away from there, before a lot more people get hurt."

EMMA RETREATED TO a back office, where she worked on a brief article about the ambassador's arrival in Montrose. She'd file the story before the deadline for tomorrow's paper, but she hoped by tomorrow she'd have more exciting news to report.

Shortly after noon, Graham found her. "I thought you might like some lunch," he said, setting a paper bag with the emblem of a local sub shop on the table beside her.

"Sounds great." She opened the bag while he sat across from her with his own lunch. "How are things going for you?" she asked.

"The ambassador's pilot filed a flight plan to leave Montrose at ten this evening and fly to Houston," he said. "Our best guess is he'll file a new plan there after refueling. We've got surveillance on the ranch, but we don't expect them to make a move before dark."

"So when will you make your move?"

"We'll go in at dusk."

"I'll go with you." It wasn't a question. She looked him in the eye and he didn't look away.

"Civilians have no place on a police operation like this." He took a large bite of his sandwich.

"I'm not just any civilian. I'm the reporter who led you to the evidence that could break open this case."

She had to wait while he finished chewing. She couldn't decide if he was weighing his answer carefully, or merely stalling. "You've been helpful," he said. "That doesn't entitle you to special privileges."

"Maybe not. Does sleeping with you?" She smiled, hoping to take some of the sting out of her words.

"That only makes me want to protect you more," he said softly.

"I'll wear a Kevlar vest, and I'll stay in the Cruiser until you tell me it's safe to leave. I won't interfere."

"Would you be able to identify Valentina Ferrari on sight?" he asked.

"I think so, yes. And Jorge Ferrari, too."

"Then that will be the official reason you're coming with us. And you'll do exactly as I say."

"Yes, sir." She gave him a mock salute, then patted his hand. "Everything will be fine, I promise."

He made a grunting sound that could have meant anything and they returned to eating their lunches. Clearly, Graham still struggled with giving her the independence she needed, but he was learning.

THE WHOLE TEAM, along with reinforcements from the Montrose County Sheriff's Department, gathered at Ranger headquarters as the sun was setting over the canyon. As the day's heat gave way to a chilly evening, Graham briefed everyone on the plan for the evening.

"We'll approach the ranch from two sides, at the front gate and through the wilderness area," he said. "Prentice's guards will try to stop us, but we have a warrant authorizing this search. If anyone interferes, place them in custody."

He assigned teams to search the old mine and surrounding grounds for any sign of recent activity. "If you locate the missile, set a guard and notify me. Remember that anyone you encounter may be armed and dangerous, so be prepared." Though his ribs were still bandaged and Emma knew his shoulder still pained him, he'd abandoned the sling and changed into black SWAT gear, complete with a bulky Kevlar vest and riot helmet. He presented a big, commanding presence that held the attention of every man and woman in the room.

She was waiting in the front seat of the Cruiser when he led the others outside. "Afraid I'd leave you behind?" he asked as he climbed into the driver's seat.

"You would if you could," she said.

"I don't suppose I can talk you into waiting here?" he asked. "I promise to give you an exclusive when we're done."

"Nice try, but I'm coming with you. I agreed to play by your rules." She patted her chest. "I'm stuffed into this ghastly uncomfortable vest and I'm ready to duck when you give the word."

He shifted the Cruiser into gear. "Then I guess we'd better get started."

Half the vehicles fell in behind Graham on the park road while the other half, led by Randall Knightbridge and Michael Dance, set out cross-country to approach the mine from the side. The canyon itself presented a natural boundary at the rear and at the other side of the ranch, making retreat that way all but impossible.

Graham turned into the private road that led to Prentice's ranch and stopped the cruiser in front of the closed gate. His headlights cut a bright path through the gray dusk, a spotlight illuminating the empty gravel drive. She peered down the driveway, expecting to see the headlights of an approaching Jeep, but saw only darkness, only the rumble of the idling engines of the caravan behind them disturbing the evening stillness. "Have you ever been here when guards didn't greet you within a few minutes?" Graham asked.

"Never." She continued to stare down the drive. "Maybe they think if they ignore us, we'll go away."

"Do you have Prentice's number in your phone?" he asked.

"I do." She pulled her cell from her purse.

"Call him. If I try, he'll see it's me and ignore the call. But he might talk to you."

She punched in the number and listened to the series of long rings. "No answer," she said. After the tenth ring, she hung up. "What now?"

Graham keyed his radio. "Simon, bring up a pair of bolt cutters," he said. "We're going to have to go around this gate."

Ten minutes later, Simon and a man from the sheriff's department had cut the fence wire and pulled up two fence posts, opening a gap wide enough for a vehicle to easily pass through.

Graham drove to the house, which blazed with light, though no guard came out to greet them. Emma waited in the vehicle while he got out and knocked on the door. No one answered. He tried the knob, but it didn't yield.

"Do you think they're all down at the mine?" she asked. "Moving the missile?"

"Could we get so lucky?" He slid back into the driver's seat and they started forward again, leading their caravan toward the old mine site.

"I've been this way once," she said as they inched along the faint trail. "The first day I came to interview him, Prentice gave me a tour of the place. He mentioned that he planned to reopen the mine one day—that a survey had revealed it still contained gold that could be accessed with new technology."

"Do you think he was telling the truth or merely bragging?" Graham asked.

"Maybe a little of both. I've heard that with the price of gold so high, some of these mines might be worth reopening."

"Or maybe he just uses that as an excuse if anyone asks about a flurry of activity around the mine."

They rounded a sharp curve and he came to a halt and cut the lights. The vehicles behind him followed suit. "No sense giving away our presence before we have to," he said.

They inched along and gradually her eyes adjusted to the dark enough that she was able to make out the silhouettes of trees and rocks. Then the mine itself came into view—a weathered wood head frame marked the opening to the tunnel. No lights showed around this entrance, and there were no vehicles or signs of activity. Graham stopped the Cruiser, though he left the engine running. "Stay here," he told her.

She watched his flashlight beam and that of the others until they disappeared behind a tumble of rock. A half circle of moon showed just above the mountains on the horizon. In its pale light the landscape looked smudged, like a charcoal drawing. The air smelled of car exhaust and sagebrush, the only sound the occasional ping of the cooling engine. Emma hugged her arms across her stomach, adrenaline making her jittery and on edge.

A shout in the distance startled her—men's voices, followed by the heavy slam of a car door and the sharp whine of bullets ringing on metal and rock. With her heart in her throat, she clutched the door handle and strained forward, squinting into the darkness.

Footsteps pounded on the hard ground—dark figures running toward her. The driver's-side door wrenched open and Graham leaped into the driver's seat. "Hang on tight," he commanded, as the vehicle lurched forward.

"Ranger one, this is Ranger three." Carmen's voice over the radio crackled with anxiety. "What's going on? I heard gunfire."

"There's another entrance to the mine," Graham said. "A side tunnel. Or maybe this headframe is just a decoy. There are at least two vehicles back there. They took off when I surprised them. I'm going after them."

"Should we follow?" Carmen asked.

"Radio Randall and Michael. Two Jeeps headed their way, occupants armed and dangerous. We ought to be able to trap them between us. You take a team in to search the mine. They may have left someone—or something—behind."

He reached behind the seat and took a shotgun from the rack in the backseat and handed it to Emma. "Do you know how to use one of these?" he asked.

"No," she said.

"It's easy. Jack the lever." He demonstrated. "And pull the trigger. If things get bad and anyone comes near you, promise me you'll protect yourself."

She didn't know if the lump in her throat was fear, or sorrow that something might happen to Graham. If he was alive, he'd protect her, so when he said "if things get bad" what he really meant was if he wasn't around to help her. "All right." She took the weapon with shaking hands and laid it across her lap.

The Cruiser lurched forward and she clutched the shotgun so it wouldn't bounce off her knees as he headed out across the rocky ground.

She tried to calm her fears by reminding herself that when this was over, she'd have the story of her career, but all she really wanted was to be home with Janey, soaking in a hot bath and enjoying a glass of wine, not rocketing across the ground, headed for unknown danger.

"There they are!" Triumph in his voice, Graham nodded toward the faint glow of red taillights. He switched on his own lights and hit the brights. Behind him, two more Cruisers did the same.

Graham sped up, the Cruiser bouncing over the rocks, barely under control. "You're not getting any closer!" Emma shouted. "We're going to wreck."

But Graham ignored her. The vehicle ahead must have realized they were following, because it increased speed, also. Emma gave up trying to hold on to the shotgun. She let it slide to the floor and clung to the dash and the door handle, her teeth clamped together to keep them from chattering. Graham steered around cacti and boulders, through dry creek beds and over hills, the vehicle's suspension protesting with every jarring landing, engine racing.

They roared over a hill and she was surprised to discover the gap between them and the other vehicle had lessened. She thought she could make out three occupants. She was about to point this out to Graham when something pinged off the hood of the Cruiser.

"Get down!" he shouted.

She dove under the dash. "They're shooting at us!" The thought refused to register at first, but a second ping shook her back to reality and anger overtook her initial shock. "They're shooting at us!" she said again.

She grabbed the shotgun and rested the barrel on the top of the lowered side window.

"What are you doing?" Graham shouted. "Get down!"

"If you have to drive, then I have to shoot," she said. With more calm than she would ever have imagined she could possess, she levered the gun and fired.

The force of the shot propelled her back against the seat and the blast echoed in her ears. She had no idea if she'd hit anything, but she'd definitely gotten the attention of the trio in the vehicle ahead. They dove out of sight. Giddy, she prepared to shoot again.

"Emma, don't!" Graham ordered. "You might hit the missile."

She dropped the rifle as if it had suddenly heated up and burned her. "Why didn't you say something before?"

"I didn't think you'd actually shoot."

He'd slowed the vehicle and the other two Cruisers took the opportunity to catch up with them. The radio crackled. "We can surround them with a flanking maneuver," Marco said. "Michael's going to try to shoot out their tires."

Graham glanced at Emma. "I mean it this time— stay down."

She dove under the dash once more, knocking her head as the Cruiser sped up again. Closing her eyes, she tried to ignore the sound of gunfire around her.

Then, as suddenly as the violence had erupted, peace descended once more. The Cruiser rolled to a stop. The shooting had ended, replaced by the rush of the wind and the slamming of car doors. Graham left the vehicle, but Emma stayed put, though curiosity compelled her to peek out over the dash.

Graham had one of the men up against the bumper of the Jeep, cuffing his wrists, while Carmen and Michael dealt with the other two. Simon and Marco stood at the back of the Jeep, examining the bomb, the nose of which stuck out of the back window.

Assured the danger had passed, Emma sat up and unfastened her seatbelt. She was debating getting out of the Cruiser—Graham would be furious with her for disobeying his orders, but she wanted to get close enough to overhear the conversation.

The question was decided for her when the man Graham had cuffed turned to face him, cursing loudly in Spanish. He shook his head and his hat fell off, revealing a fall of long black hair and a decidedly unmasculine face. The man Graham had apprehended was no man at all, but a woman.

Emma leaped out of the Cruiser and moved forward, notebook in hand. "Who are you?" she asked.

The woman fell silent, staring at Emma. "I know you," she said after a moment, in lightly accented English. "You're that reporter. The one looking for Lauren Starling."

"Yes." In all that had happened, Emma had almost forgotten about the missing anchorwoman. "Do you know Lauren? Have you seen her?"

The woman pressed her full lips together and turned back to Graham. "I want to call my lawyer."

"You'll have plenty of time for that," Graham said. "Why don't you start by telling us your name?"

The woman lifted her chin. "My name is Valentina Ferrari. My father is—"

"Jorge Ferrari, ambassador to the US from Venezuela." Emma moved closer, ignoring Graham's frown. "You're Richard Prentice's girlfriend."

Valentina's expression grew guarded. "I am not anyone's girlfriend."

"But what a coincidence that you're now on Richard Prentice's ranch," Graham said. "With a stolen Hellfire missile in your possession. Did Prentice ask you to steal it for him?"

"I refuse to say anything else. I want to speak with my attorney, with my father and with a representative from the State Department."

"Cruz!" Graham called. "Take Ms. Ferrari to the sheriff's department and book her."

As Marco stepped forward to lead Valentina away, Graham took Emma's arm and led her back to the Cruiser. He said nothing as they fastened their seat belts and he turned the Cruiser and headed back the way they'd come. Emma looked back at the trio of vehicles. "What will happen now?" she asked.

He said nothing, guiding the vehicle over and around rocks, jaw set, eyes fixed straight ahead. If not for the tension radiating from him, Emma might have imagined he'd forgotten she was there. "Don't do this, Graham," she said.

"Don't do what?"

"Don't give me the silent treatment. I didn't do anything wrong. I didn't get out of the car until it was safe to do so." So what if he hadn't given her permission to do so yet? She was an adult, and she had a job to do, too.

He slid his hands down the steering wheel and let out a long breath. "I'm not angry with you," he said. "I'm angry with myself, for not finding a way to stop

Prentice before things got this far. Now we've got a foreign national—a diplomat's daughter—involved, which
means the politicians will be all over this. She'll claim
diplomatic immunity and we'll have nothing."

"Will the US grant diplomatic immunity to someone who might be involved in a murder investigation?"

"It's been done before. Sometimes a country will
waive diplomatic immunity, but it doesn't happen very
often. Our relations with Venezuela are shaky enough
right now that I don't think anyone is going to press it.
Instead of finding the piece I need to solve the puzzle,
the puzzle just gets bigger."

"You'll get to the bottom of this," she said. "I'll help.
Maybe I can talk to her, woman to woman. Or—"

He stomped on the brake, throwing her forward.
She braced against the dash as he shifted into Park
and turned toward her. "Don't you think you've helped
enough already?"

"Wh-what do you mean?" She stared, wishing she
could make out his features better in the darkness. All
she had to gauge his emotions was the rough timbre of
his voice, anger mixed with something else she couldn't
identify.

"What do you think you were doing, firing that shotgun at them?" he demanded.

"You were driving and they were shooting at us.
Somebody had to shoot back. Why else did you give
me the gun?"

"I didn't think you'd really shoot! You said you didn't
like guns."

"I don't. But I had to protect you."

He stared at her, then began to laugh. She could feel
him shaking.

"What's so funny?" she asked.

"You are." He wiped his eyes. "I'm the cop. I'm the one who's supposed to protect you. Not the other way around."

"Maybe we should protect each other."

He gripped the steering wheel with his uninjured hand, his jaw working. "You know this isn't easy for me. I'm not used to a woman who's always questioning me and second-guessing my decisions."

"It's not personal, Graham. I do trust you, but I'm not used to having people tell me what to do."

"Even when it's for your own good?"

"I have to decide for myself what's for my own good," she said. "Wouldn't you feel the same way?"

"Fair enough."

"Did you mean what you said before—that you loved me?"

"Yes."

"I love you, too. Do you think that's enough for two such independent people to work together?"

She reached across the seat and he took her hand and squeezed it. "I think it's a good start," he said.

THE NEXT MORNING, Graham returned to Ranger headquarters early, only to find the rest of the team there ahead of him. "We got a match on those prints, Captain," Simon said.

Graham studied the report Simon handed him. Valentina Ferrari was a match for the previously unidentified print they'd found in Bobby Pace's plane. "That's one loose end tied up," Graham said. He dropped the paper onto his desk. "Not that it will do us much good."

"The bullet that killed Pace is the same caliber as the

gun she was carrying when you arrested her," Simon said. "But ballistics isn't back with their report."

"So she killed Bobby Pace." Michael whistled. "That's cold-blooded."

"Guess looks, money and power weren't enough for her," Simon said.

Graham checked his watch. "I've got an appointment at eight to talk to Ms. Ferrari," he said. "Let's see what her story is."

"If we can't prosecute her for murder, maybe we can at least get her to incriminate Prentice," Michael said.

"He's already issued a statement to the press saying he was away last night and has no idea what Valentina was doing on his property, and no knowledge of the missile," Michael said.

"His story about being away checks out," Simon said. "He and the ambassador were at a dinner with the mayor, city council members and at least fifty other people."

Graham's stomach churned. "He's doing it again," he said.

"Doing what?" Michael asked.

"Slipping out of the net. No matter how much evidence we compile against him, he builds a story to refute it."

"So he's just a misunderstood rich guy who makes poor choices in associates," Michael said.

"He'd like us to believe that. So far, he's been doing a good job of convincing everyone else." He fished out his keys. "Come on, let's see what Valentina will tell us."

The interview room in the Montrose police station featured gray walls, gray floor, gray folding chairs and tables. A couple of ceiling mics and cameras. Nothing to distract from the business at hand.

The door opened and two deputies led in Valentina Ferrari. Dressed in baggy orange coveralls and silver handcuffs, she didn't look glamorous, but there was no denying her beauty. She lifted her chin and glared at Graham, disdain in those dark eyes.

A tall, handsome man in a gray suit only a shade lighter than his hair followed her in. "I'm Esteban Garcia," he said. "I'm Ms. Ferrari's attorney."

Graham motioned for them to sit at the table. He and Michael settled into chairs opposite them. "My client has nothing to say to you," Garcia said.

"Your client is allowed to speak for herself." Graham addressed Valentina. Without her heavy eye makeup and military clothing she looked younger, barely out of her teens. "Ms. Ferrari, how do you know Richard Prentice?"

"He is a friend of my father's."

"I have a photo here of the two of you together, at a party at the Venezuelan consulate in Denver."

She glanced at the copy of the newspaper photo that Graham slid from a folder.

"You don't have to answer that," her lawyer said.

"It doesn't matter," she said. "He is someone my father invited to the party. He is nothing to me."

"You two look very friendly in the photo," Graham said.

Her lips curved in the hint of a haughty smile. "Men always want to be friendly with me. That doesn't mean it means anything."

Graham left the photo on the table between them and

sat back. "Let's talk about the missile you were carrying in the back of the Jeep when we arrested you," he said.

"That did not belong to me."

"Then why were you helping to transport it?"

She shrugged.

"Do not say anything else," her lawyer cautioned.

Graham studied her beautiful, proud face, and he had a sudden memory of Emma, regarding him with similar defiance. The image triggered an idea. "Do you always let men like him tell you what to do?" he asked Valentina.

"I let no one tell me what to do." The words came out sharp and crisp, as if she were giving an order. "I make my own decisions."

"So were you the one who decided to buy the missile, or were you just the errand girl?" Graham hoped to trip her up, and get her to tell him the missile's intended recipient and purpose.

"I am no errand girl!"

"Right. So you bought the missile and hired Bobby Pace to fly it to Colorado for you. Then you shot him."

"I object to this line of questioning." The lawyer glared—not at Graham, but at his client, who refused to look at him.

"Let the lady answer," Graham said.

She pressed her lips together, but said nothing.

"We have your prints in the plane," Graham said. "And when ballistics gets done, we'll know the bullet that killed him came from your weapon."

"Men are so stupid," she said.

"Was Bobby Pace stupid? Is that why you shot him?"

Garcia stood. "This interview is over."

Graham waited for Valentina's answer, but she stood

and followed Garcia out of the room. Graham's phone chirped and he answered it. "Ellison."

"Ballistics says Valentina Ferrari's gun killed Bobby Pace," Simon said.

"That's one more question answered," Graham said, after he'd disconnected the call and given Michael the news. "But we still don't know what she was doing with that missile or why."

"Speaking of questions," Michael said. "I didn't want to say anything until the interview was over, but the press is outside. They want a statement."

GRAHAM FOUGHT A sense of déjà vu as he stood on the steps of the police station, facing the gathering of reporters and television cameras. He searched the eager faces for a tall, beautiful woman with red hair and generous curves, and his spirits sank when he didn't see her. Maybe Emma didn't need to attend a press conference to get the story on Valentina Ferrari, but he'd expected her to be there, if only to make sure the competition didn't scoop her. Now, he didn't have even her friendly face to help him get through this.

"Why are you holding Valentina Ferrari?" A male reporter from one of the national papers fired the first question.

Before Graham could answer, a second reporter said, "Senator Mattheson claims the arrest of an ambassador's daughter is another example of harassment on the part of The Ranger Brigade."

"We have evidence linking Ms. Ferrari to the murder of Bobby Pace," Graham said.

"Have you formally charged her with murder?" asked a woman from the local daily.

"No charges will be filed."

Graham turned to see Senator Mattheson, flanked by the district attorney and another man in a dark suit, emerge from the police station. Mattheson stepped up beside Graham. "Ms. Ferrari will be returning to her own country this afternoon," he said. "This has all been a misunderstanding."

"Murder is more than a misunderstanding," Graham said.

The senator's gaze could have chilled meat. "Venezuela is a valued ally of the US," he said. "We will do whatever we can to protect and honor that friendship."

The press began shouting questions, their words blurring together. Graham ignored them. "Did Richard Prentice have anything to do with this?" he asked Mattheson.

He didn't know whether to be pleased or alarmed at the way Mattheson's neck reddened at the mention of the billionaire. "Mr. Prentice is a friend of the family," the senator said. "He spoke on behalf of the Ferraris." He turned to the crowd. "I think that's all we have time for today. Thank you for coming."

He started to leave, the other man in a suit following. Graham put out a hand to stop him. "Who are you?"

"Ed Stricker. State Department." The man didn't offer a hand.

"Are you one of Mattheson's buddies?" Graham asked.

"I'm the man who's trying to prevent an international incident, no thanks to you."

"So it doesn't matter to you that a man was murdered? Not to mention the question of trafficking in illegal weapons, even terrorism."

Stricker frowned. "International security takes precedence over one local murder, which we believe was an accident, anyway. As for the missile, we've taken that into custody and will be conducting our own investigation."

"You'll let me know what you find?"

"I wouldn't lose any more sleep over this, Captain." Stricker followed Mattheson back into the station.

Graham turned to the DA. "What can you tell me about this?"

"Our hands are tied," the lawyer said. "The orders came from well above my pay grade."

"So she gets away with murder."

"You can send the evidence you have to the Venezuelan authorities and they may choose to prosecute."

"I'm not holding my breath."

The DA clapped his hand on Graham's shoulder. "Let it go. There's nothing you can do now." He left to join the others.

Michael moved up alongside Graham. "Frustrating," he said.

"I don't like not having answers," Graham said. "And I don't believe Valentina Ferrari is the only one getting away with a serious crime here."

WHILE HER COMPETITION attended the press conference at the police station, Emma called every contact in her list, trying to track down anyone who could put her in touch with Valentina Ferrari. The story of a fashion model and diplomat's daughter turned murderer—and possibly terrorist—was the biggest of her career. But even more than that, she wondered if Valentina could help her find Lauren Starling. The fact that Valentina had connected Emma with the search for Lauren made

Emma believe the young woman had more than a casual interest in the case. Maybe she knew something that would help.

Two calls to the Venezuelan consulate, several unanswered to Richard Prentice and one each to the State Department, Valentina's modeling agent and a foreign correspondent she'd met once at a party yielded nothing, however. She stared at the phone, out of ideas and wondering if she should have gone to the press conference, after all.

The phone rang, startling her. The screen read Unknown Number. Curious, she answered. "Hello?"

"I understand you wish to speak to me." The softly accented, feminine voice was unmistakable.

"Yes," Emma said. "I'd really like to hear your side of the story."

"I am going home to Venezuela this afternoon, but if you come to the airport now, I will give you a few minutes."

Almost giddy with excitement, Emma hung up the phone and prepared to leave. She slipped fresh batteries into her recorder and stuffed it, along with a notebook and extra pens, into her purse. She grabbed her keys, but stopped when she reached the door and pulled out her phone. She had worked alone for years, valuing that independence and the ability to shape her own fate. But maybe it was time to share this triumph with someone else.

Graham answered on the second ring. "Emma! Is everything all right?"

"Everything's more than all right. Can you meet me at the airport in about fifteen minutes?"

"What's going on? Are you leaving?"

"No. Just trust me and meet me at the airport. And maybe you'd better change into civilian clothes. What I'm asking you to do is very unofficial."

He hesitated, then said. "All right. I'll be there as soon as I can."

Twenty minutes later they met outside the FBO. As she'd asked, he'd changed into slacks and an oxford shirt. Minus the uniform and utility belt, with no visible weapon, he looked a little less threatening, though no woman, at least, would mistake his muscular arms and broad shoulders. "What's up?" he asked.

"Valentina Ferrari has agreed to talk to me. I thought you might like to listen in."

"How did you manage that?"

"Persistence. And luck." She turned toward the plane parked at the edge of the tarmac. The Venezuelan coat of arms shone in the afternoon light. "Come on."

Two guards stopped them at the bottom of the stairs leading up to the plane. "Who is this?" one demanded, nodding to Graham.

"My bodyguard," she said. "He won't say anything. He's just here to observe."

Playing along, Graham kept quiet and allowed them to frisk him. Then one guard led the way up the stairs, while the other fell in behind.

They found Valentina alone in the luxurious cabin, dressed in designer jeans and a man's white dress shirt, unbuttoned to reveal a red silk shell and plenty of cleavage. Her feet were bare, toenails polished crimson. She studied Graham through narrow eyes. "What is he doing here?" she asked.

"Graham is only here to listen," Emma said. She was

prepared to argue for him if it came to that, but Valentina merely shrugged.

She motioned for them to sit on one of the two leather sofas, then she half reclined on the other, feet tucked beneath her. "I suppose you want to talk about Bobby," she said, without preamble.

Emma took out her notebook and switched on the tape recorder. "Yes. What happened with Bobby?" she asked.

"I agreed to do a favor for…for some friends. They wanted me to pick up a…a package in Newport and fly it to Colorado."

Graham leaned forward, as if to speak, but a look from Emma silenced him. Valentina fussed with the sleeves of her shirt, carefully unrolling and rerolling them, smoothing the crease. "What happened?" Emma prompted.

"He didn't want to do the job at first. He was afraid it might be illegal, since I asked him to keep it a secret." She smiled. "I told him I was a famous Brazilian fashion model, and I was trying to avoid the paparazzi. He liked that."

"You were the woman someone heard arguing with him here at the airport," Emma said. The other pilot had gotten the day wrong, but that was an easy mistake to make.

"I suppose so. In the end, he agreed to do the job. He said he had a sick boy and needed the money. We flew to Newport the next day and everything was fine. I picked up the package and we started back here. But when we got ready to land, he became very nervous. He wanted to fly to the airport and land, instead of in the wilderness area. He was being silly." She shook her head.

"Did you shoot him?" Emma asked.

Valentina smoothed her long fingers down her thighs, nails bright red against the dark blue denim. "It was an accident," she said softly. "I pointed the gun at him to scare him, but he lunged toward me, as if to take it from me, and it went off." She bit her bottom lip and shook her head, eyes glistening. "I didn't mean for him to die. If he'd only done what he agreed to do, nothing would have happened."

"Did Richard Prentice have anything to do with your 'package'?" Emma asked. "Was he helping you?"

"I don't want to talk about the package anymore," she said.

Emma and Graham exchanged glances. Maybe she could work the conversation back to the topic of the missile and Prentice later. "What do you want to talk about?" she asked.

"I called you because I heard you have been looking for Lauren Starling."

Emma's heart raced at the mention of Lauren, but she tried to reign in her excitement. "Do you know Lauren?" she asked. "Have you seen her?"

Valentina nodded. "We first met at the party at the embassy. She was…very sweet. Not all women are so kind to other women, especially when the other woman is younger and beautiful. She was different. She was a strong, American woman, but she was also very fragile."

"Fragile? In what way?"

Valentina shook her head. "I can't explain. She just looked…vulnerable."

"Have you seen her since the party?" Emma asked. "Do you know what happened to her?"

"I don't know." She worried her lower lip between her teeth, hesitating. Then she lifted her head and met Emma's gaze, her expression calm and determined. "But you should ask Richard Prentice that question."

"Richard Prentice knows what happened to Lauren Starling?" Emma's hand shook as she scribbled the words on her pad.

"I can't say more." Valentina stood. "You must go now. My flight will leave soon."

"Wait, no! I—" Emma rose, also, but Valentina turned her back and hurried into a rear cabin, shutting the door firmly behind her.

The two guards emerged from the shadows to escort them out of the plane once more. Graham looked as if he might resist, but Emma took his arm. "Come on. We've got everything we can here."

He waited until they were in the terminal before he spoke. "What do you make of that?" he asked.

"I think she's telling the truth," Emma said. "About Bobby, anyway. I don't think she meant to kill him."

"She wasn't willing to incriminate Richard Prentice."

"He's a powerful man. Maybe she's afraid of him. Or maybe he's innocent."

Graham grunted. "What about Lauren Starling?"

"I think she's the real reason Valentina wanted to speak with me. I think she wants to help Lauren."

"Are you going to talk to Prentice?"

"I don't know. It might be better to do some checking around first."

He put a hand on her arm. "Be careful."

She leaned into him. "I will. I've learned my lesson. Being independent doesn't mean I have to do everything myself."

"What's the next step?" he asked.

"There are lots of next steps," she said. "As soon as the insurance pays out, I have to buy a new car, and find another house."

His eyes searched hers. "What if I made you a better offer?"

"I'm listening."

He took both her hands in his. "Do you think you could put up with a stubborn, overprotective law enforcement officer?"

"You forgot grumpy and mistrustful of the press."

He nodded. "That, too. Though there's one member of the press I've learned to trust with my life." He squeezed her hands.

She wet her suddenly dry lips. "What are you saying, Graham? I mean, do you want to keep living together or dating or…"

"I want to marry you." He slid his hands up her arms to grasp her shoulders. "No half measures. I love you. I'm asking if you love me enough to stick with me, for better or worse?"

She wasn't sure she remembered how to breathe, much less speak, but the words came out, anyway. "You won't try to smother me or change me, even when I make mistakes, or do things that drive you crazy?"

"I might try sometimes, but I won't ever fool myself into thinking you'll let my judgment trump yours. And I won't try to change you. I love you exactly the way you are."

"And I love you—bossiness, grumpiness and all."

"Is that a yes?"

"Yes, I love you. And yes, I'll marry you."

He kissed her, then brushed his knuckle along the

side of her mouth. "This is either the bravest, or the craziest thing I've ever done," he said.

"It's the best thing I've ever done," she said. "You and I are going to make a great team. You just wait and see."

\* \* \* \* \*

# MILLS & BOON®

## INTRIGUE
### Romantic Suspense

**A SEDUCTIVE COMBINATION OF DANGER AND DESIRE**

---

## A sneak peek at next month's titles...

### In stores from 17th July 2015:

- **A Lawman's Justice** – Delores Fossen *and*
  **Lock, Stock and McCullen** – Rita Herron

- **Kansas City Secrets** – Julie Miller *and*
  **The Pregnancy Plot** – Carol Ericson

- **Tamed** – HelenKay Dimon *and*
  **Colorado Bodyguard** – Cindi Myers

**Romantic Suspense**
- **Playing with Fire** – Rachel Lee
- **The Temptation of Dr Colton** – Karen Whiddon

---

0715/46